THE GIRL IN THE CLOCKWORK TOWER

LOU WILHAM

Midnight Tide
PUBLISHING

ALSO BY LOU WILHAM

The Curse Collection
    The Curse of The Black Cat
    The Curse of Ash and Blood

The Sea Witch Trilogy
    Tales of the Sea Witch

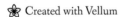

To Mom & Dad
who nurtured the story teller, the artist,
and the dream inside of me.

THE GIRL IN THE CLOCKWORK TOWER

A STEAMPUNK RAPUNZEL RETELLING

LOU WILHAM

1

_____

PERSINETTE

THE WASHED-OUT, dilapidated buildings of the labor camp spread out beneath Persinette as she floated high above it all. Drifting down toward them, Persi bobbed lightly through the narrow alleys between one building and the next, her bare feet several inches off the ground. With not a soul in sight, an eerie silence blanketed the vast vacant camp.

A soft snap drew her attention. She spun to see what the sound was, and all at once the narrow alley was full of people. A sea of dirty, tired, gaunt faces swam below her, dirty arms reaching for her. What seemed like a million bony, pale hands grabbed at her ankles, to pull her down—down into that sea of frail bodies.

Persinette's green eyes jumped from one face to the next as they tore at her hair and clothes. She recognized them, all of them. She'd seen them all before, though never in person. They dragged her lower and lower into the pushing, writhing pit of dirty and too-thin bodies.

. . .

PERSINETTE AWOKE WITH A START, her face sweaty and her breath coming in hard, shallow pants. A scream was on her lips, but she swallowed it down with a dry gulp. "Just a dream, Persi. It was just a dream," she whispered to herself, taking another deep breath to calm her racing heart. Even with her familiar room in the Tower before her, those faces still swam in her mind, each the same dirty, terrifying rictus she'd seen the first time she'd had the vision.

"Just a dream," she repeated. But a part of her asked "Was it?"

A shrill, angry noise broke the silence of the early morning, startling Persi and setting her heart racing once more. With narrowed eyes, she glared at the offending alarm clock on her bedside table. Beside it sat a piece of crisp parchment that seemed to glow in the soft morning light. In one swift motion of her freckled hand, she silenced the alarm and scooped up the paper. She rubbed at her eyes and read the schedule typed neatly on the page before her.

- 6:30 a.m.—Briefing with Agent Gothel
- 7:00 a.m.—Breakfast

After that, Persinette skimmed the rest. Other than the briefing with Gothel, nothing mattered; everything else was just trivial busywork. She dragged herself from the warmth of plush blankets and soft sheets to the washroom to prepare for her morning meeting.

After sixteen years of living in MOTHER headquarters, the long walk down the bustling corridors, the too-early meeting, the rush of passing MOTHER agents and automatons, even the hiss of steam as the door to the conference room opened—all of it was routine. When she'd first been brought to MOTHER at eight years old, it had all scared her, but Persinette found that over time, anyone could get used to almost anything.

"You're late." Even the guttural, admonishing voice of MOTHER Agent Gothel had become commonplace for Persinette. The slender, middle-aged woman with sharp features and even sharper eyes was standing at the head of the table, a clutter of papers strewn before her.

The doors to the room groaned shut behind Persinette, barely missing the long train of her skirt. "I'm sorry, Gothel," she murmured. Her long lavender hair fell into her face as she ducked her head and tried to make herself as small as possible. Gothel had never let an outright threat fall from her lips, but the implication was always there: the moment Persi was no longer useful to MOTHER, she would be disposed of, as so many others had been.

Gothel's eyes narrowed on Persinette before she seemed to make up her mind about something. "Now that you're here, sit," she ordered, gesturing to the seat across from her. The bustle of Persi's skirts let out a soft *poof* of air as she hastily complied. "We need an updated list of Enchanted in Province Four."

Gothel held out a file and Persi hurriedly reached for it, knowing full well what was inside. Still, she made a show of setting the file on the table, opening it, and flicking her eyes over population statistics, maps, and photographs of Daiwynn's fourth Province.

"We have provided you a map of the area and plenty of pictures. Any other information you may need is available upon request, of course." The agent's words were sharp and direct, as always.

Persinette's fingers conducted their obligatory flip through the pages of the file as she nodded and took in the information she'd been given. She dared not say a word, however. With Gothel, it was usually better to speak only when spoken to.

The agent gave her a moment before asking, "So, how long will this take you?"

Swallowing roughly, Persi took a moment to think. Whenever possible, she did her best to stretch out the length of time between the Collections she was involved with. She thought—however foolish the thought might have been—that by taking her time, she would give whoever she had a vision of—her target—the chance to get away. Still, even now, some annoying and logical voice in her head reminded her that these Enchanted didn't even know MOTHER was coming for them. Without that knowledge, they had no idea that they needed to run at all. She promptly told that voice to be quiet; she was doing the best that she could, after all. "A couple of months or so. Province Four is rather large," she said finally.

"You have six weeks," Gothel replied sharply, leaving no room for argument. Those cold, dark eyes narrowed on Persi as if perhaps she expected an argument. However, there would be none; Persinette saw no point in it. She would deliver what was expected of her in the time she was allotted, or else.

"Right, then. Guess I better get to work." Persi grabbed the file as she stood. She was already standing to head back to her rooms in the Tower, far away from Gothel's glare.

The agent's voice stopped her before she could push the button to open the doors. "One more thing, Persinette."

Persi licked her dry lips, almost afraid to ask the question. "Yes, Gothel?"

"They want you in the field this time."

"Excuse me?" Persinette's stomach did a sick drop

toward the toes of her buckled boots. She'd been prepared for almost anything—just not that. "I can't go into the field, that's not my job," she argued. "My job is just to find the people. You and the Steps are supposed to go on Collections, not me."

Gothel shrugged her slim shoulders, not even bothering to lift her eyes from the papers in front of her. "Those are the orders," she said simply.

"But..." Persinette frowned deeply. "I'm not even trained to go out into the field! What do they think this is going to accomplish?" she demanded as she spun to meet Gothel's eyes again. The shock of those orders brought with it a rare instance of bravery and contradiction. Never did Persinette go against orders. Seldom did she even question them.

The corners of Gothel's mouth pinched with obvious disgust, her eyes narrowing. She seemed to find Persinette's sudden bout of courage neither amusing nor admirable. "They are hoping this will speed up your process and allow increased Collection rates as you will be out in the field able to disseminate any visions that may occur on the spot."

What Gothel didn't say—and didn't have to say—was that Persinette's limited results had finally begun to draw attention to her. The higher-ups in MOTHER had noticed, and if they didn't start seeing better results from her, she would be punished.

Persi nodded so quickly her teeth clacked together, then headed for the doors. Orders were orders, and Persi knew she didn't have much choice. She was going out into the field whether she wanted to or not.

"You may be outfitted with a stunning pistol, so make sure you get down to the firing range to practice," Gothel added as an afterthought.

Swallowing hard, Persinette nodded once more eyes fixed on the closed door before her, then smacked the button to open the doors. Out in the corridor, and out of Gothel's sight, she leaned against the cement wall to take calm her pacing pulse.

"Calm down, Persi. This might be for the best."

Even as she told herself so, a small, nasty voice that sounded eerily like Gothel reminded her of all the things that could and likely would go wrong.

It took her a few moments to silence the voice and regain control over her trembling knees enough to walk in a strangely robotic fashion back to the Tower. Each step was a struggle, but she focused on the click of her hard-soled boots on the tiled floor as she fled the probing eyes of MOTHER.

ALTHOUGH PERSINETTE HAD NOT BEEN BORN THERE, the Tower was the only place she'd ever really called home. The rooms that surrounded hers housed others of her "kind": fairies, pixies, werewolves, and even a troll or two. Each was given plenty of living space and the illusion of freedom, but Persinette understood the Tower for what it was—a prison. She and the others of her kind did not *live* in the Tower; they were *kept* there.

Once back in her quarters, she opened the barred windows just a crack. There was no way to get out past the bars—and at night the windows locked automatically—but at least she was able to let some fresh air in. Persinette slumped down into the oversized chair that was perched on the rug in front of the jam-packed bookshelf. She inhaled deeply, pressing the heels of her shaking hands to her eyes to stop the panicked burn of tears.

"Get ahold of yourself, Persi. You can do this," she scolded herself. The file—which she'd picked up from the chair and flopped across her legs—sat heavily in her lap as she continued to breathe in through her nose and out through her mouth until her eyes stopped burning and she was in control again.

When her hands were finally steady, she opened the file and let her eyes flick over the printed pictures. Perhaps this could be a blessing in disguise. Maybe she could make this work for her. She could finally have a chance to do something to help the Enchanted, perhaps even stem the flow of faces that regularly haunted her. She could warn them somehow, allow them time to escape before MOTHER reached them.

But how? she asked herself.

She would have to make it look like she hadn't engineered their escapes herself. Like those Enchanted simply decided to pack up and leave. As much as Persinette wanted to help, she also knew that if she were found out, she'd be sent to the camps right alongside those she'd help Collect. Then she'd be no good to anyone. Still, in spite of her fear, she had to help. She knew that with every fiber of her being.

Yes, but how can someone like you help? That nasty little voice asked.

She shrugged the voice off, but still she asked herself: *How? How? How?* Persinette sat there in that overstuffed armchair asking herself over and over until lunch time.

No solution came to her.

When, at last, the lunch bell rang through the halls, she pulled herself to her feet and headed down to the mess hall. Tray in hand, Persinette settled at one of the little tables with a few other Assets, her mind still focused on the single question. *How?*

"You're a train wreck, 11-24-10." The snide words and the sound of her Asset number turned Persi's stomach and ripped her from her thoughts.

A rainbow-haired man with a short, dark beard stood on the other side of the table, two ruddy, brown-haired men flanking him. His name was Agnes, and he'd never said more than a handful of words to her before that night. Persi shrugged, trying to come up with a lie that would explain away the mussed lavender hair and what must have been a vacant expression. Again, nothing came to mind.

Agnes sneered at her silence. He was beautiful, painfully so—but then, unicorns always were. "Oh look, cat's got the Seer's tongue. Maybe all those visions finally addled her brain."

Persinette opened her mouth to say something, anything to get him to stop, to get him to leave her alone, but she couldn't get any words past her lips.

"Pathetic." He snorted with disgust. The two men on either side of him let out soft chortles of laughter.

"I have to hit the shooting range after dinner," she blurted out suddenly.

A short hateful bark of laughter left Agnes. His eyes lit with vicious amusement at her obvious discomfort. "Is that so? Do you not know how to fire a pistol, 11-24-10?"

Persi floundered for words again. She'd seen Agnes's cruelty toward the others, but up to that point he'd ignored her. The longer the confrontation dragged on, the harder she found it to think at all. Her palms were sweating against the table, slicking the surface. Her mouth gaped—to retort, to cut him down, to show him she was not someone to be pushed around—but the well of words in her throat was dry.

Loud chuckles rippled through the little group. In a moment of sheer panic, Persi stood abruptly from the table and made a beeline for the door of the mess hall. The laughter only grew louder, following her as she ran. "That's right, run, 11-24-10! Get lots of practice running! Or they'll kill you out there!" Agnes shouted after her.

The words echoed behind her, her heart racing and her palms getting even damper.

PERSINETTE THOUGHT of little else all evening. The memory of Agnes's words kept her awake more than the nightmares ever had, and at breakfast the next morning, she had to prop her head up on one pale hand just to keep herself from falling asleep in her porridge.

It took her till lunch to finally shake those words and focus on the task at hand once more. She still had not formulated a plan, however; all she had was a plan to formulate a plan. Which was...a start. Of sorts.

For a plan—or a plan for a plan—she'd need research.

Once she finished eating, she went down to the office that handled information requests. At the front desk sat a scowling young woman with bright blonde hair and sharp grey eyes that narrowed on Persi as she walked up to the counter. "What do you want?"

"Good afternoon," Persi said with a smile. She wasn't sure what she was hoping for—maybe a smile in return?—but what she got was a blank stare that left her feeling awkward and uncomfortable. "I, um, need to fill out a library access request form, please?

With a cold look the MOTHER agent stared Persinette down for a moment longer before she wordlessly pointed to a rack of forms beside the window and promptly ducked her head back down to whatever she'd been doing before.

"Right. Thanks." Persinette forced her smile wider and looked over the rack for the form she needed. Once she'd found it, she filled it out at one of the longer, counter-height tables. She was so engrossed in the little boxes and spaces for explanation that she didn't notice anyone else in the room until someone peered right over her shoulder—Agnes.

"I don't think a book is going to teach you how to handle a pistol," he said coolly. "At least not enough to keep you alive."

Persinette spun around, sending her long hair fluttering, and fixed Agnes with a look of sheer determination. She was going to do it. She was going to tell him off. This was it! She opened her mouth to speak and...and...and *nothing*. Nothing came out!

Agnes laughed coldly and shook his head. "I'll leave you to it then, 11-24-10. Good luck." He gave her a mock bow and strode off.

She stood there for a long moment, still trying to coax words from her mouth, but if any words had formed, the stubbornly refused to come out. Instead, Persinette's eye twitched, but she forced herself to turn back to the task at hand: getting into the library.

2

CAPTAIN MANU KELII

"LOOKIT, BENARD. THEY HAVE PINEAPPLE GIN!" Captain Manu Kelii found excitement wherever he could get it these days, but especially in all things pineapple.

"So it is sir. Exhilarating." Benard—Manu's first mate— merely blinked at the garishly yellow bottle of pineapple liquor his captain waved in front of his face.

"We're getting it," the young captain declared, as if there might have been any objection, or Benard even had any say in the matter.

"Of course, sir," the first mate said flatly.

Manu added the bottle their basket of supplies with a soft *clink* and surveyed the rows of dried meats on the shelf. "You know, Benard, you could at least pretend to enjoy shopping. With the Uprising so busy gathering intel, there isn't much else to do."

"Very boring, sir." Benard dropped a pack of yeast into the basket, then pushed the cart into his captain's side, likely trying to steer him through the aisles more quickly.

"I mean, this is not what I signed on for at all. When you said, 'Manu, let's continue the prior captain's efforts with the Uprising,' I thought we'd be going on adventures every week. Or at least every other week." Manu was rambling now, heat settling into his tanned skin with the notion of such excitement.

Benard, for the most part, seemed to be tuning him out. Over the years, it would seem that the old goblin had grown used to his captain's ravings and tended to let the captain tire himself out rather than argue with him. Benard simply continued through the aisles, adding first a ticket for flour, then one for grain into their basket while the captain chattered on.

"Are you listening, Benard?" Manu asked, cutting himself off. He'd stopped in the very center of the aisle, his tall and leanly muscled frame perfectly suited to impeding the traffic of the other customers pushing carts around the small grocer's shop.

"I'm sure Eddi will have a mission for us soon, Cap'n." Benard, considerably shorter and thinner, moved easily around his captain, and managed not to knock anything off the copper shelves in the process.

"Yeah, well, it had better be very soon." Manu huffed, adjusting his navy blue velvet top hat. Benard looked at him, head tilted in thought, before he shook his head and continued onward.

Their shopping concluded, the pair led the ticking automaton that pushed their flatbed cart of supplies back to the *Defiant Duchess*. They made their way through the traffic of the town and toward the outskirts where the airship was docked. There, the *Duchess* hovered in all her glory. Her light golden balloon held her frame a few feet off the ground while the crew bustled about the deck, preparing to embark on another voyage.

The small loading platform dropped onto the ground

with a *click* and a puff of dust. The two men and little robot climbed onto the thin plate of metal before it lifted slowly back up into the ship.

"Shame they hadn't any pineapples," Manu told Benard as they rose up the short distance into the cargo hold. "They would have made the most beautiful and tasty garnish."

"Yes, sir. I'm sure they would have."

"Fresh pineapple really is the best garnish," Manu blathered, not noticing that Benard had gone to unload the flatbed with some of the other men. "It's a shame what MOTHER has done to the fresh produce market, overall. We can hardly get anything good these days. I haven't seen a crunchy stalk of celery in nigh on six months!"

"Maybe next time, Cap'n."

"Yes, well, let's hope so because I just can't—"

A deckhand ran down the steps into the cargo hold, her hair a wild disarray and her light blue skin turning purple in a flush of excitement. "Sir." She stood at attention before the captain, bowing her head in respect.

Manu faced her, standing up a bit straighter himself. He pulled at his navy blue waistcoat, readjusting it to appear every bit the captain that he was—the man who demanded the respect of his crew, in spite of his youth and nonsense. "Yes? What is it?"

"There is a call awaiting you at the helm, sir," the little nixie said stiffly as if perhaps she were nervous to speak to her captain directly. And perhaps she was, but that wasn't at all Manu's concern.

"Who from?" The question was a perfunctory response. Manu already knew who was calling; he seemed only to take calls from one person these days, on one subject matter. Eddi, with orders from the Uprising. All he could hope was that this time the orders were to go and do something *exciting*.

"Eddi, sir."

"What is it pertaining to? Did they tell you?"

"No, sir." The girl shifted nervously under his gaze. "I'm sorry, sir. I didn't ask."

"Oh, for crying out loud!" Benard, now back at Manu's side growled. "Just go and answer the call, Cap'n. You know Eddi doesn't like to be kept waiting."

Manu eyed his first mate and idly pondered yelling at the irritable old goblin. Benard's long pointed ears twitched as he quirked one thin, dark brow—waiting, it would seem, for a reaction from the captain. It had been years since Manu had shouted at Benard like such a spoiled brat—and he wasn't a teenager anymore, he was a grown man, *damn it*. So he sucked back whatever response might have been on his tongue and nodded.

"Right, then. You all finish unloading this and send the automaton back when you're through. I won't have another grocer refusing us business because one of you decided to keep their delivery bot," Manu declared in his best *I'm in charge* voice.

"Aye, Cap'n." Benard saluted with a proud tilt of his lips and made for the pallet of supplies.

The captain snapped around and strode off, heading through the winding, wood-paneled corridors to the helm of the *Duchess*.

3

PERSINETTE

WITH THE FORM FILLED OUT, all Persinette could really do was sit back and wait. She handed in the paper and went to the dining hall for supper. She hoped that whoever reviewed those forms was feeling benevolent when they got to hers. Or that they believed the ruse she'd concocted.

Supper was quiet. Persi ate her dinner—thin soup and wilted spinach—without any complaint, as she always did, then began the long, slow trek down to the shooting range. The corridor seemed to stretch out in front of her ominously. Was she marching to her doom? Probably not, but it felt like it.

"Persi!" It was Elwyn, running toward her. The woman's long wavy hair was held back with a pair of goggles and the corners of her lips were turned up in a smile. "There you are! I've been looking all over for you." Elwyn laughed a little. "Where are you off to?"

"The shooting range, for target practice." Persinette found her shoulders relaxing and her stomach unclenching.

The smile on Elwyn's lips was infectious, or perhaps just seeing a friendly face after a long day made her smile, too.

"Oh, that's right! You're going out on mission in a few weeks, aren't you?"

Persi nodded, her heart pounding at her eardrums at the thought of the mission and the very short window of time she had to get herself ready. She gulped noisily, but did her best to hide her distress.

She must not have been very convincing, however, because Wyn wrapped her arms around her in a tight squeeze. "It'll be all right, Persi. You're stronger than you think, trust me."

Persinette allowed her friend to hold her for a moment. She let the warmth of Wyn's body press against her skin, providing her with some small amount of comfort. It was just a little support, but it was enough. When Wyn pulled back, Persi took a inhaled and nodded firmly. "Yeah, it'll all work out."

"Atta girl. Be brave!" Wyn chuckled softly. "Now, how about I walk you?"

"I'd like that."

Wyn grinned, and the pair of them started down the corridor once more. "I heard you applied for library access again."

Persinette blinked at her friend owlishly, unsure how Wyn had heard. She had only put the form in a few short hours ago—how could Wyn already know?

Wyn laughed softly. "You know how it is around here. Everything comes through the library. Plus, an Asset requesting to read books, well...you know."

Persinette did know. She knew all about how MOTHER hoarded the information of their world in that library. She knew that it was the most extensive collection of books in Daiwynn, rivaled only by the Great Library—if one believed such a place even existed. She also knew that MOTHER had row upon row of grimoires, history books, and anything else she might need to help her make a plan to save people from Collection.

"Right," Persi whispered. "I didn't mean to cause a stir." Panic settled into her gut the more she thought about how everyone likely already knew. How they were all looking at her now. Surely they'd find her out!

"Oh no, no stir. It's just been a slow week," Wyn teased with a wink.

"Oh. Okay." With that, Persi hoped that they could conclude their discussion of the library. She didn't want to lie to Wyn, but if Wyn pressed for details, she'd have no choice.

"So, what's it you want with library access anyways? Don't you have enough romance and adventure novels in your collection already?" Wyn spoke in a fond, playful tone, but Persinette's heart raced nevertheless. She'd never actually *lied* before, not to someone's face, not like this. She had stretched the truth—avoided relaying information, that sort of thing—but she'd never outright lied. Already she could feel her palms going damp and the blood draining from her cheeks.

Persi laughed nervously to...buy herself time, maybe? *Think, Persi. Think.* Could she tell Wyn the truth? Maybe. There was some small chance that Wyn wouldn't turn her over to Gothel, but that chance was tiny. Elwyn was, after all, a MOTHER agent herself. Whether Wyn was working in the library or in the field, that was still a fact. No, honesty wouldn't do it. "I just wanted to get some more detailed information on Province Four. I thought it might help me draw out a vision if I saw actual pictures of everyday life instead of surveillance footage. Besides, it doesn't hurt to check to see if there are any curses or crossed lay lines in the area. Right?"

Too much. That had been too much! Persi waited—her stomach jolting and threatening to expel her breakfast—for Wyn to call her a liar. That moment never came. Instead, Wyn shrugged and moved on. "I also heard you're being signed up for field training."

Another nervous laugh left Persi's lips. "You hear a lot, don't you?"

"Oh, you know, the library is the epicenter of information! So, as a librarian myself, of course I do."

"Right." Persi allowed herself to relax, even chuckle softly. For the time being, it would seem she was safe. How long that would last, she did not know, but she was happy to have at least these moments with her friend. "Speaking of hearing everything, you didn't happen to hear who would be in charge of my training did you?"

"Not yet. It would seem that's still up in the air at the moment. I'll let you know as soon as I know anything, though. Just don't stress too much about it, Persi. You'll do fine."

By that point they had stopped in front of the thick metal doors that lead into the training rooms. Wyn leaned in to give her friend another tight hug, and Persi soaked up the comfort like a sponge. "Thanks, Wyn. I'll see you later." She pulled back and Wyn trotted down the corridor. Persi pulled the keycard from a pocket at her waist and swiped it. The doors opened with a hiss.

On the other side of the cement walls was a vast open space divided into different training areas by partitions and half-walls.

MOTHER agents and Assets alike filled those spaces,

practicing everything from hand-to-hand combat to sword fighting. Labored breaths and the metallic clanking of weapons echoed throughout. Persinette bypassed all of these little arenas and headed straight for the shooting range. She had no desire to deal with any of the other agents.

The shooting range was mercifully empty. Persi swiped her card to open the gun locker, pulled out one of the small stunning pistols, and settled herself behind the red line.

Each time she lifted her hand to fire the kickback of the pistol jerked her shoulder painfully. Still, she kept at it. Persi lost count of how many times she tried and failed to hit the target—it felt like thousands, but could only have been twenty or so before the practice pistol lost its charge.

It was then that the feeling of being watched finally registered, the hairs on the back of her neck prickling. Slowly, Persi turned to find Agnes leaning in the corner, his long legs crossed at the ankle, arms holding another pistol in a posture of complete relaxation. Thin lips—half hidden by the short dark beard—spread into a look of smug amusement. "Oh no, do go on. This is the funniest thing I've seen all day," he drawled.

Persi pinched her brows together as that upset feeling settled into her chest once more, threatening to choke off her breath. "I'm practicing," she muttered, swallowing around the bile rising in her throat.

"No. You're not practicing. You're failing. Because you're a failure. Aren't you, 11-24-10?" His voice was cold, dispassionate, hard.

Persinette lifted her chin, doing her best to stand up taller than her short stature. "No." She forced out the word, trying to sound stronger than she really felt, but all she earned for her trouble was another derisive laugh.

"How adorably pathetic. Well, let me show you how it's done. Move."

Agnes didn't wait for her to move, however. He strode up to the line, placed his well-polished boots just so, and shoved her out of the way. He lifted his arm to aim at the target, inhaled once, and then fired the pistol he'd been holding. A harsh pop echoed off the bare cement walls, followed by a soft hiss of steam from the gun.

"*That* is how it's done." He handed her the still-warm pistol. "I hope you took notes, 11-24-10." A moment later he was gone, and Persi was still standing there, holding a pistol in each hand.

She glanced across the empty expanse from the line to the target to find a single shot right in the middle of it. He was right. She'd never be that good, and anything less than *that good* would put her in danger in the field. She was really in trouble

4

CAPTAIN MANU KELII

THE LARGE PROJECTION system was already running when Manu reached the helm. There, displayed on the dingy, antiquated screen was the black-and-white image of Eddi—the leader of the Uprising—sitting behind a desk and looking annoyed at the wait. Manu sank into the well-worn leather captain's chair in front of the screen, taking care to drape his long, lean frame across it as if he hadn't a care in the world. Removing the navy blue top hat, he perched it on an immaculately clad knee and flashed Eddi a boyish grin.

"Comfortable?" Eddi eyed the captain. Their dark eyes were set behind the usual goggles with their bug-like and terrifying appearance.

"Exceedingly." Manu shrugged, the grin spreading further across his lips. He knew that the leader of the Uprising didn't actually care whether or not he was comfortable so long as he followed orders.

"Wonderful. Then we can get down to business." Eddi turned their wrinkled face to something on the desk before them, then fixed Manu with another strangely magnified glare. "We've learned from one of our operatives on the inside of MOTHER that they are planning a Collection in six weeks for Province Four."

That got Manu's attention. If he was being informed about a Collection, that meant the Uprising wanted him to stop it somehow. Which meant action, adventure, daring... heroics at last! While he did not particularly care for the idea of Collection, he did like of idea of having something to do besides wait. "And what would you have us do with that information?"

"I want you and your crew to head in that direction. We need you to be in the Province ready and waiting." Simple and direct, but Manu got the feeling that there was more to this than just a run-of-the-mill Collection.

Manu tugged down the corners of his lips and pinched his brow as if in thought. Of course he wanted adventure, but the question remained... "Collections happen every day. Why this one?"

Eddi blinked at him from behind those goggles—an insect annoyed with the world. Manu flinched a little under that gaze; he didn't much care for the way those magnified grey eyes were looking at him like *he* was the bug about to be squashed. After a long pause, Eddi finally spoke. "We have been informed by our man on the inside that the plan is to take a Seer on the mission this time."

It was now Manu's turn to blink—in confusion. He frowned, trying to understand the words Eddi had just spoken. A Seer—in the field? It felt strange, even dangerous, to think about such a thing. "That seems a little reckless," he said, his words coming out soft and thoughtful.

"It does," Eddi agreed.

"Seers are not trained for such things, are they?"

"No. Until now MOTHER has kept their fortune-tellers safely within the compound. Possibly for fear that we may try to abduct one."

Which, Manu supposed, was precisely what Eddi intended to do.

Manu remained silent a moment longer as he processed the information. Seers were valuable. They could see into the future, into the past, and even across the present, depending on how powerful they were. MOTHER would be foolish to let one out in the open like that. "What's changed?"

The Uprising Leader shrugged their narrow shoulders and moved on. "Distance is well known to hinder a Seer's sight. Perhaps they're testing whether a Seer can better detect our kind at close range, using this Asset as a guinea pig. This might be a new tactic to increase Collection rates and purge Daiwynn of Enchanted altogether."

"Still..." The captain's frown returned. His stomach gave a twist the more he thought about it. "The Asset will be a sitting duck."

"It will," Eddi said, shrugging once more. It was clear the Uprising Leader did not care about the why. All they cared was that MOTHER was making this change, and the Uprising needed to take advantage of it.

"They haven't begun training those Assets as they do the others, have they? I mean the field Assets, they're—well, they're killing machines."

Eddi shook their grey head. "Our sources say no. Perhaps they plan to in the future, if they can prove that this would be profitable."

Manu's tanned fingers steepled in front of his face as he frowned further in thought. He had never imagined what it would be like to be one of those Assets. Each was taken by MOTHER at a young age—possibly even while still in the womb—and trained to hunt down and exterminate their own kind. Their fellow Enchanted. The very thought sent a chill up his spine.

The Uprising Leader remained silent, watching the captain as he pondered, appearing to let him think. "That will be all, Captain," they said at last. "Head toward Province Four. I'll have more for you soon." The screen winked out as Eddi closed the link between them.

Manu sat there for a while, staring at the blank screen pensively. The only thing he felt—aside from an impending sense of dread—was the churning of his stomach. His eyes flicked this way and that, wondering what this meant for their cause.

Hadn't MOTHER done enough damage to the Enchanted of Daiwynn?

Why try to increase their intake now?

THE WOODEN BOARDS of the bridge creaked under his black suede boots as Captain Manu made his way into the open air of the *Defiant Duchess*'s decks.

"We have a heading," he announced to the gathered crew with much bravado, a little smile lighting his features. In spite of the nervous state of his stomach, Manu told himself that a heading was good. It meant they had work and something to focus on. If he could just keep himself from having to sit still for too long, perhaps his mind wouldn't have time to imagine all of the horrible things this mission could mean for them.

"Where are we off to, Captain?" the bespectacled sailing master asked. Manu thought her name was Paula, but as she was a recent addition to the crew, he had no way of being sure.

"Province Four, and make it snappy. I've already plotted the course, so you just need to...enter it into the doohickey." He motioned as if typing on a typewriter.

"Now?" she asked, obvious amusement crinkling her eyes.

"Yes, now! Off with you!" He shooed the young woman off to work. "No time like the present! Off you pop!"

Could-be-Paula nodded and gave an excited laugh before heading to the bridge. They had stayed in Province Two far too long for Manu's liking, anyway. It would surely be only a matter of time before the local authorities called the air police to investigate the great ship on the edge of town. Best be on their way before then.

As she scurried off to the bridge, Manu faced the rest of the awaiting crew. If they were going to leave before night-fall, they needed to get a move on. "Is all of the cargo stored?" he asked one of the deckhands as the young man scuttled past him.

"I'm not sure, Captain."

"Well, go and check. I want everything ready to depart by dusk."

The deckhand nodded quickly and ran off to fulfill his orders. As everyone around him leaped into motion, Manu let out a breath. Yes, now he could go back to his quarters and relax with a cocktail until they were ready to leave.

"Cap'n!"

That was Benard's voice. Manu had to stop himself from cursing the goblin's timing.

With a dramatic sigh and slumped shoulders, the captain turned back to eye his first mate. "What is it,

Benard?" The words left him in a grumble as petulant as Manu felt.

Benard didn't seem the least bit fazed by his captain's sudden shift in mood. Instead of apologizing for the interruption, he just stood at nonchalant attention.

"Well?" Manu demanded, unable to stop the irritation billowing out of him. There was a bottle of pineapple gin calling his name, and the only thing he could think at that moment was all the delightful cocktails he could concoct from it...if he could just get back to his quarters, damn it!

Benard jerked his head toward the door to the space below the decks and walked away. Manu followed, and the two headed to the vacant galley. Only once the door was shut behind them did the first mate speak to Manu again. "What did Eddi have to say?"

Manu huffed as his mood soured further. He had pointedly been avoiding the thought of the Seer who would be sent out for the slaughter in less than two months. But it would seem there was just no skirting the topic now. "We're off to spoil a Collection."

Benard's brows creased. "And?"

"And MOTHER is bringing a Seer along for the ride this time. I don't know what Eddi has planned for the Seer, just that they're the reason we've been called out." He wasn't sure why this couldn't have waited till morning. Surely he could have told Benard all of this after a good drink and a nice lie-in while the *Duchess* bobbed through the air.

Benard's greenish mouth twisted into a grimace. "Why?"

"Don't know. Neither does Eddi. All we can guess is that they're trying to speed up the extermination process." His gut did another sick turn. Damn it.

"That all?"

The question hung heavy between them for a moment as Manu sucked in a breath to calm his stomach. No such luck; it fluttered uneasily. "That's all we've got so far."

"Right, then. As you were, Cap'n," Benard said, dismissing the young captain.

"No, as *you* were Benard," Manu grumbled, and stomped off to his quarters.

Before the day was out, they'd be setting sail for Province Four. Off on a mission that even Manu wasn't sure about. He and the crew would get to see some action for the first time in a long while, true. But before all of that...he desperately wanted to try out that pineapple gin. Hopefully, that cocktail and some much-needed rest would calm the niggling feeling of dread at the back of his mind.

5

PERSINETTE

LATER THAT WEEK, Persi was walking alongside Wyn toward her early morning meeting with Gothel when she saw Gothel all but skipping down the corridor.

"What's gotten into her?" Wyn asked, her nose wrinkling as she watched the retreating form of Agent Gothel.

"I don't know, but whatever it is, it's probably not good," Persi replied with a sigh. It seemed to Persinette that Agent Gothel enjoyed giving people bad news. Her dark eyes would twinkle with twisted joy whenever got to deliver some terrible tiding, and a moment later the corners of her lips would stretch up, up, up, the way a villain's would in the few comic books Persinette had read. Worse yet, it seemed that her favorite person to deliver bad news *to* was Persi herself. Gothel never seemed so delighted as when she was telling Persi something truly horrible.

Wyn shook her head and patted Persi's shoulder. "Whatever it is, it can't be so bad."

Her friend was trying to be comforting, Persi knew, but it didn't tamp down her rising feeling of dread. "Right, well, I'll see you later?"

Wyn nodded. "Chin up, Persinette, my dear. You'll be all right."

She left for the elevators. Persi faced the meeting rooms Gothel had disappeared into, took a inhaled a steadying breath and swiped her key card. The door opened with a soft hiss and a clanking of gears to reveal Agent Gothel sitting at the table. The older woman's face was *almost* lit up with a smile as her dark eyes landed on Persinette. "Ah, Persinette, you're late!" Her voice rang out with a verve that was practically cheerful compared to her usual tones.

"Sorry, I was talking to Elwyn in the hall." Persi sat carefully in her usual chair across from Gothel, her ankles tucked one behind the other to keep from kicking her feet as they dangled above the floor.

Gothel snorted. "It would seem that the higher-ups don't want you to die out in the field after all, much to my chagrin," she said with a little sneer. "You've been assigned a trainer to oversee your field training."

Persinette swallowed roughly and nodded, tucking a strand of soft hair behind her ear with a shaking hand. She did her best to breathe through the feeling of impending doom and terror that had settled over her When her hands dropped into her lap, she clutched them together to hide their tremors. "Well...that's good. Who is it?"

"Our best field Asset has been assigned to you," Gothel went on, and Persinette waited for the name, her slightly gapped teeth digging into lower lip nervously as she did her best to remain still. "After dinner, you will meet him in the training rooms."

"Yes, of course. But who is it?" Persinette asked again, the suspense getting the better of her. The question earned her a glare from Gothel.

"Asset 95." The words left Gothel's lips with what was nearly a delighted cackle.

All movement stopped, even her heartbeat—or so it felt anyway. "Agnes?"

"Yes, Agnes." The older woman was visibly and positively giddy with excitement. It was common knowledge that Agnes could be ruthless, and even downright cruel, to members of his own kind, especially those outside of his most intimate circle. "Oh, and I see you've put in a request for access to the library," Gothel added offhandedly.

Still reeling, Persinette did her best to turn her mind to the lie she would have to tell. "Yes, I did."

"What for?" Gothel's dark, beady eyes narrowed on her Asset.

Persi squirmed. She always felt something like prey when Gothel looked at her that way, but she couldn't indulge that instinct now. She had lied to Elwyn already; she just needed to use the same lie. She repeated it to herself. *Research. I just want to do more research on the area.* As lies go, it was a comfortable one, and close enough to the truth that it should have been easy to tell. So why couldn't Persi get it passed her tongue? Gothel just watched her, that hawk-like expression cut into the hard lines of her face.

"Well?" Gothel asked, impatient.

"I-I just wanted to do a little more research on the Province before I was out in the field. You-you know...to be safe," Persinette stammered, in spite of her best efforts to remain calm. *It's not technically a lie,* she told herself. She just had to make Gothel believe it.

Those dark eyes held Persinette, perhaps looking for any indication of a lie, or perhaps simply because Gothel enjoyed making Persinette uncomfortable. After what felt like forever, Gothel shrugged. "Fine. Your request is approved."

"Thank you Agent Gothel." Persi ducked her head, relief washing over her. She had gotten away with this much. *But can I get away with the rest?*

"But any books you take out of the library will be monitored, as usual." There it was, the underlying threat. *Sit up straight, Persinette. Fly right. Behave yourself and do as we say, or we'll dispose of you as we have so many others before you.* Persi had heard the same message so often she was almost numb to it. Almost.

"Of course." Persi nodded. Then she rose and left slowly, hoping it appeared like everything was normal.

ALTHOUGH THERE WERE other things to be done—like research and planning—Persi could not get the thought of training sessions with Agnes out of her mind. He was by no means going to go easy on her; she knew that. The bitter old unicorn may make her life doubly hard simply because he could. Still, there was one bright spot: she had been given the go-ahead to do her research in the library.

Persinette loved the library. Walking into the large upper-level west wing of MOTHER headquarters was like stepping back in time. She closed her eyes and inhaled deeply, breathing in the scents of years past. Every other part of MOTHER felt dim and sterilized compared to the library. They could not scrub books as one might metal, leaving the past lingering on their pages. This was her haven.

"Morning Persinette," Wyn greeted from the front desk, a grin crinkling her cheeks.

Persinette waved cheerfully and headed deeper into the library. She let her freckled fingers skim the spines of one shelf, practically feeling the knowledge hum beneath her fingers. She grabbed as many books on Province Four as she could carry—to sell her ruse, of course—while slipping a few books on communication spells into the stack here or there.

She found a secluded spot in the back of the library, where hopefully no one would pass by, and took her time poring over the books she'd found. With all the titles spread out on the table before her, it would be hard to tell which were spell books and which were history books—she hoped so, at least. After a few hours, Persi found a spell that might work, and flicked her gaze around to make sure no one was looking. She sent up a prayer and an apology to whatever deity was in charge of books, hoping that they would understand the necessity of this act, and then ripped the page from the book. The paper crinkled under her shaking fingers as she folded it and stuffed it down the front of her dress. *Desperate times*, she told herself. She gathered up all of her books and returned them to their designated shelves so no one would have any need to go through the books she had chosen.

Just for good measure, she took a book on Province Four history to the counter to check out. It would have looked suspicious if she didn't check anything out, right?

"Is that all? All of those books you grabbed, and you're just taking out this one?" Elwyn teased, one dark brow quirked up toward her tightly curled hair.

Guilt tugged at Persinette's lower back, nearly pulling her into an awkward hunch. She didn't like having to trick her friend, but she didn't really have a choice. So she swallowed down that feeling and shrugged. "I figured I have six weeks; I can pace myself a little."

"You're stressed about training with Agnes," Wyn offered. She must have misinterpreted the strain on her friend's face, but Persi wasn't going to correct her.

"A little," Persi admitted, grateful for the out, and handed over her library card and the book to be scanned. "But maybe it won't be so bad. I mean, no one can be that horrible all the time, right?" There was no point in asking Wyn how she knew Agnes would be training her. She was a librarian; she knew everything.

"I don't know, Persi. He seems pretty terrible to everyone except his two cronies."

"Still, you can't fault me for trying to be optimistic." As Wyn finished, Persi took the book and her card and tucked both into the empty satchel hanging from her shoulder.

Wyn sighed loudly and shook her head. "I can't help but feel that you're just going to get your feelings hurt that way."

"It wouldn't be the first time. And it probably won't be the last, either. Don't worry about me, Wyn. I've got this covered." Persi stretched her lips into a wide, confident smile, big enough to dimple her cheeks. She forced a brave wink that she didn't really feel. "And who knows, maybe I'll drive him crazy with my niceness and he'll just quit."

Wyn laughed loudly at that. "We can only hope. Well, good luck killing him with kindness."

"Oh Wyn, I don't need luck!" Persi allowed herself a soft chuckle, letting it relax her. She headed back toward her quarters, where she dropped off the book and tucked the spell away under her mattress before leaving for the dining hall.

There, in the center of the Enchanted dining hall—at a mostly empty table despite the crowded other tables—sat Agnes and his two cronies. Persinette felt her nerves nearly choke her as she watched the trio laugh about something Agnes had said. Soon, she'd be off to the training room. Soon, she'd be facing off with Agnes. Persinette's stomach gave another sick lurch, and suddenly she wasn't very hungry.

Instead of filling her plate as she usually would, she looked to the automaton behind the counter and asked, "Can I get some toast and blackberry jelly?" The blank eyes of the robot stared back at her for a moment, trying to register her question. "I'm sorry if it's outside of your normal programming," she said guiltily. The poor robot's innards whirled and ticked as it processed her request.

"Not to worry—Persinette," it responded in a stilted, awkward fashion. The automatons MOTHER put in the kitchen weren't the best machinery in the world, but their job wasn't overly complicated, and they did all right so long as they weren't asked to do something outside of their normal protocols. "I will have someone bring your—toast— to the table."

"Thank you." Persi took the little metal number the robot held out stiffly to her before plunging into the daily struggle of finding a place to sit. Although she liked to think of herself as friendly, she didn't have many friends, and the ones she did have were humans, which meant they ate with the other humans in a separate cafeteria. Why? MOTHER never really gave a reason; it was just the way things were. The humans and their Enchanted Assets ate separately, had separate bathrooms and even separate living quarters, the designation denoted on the doors with either a starburst or a person shape.

Perhaps to others it would be strange, even disturbing, but it was all Persinette had ever known. And, she supposed, it was the way of things. In all of the history

books she'd read, humans had always found a way to separate themselves into categories that didn't mean anything.
Enchanted themselves hadn't been much different. In their
history, fae, trolls, werewolves, and all the others had kept
themselves separate from each other as well. Different
lands. Different rulers. Different cultures. She sometimes
wondered how much of that was from the humans' influ-
ence on the realm of the magical, but it didn't matter now.
Now, the two had merged, and the categories were *human*
and *other*.

She found a seat against the wall on the edges of the
cafeteria's main seating area. A kitchen robot ticked along to
her table and dropped her plate onto it with a soft clatter.
Persinette took a moment to spread the jelly and then
nibbled the burned bread, hoping it would settle her nerves.
It didn't. But it was nice to have bread in her stomach. It
made her feel whole and centered in a way that wilted
canned vegetables probably wouldn't have.

At some point, the noise from Agnes' table drew her
attention again. He and his cronies were loud, carrying on
the way football players or frat boys did in some of those
human movies she'd watched with Wyn.

As if he sensed her staring at the back of his rainbow
head, Agnes turned to her and sneered. "Awwww, what's
the matter, 11-24-10?" he shouted over the din of the cafeteria. "Don't have any friends?" The whole hall fell silent as
everyone followed the gaze of Agnes's dark, cruel eyes.

"It's Persi." Her voice sounded clear and firm over the
space between them in a rare act of bravery. "Or Persinette
to you." She wasn't sure where her courage had come from,
but she found herself thrilled at the ability to bite back,
finally. Even if it was just this. Even if no one else would
think it was brave.

A loud snort, followed by uproarious laughter, was the only response. "Right, then. I'll see you in the training room, *Persinette*." Agnes's taunting look twisted his beautiful features into something ugly. Everyone around him chortled along, and Persi decided she'd had enough for one day. She slathered the other half of her toast in jam, grabbed her bag, and left the dining hall. The harsh sound of collective laughter seemed to engulf her until the doors shut behind her with their usual hiss.

6

CAPTAIN MANU KELII

A CRYSTAL GLASS of gaudy yellow liquid perched on one edge of stacks upon stacks of charts, holding down the edge of the pages and keeping them stretched flat across the worn wooden desk. Manu rubbed at his eyes, lounging further back into the oversized leather chair before glaring down at the stained papers once more. It had been a few days since they had left Province Two, and his stash of pineapple gin was getting low. Pineapple gin and tonics seemed to be the drink of choice for this mission, heavy on the gin. They would need to stop to refill his stores soon.

Manu sipped the from the glass slowly, savoring the tartness of the pineapple as he looked over a particularly detailed map of Province Four. They'd need to anchor just far enough away from the action not to be suspicious, but close enough to be of use. And, of course, Eddi had been none too specific about where in Province Four they needed to be. Home to the capital city where the queen resided, Province Four was the largest of the seven Provinces of Daiwynn. It would take them a week to cross from one side of it to the other, so something a *little* more specific was badly needed. The young captain grumbled as he looked over the map again, furrowing his brow.

"Something wrong, Cap'n?" The voice startled Manu out of his thoughts. His typically dark brown eyes flickered gold with irritation.

"Don't sneak up on me like that, Benard!" Manu growled and wadded up a bit of parchment to chuck at the first mate's head.

Benard ducked, long accustomed to dodging items hurled at him by the captain. As Manu fell into a melodramatic pout—shoulders slumped, arms crossed—the goblin's lip curled just so.

"Well?" Manu asked, letting irritation lace his tone.

"Eddi has sent another message. We are to head to Hoggle. The Uprising is sending a unit to meet us there."

Manu blinked at Benard in disbelief. "A unit!" he shouted and threw his hands up in agitation at the very thought. "What in gods' name do we need a unit for? We are *more* than capable of getting the people out without help!" He rose from his chair and paced the room. *Who did they think they were talking to? Some rank amateur?* Manu had run interference enough times in the last six years that he hardly needed an Uprising unit to help him extract a couple of Enchanted civilians!

"I have no idea, sir," Benard responded calmly. "Perhaps just to be safe?" He shrugged and looked at the maps sprawled out on the table, his glowing green gaze falling to the exact location of Hoggle. One long ear twitched. "It doesn't look like much."

The captain sighed—releasing some of his annoyance—and came to stand beside Benard, looking at the map as well. "That's because it isn't much. Hoggle is the smallest town in Province Four. What would they want with that place?"

Benard shrugged again, lifting his eyes back to the captain. "Must be someone important there."

"Either that, or this is just a test run for their Seer. To see how good the Asset is before throwing them out into the fray." It still didn't sit quite right with him, bringing a Seer out into a potential combat situation. MOTHER didn't train Seers for that, which meant an innocent Enchanted was likely to get hurt. What was MOTHER trying to do?

"You think this is a new trend?" Benard asked.

"Unfortunately, yes, I do." Manu all but hurled himself back into the overstuffed chair, scrubbing at his face. "It seems MOTHER is getting desperate to finish rounding us all up."

"It's sure taken them long enough. They've been at this what, a hundred and fifty years?" Benard snorted softly and rolled his eyes.

He was right, of course; it had taken them long enough. For as long as Manu had been alive—some twenty-six years or so—MOTHER had been rounding up Enchanted and putting them into the camps. The trouble was that magical beings were hard to track and even harder to pin down. Now, it would seem, MOTHER was looking for ways to speed up the process. The thought unsettled Manu.

"Should we be worried, do you think?" Benard's ears twitched again in clear concern.

"I wish I knew, Benard." Manu sighed and ran a hand through his hair. The young captain didn't know much about what the hell was going on in the kingdom of Daiwynn politically. He spent much of his time floating above it all and very little time walking among the people.

But there was one thing he did know, and that was this. "There's a war coming. I can tell you that much."

Benard nodded. It seemed that every person in Daiwynn had come to terms with this fact. The kingdom had been on the brink of a second magical war with the humans since the practically the end of the War of 2050. However, that brink had never been closer than it was now. "Question is, are we on the winning side?" Benard's eyes lit with mischief. Goblins loved a good fight.

"Maybe, maybe not." Manu shrugged and took up his now lukewarm glass of gin and tonic. "But we're on the *right side*."

The pair was silent for a what felt like hours as they both stared down the maps, captain and first mate thinking the same thought: *this might be the end of everything.*

"How far out are we from Province Four?" Manu asked at last, breaking the silence.

"Eh, about a day. Should be to the border before tomorrow evening."

"Right, then. I want to make a stop for gin." Manu didn't stop the grin settling onto his lips as he held up the small empty bottle for Benard to see.

All this earned him was an eye roll, a soft scoff, and not a single word as the first mate departed.

"Is that a no? Are you sassing your captain, good sir? I should have you walk the plank!" Manu shouted. But that didn't stop Benard. The goblin just kept walking.

Manu grumbled as he reclined in place once more. The door shut with a soft click.

MANU MUST HAVE FALLEN asleep in that chair looking over the maps, because the next thing he knew the sun was beating in through the large bay window opposite him. A soft growl left him as he lifted his head to glare at the open curtains. He distinctly remembered closing those before he settled in with a drink to chart a course the night before—

"Morning, Cap'n." Benard's voice rang out cheerfully. *Ah, there's the source of the damnable curtains brightness.* "Breakfast is porridge and bratwurst, and you have a call waiting for you on the flight deck."

"Who on the gods' green earth would be calling at—" Manu looked around for his pocket watch, patting the sides of his waistcoat and shifting the papers on the desk before him. The blasted thing was nowhere to be found.

"Seven o'clock in the morning, sir," Benard supplied helpfully. He reached for the front pocket of Manu's rumpled periwinkle waistcoat, extracted the watch, and set it in Manu's hand.

Manu squeezed it, sat up straighter, and tucked the watch back into the waistcoat pocket. "Right. Right. Seven o'clock, of course it is. The question still remains."

The goblin's eyes swept over his captain. He frowned. "You may want to wash up first, Cap'n. It's Eddi, and I doubt you want to see the leader of the Uprising when you're all—" He gestured to the captain's disheveled appearance.

"Right, then. Go keep them occupied and leave me to it." Manu stood and shooed the first mate from his quarters. He sighed, scrubbed at his face once more, and headed to the bathroom to shower and get himself into a fresh set of clothes.

Just as he was buttoning up a clean waistcoat, there was

a knock at the door. "What is it now?" he called, annoyance dripping in every word.

One of the young cabin boys peeked around the door, looking for all the world thoroughly terrified. "Mister Benard says to hurry up, sir. He says you've already kept Eddi waiting an hour, sir," he whispered.

"Tell him that perfection takes time!" The captain roared, his eyes flashing golden in irritation at the young boy, who yelped, slammed the door, and ran off.

It was a while longer before the captain finally decided to grace the flight deck with his presence, but his leisurely arrival only seemed to amuse Benard, rather than annoy him as Manu had hoped. Manu's hair was now neatly combed and his clothes were immaculate—a royal purple waistcoat with a crisp white shirt underneath and perfectly matching purple trousers. He looked every bit the suave and debonair captain that he was, if he did say so himself.

"Clear the room," Eddi ordered. Everyone rushed to comply, not wanting to upset the leader of the Uprising any more than their captain already had. Once the crew was gone, Eddi locked those magnified grey eyes onto Manu, who froze for half a second too long. "You kept me waiting."

"But I look damn good doing it," Manu said, mustering all the bravado he could. He needed it now more than ever, because he knew what was coming. Eddi would give him the rest of his mission and he would have to reconcile himself to whatever misery he was assigned.

Eddi stared at him, not even a little hint of amusement on their face. Manu's ego deflated a little—not enough to force the smirk from his lips, but still. "Are you quite finished joking around?"

"Yes, sir." Manu tumbled into the captain's chair with a heavy sigh. He grabbed a bit of parchment from the table nearby to jot down whatever information they would give him.

"This is your target." A black-and-white picture of a beautiful, fair-skinned young woman appeared on the screen. The girl's skin was littered in more freckles than the sky had stars, and soft ringlets of light hair neatly framed her face.

"Since when did MOTHER Assets get so pretty?" The question left Manu of its own accord, his mind stuttering at the image of the girl.

Eddi's wrinkled face quickly replaced the girl's. "Her name is Persinette. You are to make contact. Our operative on the inside says that Persinette is open to helping our cause. If she does prove willing, you will be her point of contact."

Manu nodded as he jotted everything down. With a whirring and clicking noise, the NON printer beside him spat out a grainier, picture of Persinette. "And if she isn't willing?"

"Then your orders are to shoot her," Eddi said simply, and then the transmission cut out.

Manu grabbed the picture and sat back in the chair, his dark eyes flicking over the girl's features. His fingers trembled, the paper shaking in his grasp. "Then you shoot her," he repeated, trying to come to terms with that idea. He knew why Eddi wanted that. If the Uprising couldn't have her, they'd rather she die than work for MOTHER, and so there was logic to the order. Still, he couldn't imagine putting a bullet in the freckle-faced girl staring up at him from the picture. "I wonder what color her eyes are."

7

PERSINETTE

AN HOUR LATER, the flouncy bustled skirt and tightly
fitted corset had been replaced with a pair of leggings and
form-fitting camisole so Persi could prepare for training. She
tied her long hair back in a braid, steadied herself, and
headed to the training room. Gears clanked softly as the
training room doors opened. Inside, the room was a wash of
sounds of people fighting—grunting and panting, and
weapons smacking one another or firing ammunition.

"Oh look, she showed up." The cold words were all that
greeted Persi when she walked in. Agnes was leaning
against a wall, waiting, his long, slim form stretched out
lazily. He wore his telltale rainbow mane tied in a tight bun.
"And you actually came prepared this time. Good." That
sneer was on his face again. Dread seeped into Persinette's
very bones. "Where shall we start, do you think?"

Where shall we start? As if she knew! Persinette had
received no weapons training whatsoever in her time with
MOTHER. She barely knew the names of half of the
weapons, let alone how to use them. So she merely shrugged.

All that earned her was a stony glare from Agnes. "Very well then, we'll start with hand-to-hand. Come along." He turned abruptly and headed deeper into the training room to find a combat arena that was open. He never once glanced back to make sure she was following, nor did he bother to slow his long strides so that she could keep up. When he found a vacant arena, he led her inside. Then Agnes turned to her while standing in the middle of the mat. Arms crossed over his leanly muscled chest, he watched her as if waiting for something. For what? She wasn't sure.

"Now what?" Persi asked, shifting awkwardly from foot to foot at the edge of the mat.

"Come at me," he instructed simply. His blue eyes remained focused firmly on her, watching for any twitch of movement.

Persi's eyes widened. She blinked at him. "I'm sorry, what?"

"I said, come at me," Agnes repeated, glaring at her. When she didn't react right away, he let out a long-suffering sigh. "This is the best way for me to judge your skill level. Attack me."

"I can't just...a-attack you," Persi stammered. She recoiled, her shoulders hunching.

"Damn it, 11-24-10! Attack me!" Agnes growled. His eyes flashed with danger. "Attack me or I'll attack you!"

Terror jolted her into action. If there was one thing Persinette did not want, it was for Agnes to attack her. He had far more training than she did, and the desire to inflict real damage. Without another thought or any kind of plan, Persinette ran at Agnes as fast as she could.

It took Agnes less than a half a second to use her

momentum against her, leaving Persinette in a breathless heap on the mat as he glared down at her.

He glared down at her. "That was pathetic." He nudged her with one polished boot before stepping some distance away again. "Get up and do it again."

She laid there for a moment, trying to fill her lungs with air as they squeezed tight from the impact, her eyes fixed on the cold ceiling of the training arena. Maybe if she didn't get up, he'd write her off as useless, and they could end this now.

"I said get up, 11-24-10!"

With another gasp, Persi pulled herself to her feet and turned back to Agnes. Her hands tightened into fists at her sides, and she took a moment to size him up, forcing herself to slow down and think. *Focus, Persinette.* Another breath, giving herself time to come up with an inkling of a plan, but there was nothing. So she ran at him again, the time letting out a shout of determination as she went.

It ended with her in the same place—on her back, on the mat, gasping for breath. He was *so* fast.

"Again!"

It went that way for a while longer until Persi was sure her back was bruised from the force of being thrown onto the mat. When she pulled herself upright, Persi panted and let out a soft whimper of pain as an ache settled bone-deep into her spine.

"You just keep doing the same stupid thing and expecting different results," Agnes said. "Try something else!"

"Can't we just be done for tonight?" Persi hunched forward to brace herself on her knees.

"No." Agnes watched her. He looked every bit the neatly coiffed man he'd been when he'd walked into the arena—not a hair out of place—whereas Persi's hair was mostly free of its braid and she was panting roughly. "Again."

This time Persi took her time. She circled him slowly, thinking of the best way to attack. This time, instead of just charging straight at his middle, she came at him from the side and leveled a kick at his stomach. In a flash she was on her back again, the wind knocked from her once more.

Agnes leaned over her with a brow raised. "That was better. I'll see you again tomorrow." With that, the unicorn left Persi laying in the middle of the mat, still panting.

When Persi finally pulled herself to her feet, it was with a groan. She dragged herself back to the Tower, and even as her body begged for rest, she pulled the spell from under her mattress and began to practice the words.

MAGIC WAS NOT AS easy as Persinette had thought it would be. In the books she'd read it always sounded so simple—one could pick up a spell, recite it a couple of times, and make it work. However, like all other Enchanted who had been abducted as MOTHER Assets, Persi had no formal magical training. Every Enchanted had access to that power, but without proper training none could wield it, let alone even find it.

She spoke the words and reached for the magic, but it refused to come to her. It felt as if there were a sheet of glass separating her from her power, and the more she reached, the thicker the glass became.

"Ugh, come here," Persinette muttered to the power, feeling silly as it stubbornly refused. It was almost like she was talking to herself. And what was doubly ridiculous was that the spell itself required two people.

Exhaling, she eyed the page before her again. At the top, written in scrawled untidy handwriting, were the words 'Fire Message' and a list.

Items required:

Candle

Paper

Pen

Candles were in short supply in MOTHER headquarters, but every Enchanted was still supplied one for emergencies; power outages in the Tower were a semi-regular occurrence. Persi supposed she'd just sit in the dark next time.

The instructions were relatively simple: light the candle, write your message, and recite the spell while the paper was burning. The trouble with all of that was that Persi had no one to send a message, and therefore no way to check if the spell was working. After some thought, she decided to send a message from her bedroom to the over-stuffed chair in front of her bookshelves and prayed that was enough distance to test it.

Things were not going well. So far, she had not managed to get the messages even that far. All she had to show for her efforts was an awful lot of wasted parchment, a room full of the stench of burned paper, and singed fingertips.

"Damn it." She winced, dropping the latest bit of flaming parchment to the desk and lifting her fingers to her lips to try to cool them. Once the paper had burned away, she stood, ran to the chair, and found no signs of the message having transferred—again.

Persi sighed, looking down at the torn page once more

as she shook her head. She hadn't thought much of it before, but if she could get this to work—this one tiny spell—then perhaps she could do other magic. Maybe she could even escape using magic.

She bit her bottom lip, then she tucked the torn page under her mattress with the silent promise that she'd try again tomorrow.

PERSINETTE SOON FOUND that that failure would set the tone for the whole next week.

First, there was a breakfast of soggy toast and canned eggs, the very sight of which turned Persi's stomach. "You'd think they could at least give us dry toast," someone behind her complained to his friend. "I mean where has this stuff even been?"

She tried not to think about that as she headed for a table near the doors. Her skirts rustled when she sank into her chair and proceeded to push the slimy eggs around her plate. A tray clattered at her elbow, followed by a second, and third, announcing that three people had joined her at the table. When her eyes flicked up, she found Agnes and his two friends sitting across from her.

"11-24-10." Agnes looked terribly smug as always.

Suddenly, Persi felt she was not very hungry. Without a word she stood, took her tray and left.

Then there was the third meeting with Gothel in as many days.

"Your training is not going well," Gothel said, not giving Persi the time to sit. Before her lay a paper which was no doubt a report on Persinette's abysmal progress with Agnes.

Persinette settled into the chair and shifted uncomfortably. "Well, it has only been a few days."

Gothel gave a soft snort. Her dark eyes flicked up from the paper, examining Persinette in much the same manner as a scientist studying bacteria under a microscope. "We expected more of you, Persinette."

Of course they had—though Persinette wasn't sure *why* they had. She'd never trained as a field agent and had a history of being nonconfrontational. It had always been her understanding that she was an Asset who would remain at a safe distance from any type of combat. "Well, I still have five whole weeks to get it right," she said, trying to sound hopeful.

"We're going to lengthen your training sessions with Agnes. Four hours a day instead of two." It was clear from the look on Gothel's face that she not only knew how uncomfortable this announcement would make Persinette, but also delighted in it.

"Four hours? But I still have research to do!"

"Then I suppose you'll have to skip lunch, won't you?" Gothel's tone was almost gleeful.

Persi bowed her head instead of arguing. Nothing she could say would change the situation, so what point was there? "Yes, ma'am."

Then, right before lunch, Persinette reported to another training session with Agnes. As much as he seemed to enjoy beating her to the ground, she had to wonder why he bothered even trying to help her. It was evident he did not like her, and likely would be just as happy if she were to die in the field with no training at all. Yet, there they were again, standing in the middle of a squishy mat, staring each other down.

Persi was panting from another round of hand-to-hand

combat in which she'd ended up on her back at least ten times.

"Why are they even putting the effort into you? They should just let someone shoot you," Agnes said coolly. He didn't wait for her response; he just grabbed two bo staffs from the weapons cabinet and threw one at her. He laughed as she fumbled to catch it before it landed on the mat with a muted *thunk*.

Persinette didn't respond. She picked up the staff, held it in front of her like one might a bat, and waited. Agnes didn't keep her waiting long—he came at her with all of the force he could muster, smacking the staff from her hands and sweeping her legs from under her in one fluid motion. Her back smacked against the mat, and she coughed loudly as the wind fled her lungs. As she choked to regain her breath, tears burned her eyes.

"You're not even holding it right! It's not a bat." Agnes held up his hands so that she could see how he was handling the staff, but a fell back into a fighting stance almost instantly. "Again!"

It went on like that for another hour and forty-five minutes before Agnes finally dismissed her and Persinette was left to drag her tired and worn body down to the mess hall to grab some toast. Then it was off to the library for more research.

"You all right, Persi?" Wyn asked as Persinette limped past the front desk.

Persi merely nodded and kept walking toward the rows of books. She didn't have time to be injured right now. There was too much at stake. With just five more weeks until they headed to Hoggle for the Collection, there was no time to waste.

"Oh no you don't. I'm taking you to the medic. Right

now." Wyn wasted no time in coming around the desk and dragging her friend back down the hall.

The medic offices were stark and cold, lacking much of the character and warmth of the other departments in MOTHER headquarters. The walls were a washed-out white and the furniture was something that Persi might have been called "modern" in the time before the war.

"Name?" the bored-looking woman with the overly-large spectacles behind the counter asked, not even glancing up from the paperwork in front of her.

Persinette sighed and handed over her badge. Then she settled onto one of the cold, hard, too-white chairs in the waiting room.

8

CAPTAIN MANU KELII

THE PICTURE of the girl named Persinette fluttered lightly with the motion of the ship underneath the bit of tape holding it next to the captain's desk. Manu hadn't ever been given such a mission before. Most of the missions the Uprising sent him on were simple extractions—get in, get the people out, get away, and all as quickly as possible. In all honesty—though he would never show it—Manu was a little nervous to become a point of contact for an agent on the inside. It was a huge responsibility. So, he did his best not to think about that.

Instead, he focused on the sheer annoyance he felt at being instructed to pick up a unit in the border town of Olaf.

"Perhaps they'll come in handy, sir," Benard offered, sounding somewhat optimistic.

"Come in handy? Doing what? Mutinying? Taking my ship? Making me do all the things I don't want to do?" Manu's tone grew shriller the longer he talked, and he felt the control slip, the subtle shift of brown to golden in his eyes, but he couldn't stop it. "I have no desire to have such treasonous vipers aboard my ship!"

Benard let out a heavy breath at Manu's antics. "I think you're just paranoid."

Growling, Manu narrowed his flickering gaze on his first mate and bared his now-sharper teeth. "Paranoia is what keeps a pirate captain in control of his ship, good sir."

"Right, pirate captain," Benard muttered.

"What was that, first mate?" Manu surely looked for all the world as threatening as a tiger waiting to pounce, but Benard seemed unruffled.

"Nothin', Cap'n. I was just wondering when you were heading to the meetup, sir? Shall I rally the troops?"

Manu snorted, but his control had returned, and with it the shrinking of sharp incisors and darkening of irises. The decision was made; he would take on the unit whether he liked it or not (he did not) and he would prove to Eddi that he was capable. Hopefully, after that, he would be allowed to drop Eddi's spies off somewhere and complete the mission with just his crew. Till then, he'd follow orders.

"They should be ready when we touch down in Olaf. I want none of the Uprising to be able to run back to Eddi and say we were late." Manu's tone was restrained, tight, but he'd managed to reign in his anger for the time being.

Benard nodded before hustling out to gather up those they had decided would be backing up the captain for the rendezvous.

A FEW PASSING hours found the *Defiant Duchess* settled gracefully into a hover a few feet above the ground, her crew ready and waiting for the final order. Captain Kelii and his first mate had hand-selected some of their best shipmates to join him at the meeting with the Uprising Unit and ensured each was laden down with enough weapons to combat an attack by the Uprising, daggers and pistols tucked safely away beneath long cloaks and overcoats. Manu was taking no chances.

The small group filed onto the platform, which descended with the soft clicking of gears. As they touched down, the puff of dry earth took a moment to settle, but once it had, the captain and his crew set off for town. The meetup spot was an abandoned office building full of pressboard furniture and old computers that had long ago been ransacked for parts. Disintegrating ceiling tiles long fallen crunched beneath their feet as they traipsed over to, and then up, the stairs, headed for the fifth floor.

"They sure wanted to be certain we weren't followed, didn't they sir?" one of the older crew members—a werewolf named Sebastian—asked as he climbed the steps.

Manu shook his head, frowning. "No, I don't think that's it. I think they didn't want the chance of us ambushing them." He blinked, surprised at his own words. Maybe Benard was right; perhaps he was getting ridiculously paranoid.

"Something wrong, sir?"

"No, nothing." The door to the fifth floor opened with an annoyingly loud creak, so loud they couldn't have snuck up on the Uprising Unit if they had wanted to.

There, in the middle of a room strewn with broken office furniture and mostly disintegrated paper, waited a group of five Uprising agents, all dressed from head to toe in black and eyeing the crew of the *Defiant Duchess* with varying amounts of disgust. At the front of the group was a green-haired witch, one brow cocked and her red-painted mouth twitching at the corners.

"Ah, Captain Kelii. How nice to finally meet you," she said smoothly.

Though her lips said the words, her eyes said something else entirely. It put Manu's teeth on edge. As did the fact that she knew his name, but he had no idea who she was. He narrowed his eyes—to cover the fact that the whole thing discomfited him—and approached the woman, boots crunching as he went. Now in front of her, Manu offered one of his trademark roguish smiles. "I'm afraid we haven't been formally introduced. I'm Manu Kelii, Captain of the *Defiant Duchess*. And you are?" He held his hand out to her, more out of politeness than an actual desire to shake her hand.

"Ivy Warner." She extended one lightly tanned hand but didn't shake his. Instead, she let it hang there, limp at the wrist—waiting.

Manu seized the cue, taking her hand carefully in his own and kissing it, a gesture so antiquated and foreign that he had to wonder how old Ivy Warner actually was. "Right, then," he said, straightening and dropping her hand. "I suppose we ought to head back to the ship. We have quite the journey ahead of us to Hoggle."

Ivy studied him, dark eyes thoughtful as she seemed to calculate something. Her odds, maybe? He had no idea. Either way, he decided very quickly he did not trust Ivy Warner. He did not trust her at all.

"Do you not have any questions about our purpose on your ship?"

The captain tilted his head, examining her in return. "I have many questions about your purpose on my ship," he responded flatly. "But all of them can be answered in the reasonable safety of the *Defiant Duchess* once we are on our way. Don't you think?"

Another long silence passed as Ivy examined him. Then she nodded in agreement. "Very well. Let's move out."

The group retired down the stairs, and once more to the outskirts of Olaf, where the airship waited for them, bobbing pleasantly in the breeze.

ONCE THEY WERE EN ROUTE, the captain settled into his quarters, hoping, if he could, to avoid the Uprising Unit and its leader. There hadn't been a confrontation—not yet—but he was not sure how long the preemptive détente between himself and this Ivy woman might last.

"You can't avoid her forever, you know," Benard said as he entered the room, bumping the door shut with his hip. "Besides, isn't she your type?"

"Excuse me?" Manu asked, looking up from where he'd been scowling at the worn floor of his quarters. "My type?"

The scathing tone from his captain only seemed to make Benard snicker. "Yes. Beautiful, powerful, and very likely to shoot you when it all goes horribly wrong. Exactly your type."

"That was one time, Benard!" Manu narrowed his eyes at his snickering first mate. "Honestly, I can't believe you're still bringing that up. It was *years* ago." He settled into a sulk, arms crossed.

"It was six months ago," Benard reminded him.

The captain huffed and intensified the ferocity of his glare. "Still."

"Just trying to keep you grounded, sir," the goblin said with a soft chuckle. His words only made Manu pout more.

"So, this is what the great Captain Kelii does in his spare time? Sulk like an errant child?" A female voice interrupted their staring match. Both men looked up to find that Ivy had joined them without so much as a knock.

"Do you—" Manu snapped, but Benard stepped between them.

"Miss Warner, how delightful to see you. Please, do come in and join us; we were just discussing which route was best to get to Hoggle and where to dock once we reached the town." There was a false politeness in Benard's tone that no one but those who knew him best would catch. Manu turned up his nose in disgust at Benard's cordiality, but quickly schooled his expression and sat up from his slumped posture, not wanting to draw a scolding from Benard. "Yes, please do come in. We'd appreciate your input."

Ivy nodded and took a seat on the other side of the desk, facing Manu. Her dark eyes flicked over the untidy surface before they fell upon the picture of Persinette taped to the wall. "Do you frequently hang up pictures of potential Assets?"

Manu shrugged, not even glancing at the picture, as though it were of no importance at all. "I want to be sure I don't forget who I'm looking for once we reach Hoggle. It helps me focus." Maybe it was the truth; perhaps it was a lie. In all honesty, Manu had no idea why he'd hung the picture up.

"I see," Ivy responded, eyeing him suspiciously. "As if the host of MOTHER agents surrounding her wouldn't be enough of a clue." Her too-red lips twitched upwards as they had earlier.

"Yes...well." Manu gave another awkward shrug. "That's not really important, is it? What's important is how are we going to set up camp just outside of Hoggle without being noticed. The town is relatively small, and MOTHER is sure to take notice of an airship parked just outside."

Ivy settled back into the chair, crossing one leg over the other and taking her time to arrange her skirts, in no apparent hurry to provide anything of use. "Why not just use a cloaking spell to cloak the ship?" she asked finally.

The two men blinked, and a brief silence passed before Manu said, "Because we don't have a witch aboard with enough power to cloak the entire ship."

Ivy twitched those red lips again and released a soft chuckle. "Well, it was lucky that Eddi sent me to you, wasn't it? Perhaps for this very purpose."

"Right. *Lucky*," Benard muttered.

"Is that the only reason Eddi sent you to us? To provide cloaking for Hoggle?" That was a terribly convenient excuse. Manu was suspicious.

"And to make sure you follow orders, of course," Ivy added with a little shrug of her own. "Eddi is worried you'll go..." Her words trailed off, as she flicked another glance at the picture of Persinette. "...*soft* on the Asset."

"Of course." Manu clenched his teeth, jaw ticking in annoyance.

"I wouldn't take it too personally, Captain. You hardly have a track record of being our most brutal man on the ground." There was a hard glint in her green eyes that made Manu a little queasy.

"And what is *your* track record?" He couldn't help but ask, but once he'd voiced the question, he had wished he hadn't.

She gave a careless chuckle as she stood and made for

the door, heeled boots clicking softly against the floorboards. "I'd get some rest if I were you, Captain. We have quite the journey ahead of us."

9

PERSINETTE

AN INHUMAN howl came from the other side of the heavy iron door before her. In spite of her rising fear, Persi lifted one pale and freckled hand lifted to push it open. The door swung inward with a screech of hinges that echoed off the cold cinderblock walls inside. Something moved in the darkness, rushing from one side of the room to the other. As soon as Persinette picked her way inside to see what it was, the door slammed behind her. A moment later, an emaciated, pale, bleeding face filled her vision so that she could see nothing but—that face, those screaming, tortured eyes.

PERSINETTE JERKED AWAKE WITH A SOB.

"Silas!" she panted, clutching at the sweat-slicked fabric of her camisole. "Poor Silas."

She brushed sticky strands of hair back from her forehead, allowing herself a moment to remember Silas. She'd been ten years old when the vision had left her frozen in her seat in the cafeteria. That vision had sent a little boy to the labor camps, a boy scarcely two years her junior. Although she had been terrified for her own safety, fear didn't excuse the fact that she had given that little boy's name and location to MOTHER, condemning him to spend the rest of his short life slaving away at backbreaking work for MOTHER's profit.

She remembered his face even now, just as she remembered them all. Silas had been eight, with the pale green skin and slightly pointed ears of a pixie. Closing her eyes, Persi could still summon her original vision of him.

There he was on the hill just outside of town—all blonde hair and big brown eyes—flying his kite and laughing. Not a single care in the world. No idea that in only two days' time MOTHER would come and Collect him.

Persi shook her head, pulling herself from that image and the guilt that gnawed at her. Her eyes flicked to the clock on her bedside table.

The softly glowing metal hands of the clock showed the time even in the darkened room: 3:00 a.m. For a moment, she thought to shut her eyes and try to go back to sleep. Maybe she could get a bit more rest before the long day ahead. But the moment her eyelids closed, she saw Silas's gaunt face again, and she abandoned that hope entirely.

"All right, Persi. May as well do some practicing." She rolled out of her bed and headed back to the desk, where she'd perched the candle. She lit the wick, scribbled her name on a bit of parchment, and set it aflame as she whispered the spell again.

For the first time in weeks, the paper didn't just burn—it flashed a brilliant violet color. Surprised, Persi yelped and dropped the parchment to the desk, where it disintegrated into a smoking pile of ashes. Her eyes remained fixed on the small, smoldering heap for a long time, still shocked by the brilliant flash of light. Then she leaped to standing, knocking the chair to the floor in her haste.

Her stocking feet skidded across the threadbare rug as she came to a stop before the well-worn leather chair. There, sitting in the middle of the slightly sunken leather cushion, was a charred bit of paper. On that blackened piece of paper read the word *Persinette* in an untidy scrawl.

"Yes!" Persinette whooped, bouncing in her excitement. "It works! It really works!" A half-awake delirious giggle bubbled out of her, the sheer joy and amazement setting her body humming. "I can do magic," she whispered excitedly, still bobbling on her toes. "I can do magic!" She shouted it this time, her limbs flailing in a ridiculous victory dance that would be thoroughly embarrassing if anyone were to see it.

Once the glee had subsided, and she'd stopped her dancing, Persi returned to her desk for a fresh bit of paper. She tapped the pen to her lips in thought, pondering just what to say. The sending of the messages would have to wait, of course; no one would be awake to receive them at this hour. But that was something she could worry about later. For now, she just needed a message to send to those unlucky few whose faces were on the list she'd given Gothel.

What she finally scribbled onto the parchment was this: 'MOTHER is coming. Get out.'

IN THE TIME between writing the message and daybreak, Persi had practiced the small collection of spells she'd amassed over her last few weeks. None of the other spells worked, but she told herself she just needed more practice.

After all, it had taken her five weeks to get the fire message spell to work.

Five weeks—five *long* weeks—had passed in what felt like an instant. Between regular training sessions with Agnes and her research, she barely had time for meals, much less magic practice. Although she'd been able to use some magic in that five weeks, her training with Agnes was not going any more smoothly than it had at the outset. She did not ache as she had the first couple of weeks, true, but she was no closer to fending off Agnes or his attacks—a fact she was reminded of as she once again entered the training arena.

Agnes was standing there as always, a bored expression on his face.

"Should I get the bo staffs again?" she asked as she tried to prepare herself for what would no doubt be an onslaught of whacking with the hard, wooden pole. One would have thought that after five weeks of being beaten with the damn thing, she'd have learned how to fend it off. But she hadn't, and it still hurt like hell every time he smacked her with it.

"No."

The world jolted Persi to a sudden stop, her lavender brows lifted in surprise.

"Go get a set of pistols," Agnes continued. "We are heading down to the firing range."

Persi felt all of the color drain from her face. "We don't need to do that. They're probably not going to issue me a pistol," she argued weakly.

The unicorn's lips twisted into something like an irritated grimace. "Did I ask that?"

Five weeks ago, the annoyed expression would have glued her tongue to the roof of her mouth. Not now. Not today. That small victory early in the morning had left

Persinette feeling powerful in a way she'd never felt before. So instead of bowing and taking Agnes's abuse as she usually did, she frowned and shook her head. "No, but it still seems like a waste of time. They aren't going to issue me a pistol, so I have no use for knowing how to fire one."

"Yet not even a month ago you insisted on practicing at the firing range yourself," Agnes responded coolly.

""Well, yes, but that was only because Gothel said I might be given a stunning pistol. I don't really think I will, though." Persi's hands clenched at her side, her feet steady on the ground beneath her.

Those dark blue eyes stared her down coldly. Perhaps Agnes expected her to cave, just give up and do as she was told. But she did not, because she *would* not, and so he snorted softly. "Trust me, little Seer, you will want the target practice. Whether you're given a stunning pistol or not, the ability to hit a target at a distance will come in handy. For all you know, you'll use it to chuck a shoe at someone in self-defense."

The image of herself hurling a shoe at an enemy to defend herself almost made Persi giggle. Instead, she opened her mouth to argue once more. "I hardly—"

"That is enough! Go and get the damn pistols, 11-24-10!" Agnes snapped. "Before I write you up for insubordination."

Persi's mouth clapped shut, and she nodded quickly. Insubordination was not something she needed added to her file. Instead of launching more arguments, she checked out two practice pistols from the firearms locker and headed down to the firing range to meet Agnes.

His face was blank with boredom again as he held out a long-fingered hand. After she'd given over the pistol, they both advanced to the yellow line painted on the floor.

"Watch me closely this time," Agnes instructed. He squared off his body just so, narrowed his eyes, and fired. Persi's eyes flew from him to the target in amazement. There, in the dead center in the paper, was a small, smoking hole. "Now, you try."

Persinette nodded, drawing back her shoulders and puffing out her chest to appear bigger than her diminutive form. Then she did her best to square her feet as Agnes had, lifted the pistol, and aimed.

"No, no, no!"

Persi stopped, alarmed, her finger still on the trigger.

"That isn't how you hold a pistol, you idiot," Agnes said. "You're going to break your damn hand doing that." He moved to her, his whole demeanor exasperated, and pulled the wrist of her free hand where it was relaxed at her side. "Both hands, moron. Both hands." His fingers curled over hers hold them in place around the weapon. "This will also keep the gun steady when it recoils."

Persinette stayed silent, but noted where he'd positioned her hands.

"And square up your feet more, shoulder-width apart. You should be able to brace yourself against the ground." He kicked at her calves to widen her stance, and she shifted stiffly. "It might feel weird at first, but you'll get used to it." He moved around her, correcting the angle of her hips and shoulders more. "This is also prime shoe-chucking stance."

She wasn't sure if he was joking or not, but on the off chance that he wasn't, she didn't laugh. Instead, Persi glanced down at her feet to memorize where he had placed them and focused all her energy on not budging an inch.

"Now, lock your elbows in against your body." Agnes tugged her arms close to her torso before leaning over her shoulder to squint through the sight. "All right, aim and fire.

But wait till I move off," he added quickly with a giant step back.

She nodded and waited. In the new position, the recoil jerked her whole body, not just her shoulder. She winced.

There was a little tsk-ing noise as Agnes surveyed the target, which she had missed entirely. "You didn't anchor down through your toes," he chided, pushing her into the stance once more. "Spread your toes out in your shoes to grip the ground."

"This is pointless," Persi muttered, even as a violent flush reddened her cheeks.

"Protecting yourself is never pointless. Again!"

10

CAPTAIN MANU KELII

THE ORDER HAD COME as they neared the city of Flit:
They were to head into the city to stop one of MOTHER's
raids on an underground produce market.

"So, what's the plan?" Benard asked as he, Ivy, and
Manu sat in the captain's quarters once more. The meetings
were becoming a regular thing, and one that Manu did not
much care for.

"We are going to cause a diversion while Ivy and her
unit go in and get everyone out of the market. No muss, no
fuss, no unnecessary bloodshed." It sounded so simple when
the captain said it like that. Even Manu himself believed
that it would be that easy; somehow saying it out loud made
it seem entirely possible.

Ivy looked at him blankly. "No."

"No?" Manu furrowed his brow. "Then what's your plan,
Miss Warner?"

"We plan an ambush and dispense with the MOTHER
unit before they even reach the market." The words were
said in such a way that told Manu that the idea of killing
people didn't bother her at all. It almost sounded as if she

might enjoy it. "I see no reason to spare the lives of our enemies."

"And I see no reason to draw unwanted attention to my crew or my ship when we are about to go on a mission where stealth is of the essence," Manu spat back without skipping a beat. Out of the corner of his eye, he saw Benard grin, but Manu's gaze didn't drift from Ivy. She stared back at the captain—unblinking—as if perhaps she could change his mind merely by looking at him. "Is that clear, Miss Warner?" His tone left no room for argument.

She nodded. "Yes, sir. No bloodshed, sir."

"Are you mocking me, Miss Warner?"

"Wouldn't dream of it, Captain." She stood. "If that will be all, I will go prepare my unit. When will we be touching down in Flit?"

"0300," Benard answered for his captain. The goblin's eyes had narrowed on her, but he said nothing more.

Ivy dipped her head in farewell and left. Once the sound of her retreating boots had faded, the two men faced each other.

"I want a small unit of our own to go along with them," Manu said.

"You don't think she'll follow orders?" Benard asked with a frown.

"I'd rather not take the chance."

Benard nodded. "I'll gather up some of the men," the goblin said, and left the captain to his thoughts.

IT TOOK them two days to reach Flit, and all the while Manu and his crew prepared for the task ahead. A small group of men, led by Benard, had been instructed to keep an eye on Ivy and her unit while another group was assigned to cause a distraction.

The morning of the mission, the whole crew was outfitted with stunning pistols before they filed down into the city.

"This way," Manu said as he led his small unit to where reports had indicated MOTHER would enter the city. An elementary school and small boarding house for low-income families were the only highlights of this part of Flit. The ever-present thin veil of steam drifted through the streets in the early morning, reflecting only the soft glow of street-lights as the city lowered deeper into its sleep. Then a flash of light drew the captain's eye. Through the steam, he and his unit could see the shimmering air indicative of a portal opening, which a handful of MOTHER agents came through and onto the empty street. Someone shifted behind Manu in anticipation, but he held up his hand—*wait*. The small envoy of MOTHER agents slipped through the streets of Flit, and Manu and his crew followed along parallel alleys and side streets, tracking the agents' every step.

"Now!" the captain whispered. He and two other crewmates went ahead to duck into a well-lit pub to lie in wait. A few minutes later, the signal came in the form of an unmanned carriage rolling past the front windows. Then Manu and the two men sprang into action. The quiet hum of the pub erupted into harsh yells and harsher fists.

"What did you just say about my mother?!" Elliot shouted, shoving Manu through the door, out into the street, and right into the path of the MOTHER agents.

"I said she smells like pig lard!" Manu shouted back.

Elliot snarled, drew back his arm, and punched his

captain square in the jaw—conveniently sending Manu staggering into one of the agents.

"Watch where you're going," the man growled.

"Why don't *you* watch where you're going?" Archer, who up to this point had remained silent, cried.

The agent hissed before he thrust Archer to the ground and kicked him with the hard edge of his boot. From there, things descended into an all-out brawl. Manu couldn't tell whose fist landed where and which side was winning. He allowed himself to dive into the fray and enjoy the small battle happening right in front of him. His only regret was that Benard wasn't there; the goblin always loved a good bar brawl.

As the two groups pummeled each other, Manu fully lost track of time until a shot rang out, echoing down the empty street. One of the MOTHER agents stumbled backward, clutching at his chest and gasping. Another crack of a rifle followed, this one crumpling a second agent to their knees.

"Ambush!" someone shouted. All of the MOTHER agents drew their weapons.

What followed was a mad scramble as the crew of the *Defiant Duchess* hurried to get away before the agents fired. The small band of air-pirates broke apart and headed back to the ship in different directions—which had been Manu's plan for whenever agents inevitably turned on him and the crew. What he hadn't expected, however, was that the MOTHER agents would be shooting at them *as* they ran off. He heard a shot and looked over his shoulder to see who might be firing at him, but saw no one and felt nothing.

The young captain didn't stop running until he'd reached the ship. "Has everyone made it back?" he asked Benard between ragged breaths.

Benard frowned deeply at him, his eyes fixed on Manu's side. "You need to see the medic, sir."

"What?" Manu looked down at the growing splotch of red on his shirt. "No. I need to do a roll call and get this ship in the air!"

"Sir, you're bleeding," Benard said flatly, still eyeing the wound.

"It's just a graze, Benard. Now answer the damn question!" Manu covered the wound that was only just then beginning to sting with his hand, if only to take Benard's eyes off it.

"Everyone is accounted for, sir," Owen the Boatswain said softly. "Including our...Uprising guests."

"Right, then. I want this ship in the air *now*."

"Won't that look a mite suspicious, Captain?" came a voice from the stairs to the upper decks. Manu looked up: Ivy, who appeared entirely too relaxed after everything that had happened. Not a single hair on her head was out of place.

"And what would you suggest, Miss Warner?" The adrenaline was fading and the wound at his side was fast becoming more than a sting.

"We should wait until this afternoon. Then we'll know that the market is in the clear and that MOTHER hasn't linked your ship to the attack this morning." There was an annoying amount of sense in her words, but it didn't make him feel any calmer.

"And whose fault was that attack this morning, Miss Warner?!" he shouted. Everyone in the cargo hold stopped to watch as Ivy stared down the captain. They both knew she'd had a hand in the attack. They both knew he couldn't prove it.

Framed by her green hair, Ivy's brow creased in disbelief. "Surely, Captain Kelii, you don't think I would go against your orders?" One lightly tanned hand pressed to her heart as if she were hurt.

The captain narrowed his eyes at her, but before he could open his mouth to tell her that he did, in fact, think precisely that, Benard stepped between them. "Of course, we don't think that, do we sir?" Manu's first mate gave him a sharp look and a quick shake of the head.

"No, of course not. But we still will be ready to leave by 0600. That is final. Now, if you'll excuse me, I believe I need stitches," Manu said in a careful, measured tone. He stood taller, wincing slightly. "Benard, get the ship ready to leave. Miss Warner, I assume your unit has all returned by now?"

"Yes, Captain, we are all aboard," Ivy murmured as she bowed her head. "Please do get yourself seen to—we wouldn't want anything to happen to you." With that, she left the cargo hold.

"Yeah, sure you wouldn't," Manu muttered darkly. The open wound throbbed again, and he hissed.

Owen moved to Manu, his large form dipping low beneath Manu's arm to tug it over his shoulder in support. "Just think Cap'n, after Hoggle, we can dump her wherever and watch her disappear into the distance like a tiny ant." Owen offered his captain a wide smile of encouragement.

"Not soon enough," Benard muttered, shaking his head. "You can take him to the medic?"

Owen nodded. "I've got this. You start getting us ready to leave."

"I can walk, you know! I'm not a child!" Manu cried. The wound was making him lightheaded.

"Of course, not Cap'n. But let Owen see you there, just for my peace of mind?"

Manu felt like he was being patronized—he was sure Benard had used that exact tone to a twelve-year-old Manu who hadn't wanted to eat his vegetables. "Oh, fine," he said, and let the taller man lead him up into the main decks and to the medic. "You're too good for him y'know, Owen?" Manu asked, now genuinely woozy from the blood loss.

"Yes, I know, Cap'n." Owen chuckled and half-dragged the captain down the rest of the hall.

11

PERSINETTE

THE COLLECTION in Hoggle was in just two days. Forty-eight short hours. Persinette would be lying to herself, and everyone else, if she said that she wasn't apprehensive. When she did have time to eat between training and research, she found it difficult for her stomach was in gnarled knots. Even as she tried to save them, the people whose names she had listed for Gothel haunted what little sleep she was able to get. They went about their days and nights as if everything were normal, not knowing the danger that lurked ahead of them. Persinette wished she could scream out to them, warn them, but they remained in her dreams, oblivious. During her waking hours she was plagued by all of the things that could, and inevitably would, go wrong. That seemed to be her luck as of late.

Her sessions with Agnes did nothing to ease her nerves. Training had gotten easier over the past weeks—that much was true—but she still felt in no way prepared for the mission ahead. She likely never *would* be ready, no matter how much combat training she went through, simply because the idea of hurting another person, even in self-defense, even with a shoe, made her queasy. In her mind she could hear Agnes' words over and over: "you hesitate too much, Persinette. You're as good as dead."

Maybe he was right—she *was* as good as dead. Perhaps this was MOTHER's clean and drama-free way of getting rid of her so they didn't have to make a scene. No one talked about an Asset once they were deemed not useful anymore. Most of the time that Asset simply disappeared without so much as a goodbye. Still, there had been more than one occasion when Persi had witnessed MOTHER's methods of disposal.

The first time she'd ever witnessed an Asset being "erased" had been ten years ago. Persinette was fourteen, and had been with MOTHER for six years at that point, but had not yet had reality of her disposability so rudely thrust in front of her.

It was dinnertime, and the mess was full of buzzing chatter as fairies, unicorns, witches, and other magical beasties all enjoyed their last meal of the day. All companionable talk stopped dead as the doors to the hall opened and a small group of MOTHER agents strode in.

"Asset number 10-22-81." The tall man leading the group read from a file in his hands. His dark eyes flicked around the room trying to find whoever it was, and everyone in the room followed suit, all eyes looking from face to face to suss out this 10-22-91. "I said, Asset number 10-22-91," the man repeated.

After a few tense seconds, a woman stood from a chair two tables over from Persi. She tipped her chin upward, making her wild mass of light brown curls seem even longer, and her bright, bespectacled eyes took in the MOTHER agents without an ounce of fear. "Is this about my trial?" she asked.

"Trial." The tall man snorted softly. He motioned to the agents behind him, who leaped forward, shoved the woman's face again the table, and cuffed her wrists in iron manacles. "Asset number 10-22-91, you are sentenced to a life of service to the crown of Daiwynn for crimes against humanity under section 3B of the—"

"My name is Rose," she cut him off as the agents tugged her to her feet. She held her chin high once again. "My name is Rose, and I don't give a shit what law you say I've broken. I didn't do anything wrong." Her tone was even and soft, but it carried across the whole hall.

The tall man towered over her and backhanded her with the full force of his well-muscled frame, knocking the metal-framed spectacles from her face. "You're disgusting."

A soft laugh fell from Rose's busted lips as she faced him again. "Oh, Gaston, no one will ever be as disgusting as you."

The next blow was not backhanded, and it sent Rose to her knees. She laughed, still, even as Gaston kicked her, merely coughing between her giggles. But the laughter eventually faded. And when it had, the MOTHER agents dragged her unconscious form away.

Persi remembered spending the next week trying to figure out what law Rose had broken; she needed to know so that she didn't break it herself. But no one would tell her. They said she was too young to understand.

Now, she gulped roughly, trying to rid herself of the memory. That woman would be her if MOTHER ever found out she was working against them.

"Persinette." Agent Gothel's irritable voice broke through her thoughts. "Are you listening to me?"

"I'm sorry Agent Gothel, I must be nervous about the mission." She lied—something that was becoming all too common for her these days. Now was not the time to think about the inevitability of MOTHER finding out, nor was it the time to let fear take over. For if she let it, she knew it would paralyze her into inaction.

"May I continue now?" Gothel's expression was more pinched than usual, so instead of speaking up, Persi just nodded and forced herself to refocus on the images playing out on the screen. "You'll be headed to Hoggle, as you well know. You've given us information on two Enchanted in the area. A werewolf and a fairy."

As if she needed reminding, images of the two people she'd had visions of flashed on the screen. Some Seers just got a location, some got a name, but some got it all—a name, a face, a place, and even a hint of what the person was like—in their visions. Persi was damned enough to be the last sort of Seer. The fairy's name was Roman, he lived above the grocer he worked at, and he fed the stray cats that frequented in the alley behind the place. He was sweet. The werewolf was a woman named Heather; she'd just moved to Hoggle. She was pretending to be human so she could work at a butcher shop and rent an apartment the size of a closet on the outskirts of town.

Persinette shook the visions away. *Focus.* "Yes ma'am," she responded softly.

"Your mission, while in Hoggle, is to help us find any others in the area. Hopefully, your proximity to them and their daily lives will help," Gothel continued as if Persi hadn't spoken at all. "Now, have you had any other visions since our last meeting?"

The screen shut off with a soft hiss as its steaming gears slowed to a halt. This question was common, especially this close to a Collection. Gothel just wanted to "check" to make sure they hadn't missed any Enchanted.

Like this whole thing was some carnival game of whack-a-mole.

"No ma'am," Persi lied. The reality was, she could, in all likelihood, lead MOTHER to every Enchanted in Hoggle. The town was small, and she'd had visions of a small clan of mountain trolls who worked as carpenters, an old goblin who hoarded cats, and a very young nymph girl trying to make a living as a pickpocket. None of whom, in her estimation, stood a fighting chance against MOTHER—but this werewolf and this fairy might.

Gothel nodded, jotting *nothing further* in the file that sat before her. "Your training sessions with Agnes have been suspended until you return. We leave just before dawn, so rest up." With that, the agent dismissed her.

The young woman nodded, stood from her chair robotically, and headed through the hall and back to the Tower. She spent the rest of the day there, under the guise of resting up for the mission. In reality, she did anything but. She worked all day on the spells she'd gathered until she was able to conjure a small glowing ball of fire about the size of a thimble. Not enough to do any real damage, but it was a start.

Persinette ordered dinner and had it delivered to her door by one of the automatons—not something she'd regularly be allowed to do, but with a mission looming over her head, she'd argued she needed time to mentally prepare. Distracted, she merely nibbled at the food as she worked at the spells. Once she was able to conjure the small ball of fire with ease, she practiced on a spell to move objects.

"Start small," she reminded herself as she tried to push the pen across her desk with nothing more than magic. Little by little she nudged it until it fell to the floor.

She spent much of the next morning trying to move a

book across the floor the same way. After lunch, she attempted to push her desk chair, since it was probably lighter than the chair in front of her bookshelf.

Persinette worked her magic to its breaking point and beyond. So much so that the night before the mission, she poured herself into bed and, for the first time in her sixteen years with MOTHER, slept a nightmare-less sleep.

12

PERSINETTE & CAPTAIN MANU KELII

IF PERSINETTE THOUGHT that the morning of their mission would offer enough chaos for her to slip away unnoticed—although what she'd *do* once she slipped away, she didn't yet know—she was wrong. That morning was a thing of planned precision at its finest. Everyone in the small platoon of MOTHER agents knew where they needed to be and when they needed to be there. The only person who seemed to be at a loss for what to do was Persinette herself. Clearly, she was the only first-timer in the unit.

"Stand here," one of the agents snapped after Persi had asked him when they would be leaving. He took her by the shoulders and placed her in the spot, his face twisted in agitation. "And for gods' sake stop asking so many damn questions."

"Right. Sorry," Persinette muttered as her fingers fidgeted with the buckles of her corset. She chewed on her lip anxiously, watching the agents around her collect their preferred weapons, from swords to revolvers, and line up to head through the portal.

"Quit your fidgeting," he said under his breath.

"But what should I do with my hands?" she asked softly. The question was more for herself than for the irritated MOTHER agent beside her, but he answered anyway.

"I don't give a damn. Just be still." He narrowed his eyes in a way that made Persinette want to run and hide under her bed.

She nodded quickly and willed herself to be motionless. With the pull of a lever, the sound of rushing water filled the air, the portal opened, and they all filed through. A set of agents had already been to Hoggle and set up a perimeter around the little town. Gothel and the cranky older man flanked Persinette as she exited the portal and took her first steps in sixteen years onto real soil. The dirt beneath her feet felt alien, but she had no time to ponder it as they pushed forward.

"You will be set up in an apartment complex that we have secured as a safehouse with a twenty-four-hour guard until tomorrow morning. We hope that this will give you plenty of time to have another vision." Gothel recounted the plan as they walked, but Persinette found it increasingly hard to focus on the words. The ground squished beneath her boots in a strange way that the stone and cement floors of MOTHER headquarters did not, while the air was full of too many smells—both good and bad—that left her mind spinning as she tried to discern one from another. The scents out there just mingled and mixed and blended in a way that was distinctly other from the filtered, stale air of MOTHER.

"Persinette, are you listening?" Gothel snapped.

Persinette's eyes flitted from the towering building she'd been surveying back to Gothel. "Yes, Gothel."

Gothel nodded, and they mounted a hissing, groaning

elevator to what was revealed to be a tiny, one-room apartment.

"Is there any way I could maybe...get out? Go to one of the bookstores? See the town?" As soon as she said it, Persinette knew it was hopeless. Wishful thinking, that's what that was, confirmed by the sole response she received: the slamming of the door. The bang echoed off the four bare walls of the room, which felt more like a cell than an apartment. Persinette forced herself to be calm.

"So here we are," she said to herself, spinning to look out the window. A new city, a new room, a whole new *world* outside the dust-coated window, and she was trapped in a musty room without any means to explore it.

Her eyes drifted to the street far below. Gothel had made sure to get her a room without any means of climbing out. She was so high above the town that if she attempted to escape, *failed* to escape, and fell, she'd surely die. Still, she was not quite so high up that she couldn't see the ant-sized people going about their lives.

Pressing one hand to the window, she leaned against the glass to get a better look. "They're all so tiny down there," she whispered to herself. "Hello down there, people of Hoggle!" she said, as if perhaps they might hear her and wave. They did not.

MEANWHILE, on the outskirts of Hoggle, the young Captain Manu Kelii was sitting in his quarters bored out of his bloody mind as he listened to Ivy's little analyst drone on and on and on about what he should and should not do.

"I think I know how to talk to a girl, Ivy," Manu sighed as he rubbed at the bridge of his nose.

Ivy snorted. "Could have fooled me."

"This isn't just about talking to a girl, Captain." The analyst sounded annoyed. "Please do take this seriously. We don't know if this girl is dangerous or not."

"Yeah, she looks like a real cold-blooded killer. Oh wait, no—that's Miss Warner." A cheeky grin split the captain's face, earning him only a glare from everyone in the room. He relented. "All right, fine. I'm taking it seriously. I will go. I will be armed. I will have a handful of men as back up."

"And a sniper. *And* I will be a part of the meeting," Ivy added.

Manu laughed loudly. "In your dreams. After what happened in Flit, I'm not taking any chances. You and your unit will sit your pretty asses on this ship and not move until I'm back."

"We had nothing to do with what happened in Flit," the analyst protested, straightening his waistcoat.

"Furthermore, this is what we were brought on to do. To help you secure the Asset," Ivy said.

The captain shrugged, his own goldenrod waistcoat scrunching up a little. "I'll make sure Eddi knows you were a huge help. Don't worry about your orders."

"That is not the issue here!" The witch's eyes blazed, and her fingers sparked with green magic. "I am here to do a job, and I will not let some ignorant...*child* of a captain impede my fulfilling a direct order!"

"Captain..." Benard's soft warning drifted across the room.

Manu sighed. "Fine. I'll give it some thought." Except he wouldn't.

And that is how the young captain and his first mate found themselves sneaking from the ship late at night.

"This is a stupid idea, sir," Benard hissed as they slipped into an alley on the edge of town.

"They didn't give me much choice, Benard. Ivy is trigger-happy," Manu reminded him as they slunk through the mostly sleeping city.

"I didn't mean that, sir. I meant trying to pass yourself off as food service to get close to the girl. It's just not a good plan, sir." They came to a stop in an alley across from a tall apartment complex.

"What are you talking about? It's an excellent plan!" Manu's dramatic exclamation came with much huffing and flailing of the arms.

Benard looked him over. "You won't be able to pass yourself off as food service, sir."

"And why not? Don't I look the part?" Manu wasn't sure *why* he was so offended that Benard seemed to think he didn't look the part of a waiter, but he was very offended indeed. Or perhaps he was just perpetually offended these days—having an Uprising Unit on his ship had thrown him into a tailspin that made life as a whole quite annoying. "Gods, why is it so bloody early? Whose idea was it to come out here so damn early?"

"Yours, Cap'n," Benard reminded him. He gave Manu another, longer look. "No. You do not look the part."

"Then what, good sir, do you suggest?" Another huff of indignation followed the question as the young captain crossed his arms over his well-tailored waistcoat.

"You look like a pampered dandy. Go muddy yourself up a bit, maybe."

The young captain practically choked on his own tongue at the mere suggestion. "Muddy—muddy myself up a bit! You expect me to get dirt on these clothes?" Manu felt a look of utter revulsion cross his face at the mere idea of such a thing.

His first mate shrugged. "Then come up with another solution, sir."

"I will not," the captain replied obstinately, puffing out his chest and standing taller.

Benard rolled his eyes. "Suit yourself," he muttered.

They both walked to the mouth of the darkened alleyway to look up at the looming apartment building. With its strangely stiff construction—as if a child had cobbled it together from building blocks—it looked left over from a bygone era, long before the realms had merged and so-called "modern" architecture had been all but abandoned. In the early morning light, it resembled a tower from one of those stupid old fairytales more than anything else. As though high above—on whatever floor they had decided to put her—was a princess.

"It's still a stupid plan," Benard said, just loud enough for Manu to hear. The captain decided to ignore it as he slipped a false moustache from his pocket and stuck it to his upper lip. It *was* a good plan—a solid plan. It would work. It would work because Captain Manu Kelii was a smart man, damn it!

It didn't, in fact, work.

The guards saw right though Manu, and although they didn't realize that he was there working for the Uprising, they could tell he was suspicious enough—as there was no need for a waiter to be wandering the halls at such a time, even if said waiter was "just getting off work," as per Manu's backstory. So despite his ridiculous French accent—which Benard had called insulting when he was practicing it—Manu was not allowed into the building, let alone onto the same floor as Persinette.

"I told you it wouldn't work," Benard seemed to take great pleasure in stating the obvious. Manu pulled the moustache off his upper lip in silence. "And why did you wear that ridiculous caterpillar on your face anyway?"

"Bite your tongue, Benard. This is a sophisticated disguise!" Manu tucked the shaggy thing into his pocket.

"A disguise?" the goblin shouted, laughing at the ridiculousness of the statement as they retreated to the ship. "What in gods' names do you need a disguise for? You're not a wanted man! No one even knows who you are, Manu!"

"Shut up, Benard," Manu said. He needed to rethink his plan and pour himself a drink. Maybe he'd do the latter first. "It helped me get into character."

They climbed the rope ladder back up to the ship, Manu first and Benard cackling loudly beneath him. "Into character, he says!"

Shhh, you're going to wake everyone up!" the captain said crossly. The rest of the walk to the ship and their quarters passed in silence.

By the time Manu returned to his quarters and draped himself into the chair behind his desk, he had decided one thing—he needed to draw the girl out. Getting close to her while she was under the watchful eye of MOTHER had proven too risky. And then he had to pray she didn't raise the alarm. The question was—what would draw her out? And even once he had...how could he convince her to help them?

He pulled his pocket watch from his rumpled waistcoat and sighed heavily. There were but a few hours until MOTHER finished their Collections and took Persinette back to headquarters where he had no hope at all of contacting her, and he had to figure something out. He needed a reason for MOTHER to take Persinette along to the Collection. Something that would make them think it wasn't safe to leave her sitting in the apartment waiting for them to get back.

"A distraction," he murmured, deep in thought.

By the time the sun rose, he had thought of a plan. Was it a good plan? Maybe not. But it was something, at least.

THE FIRST THING Persinette had noticed about the world outside of MOTHER headquarters had been the strange feeling of the ground, but the second—all of the different smells—was by far more remarkable. The world was so smelly! There was everything from the unwashed smell of the person who had slept in the tiny apartment before her to the tempting scent of something baking in one of the nearby apartments. And then there was all of the noise! Persi had always thought that headquarters was loud, what with the hustling and bustling of agents, Assets, and robots going to and from this or that, yet headquarters seemed positively muttered in comparison to the real world outside its walls.

Persinette could hear people down on the streets shouting at one another, horns honking, the couple in the apartment below chatting over dinner, and someone in the apartment above dancing to soft music. It was all so loud—but nice, she decided. It felt like there was life here. These were ordinary people, just trying to live their lives, and she liked that thought.

For a moment, Persi considered what she would have been doing right then if MOTHER hadn't abducted her. Perhaps she too would be dancing with someone special across their one-room apartment in the middle of a town much like this one. "Guess you'll never know," she said to herself, and shook her head.

Persi didn't sleep that first night. She didn't dare shut her eyes and waste a moment of the rare bit of freedom she'd been given. Instead, she perched herself in a straight-backed chair at the window and watched the people go this way and that in the street and the steam that fogged it. She watched as a loud clockwork car ticked its way past the building carrying perhaps the only wealthy people in Hoggle and splashing a young woman who was selling something on the curb. Yet although Persi could imagine what these people looked like and sounded like, they were much too far off to really know anything about them. Still, she wondered where they were going and what they were doing at such a late hour.

Even as she imagined the lives of the townspeople, Persi found her eyes were continually drawn to the horizon. Gothel had—perhaps intentionally— chosen the tallest building in Hoggle. Meaning that even though Persi was not on the top floor, she could still see out over the tops of most of the other buildings.

Past the edge of town was the country: a vast open space of farms and hills, and, Persi hoped, freedom. Except that idealized country was ruined by the hulking grey build-ings of a labor camp that sat just outside of Hoggle. A thick cloud of steam and smoke drifted up from one of the taller buildings, presumably the factory where even at such a late hour the Enchanted trapped inside worked away.

Persi lost herself staring at it as she imagined all of the faces of the Enchanted she had sent to camps just like that one. Her mind wandered so far that she didn't hear the door creak open.

Persi jumped, nearly stumbling from the chair, as a woman touched her shoulder. Gothel. "Is it time to go?" she asked in a voice much higher than usual. "Back to head-quarters?"

"No. We're headed over to where the fairy lives. We've been ordered to have you on site when it happens." Gothel tugged Persi to her feet by the wrist without further preamble, and panic the likes of which she'd never felt before rippled through Persi.

Persinette's breath grew shallow and her heart raced in her chest. This was it. This was the end of it all. MOTHER probably had plans for her to be shot in the line of duty. That way they could write it off as just an accident. Or maybe—maybe something much worse was going on. Maybe Gothel was telling the truth and they were just going to Collect the fairy. Persi took a moment to try to decide if that were worse or better. *Worse. Definitely worse.* To have to watch as another Enchanted was Collected, left helpless as they were dragged away to one of MOTHER's camps...

Persi's stomach did a sick lurch, and her knees nearly gave out as Gothel half-dragged her to the old elevator. "Hurry up, Persinette! I don't have time for your bullshit."

The girl closed her eyes and pulled herself up straighter before she followed. If this were to be her execution, then so be it; she would head to it with her chin held high as Rose once had. If not, well, maybe the fairy had gotten one of Persi's messages and managed to escape. Then, at least, Persi wouldn't have to watch as the woman's eyes faded to a lifeless hue like those she saw in her dreams.

With Hoggle being such a small town, the unit of MOTHER agents and their Enchanted charges arrived outside the small building that was their destination not ten minutes later. The group marched up a set of rickety wooden steps and stopped on a landing just outside a thin-looking door which one of the MOTHER agents promptly kicked in. Through the settling dust, Persi watched as they charged into the fairy's home and set about checking the rooms one by one. Although the apartment was not as small as the one Persi had been housed in the night before, it took only a few minutes for the agents to clear it and return to Gothel to report.

"Looks like the place is clear ma'am. It seems the Enchanted left," one young agent reported, his face scrunched up in displeasure at the mere idea of an Enchanted escaping.

Persinette felt her stomach settle a little. He'd had gotten away and there was no evidence that he had been tipped off. It looked as if he had merely decided to leave on his own. Persi thanked her lucky stars for that.

"Any sign where the damn thing may have gone?" Gothel asked as her dark gaze swept the room.

The agent opened his mouth to say something, but a loud bang cut him off. Persi turned quickly, unsure of what it was, or where it was coming from. It took her several seconds to realize that someone was shooting at them. During those seconds one of the agents shoved her back to the steps as a bullet whizzed past her head, just grazing her ear. The sting of pain made Persi yelp, and then she was off like a shot herself—down the rickety steps, through the narrow alley, and out onto the busy city streets.

Panic raced through her. She didn't stop on the street; she kept running. Persinette ran until her lungs burned and she could barely feel her legs. She panted hard, eyes looking around wildly until she realized that she had no idea where she was or how she'd gotten there. The boarded buildings and dirt road did not look at all familiar. Dread returned with a sob, threatening to choke off her air. Before she could even move, someone grabbed her wrist and yanked her into a boarded-up shop. Just as her lungs filled to scream, a hand covered her mouth to stifle it, and the door to the shop slammed shut.

13

PERSINETTE & CAPTAIN MANU KELII

BENARD'S PLAN was far less elegant than Manu would have liked, but it got the job done—surprisingly. Ivy had been itching for a chance at some more MOTHER agents, so she and some of Manu's more trusted men had been sent to wreak havoc on the small unit they had followed to the fairy's home. Then all they needed to do was hope that Persinette would head for the hills in fear, and so she had—a move Manu wasn't quite sure how Benard had predicted. But here they were.

Manu waited, holding the terrified girl until he was sure that no one was coming after her. "Shh. Shh. Relax. I'm not going to hurt you," he whispered soothingly.

There was a muffled growl, and then the girl trod hard on his instep. Manu yelped, and the girl was across the room in seconds, reaching for the door to the street. Manu lunged for her wrist and did his best to hold onto her while she struggled to get away again. "Persinette...Persinette..." He said her name in as calming a tone as he could manage with a thrashing girl clawing at his arm. Still, she fought. Eventually, he had to shout. "*Persinette!*

That seemed to stop her. Finally, Persinette turned her wide green eyes to look at him.

"Who are you? And what do you want with me?" Persinette felt terror rise in her throat, but she swallowed it and did her best to channel Agnes. How would he act in such a situation? Well...the man who had grabbed her would probably be on his back, but she'd missed her chance for that.

"Captain Manu Kelii at your service, ma'am," the young captain said with a flourish and a bow that seemed to her a bit more than the situation called for. "I'm a part of the Uprising and am here to recruit you to our cause."

Between the bow and the extravagant introduction, Persinette's mind stuttered to a halt. All panic and residual anger faded and she blinked owlishly at the man, trying to understand the words that had just come from his lips. "I'm sorry, you're what?"

The handsome man huffed as he righted himself, straightened his waistcoat, and narrowed dark brown eyes on her, giving Persinette a moment to look him over. Even in the dim light she could see tanned skin stretched over a strong jaw and mussed dark hair.

"Captain Kelii, Uprising, here to recruit," Manu repeated. Maybe she was still coming to her senses after the whirlwind of being grabbed up by a stranger. Hopefully his breakdown of the information into bite-sized bits would get through to her. Then she would see the seriousness of the situation before her and be impressed, damn it!

Persinette snickered softly into one freckled hand. She couldn't help herself. What with the colorful introduction, and the entire idea that the Uprising had sent this man to recruit her—well, it was all quite funny.

Manu's face fell into an expression of complete horror. "Are you—are you laughing at me?"

Persi bit the tip of her tongue to quell the laughter that was bubbling up inside of her. "No, no. I...you're a captain who works with the Uprising? You don't look like much of a rebel to me..."

The captain gaped as he tried to comprehend how anyone could be *laughing* at him in such a way! He had never in his entire life been laughed at! Well, not to his face anyhow. Unless you counted Benard. "And what *do* I look like, pray tell?"

She shrugged, swallowing down the remnants of her laughter so she could inspect him properly. "Some kind of fancy lordling, or something?"

Those words brought a grin to the pirate's face—a lordling. Lordling, now that was a new one! "And have you met many lordlings, Miss Persinette?"

"No, none at all in fact. But I've read about plenty of them, and you're exactly what I always imagined they would look like." She flicked her eyes over him again, drinking in the well-tailored kelly green waistcoat and trousers and the way he held himself with no small amount of arrogance. Definitely a lordling—possibly handsome enough to outpace even Mister Darcy. Even in the dim light of the boarded-up shop, she could see how attractive he was, from the time he put into his appearance to the strength in his jaw.

A soft grumble resonated from somewhere in the shadows before another man emerged. "Stop flirting, Cap'n. We don't have all day. MOTHER will track her down soon and find us."

Oh no. Like a smack to the face, it all came rushing back.

She had run from the MOTHER agents. She was likely going to be in trouble when they found her again. Persinette felt the blood drain from her face. What would Gothel do to her for running? Would they throw her into one of the camps without so much as a moment to explain herself, left to rot? Or worse, would she be shot down as so many others had been before her? Her stomach twisted into vicious, angry knots, threatening to expel whatever was inside of it. With a hard gulp, Persinette tried to keep it all from spilling out onto the floor.

"Don't worry about MOTHER. They'll think you just got scared and ran off. You're new at this. They can't blame you for that," the captain said, trying to calm the fear that had written itself across the young woman's face. Benard nudged him, grumbling something under his breath, and the captain cut him a dirty look. "All right, all right, I'm getting to it. Off with you, you horrendous little goblin, before you terrify the poor girl further."

In spite of the looming fear that had taken over, Persinette found herself laughing softly at the two men. Their quibbling eased some of the tension that had drawn her shoulders up to her neck and allowed her to focus more on what this captain was saying. "You said you were here to recruit me for the Uprising?" she hinted, hoping she could get the captain back on track.

"Right. The Uprising." The captain gave her a firm nod and a grin that could charm a cat.

Persinette squirmed. There was something dangerous about that grin and all the promises that came with it. She cleared her throat, refusing to be distracted by a pretty face in the face of everything. She lifted her chin. "What would the Uprising have me do? Am I leaving with you right now on your ship to join their forces and help combat MOTHER?" In spite of herself, some of her excitement seeped into the questions. The idea of flying away from Hoggle on a pirate ship to join the forces of the Uprising was thrilling. It was the kind of adventure she had spent her entire life dreaming of. It smacked blissfully of freedom, the kind of which she'd never experienced before and might never get another chance at.

A single word dashed all of those hopes. "No."

"No?" she repeated, her far-off visions of running away and revolution fading in a puff of steam. Her shoulders sank in disappointment. "Then what does the Uprising want from me?"

"No," Manu repeated. A frown tugged at his lips as he saw the sadness marring that pretty freckled face. "Your orders are to return to headquarters with the MOTHER agents and feed us intel from the inside. I will be your point of contact in this endeavor." His chest swelled perhaps a bit too much with pride at his role in this mission. It was quite the responsibility, in his mind, and he vowed to be as serious as the situation warranted.

"So, g-g-go back and pretend like everything's normal while feeding you any information I can from MOTHER?" Persi said the words slowly, processing them—or perhaps questioning the wisdom of the idea itself. Well, she *was* questioning their wisdom, in a sense. For she knew something that the Uprising and Captain Manu Kelii did not: she was a lousy liar.

"Exactly." The captain nodded with a little smile. She seemed to have finally understood, and this pleased him. "Any upcoming Collections you're told about, you tell us. And before you give them a list of where and who to collect, you give us a heads-up. Then we can get them out before MOTHER comes knocking." It sounded like a fantastic plan to him. What better way to stem the flow of Collections than to have one of MOTHER's own Seers give them the information directly?

Persinette wrinkled her brow, pondering the plan. The captain was still smiling confidently at her, but there was a problem wasn't seeing. *He* didn't have to return to MOTHER and act as a spy in a pit of vipers all the while praying not to be found out—she did. She, who was a lousy liar. This was not a decision to be made lightly.

"So, what d'ya say?" the captain asked, that beautiful smile replaced with an expression of seriousness. He held out his hand to her for them to shake on it.

Persi's eyes flicked down to his well-manicured hand as she pondered the offer. It wasn't freedom—not by a long stretch—but it was a chance to help the people who needed it most. Maybe it would end some of the nightmares that had haunted her regularly since she'd begun working with MOTHER. Maybe then Silas wouldn't come to her nearly every night with his gaunt face and dead eyes. It wasn't freedom, true, but it was something. Maybe something better. It was an opportunity to do some good.

So, she shook on it, her small hand firmly engulfed by his. "All right, I'll help you. But how do I contact you?"

The captain's face split with a grin even more massive than the last, and as his dark eyes sparkled, Persinette wondered if she'd struck a deal with a very handsome devil. Manu held her hand for a moment longer than was necessary before he pulled from his pocket a small compact mirror. "With this," he declared, and held it out to her.

It was a beautiful little mirror fashioned out of brass. On the lid sat a simple ivory cameo of a delicate lily of the valley surrounded by engraved scrollwork. "It's lovely," she whispered, reaching for it. Just as her fingers brushed the cool surface of its lid, there was a soft *tink* of metal, and

Persi felt a sharp prick at her fingertip. She yelped and yanked her hand back, examining where a red droplet of blood was forming. "It bit me," she said, narrowing her eyes on the little mirror.

Manu frowned and shook his head. "Sorry, I meant to warn you. It works on blood magic. That was just to ensure that no one else can use it. Here—it won't bite this time, I promise." He offered it to her again.

Persi reached out more carefully, alert for any sign that it would draw blood again. The captain sat it in her palm, and he was right—it didn't bite. She supposed it had gotten the pound of flesh it needed to sustain itself.

"Now all you need to do is say my name and it'll call me up so we can chat!" Manu let the charming smile overtake his face once more in an attempt to reassure the girl. "It'll be easy. Just say *Manu Kelii* and it'll ring me."

Persi nodded slowly, looking down at the little mirror. It was amazing to think that such a small trinket could be her key to finally doing something to change the tides. Her fingers brushed the little flower buds in reverence.

"You should be off, miss. We don't want them to realize you've been to see us." The other man appeared from the shadows once more—where he'd presumably been keeping an eye out between the boards on the window—and held open the door. "It wouldn't serve any of us if you were found out."

"Oh, right," Persi said, looking up from the compact. She tucked it into the little pocket resting at her hip and turned to the door. "I'll be in touch."

"I'm counting on it." Manu winked.

A little *eep* left the girl as she flushed brightly and rushed out the door.

14

PERSINETTE

IT'LL BE EASY, he'd said. Persi thought back to that conversation a day later and realized that Captain Kelii must have never had to do anything of this sort in all of his life. That was the only explanation for why he thought this kind of infiltration mission would be so *easy*. Or perhaps he *had* done such a thing, but he was a good liar, which would make the whole thing come more naturally to him. Persinette, on the other hand, was not a good liar. She was an honest person and had been all her life. Dishonesty tended to make her twitchy and uncomfortable.

So, when the MOTHER agents found her wandering the streets of Hoggle, she did her best to answer their questions as directly as possible, being careful to tell the truth, but not the whole truth.

Where had she been? She wasn't entirely sure.

Why had she run away? All the gunfire had terrified her.

These answers seemed to be enough for them, and Gothel had grunted before taking her back to the portal and pulling her through it and back to headquarters.

"Well, that was a bust, aye, Gothel?" one of the other agents asked as they headed to the door of the portal room. The young woman looked far more jovial about the whole thing than Gothel did. Maybe because she'd gotten to participate in a gunfight; that seemed to have gotten everyone excited.

Gothel just growled and dropped her hold on Persinette's wrist. "Go back to the Tower and stay there until I call for you," she hissed. Persi nodded quickly and scurried off before someone decided to interrogate her again.

Once back in her quarters, she leaned against the thick metal door and allowed herself the first easy breath she'd had in hours. For now, it would seem, she was safe. She had fooled the MOTHER agents into believing every lie she spoken. She wasn't sure how long she'd continue to fool them, but she was not going to think about that right now. Instead, she sunk to the floor, her stocking-clad legs pulling up to her chest as the bustle of her dress rustled and her corset pinched the skin around her ribs. Even if she was safe, at that moment she wanted nothing more than to curl up into as small a target as possible.

Persi gave herself time to calm her mind and the racing of her heart. After a while, unsure how long she'd been sitting there, a soft tinkling sound drew her attention to the pouch at her waist. It took a moment to realize that the sound had to be coming from the little compact the captain had given her. With cautious fingers, she opened the lid and found herself blinking hard at a tiny Captain Kelii standing in the middle of the glass. Or, rather, a *hologram* of the captain standing in the middle of the mirror, just as a ballerina would inside a music box. "Umm...hello?"

"Oh! Hi there! It took you so long to answer that I got

distracted." He offered her a little wave and began to walk, the hologram seeming to float in place as his steps took him to a large chair. He dropped down into it and grinned up at her again.

Persinette could only stare blankly as the pocket-sized version of the man she'd met just hours ago leveled a smile at her. It felt strange, surreal, a little like she was going insane, but there he was all the same. Persi found herself struggling to find words to say to him.

"Miss Persinette? Are you there?" The captain tilted his head. "Is it broken? BENARD! I think it's broken!" He turned his head and shouted at someone else who was presumably just out of sight.

The shouting jerked Persi from her stupor. "No—no, it's not broken." She shook her head to clear any residual feelings of disbelief and tried to focus. "I'm sorry. This is all just a bit strange to me."

The tiny captain nodded. "Right. Well, I was calling to check to make sure that the line was working, and that you didn't get, you know...found out." He shifted awkwardly in the oversized chair. His miniature size made it hard to read the expressions on his face, so she had no idea what could be causing the fidgeting. She decided that she did not like this mode of communication, but given the circumstances, she would have to make do.

"No, I'm quite all right. Thank you for checking. That was very kind of you." She felt herself flush a little as she spoke.

"Ah. Good." His words came out strangely stilted as he shifted in the chair once more. "I'll just leave you to your evening. Enjoy." Then the image of Captain Manu Kelii sitting in his chair blinked out.

Persi stared at where he'd been, unsure of exactly what

had just happened. Then she shut the compact and stood. "Where to put you?" she wondered to herself, as she searched her room for the perfect hiding spot.

Ah! Tucked among the books on her shelf! Perfect.

THE NEW DAY brought a return to normal. Persi's schedule was waiting for her on a piece of parchment slipped through the heavy door to her rooms: an early morning debriefing with Gothel and then her training with Agnes.

"And what if I hadn't woken up early?" she asked the piece of paper, irritation lacing her tone. She scrubbed at her face. The parchment did not answer—not that she'd expected it to—so she hauled herself to the shower to ready herself for the long day ahead.

MEETING WITH GOTHEL was always *such* a treat, but that morning it seemed like the MOTHER agent was even more irritable than usual. Her face pinched in frustration as Persinette entered the room, and she tapped her stack of documents on the table rather violently to straighten them. After sixteen years, Persi had seen this mood more times than she cared to count. The mission had not gone well, judging by Gothel's face.

Persinette knew it was best not to ask why Gothel was in such a foul mood, so she sat in her usual chair and braced herself for the inevitable lecture. A tense silence settled between the two women that felt as if it might go on forever.

Persi vowed not to speak until she was spoken to, and Gothel glared bitterly at the papers in front of her.

"That mission," Gothel finally said in a tone that was nothing short of furious, "was a colossal failure."

Persinette bit her tongue and nodded silently. She did her best to look grave about the entire situation, but as Gothel wasn't looking at her, she couldn't tell if it was working.

"We did not Collect either of the Enchanted we went to collect. Both, it seemed, had left the area before we arrived in Hoggle."

It was hard—so hard—to sit still and not break into a victory dance. The agents hadn't told Persinette till that moment that both Enchanted had escaped, but now all she wanted was to whoop with joy. There was no way to know if it was because of the message she had sent, but that didn't matter. The fairy and the werewolf were two Enchanted who would not be haunting her dreams that night. There was relief in the knowledge that at least two people were still alive. It lit a spark of hope within her that hadn't been there before. Maybe she *could* do this. Perhaps she could help some people—not all of them, but some.

Gothel's eyes were trained on her now, taking in every slight movement. As if, perhaps, she were waiting for Persinette to slip. "What do you have to say for yourself?"

The words killed any lingering happiness Persinette felt at her success. She knew there was no possible way that anyone could have found out about her involvement. Yet her stomach sank as Gothel inspected her with those dark eyes. MOTHER was going to find out. If not today, then eventually. "Excuse me?"

"You took so long getting us the names and their locations that they fled before we could Collect! You made the entire mission a complete wash," Gothel said. She was clearly looking for someone to blame—a scapegoat—but there was no obvious person at fault. Which meant one thing: as per usual, this would all be blamed on Persinette, whether Gothel had proof or not.

"I had no way of knowing they would decide to leave Hoggle," Persi said in her defense. It was not the strongest argument to prove her innocence, but it was the truth, at least, and so it came out quickly. Because, truthfully, she *hadn't* had any way of knowing if her messages had been received, or if those she'd warned would take them seriously if they did make it through. So, still truthfully, she had no way of knowing whether or not they would be in Hoggle when MOTHER arrived.

"Your training sessions will be increased to three times daily." Gothel nodded as if this were a just punishment for the trouble Persinette had caused. "Then maybe next time you won't run from a fight like a disgusting little coward."

There was a snappy retort on the edge of Persi's tongue —something that would make Elizabeth Bennet proud and likely get her thrown directly into the dungeons—but she swallowed it down. She would be no good to the Uprising or the Enchanted they were trying to help if she ended up in the labor camps herself. "Yes, Gothel," she replied softly, ducking her head in submission. "I'll do better next time, ma'am."

"You're damn right you will. Now get out of my sight. You have training with Agnes in an hour." Gothel waved her away, that pinched look still on her face. Persi needed no prompting; she left the room as soon as Gothel dismissed her.

EVER THE OPTIMIST, Persinette had fooled herself into thinking that as the day progressed things would look up. Surely she had already seen the worst that day had to offer. She went back to her quarters, changed, and headed down to the training rooms for her first session of the day with Agnes.

He was waiting for her, as he always was, only this time instead of the bland, bored look he usually sported at the session's start, his lips were twisted into a sneer. "Ah, if it isn't MOTHER's top coward."

"What?" Persi asked softly.

"I told you. You're going to die out there, whether you run the moment things get hard or not." His chuckle made her hair stand on end.

Persinette narrowed her eyes, took a deep breath, and lifted her chin. "Are we going to train or what? I don't have all morning."

Agnes shook his head, clearly amused. "Someone got sassy while they were out in the field. Shame you can't use that spine to do anything useful."

""Are we training or not?" she repeated.

"Sure, we'll train. Hand-to-hand today, since you're terrified of guns now." He was still laughing softly, seeming to find enjoyment in her discomfort.

"I'm not afraid of guns!"

Agnes laughed loudly this time, his blue eyes bright with mirth. "Yeah, sure you aren't, 11-24-10." He strode to the center of the mat and lowered into a fighting stance, facing Persi.

Persi stepped onto the mat as well, planting her feet firmly to keep herself level. "My name is Persinette."

"You want me to call you that, you yellow-bellied little

girl?" He quirked one dark brow at her. "Earn it. Show me what you're made of, coward."

He was goading her, Persi knew, but knowing didn't quell the rage that filled her to the brim. She had never felt anger like this before, but everything in the past few days seem to have stacked up, overlapping and multiplying, and suddenly she couldn't seem to help it. She swung hard at his shoulder. Agnes ducked quickly out of the way, and she stumbled, tripping and falling onto the mat.

"Gods, 11-24-10, you're pathetic. You can't even throw a punch right." He was laughing still, bouncing from foot to foot as he waited for her to climb to her feet and try again. "Again."

Persinette bit the inside of her cheek hard and settled into her stance a second time. She took another swing at him and landed on the mat face-first once more.

The morning progressed that way until at last Agnes announced, "Enough's enough. I can't take watching you make a fool of yourself anymore 11-24-10. Go get some breakfast and get out of my sight." His tone was disgusted as he left the room.

By the time she arrived in the mess hall, Persinette wanted nothing more than to hide away in the Tower for the rest of the day. It felt as if everyone there was watching and talking about her, a paranoid thought confirmed by another Asset walking past her and mimicking the sound of a gun. Another aimed at her with his hand and mimed pulling the trigger. The pair of them dissolved into snickers.

Once she had a table to herself, Persinette forced herself to focus on the plate of stale bread and synthetic eggs instead of the people watching her. She just needed to get some food into her belly and then go about her day. Everything would be better if she just ignored them.

A tray slammed opposite her, and she looked up to find Agnes settling into a chair flanked by his two cronies. "You know, 11-24-10, if you weren't such a cowardly little gutter-snipe maybe you'd actually have some friends." He shot her a taunting smile.

Persi ducked her head once more to her food. She stabbed at the rubbery eggs, forcing herself to ignore Agnes and his friends. He was right, of course. The Assets had a hierarchy, and he was at the top of it, a fact that had never bothered her before. But now that she was Agnes's new punching bag, she found her low rank rankled.

"Shut up, 95." A sharp voice drew Persi's attention from her unappetizing meal. It was Wyn, striding across the mess hall. "Leave Persinette alone."

"Why don't you make me, Agent?" Agnes asked with a soft snort and rolled his eyes. "As if you're any better. All you do is hide up in that library. You've never been out into the field either. Two yellow peas in a pod, you and her."

Everyone in the hall snickered at this, but they didn't dare laugh as loud as they had when Agnes had been tormenting Persi. It was different when the target was an agent.

Wyn lifted her chin, a dangerous grin lighting up her face. "I wonder what Agent Kore would say if she knew you were insubordinate to one of your superiors? I'm sure she'd be all too happy to find a suitable punishment for you. Don't you think, 95?"

Agnes glared at her, his mouth thinning into a hard line beneath the dark brown beard. "No, ma'am," he said begrudgingly.

Wyn nodded, took Persinette's hand, and tugged her to her feet. "Come along, Persinette. We have things to discuss."

Persi nodded, confused, and followed her friend out into the corridor, leaving the tray behind for the kitchen bots to handle. "What's so important that you had to come into the Asset mess hall to get me?"

"You shouldn't let him talk to you like that," Wyn said, not answering the question.

"He doesn't bother me," Persinette lied. "He's just a bitter old unicorn."

Wyn eyed her and shook her head. "I came to tell you that you need to be more careful when you're out in the field."

Persi's eyes widened. Her friend had never warned her like this before. "Why?"

"Gothel is looking for someone to pin that disaster of a mission on, and word is she's telling everyone it was your fault. I know you didn't do anything on purpose to sabotage the Collection and let those creatures escape. But there's been talk about a formal review of all of your previous Collections."

Persinette felt her heart leap into her throat. "A-a-a formal review?"

Wyn nodded gravely.

"They don't do those unless...."

"Unless they're thinking of sending an Asset to the camps. So please, keep your head down. And if you need anything, let me know. I'll help you in any way I can." Wyn's words were hushed, but earnest. Persinette hugged her friend tightly.

"Thank you, Wyn. I will be careful." Persinette gave Wyn a final squeeze before pulling back and smiling at her.

"You can trust me, Persi," Wyn said.

FOR THE REMAINDER of the day, that conversation lingered in Persinette's mind. Through meals, training, and even a trip to the library, she couldn't seem to shake the feeling of being watched. Like someone was breathing down her neck, spying on everything she did. That was what a formal review would mean, after all. They would look at everything Persinette had ever done and then decide if she were useful to MOTHER. They would pick her life apart and examine it at a microscopic level until they reached a verdict—a guilty verdict, usually.

Before the paranoia got the better of her, she decided to bring all of this up with the captain. Surely, he would have some answer as to how to handle it.

After she dragged her tired, sore body back to her quarters that evening, she pulled the mirror from its hiding spot and staggered to her chair. "Captain Manu Kelii," she whispered to the little compact, then waited.

He did not keep her waiting long, however. A moment or so later the captain appeared in the middle of the glass once more, sitting in his overstuffed armchair. "Persinette!" he exclaimed cheerfully, a broad smile on his lips.

Persinette wondered if he always acted like he'd just won some kind of carnival game or if that was just a show for her, but decided not to ask. Instead, she shook her head and allowed his excitement to infect her, smiling back at him a little. "Good evening, Captain."

"It's so good to see you again. I have made pineapple manhattans! They are quite delicious. Though not as good as the pineapple gin and tonics we had last week..." Manu let the words trail off and shrugged. "How has your day been?"

The question ripped the smile from Persinette's face, a reminder of why she had contacted the captain in the first place. "It would seem MOTHER Gothel has taken note of my actions and is lobbying for a formal review of my status as an Asset."

Manu knit his brows and fell silent for a time before he nodded. "Not to worry. We'll sort something out. I'll talk to the higher-ups of the Uprising and get back to you with a plan."

Relief washed over Persinette as she nodded back. The knowledge that she was not doing this alone settled her a little. The Uprising would come up with a solution for this; they would not want to lose an inside Asset so quickly. All she needed to do was wait for them to formulate a plan. "Thank you," she said softly.

Manu nodded. "Of course."

"So, umm...what is *pineapple*?" she asked, figuring a change of topic might relax her further.

The question ripped a gasp of sheer horror from the tiny captain in the chair. "You've never seen a pineapple before?"

Persinette blinked at him. "I've never even heard of one before."

There was another loud gasp as the captain leaned forward to get a better look at her. "You, my girl, have been deprived! What do they feed you in that dreadful place? Any fruit at all?"

A soft laugh left Persi. She shrugged. "We get a lot of canned fruits and vegetables, but never anything exotic. Mainly apples and peaches."

"This is a complete and utter travesty. We shall have to remedy this immediately. The next time you're in the field, I'm taking you to get a pineapple." He nodded firmly.

Persi felt a frown twitch at the corner of her lips. "I don't know that that's really possible, Captain."

"Manu, please," he insisted.

"Manu," she corrected. "I don't know that that's really possible, Manu."

"You leave that up to me. I promise you, next time you're out on mission, I will take you to get a pineapple. You have my word."

She looked at the serious expression on his face, and a little giggle left her. "I'm going to hold you to that, Manu," she said. Was she getting her hopes up for nothing? Perhaps. But what was life without hope? Even if it was hope for something as simple as trying a pineapple.

"You do that, dear girl! I am a man of my word. You can trust that." Manu gave another, firmer nod.

"Thank you," she said softly. A warm flush settled into her cheeks.

"Th-thank you? Whatever for? I haven't even given you the pineapple yet!"

"For getting me out of my own head for a little while. I needed that."

Manu nodded and offered her another broad smile. "Until we can try that pineapple, you stay out of too much trouble, won't you?"

"I will do my level best, Captain," she said, allowing herself a grin.

"Attagirl." He winked at her. "Now get some rest. Good night, Persinette."

"Good night, Manu." With that, she shut the compact and ended the contact.

Persinette curled up under her covers, her fingers tracing the cold surface of the mirror. She allowed the conversation to play over and over in her mind until eventually, she fell asleep.

15

CAPTAIN MANU KELII

THE LINK between the two mirrors closed, and the young captain sat back in his chair. Manu's dark eyes fell upon Benard's face as the goblin shook his head disapprovingly. The captain lifted a brow, questioning, but all he got for his trouble was another shake of Benard's head.

"Well? Out with it!" Manu snapped.

"I'm just not sure it's a good idea to get that friendly with her, is all," Benard said plainly.

"Wh-what?" Manu was dumbfounded. *Would* there be consequences for getting too close? Yes, in all likelihood there would be. But Manu was willing to deal with them when they came, he decided. He just wanted the poor girl to feel like she wasn't alone in there.

Benard stepped in front of his captain, letting out the kind of deep sigh that indicated whatever came next was not something he wanted to talk about, but would do so anyway. "It's inappropriate to get too attached to her. And heaven forbid if Ivy were to find out—"

"Inappropriate? Why? She's my responsibility. And why should Ivy care? Eddi gave me this mission, not her. I was ordered to befriend Persinette and help her through this." Manu's frown deepened as he spoke. He couldn't seem to stop himself. The more he thought of it, the more upset Benard's words made him. Why shouldn't he be friends with Persinette? It would make their working together so much easier. "If this is because she's a woman, and you don't think I can take this seriously—"

"No, that's not it." Benard cut the captain off mid-tirade with a shake of the head. He took his time settling into a chair before continuing. "It's just that, well, this mission is potentially deadly, Manu. There is a high probability she won't survive it, and if she does, there is a chance the Uprising could deem your relationship with her too much of a risk." The goblin's face was drawing into a tired, worn expression.

Benard had never once looked his age—even during Manu's teen years, when the goblin had been chasing the young man around town and city—but in that moment, he did. The worry he seemed to feel was sagging his shoulders, and Manu wanted nothing more than to reach out and soothe it away. To tell Benard that everything would be all right in the end. It had to be. There was just no other option.

Before he could say any such thing, Benard went on. "I know you, Manu, perhaps better than you know yourself. You're flippant, ridiculous, and silly. You've been that since we found you. But beneath all of that, you care for every person you encounter. And I just—I just don't want you to get your heart broken by all of this."

It was the first time in many years that Benard had spoken so straightforwardly to his captain. Manu looked at him, considering his expression and words. Then he let out a laugh. "That's complete tosh, Benard! Of course she'll make it out of this! She's got *me*! How could she fail?"

Benard blinked at his captain, clearly not swayed by Manu's bravado, even though that same bravado had gotten the captain through the hardest times in life, thank you very much. "And what about Ivy?"

"You don't actually think the Uprising would hurt Persi just because we were involved?" Manu asked. Now his bravado had faltered. Although he knew the Uprising—and Eddi in particular—could be ruthless, he'd never thought that they would do anything to hurt one of their own. And Persinette was one of their own now that she was helping them. So why would they have any reason to hurt her?

"If you get too close and it risks the mission? I wouldn't put it past them. The Uprising has done worse for the greater good than kill one Seer." Benard's were soft, but they carried with them the weight of the truth. Manu felt each syllable settle into the pit of his stomach.

"You let me worry about Ivy," the captain said finally, pulling up that shield of confidence once more. "I'll have her off this ship in no time. Till then, we need a new heading. Someplace warmer, methinks." He smiled a little as he sipped his drink. "What say you, First Mate Benard? Any preferences?"

"No, sir." Benard leaned back in his chair as well. "But don't you have a call with Eddi before we head out?"

The captain sighed, bristling under the coarse realization that he was not free to go where he wanted, when he wanted. "Yes, I suppose so. Tell me, Benard, when precisely did I give up my freedom as a pirate?" He huffed dramatically.

"Since you joined the Uprising to search for adventure and save the world, sir," Benard said mildly.

"Damn this big ol' heart of mine," the captain said with a sigh, downing the rest of his drink. "Another, Benard! I don't have to deal with Eddi until the morning, and these pineapple martinis are delightful!"

"They're manhattans, sir, and as you are now responsible for the life of Miss Persinette, it might be best to forgo the hangover," Benard remarked, plucking the glass from his captain's fingers and setting it aside instead of filling it.

"Ah Benard, you are a wise man!" the young captain exclaimed with a soft chuckle. He wiggled his eyebrows playfully as he rose from his chair with a little wobble. Benard moved to steady his captain, but Manu brushed off the aid and pulled himself to his full height with something akin to swagger.

"Might I suggest heading to bed, sir?"

"Yes, yes, to bed," Manu agreed with a nod. "As I said, so very wise, Benard. So off to bed I am." The captain swayed toward the door humming a soft tune to himself. "Have a good night, Benard."

"You too, sir."

Manu nodded and headed to bed, but even with fatigue and drink dragging him with exhaustion, it was a long while before he drifted off. His mind raced, repeating Benard's warning over and over again. For all her innocence and naivete, Persinette was still putting herself in danger to help others. She knew the consequences should she be found out, and that meant she was willing to die for her cause. Manu found himself smiling a little as he marveled at the thought. He had to believe that he could protect her, no matter what. He wouldn't fail another person; he'd sworn himself to that so long ago. He wouldn't fail anyone else as he had failed his sister.

THE NEXT MORNING was perhaps the first since he was a child that Captain Manu Kelii sprang from his bed. Manu was by nature not a morning person; he hadn't been a morning person since those early days of adolescence when he had learned the luxury of a good lie-in. But now—well, now he couldn't explain it. This whole mission with Persinette, and the thrill of finally having an active role in the Uprising, had him excited enough to greet the day. His pulse was racing, and his mind was running a million miles a minute. He couldn't just lie in bed and while the day away!

So, yes, he sprang from his bed with a whistle on his lips and a bit of pep to his step. It took him no time at all to ready himself for the day ahead before he proceeded to the galley for a quick bite of breakfast.

When he entered, the entire crew stopped dead at their various tasks, jaws slack and eyes wide. One deckhand still had his fork held midair, gaping.

"What? What is it? Do I have something on my face?" Manu asked. He sidled up to one of the windows lining the wall to get a glimpse of his reflection. There was no reflection, however, as it was far too bright outside. Still, he scrubbed his face self-consciously.

Benard came from the kitchen, presumably to see why the room had gone eerily quiet. The goblin's brows lifted in surprise at the sight before him: his captain, awake before noon, dressed to the nines, and scrubbing a red patch into his cheek. "You're up early, Cap'n."

Manu's hand stopped, and he gave his first mate a toothy smile. "It is a beautiful morning, isn't it, Benard?"

"I s'pose it is, Cap'n." Benard nodded. Meanwhile, the

entire crew was still watching their captain, as though at any moment he would pull a tricycle out of his ass, sit astride it, and ride about the galley singing show tunes. "Can I get you something for breakfast, sir?"

"Just some toast, I think. Thank you, Benard." Manu's smile crept further up his cheeks, his energy reaching near-manic levels. He flicked his eyes from Benard to the crew all about the room, who were still frozen and staring. "Well? What are you all gawking at? Eat!"

There was a collective blink as the crew gawped for a moment longer, then promptly returned to whatever they had been doing before the captain's arrival. Forks clattered against dishes and the soft chatter of morning conversation filled the air once more. Benard emerged from the kitchen with a small plate of toast, which Manu took. "I'll have my breakfast on the flight deck. Where I won't be stared at like I've got a sixth head," Manu said, giving the crew a pointed look. "My call with Eddi is soon, anyway."

"Sixth? What happened to head two through five?" someone muttered. Everyone snickered.

"Whoever that was just won themselves deck-swabbing duty for the next week," the captain announced. Everyone quickly pointed to a young man who was called Stephen, or possibly Jackson. Harrison? Something like that. "You," Manu said imperiously. "You report to Ethan after breakfast. I'm sure he has plenty for you to do."

"Yes, sir." The young man nodded and ducked his head back to his food.

"Now, as I was saying, my scheduled call with Eddi is soon. I want no disruptions, Benard."

"Yes, Cap'n." Benard nodded.

With that, Manu headed out of the galley toward the helm. He dropped unceremoniously into the captain's chair, rested the plate of toast on his knee, and set up the call to Eddi. The screen rose up from the floor with a grind of gears and wheeze of steam. Manu nibbled at his toast as the screen made its slow progress, his long fingers clicking a couple more buttons and flipping a switch or two before the screen lit with a fuzzy static and Eddi appeared, sitting behind their massive wooden desk as usual.

"Do you ever move?" Manu asked abruptly.

"Excuse me?" The Uprising Leader looked nonplussed.

"I mean, are you always just sitting behind that desk waiting for someone to contact you? Don't you have places to be? People to see? Or some such?" Manu continued, letting himself grin. He set his half-eaten toast aside and sat up in his chair. After this little joke, he'd get down to business, he told himself. He'd had his fun, and there was too much to do to joke around all day.

Eddi's wide, dark eyes blinked behind those same goggles that seemed to magnify them a million times over. The leader of the Uprising was not amused, to say the least, but then again, that wasn't saying much, considering Eddi was likely *never* amused. "What do you want, Captain Kelii?" Eddi's tone held no hint of irritation, but no trace of laughter or excitement, either.

"Oh, come now, we are on first name basis now, aren't we? Manu, please." All right, after *this* joke he would be serious. Manu swallowed a laugh.

"Captain Kelii," Eddi said. Now *there* was that hint of warning. "Your message indicated this was an urgent matter. Now, either this call is critical and you should not be playing games, or it is not critical and you are wasting my valuable time. Which is it?"

Eddi blinked at him. Manu wondered if it was running the Uprising that had given Eddi all of those wrinkles. Had his leader been young before all of this had started? Had Eddi grown old, crusty, and mildewed sitting behind that desk?

"Well?" Eddi asked, noticeably impatient now.

The captain shook himself—mentally, not physically—and turned his attention back to the task at hand. "Right, then. I spoke to Persinette, and she is on board with helping us in any way she can. We made contact last night via the mirror, so the mirror is working properly." He worked hard to keep his demeanor more businesslike. He *did* need to take this mission seriously, Manu knew, more so than any other he'd been on. Persinette's life was on the line here.

"Good work, Captain Kelii." Eddi said curtly, but that was it as far as congratulations or compliments. Manu supposed he hadn't expected a pat on the back, so he shouldn't be disappointed that he hadn't gotten one. But he was. Disappointed, that is. "Was there anything else?"

"Yes," the captain said gravely. "During our talk last night, Persinette expressed concern that MOTHER is reviewing her quality of work as an Asset. She fears that upon review MOTHER will decide she is of no further use."

The wrinkles on Eddi's face deepened at the news. They seemed to realize immediately how dangerous that could be for Persinette, and already looked as though they were thinking of a way out. "Then we will just have to supply her with something for MOTHER to hunt."

Manu blinked, a confused frown pulling at his lips. "I'm sorry, what? We're going to give MOTHER people?"

Eddi's eyes rolled. "No.. We're going to place a couple of our operatives and send their locations to Persinette. She can then feed them to MOTHER. The agents will feel like they got close to catching someone, and we won't have to worry about them Collecting any civilians. All we need is for Persinette to tell us where their next Collection party is headed."

"Oh, right, of course," Manu muttered, feeling like a complete idiot. *Of course* Eddi would have a plan to protect the civilians and anyone else from being Collected.

"Find out where they're sending her next and we'll get it set up. Who knows—maybe we'll catch a couple of MOTHER agents in the process." That idea seemed to thrill Eddi, as much as *anything* ever thrilled Eddi, anyway. An eerie smile crept up the Uprising Leader's lips.

"Uh—right." Manu nodded and ended the call. He hoped that smile wouldn't linger in his memory till the evening. It was sure to give him nightmares.

16

PERSINETTE

"SO THAT'S THE PLAN?" Persinette asked Manu for perhaps the third time since the call had begun. He'd contacted her to inform her of what the Uprising was plotting, and now she was wondering what exactly she'd gotten herself into. "Isn't that dangerous?"

"Of course it's dangerous." The captain chuckled as if any danger involved didn't concern him. "But it seems the best method of protecting your cover and that of the civilians."

Persinette shook her head a little. She couldn't help but feel that perhaps this plan was not a particularly good one. She hated to think that someone else might be Collected or hurt because of her. Then there was the question of how effective this plan would be in the first place. Would it get her into more trouble than she already was?

"Listen, don't worry, Persinette. We've got you covered, okay? I'm not going to let anything happen to you." Manu's words were quiet but firm, as though he meant every single one of them.

Persinette nodded slowly. "I know you won't," she said.

"But..." She paused to swallow roughly. "But what about the Uprising? What if they've already decided I'm more trouble than I'm worth?" The words left her unbidden, thoughts she hadn't acknowledged until she spoke them aloud. She supposed all she could do was hope. Hope that the Uprising needed her more than she needed them. Pray that MOTHER wouldn't figure her out. Believe that somehow this would all sort itself out.

Manu inhaled and met her eyes. "I will not let that happen. If they decide you're more trouble than you're worth, I will get you out." Then his face lit with a smile and he winked at her. "Now cheer up—soon enough you'll be tasting pineapple!"

Persinette laughed. "You're ridiculous. I don't even know how you're going to do that."

"You leave that to me, miss. I am a man of my word, and I promised you a pineapple!"

In spite of herself, Persinette relaxed. "Anything has to be better than stale toast and rubbery eggs."

The captain gasped loudly, his hand flying to his heart. "How dare you even compare the two, madam!"

She rolled her eyes and let out another soft laugh. "All right, all right. I have to get going. I have a meeting with Gothel." The trepidation returned to her chest, where it squeezed tightly.

"Right, you go and do that. And don't do anything I wouldn't." The captain winked again, a wink that was so close to flirtatious that she felt a bright flush to heat her cheeks.

"That is a very short list, Captain," she said. Manu laughed and closed the connection between the two mirrors, leaving Persinette staring at her pink cheeks and the easy smile that had spread over her lips. Shaking her head, she stood and headed to prepare for the day ahead.

Persi's hands trembled as she pinned back her long lavender hair and smoothed any flyaways before donning a pair of goggles. In her rush to get to the door, her corset had been tied perhaps a little too tightly, but that was all right. Perhaps it would keep the butterflies in her stomach from fluttering so madly.

It had only been a week since their last mission and already MOTHER was planning another. That would be the way of things now, she supposed. There would be no break time in between. She slipped down the corridors as quickly as she could without drawing attention to herself.

One. Two. Three. Four. Five. Six.

Persi counted the clipped sound of her boots on hard tile to keep herself from sprinting to the conference room.

Gothel appeared shortly after and motioned for her to sit. Persinette sat across from her and held her breath, waiting for the briefing to begin. Hopefully they would not be sending her out into the field so soon.

"I would like to preface this briefing by making it known that I think taking you on another mission in the field without first holding a formal review is a mistake," Gothel said tightly.

"Uh...noted," Persinette murmured, unsure of what Gothel expected such a declaration to change. There was no way that Persi could tell them she wouldn't go on the mission, and as Gothel had been ordered to take her there, there was nothing left to be done.

Still, it seemed just acknowledging Gothel's words was enough to pacify her, and so the woman moved on. "Good. Now that we're on the same page, we can begin." A loud clicking sound filled the room as the rickety projector booted up and then lit the wall with its first slide: a close-knit crop of buildings surrounded by the haze of steam so commonly seen lingering around larger cities. "We will be headed to Pascal for our next mission."

Persinette squinted a little, trying to make out the buildings better through the steam, but came up short. She supposed it didn't matter what Pascal looked like—the outcome would be the same.

"How long do I have?"

"Four weeks. We have had success with other Seers using this method, so if you cannot produce results in four weeks we will continue with my plan—a formal review." Gothel's words were even and smooth, but Persinette heard the underlying danger. She would produce names in four weeks, or her *own* name would be added to the list.

Persinette nodded, swallowing around a lump that was quickly forming in her throat. "Yes, sir."

Gothel slid a file folder over to her. "Now go. Have a vision. Bring me back the details so we can form another Collection party."

The girl nodded again and turned robotically from her seat to the door. Once out in the hall, she let herself take a steadying breath to calm her racing pulse. "Well, at least Manu will have a location now," she told herself. That was the upside, she supposed. She wasn't alone. Not anymore.

THERE WAS a long day ahead of Persinette before she was able to retire to her rooms and contact the captain again. Three training sessions, three meals, and a short stint in the library during which she ripped a page from a grimoire about shield magic, just in case. Once she made it back to her quarters, all she wanted to do was sleep, but she couldn't—not yet.

Instead, she curled up in the chair before the over-stuffed bookcase, pulled the mirror from its cushions, and murmured, "Captain Manu Kelii." She let the name bring a happy flush to her cheeks.

The captain answered immediately, and for the first time in a week, he wasn't sitting in his captain's chair. The tiny image in the mirror showed just his shoulders and head leaning against what Persi could only guess was the arm of a tufted leather sofa. "Good evening, Miss Persi." He offered her a sly smile and a bow of his head. "What can I do for you tonight, pretty lady?"

A nervous laugh left Persi as her cheeks heated softly and she smiled more. "Good evening to you too, Captain." She allowed the easy playfulness to ease the part of her that had remained clenched all day.

"Is this just a social call? Shall we chat more about pineapple cocktails? Or do you have an update for me?" Over the last week, he had asked that same question every evening, with the same secretive little smile on his lips, as if he were flirting with her and she didn't know it yet. She wondered if he were, or if that was simply his nature.

Every other time she had laughed off the question, and they had moved on as if she hadn't thought anything of it. It was more comfortable that way, Persi found, since she had no idea at all of how to reciprocate such flirtations (if they were flirtations at all). Unless, of course, she was to count the ideas she'd picked up from those romance novels she read. Persi supposed she could draw on those, but then she was sure she'd muck it up. "I have an update." The words flowed from her more seriously this time.

The flirty smile slipped from Manu's lips, and he sat up to give her his full attention. "Right, then, let's hear it."

Nodding, Persinette set to work filling him in on everything that Gothel had said during the briefing—which admittedly had not been much. When she was through, she let out a long breath in a whoosh. She supposed that was it; her fate was in Captain Kelii's hands.

Manu nodded and offered her an encouraging smile. "I will have some details for you as soon as I can. Until then, you sit tight and try to relax."

"All right," Persinette let her shoulders relax a little. There was nothing more she could do at that point but hope that the Uprising and Manu would look out for her. "Thank you."

"No need to thank me, my dear lady Persinette. It's my job!" He winked at her, eliciting a soft giggle from her. "Now, I'm going to see if I can get a hold of the Uprising, and you should get some rest. I'll get back to you as soon as I have something for you."

"Okay," Persinette said, nodding again. "Good night, Manu."

"Good night, Miss Persinette. Sweet dreams." With that, he closed the connection between them, and the mirror reflected only herself once more.

Persi tucked the mirror back into its hiding spot and rose from her chair. She stretched for a moment, then walked into her room to dig out the slips of paper she'd buried deep under her mattress.

For the next few hours, until her speech slurred and her eyes drooped, Persinette practiced her magic. She focused her attention on the pen perched atop her desk and pushed it across the smooth wood surface over and over again with magic. Once the pen was so easy to move that she hardly had to try, she grabbed a book and sought to lift it from the desk. By the time she finally permitted herself sleep that night, she had raised the book an inch off the desk and held it there for a full ten seconds. Then she poured herself into bed and slept what she hoped would be a dreamless sleep.

AT SOME POINT, the blissful blackness of sleep gave way to a long narrow hallway. A softly flickering glow came from the end of the hall, drawing her toward it, and a faint sound grew louder as she approached. By the time she reached the light, she had realized that the sound was a wail of agony. Just as she came upon the room, Persinette woke with a start, panting hard.

Persinette groaned and rubbed her sweaty face as she looked out the window of her quarters. The sun was just beginning to peek in through the bars. "Training," she muttered to herself, and pulled her still-tired body from the bed.

She was ready and waiting in the training rooms by the time Agnes appeared. He looked for all the world well-rested and wide awake.

"Hand-to-hand," was all he said as he assumed his post in the center of the mat.

This training began the same as it had every other time, with Persinette doing her best to try to attack Agnes and inevitably winding up on her back. Only this time, it was even worse as she was distracted by the events of the previous week's mission, Manu's words, and thoughts of what she would do if the Uprising's plan failed.

Choking on her breath, Persi sat up slowly as Agnes

glared down at her. "Where's your head at, 11-24-10?" he asked.

"Sorry, Agnes," Persi panted as she rose to her feet. "I'm just...worried about the mission to Pascal," she lied. "I'll pay more attention."

"See that you do. I'm not training you so you can go out there and make an ass out of me by running off again! My reputation is on the line too," Agnes said. He brushed some rainbow hair behind his ear and crouched at the center of the mat again.

Persinette blinked at him. His words made something suddenly click into place. Of *course* Agnes's reputation would be damaged if she were to fail. That's why he was pushing her as much he was. Not because he cared if she survived or not, but because if she did not perform well, it would reflect poorly on him.

"Forget whatever the hell it is you're worried about. Get your head out of your pert little ass and let's work. I want to see you throw a punch—a good one this time." He squared his shoulders and motioned for her to come at him.

Nodding, Persinette launched herself toward him and aimed her fist at his arm, ready to power forward as hard as she could. She threw all her weight behind it, focusing all the fear and worry she felt into her punch.

Agnes stumbled a little, releasing an amused chuckle. "Better, 11-24-10. Again!"

With that success, they went on like that until Agnes dismissed her. Afterward, as Persinette headed down to the library, she thought more about his words. If she failed, Agnes' life was on the line too. The thought twisted her stomach. She'd never particularly cared for the ornery unicorn, but she didn't want to be the reason he went to the camps either. "I'll have to train harder," she whispered to herself and gave a firm nod.

BY THAT EVENING, Manu had sent a short list of names and locations she could feed Gothel. Now, she told herself, the real work would begin.

17

CAPTAIN MANU KELII

""YOU CAN'T POSSIBLY BE SERIOUS!" Manu shouted, exasperated, as he looked down at the cards lying face-up before him. The captain and his crew had set up a table in the middle of the rec room to pass the time as the *Defiant Duchess* made its way to Pascal. And it was at that table that Manu and five of his crew members were presently sat playing a game of Texas Hold'em. "How the hell do you win with a pair of fours? That's not even...is that even a thing, Benard?"

"It is, sir." Benard nodded from his chair, a good deal away from the table, without looking up from his reading.

"But how?"

"Because you only had a pair of twos," Could-be-Paula said, eyes twinkling behind her spectacles.

"Yes, but you didn't know that," Manu said, drawing a loud laugh from the five crew members around the table and even a few of the others. "What?" The captain's eyes swept the room accusingly.

"Nothing, sir," Ethan said, gathering up the cards so he could shuffle them for another game.

"No, what is it?" Manu frowned. The five sitting at the table, including Could-be-Paula, Ethan, Sebastian, Might-be-Henry, and Samantha all shrugged and shifted uncomfortably under their captain's gaze. "Out with it!" he demanded.

Could-be-Paula shifted again, busying herself with her chips. "Your bluffing is abysmal, sir."

Manu blinked, entirely aghast at the mere insinuation that he wasn't good at bluffing. "Excuse me? My what is what?" he asked, almost daring her to repeat it.

Could-be-Paula ducked her head, cleared her throat, and refused to say any more.

Benard broke the tightening silence with a laugh. "Oh, come on, Cap'n. You can't be good at everything."

The captain huffed and stood from the table with a loud scrape of chair against floor. "Well, if you all are entirely through bashing your dearly devoted captain, I shall just retire to my rooms, shall I?"

Benard rolled his eyes and finally looked up from his book. "Don't be dramatic, sir. It was only in fun."

"Yes, please sit back down and let us take more of your money." Ethan snickered as he shuffled the cards smoothly. "We promise we'll go easy on you this time."

Manu stormed from the room in a snit. He didn't turn back once as he made his way down the hall and toward the flight deck with its floor-to-ceiling windows that showed beautiful views of the night sky. Once there, he moved to the glass and looked out at the stars. It was almost instinct, pulling the little compact that so perfectly matched Persinette's from his pocket and popping it open. He had no idea if she'd be awake at this hour, or if she'd even be in her rooms, but it was worth a try.

"Persinette." He murmured the name fondly as a smile crept up his lips.

The seconds ticked by into minutes as he waited, holding the compact out with only his reflection staring back at him. Just as the captain was about to snap the little mirror closed, Persinette's freckled face appeared in the mirror, staring back at him. "Captain Kelii! Is something wrong?" Her bright green eyes were wide with worry.

"No, nothing is wrong, Persinette. Everything is lovely." He relaxed as he drank in her features. It was strange to consider how seeing her brought him a greater and greater measure of relief as time wore on. He had only been her point of contact for a little over a week, and already he felt as if they were friends. "I just thought maybe I'd check in."

"Oh, all right." She nodded, smiling slightly, and relaxed back into whatever chair she was sitting in.

"It's nice to see you," he said without really thinking about the words. "How has your day been?"

"It's nice to see you too," Persinette admitted, a blush coloring her cheeks. She always seemed to be blushing when they talked. He liked to think it was because he had that effect on her, but if she was just blushing all the time regard-less...well, no, surely that wasn't the case. Still, rather than allow that thought to bolster his ego, as he would have any other time, Manu ignored it. "My day has been...long." She breathed the last word out like she'd been holding it in all day.

Manu frowned a little as he settled in the chair at the center of the room. "I'm sorry. Anything you'd like to talk about?"

Persinette shook her head and scrunched her nose. "No, just the usual training sessions. It's all right. How was your day?"

Now it was Manu's turn to wrinkle his nose. "We were playing Texas Hold'em in the rec room and Could-be-Paula kept beating me. I got sick of it, so here we are."

She blinked at him a few times, as if struggling to comprehend his words. "Who's Could-be-Paula?"

Manu let out a delighted laugh, shaking his head. "One of the crew. She's the sailing master."

"And her name is Could-Be-Paula?" Persinette asked slowly.

"Well...no. I don't...I don't exactly, er, know her name. But I think, you know, it...could be Paula." The captain creased his brow in thought. "Come to think of it, I don't think I've ever asked her her name before."

"Shouldn't you know the names of your crew?" Persinette's words were soft, as if she were a little afraid of contradicting him, and her eyes flicked downward so that they were no longer meeting his.

He took a second to look at her. He wondered if the sudden submissiveness were a symptom of being raised in MOTHER. "I suppose I should, shouldn't I?"

Persinette's bright green eyes met his once more, and she nodded. "I think so."

"Right, then. I'll find out, and I'll report back."

She smiled widely, revealing gapped front teeth and dimples on her cheeks. "You do that."

Manu was sure that, even if he had tried to, he wouldn't have been able to stop the grin that stretched his lips upon seeing the smile lighting up Persinette's face. That smile had infected him in a way he couldn't explain. And since he couldn't explain it, he decided not to think about it. Surely that would be easier.

"Now, what's...Tex-as hold them?" Persi stumbled over the words in confusion.

"You've never heard of Texas Hold'em before?" Manu chuckled softly at her confusion. "Well, of course you haven't! Those stuck up so-and-so's wouldn't play poker. My girl, I am going to teach you!"

She laughed. "You are?"

"Yes, I am! Just let me head to my quarters and get my cards out, and then we'll play." His feet, as if of their own accord, were already taking him to the door of the flight deck and out into the corridors of the *Duchess*. "Hold'em is probably the easier one to teach you, anyways. Five-card draw is way more complicated, and I don't think we can play via a mirror."

"Okay. Where are you going?"

"To my quarters. Oh! But I should show you some of the *Duchess* first." He laughed as the idea occurred to him, and he turned the mirror around so she could see the path down the wood-lined corridor. "This is the hallway. Very glamorous, I know."

"So much wood." Persinette's voice sounded awed.

"Of course, my dear. The entire ship is wood. The *Duchess* is modeled after one of the old pre-war pirate ships we found, called the *Black Pearl* or some such. It was in the Americas, in a place called Hollywood," Manu told her proudly. "An old military base, we think. If it worked for the pre-ward pirates, it's good enough for us."

"Right, of course. And what are we passing?"

"Oh. Right." Manu turned the mirror back to face him so he could look down at her and walk more slowly. "That's the medic's office," he said, turning the mirror toward a set of double doors. "And that's the door down to the cargo hold."

Persinette was nodding along, her eyes flicking around to drink in as much of the ship as she could with, a soft smile on her face. "This is what I always imagined a pirate ship would be like on the inside."

Manu laughed. "You imagined what a pirate ship would be like on the inside?"

Persi shrugged. "I've read a lot of novels, and some of them had pirates in them."

"What kind of novels? The steamy kind?" Manu grinned knowingly at her. He supposed being trapped in MOTHER as she was, she would need to find some form of amusement. Why not books?

A deep flush settled onto her freckled cheeks, and she averted her eyes. "I...w-well...I..." she stammered softly.

Manu wasn't sure why he cared, or where he thought it would go if she *did* say that she read raunchy romance novels, but he couldn't let the topic go. It was in his nature to be flirty, and this seemed the perfect opportunity to forge headfirst into some very serious flirting with his pretty new charge.

His attention was so focused on Persinette and her quickly reddening face that he didn't notice Ivy coming from one of the rooms. In fact, he bumped right into her, nearly dropping the little mirror as he stumbled to keep himself upright. "Ivy," Manu said, offering her a respectful nod.

"Captain." The green-haired witch nodded back. "I do hope that is an Uprising-related communication and you are not wasting valuable magic on something...frivolous." Her dark eyes flicked to the mirror still clutched in Manu's hand with Persinette's face floating in it.

"No, of course. Persi and I were just going to go over that list of names and addresses once more," Manu said quickly. As Ivy's eyes scanned his face in their slow and calculated manner, he knew she was judging him.

"Right, of course. I'm glad you aren't flirting with your Asset. I'd hate to have to tell Eddi that you aren't taking this seriously." With that, Ivy slinked away back down the hall.

Manu huffed a sigh and spun toward his quarters once more. "Apologies. Where were we?"

"You were going to teach me to play Texas Hold'em," Persi said.

"Right. Onward!"

THE NEXT TWO days brought meeting after meeting with Benard and Ivy and her tactical advisor about the mission ahead of them. After so many hours of being trapped in conference with them, Manu was quite sick of the sight of his own office, and even more sick of the sight of Ivy and her little crony. The discussions had become so unbearably boring that he found himself daydreaming about Persinette and what she'd say when she was finally able to taste a pineapple. He just knew she'd like it, whether she herself knew it or not. He knew that she'd smile and tell him it was the best thing she'd ever tasted. She seemed the type to enjoy sweet things.

"Captain Kelii." Ivy's annoyed voice cut through his thoughts.

"Hm?" Manu lifted his chin from his hand. "I'm sorry, what were you saying?"

"We were discussing who would be the best to place at the Collection sites. Ivy has suggested that all of them be from our Unit," the tactical advisor said, his pen stopping its scratching at the notebook in his lap. Unlike Ivy, he seemed utterly unbothered by the captain's obvious distraction.

Manu frowned at the young man's words and shook his

head. "No, I think not—I don't trust your Unit not to get trigger-happy. I'd rather none of you shoot Persi in the process."

"Persi," Ivy repeated with a quirked brow. "And what of your other plans with *Persi*?"

"Excuse me? I don't have any other plans with Persi. We have the mission ahead of us and that is all." Hopefully, he was bluffing far better at that moment than he had been when he'd been playing cards.

"Right, of course it is." She nodded with a knowing look. "Now, as I was saying, my Unit is more than capable of handling a mission of this sort. We have been trained in MOTHER tactics and know how to make sure it looks like a very near miss."

"Which still does not negate the captain's worry that you or one of your people will try to inflict more damage on the MOTHER agents than necessary, and Miss Persinette might get caught in the crossfire," Benard insisted.

The tactical analyst—who Manu thought might be named Elijah, although there had been no formal introductions—snorted. "I really don't understand your concern. If a MOTHER Asset's blood is spilled, then so be it. MOTHER would not hesitate for a moment to kill any and all of the Uprising agents on this ship if given the chance."

"That is not the point," Manu growled darkly, his jaw tensing.

"Then what, pray tell, is the point, Captain?" Ivy asked with one green brow quirked. "That you're worried about your pretty little *Persi*, perhaps? More so than you are worried that the mission might fail?"

"No," Manu ground out, doing everything within his power to keep his anger in check. "My point is that there is no need for innocent blood to be shed, whether it be

Persinette's or that of a non-Enchanted civilian. Our goal in this mission is to make MOTHER think Persinette is still doing all she can to aid in their Collections, and in doing so, to save innocent Enchanted lives. That is our mandate. Nothing more, nothing less."

Ivy scoffed. "I hardly think Eddi would mourn the loss of a couple of non-Enchanted civilians. They are the reason we're all being hunted down, after all."

"This is not open for discussion, Ivy! You will follow my orders, or we will drop your sorry ass and your sorry-ass Unit off at the next town and be done with it!" the captain shouted as he leaped from his chair, slamming his hands so hard on the desk that the tactical analyst nearly dropped his notebook. Manu let his eyes flash their dangerous golden color, agitation lengthening his nails down into claws that left deep scratch marks along the smooth surface of his desk. "Have I made myself perfectly clear?"

Ivy inhaled sharply, as though debating whether it was wise to push him further, then shrugged. "Very well. So long as the *Duchess* is your ship, we will follow your orders."

Manu settled back into his seat, pulling a calm expression over his features. He focused, with some difficulty, on retracting the claws and shifting his golden irises back to brown. The beast in Manu's head growled irritably at being forced back, but the captain regained control. "Yes, this *is* my ship, and so long as you are on *my ship*, you will follow *my* orders," he agreed, ignoring the apparent threat underlining her words. The *Duchess* was and would always be his.

Ivy nodded once more. "How many of my men would you like to include in this mission, Captain?"

"One."

"One?" she asked, her face pinching in disgust. "That hardly seems an adequate way to utilize our capacity."

"The remainder of your Unit, along with a small selection of my most trusted men, will remain inside the Collection radius as backup should something go awry," Manu continued, as if she hadn't spoken at all. "If something *should* go wrong, you are to extract Persinette from the situation and get her to safety, along with any of the other Uprising agents set up at the Collection sites."

Ivy's face paled as she listened, but she voiced no further arguments or complaints. If Manu were a wise man, perhaps he would have found that worrisome, but he was a reckless soul, and so he took no notice of it. "Yes, sir," she said with a nod. "How many do we intend to set up for Collection total?"

"Six. We've given Persinette the addresses and species of four of my men already. The plan is to provide her with the final two when we meet in Pascal. Hopefully, it will be enough to make MOTHER decide it is beneficial for her to continue to be out in the field with them."

"We also hope that in doing this MOTHER will decide to bring more Seers out into the field. Which would make them accessible to the Uprising, and perhaps we can add to our list of operatives in headquarters," Benard added.

Ivy and Possibly-Elijah listened intently. Possibly-Elijah took detailed notes as they spoke, and once his pen stopped moving, he nodded. "That seems reasonable enough. Have you relayed this hope to Eddi?"

"Not yet. We want to make sure we are successful in running a few missions with Persinette first. Then we will broach the topic of subsequent operations of this type." Manu peered at what Possibly-Elijah had written. He didn't trust the young man's compulsion to jot down everything that had been said, but did not say as much, lest Possibly-Elijah write *that* down, too. "And with that, I think we are done for the evening. We will be in Pascal in a couple of days. You all should get some rest."

The two Uprising Agents nodded and saw themselves out of the captain's quarters. Once the door was shut behind them, Benard turned to his captain. "You heard that threat. Ivy intends to take your ship if things don't go well."

"We'll just have to make sure they do go well, won't we, Benard?" Manu leaned back in his chair and propped his feet up on his desk.

"Yes, sir. We will."

18

PERSINETTE

THE LABOR CAMP was silent and empty but for a lone pale figure several feet away. As Persinette drew closer, she saw the person more clearly.

There was Silas, only this time, instead of grabbing for Persinette, he merely stood before an open doorway, waiting for her. His eyes, though drooping with exhaustion and hunger, remained fixed intently on her as he stood there holding the heavy-looking door open with ease, revealing a gaping chasm of darkness on the other side.

"Silas, please, I don't want to go in there," Persinette protested, her voice echoing through the stillness of the camp.

Silas made no move to force her and did not say a word; he just stood watching her expectantly. In spite of her heart hammering with fear within her chest—and without any conscious choice to do so—she moved toward him. It was as if her feet were moving of their own volition. Her dread grew as the gaping darkness of that doorway drew closer and closer, threatening to swallow her whole.

"Come on, Persi," an eerily childlike voice called playfully.

When she got close just to the threshold, the world tilted forward and flung her into the darkness. Then she was falling—down, down, down through an endless inky blackness with no end in sight.

PERSI AWOKE with a start before she could hit the bottom of that pit. She sat up in her chair, coughing on all of the air she'd just gulped in as her eyes flew open.

"Oh, thank gods, you're awake," Wyn said, drawing her hand back from Persi's shoulder. "You were whimpering in your sleep and it was really worrying me. Are you all right?"

Persinette brushed her loose lavender hair back from her sticky face and nodded mutely. She cautiously flicked her gaze around the library to make sure no one had seen her sleeping at the table, but the place seemed empty. "Yeah, I think so. It was just a nightmare."

Wyn frowned and sat down beside her friend. "Do you have a lot of nightmares?"

As Wyn sat, Persi's head ducked to hide the feeling of blood draining from her cheeks, and her eyes jumped nervously over the books in front of her—one of which was a grimoire. Thankfully, it was propped open, and might be mistaken for a journal of some kind if Wyn didn't look too closely.

Persi hoped Wyn wouldn't look too closely. It was bad enough that she might get herself thrown into the camps because of her desire to learn magic, but she had no idea what MOTHER would do to Wyn if they thought she'd been helping. What happened to Enchanted sympathizers? She didn't know. Human didn't get sent to labor camps. They just—

"Persi?" Wyn asked, a worried frown still in place.

"Huh? Oh, yeah, sometimes. I mean not all the time," she lied awkwardly and hoped that it would seem she was just disoriented from being awoken so abruptly. "But sometimes." Persi wasn't sure why she was lying about her dreams. Wyn was her friend, and it wasn't like MOTHER could punish her for having nightmares. It was perfectly natural to have bad dreams after a traumatic experience. Still, she didn't want to give MOTHER any reason to leave her behind when the next mission began.

Wyn examined Persinette for a moment, her brown eyes thoughtful, and nodded. "Do you want to talk about them?"

Wyn was trying to help. She was a good friend, and that's all she was doing: helping, providing Persinette with some comfort. For a moment, Persinette thought about telling another lie, but there were already so many of them between her and Wyn. So instead she opted for the truth. "They—they're about the camps, and the people I've sent there. It's like they're haunting me," she whispered.

The librarian let out a soft sigh as she brushed dark curls back out of her face. "You don't feel guilty for helping with Collections, do you?"

Persi gave a half-hearted shrug. "I mean, a little bit," she murmured. "Is that bad?"

Wyn shook her head. "No, it's only to be expected. You're Enchanted, and they're Enchanted, so you empathize with them. But you need to remember, Persi, that what we're doing here is good work. The Enchanted out in the world aren't like you. They take advantage of their power and use it against mortals. They aren't good people." Wyn squeezed Persi's hand.

Persinette tried to ignore the intense look Wyn was giving her and how it made her stomach roll with nausea.

There was something sickening about Wyn's insistence that Collecting Enchanted and locking them away in labor camps was "good work." In all the books Persinette had read, people were tried before they were punished, but the Enchanted that MOTHER Collected were never allowed the chance to defend their actions. They were never allowed to explain themselves, or even refute what MOTHER accused them of. They were simply locked away and forgotten. Worse still, Persinette didn't see how every Enchanted could possibly be that bad. Magic itself wasn't inherently evil, nor were the beings who could wield it.

Persi forced herself to nod in agreement. "I just wish the ghosts would leave me alone," she said. That much, at least, was not a lie. She did wish that Silas and the others would let her be. Especially now that she had decided to help them as best she could.

Wyn patted Persi's freckled hand in a gesture that should have been comforting. "Just do your best to remember that we're doing the right thing here. We're protecting people who can't protect themselves."

"Right." Persi swallowed down the feeling of bile rising in her throat. "I, umm...I think I need to go lie down for a little. I'll just put these back." She stood and gathered up the books, quickly tucking the grimoire among all the history books before Wyn could see it.

"Oh, let me. You go and rest," Wyn insisted, trying to take the books from her hands.

Persinette held fast to them, refusing to relinquish the stack to her friend. "No, it's all right. It'll give me something to focus on while I get my head back on right. And you have all those to put back," she said, nodding to the cart that Wyn had apparently abandoned to wake her.

"Okay," Wyn said. "Well, feel better, all right?"

Persinette nodded once more and rushed away from her friend. Once she was sure that Wyn was out of sight, she stopped and leaned against one of the heavy metal shelves to try to catch her breath. "Close. Too close," she whispered. She stuffed all of the books onto one of the shelves beside her and left the library before Wyn could find her again.

THE EVENING'S training with Agnes left Persinette nursing a very bruised backside. At least an hour getting the crap kicked out her had shaken the image of Silas from her mind, if only for a little while. Persi was grateful for that much, and she reminded herself of that fact as she sat at her desk with a wince.

"Still, I wouldn't want him to go easy on me," she said. It was true; Persi *wouldn't* want Agnes to go easy on her, and not just because her failure reflected poorly on him. Although the MOTHER agents would not let anyone near her while she was out on Collection, all the caution in the world couldn't guarantee something terrible wouldn't happen. Plus, Persi reasoned that if she ever wanted to escape MOTHER and make it on her own, she'd need to be able to fight.

Persinette shook her head to clear her thoughts. "Focus, Persi. Focus." She smoothed out the wrinkled bit of book that a displayed a spell for telekinesis.

After the first few weeks of toying with the pronuncia-tion of the words and learning to focus her energy, she'd been able to float a book above the desk for ten seconds. That was it, though; that was where her progress had stalled. Every time, she would raise the book off the desk with her magic and count—one, two, three, all the way to ten—and at ten, the book would drop with a thud onto the smooth wooden surface.

"Maybe I'm just not strong enough," Persi said, feeling dejected. The spell sat there, mocking her, as she glared down at it. Or maybe she was putting too much pressure on the magic, she thought. Perhaps it would have to want to come to her, not be forced from hiding as she was trying to do now.

Regardless, she looked down at the book again and reached for the magic within herself. The first several times she had reached within herself, trying to coax the magic out with words and prayers, she'd felt silly. Of course there would be nothing in there. Of course nothing would reach back. She was just a Seer, after all—nothing more, nothing less. She had only enough magic within her to find others of her kind; that's what she'd always been told. But gradually— over the weeks that spanned from that first fire message spell to the telekinesis spell sitting in front of her—she'd found the magic reaching back.

None of the grimoires she'd looked through had talked about how it would feel to use magic, or how best to get the magic to cooperate; they were just full of spells. She imagined that was because when they'd been written, magic had been so abundant and common for her predecessors that it was like breathing. She hoped this was what it was supposed to feel like, as if the magic were a creature living inside of her more than a power. The ebb of it stretched lazily when she reached for it again, like a large cat napping.

With that thought in mind, Persi decided to treat the magic how she imagined someone might a stubborn animal. She closed her eyes and turned inwards to face the creature head-on. Then she inhaled deeply and asked, as politely as possible, "Please, work with me?"

The creature lifted its head, and a moment later, the magic reached back. She felt the buzz of electricity warm every inch of her to the tips of her toes and fingers. One corner of her lips twitched into a lopsided smile.

"Hello there," she said, opening her eyes to look at the book she'd been trying to float. As she softly murmured the incantation, the book rose slowly from the table, and where once it had stopped to hover a foot from the desk, it continued to rise. Soft sparks of light purple magic pressed it up, up, up until it *thunked* lightly against the ceiling.

"Well, well, well." She grinned to herself. Her finger twitched, and the book slid across the ceiling until it hit the wall with another thump. With a sharp tug of her hand, like one might pull on a rope, she yanked the book down to hover in front of her face.

An almost-drunken giggle left her as she jerked her head and the book flopped open. "All right, let's try something harder," Persi said. There was a thud as she released the magic holding the book aloft and it landed once more on the desk. She made her way into the main room of her small living quarters and turned her attention to the heavy leather chair before her bookcase. She remembered when Wyn had given her that chair; it had taken three robots to get it to its current spot, so it was by no means light.

""We can do this," she told her magic, which did not protest in any way. Murmuring the spell once more, she watched as the magic lifted the chair with ease into a controlled hover a few feet off the floor. Another squeal of delight left Persinette as she bounced in place. "Oh, my gods!"

In her excitement, she lost focus, and the chair settled

back to the rug with a dull bang. Persi righted it, sank into the soft leather cushions, and let out a breath of relief. Now that she knew how to get the magic to come to her more easily, she could use it in the field. But in this particular moment the sheer exhilaration of having accomplished such a thing at all, even if it was just a chair, had her mind humming with distraction from anything mission-related. She needed to share this with someone! She needed to tell someone about her success! But who?

Persinette had barely asked herself the question when an image of Manu came to her mind. She pulled the compact from where she'd hidden it in the chair and popped it open. "Captain Manu Kelii," Persi demanded of the mirror and settled in to wait for her reflection to fade away and show Manu's face instead.

He didn't keep her waiting long. Only a few seconds ticked by before his handsome face was before her, wearing its wide, roguish smile. He must have been holding the mirror, Persi reasoned, as his head and shoulders appeared before her again.

"Well, Miss Persi, I didn't expect to hear from you this evening. I thought you'd be quite busy preparing for our mission in a few days."

"I need to tell you something." The words came out in a rush as Persinette did everything in her power to swallow another drunk-sounding giggle—and failed.

Her words wiped the grin from the captain's face and made concern wash over his features. "Is something wrong? What can I do to help?"

Persi laughed as the lightness took over her body and everything inside her felt like it was floating. "No, nothing is wrong. But—you're sweet for worrying."

Manu let out a relieved-sounding sigh as he settled back

into the chair he was sitting in, his grin returning slowly. "I'm sweet," he said, laughing softly. "All right then, what is it you need to tell me?"

"Well, it's more of a show than a tell." She stood from the chair, prompting a questioning look from Manu, and turned the mirror to face the chair. She muttered the incantation again, and the chair dutifully lifted several feet off the ground once more.

Manu gasped.

Persinette let the chair settle back to the floor slowly and gave another soft whoop of excitement before turning the mirror back to face her.

"Did you just...? Since when did you...? Persinette! I didn't know you could do spells! You're amazing!"

Persinette shrugged and sank back into the chair again. "After the last mission, I decided I needed something to protect myself, and this might be the best way. I've been practicing. I only know like three spells, but..."

Manu's grin was one unlike she'd seen on his face before—she wasn't sure, but she thought he might be proud of her. The notion sent a little thrill through her belly, kicking up the butterflies that had settled there. "Nonsense. You're well on your way to be a full-blown witch, then. Give it another month and you'll have memorized an entire grimoire."

"Maybe, but I'd have to get my hands on an entire grimoire." She shifted uncomfortably, not used to the praise in spite of the pride she felt at what she had accomplished. "MOTHER keeps those locked up in the library. I've only been able to get the spells I have by ripping them out of books and bringing them back to my room. Only the witch Assets are supposed to use them, and even then only when supervised by an agent."

"Well, we'll have to get you your own grimoire when you get out, won't we? Then you can start keeping track of your spells and making up new ones," Manu said confidently.

"Making up my own spells..." Persi murmured as if she were tasting the idea. She'd never really thought about it: using her magic to do whatever she wanted by just picking a word for it. Was that how spells were made? She'd have to do some more research.

"But for now, I think you should get some rest. You look tired," Manu said, not unkindly.

Persi nodded. "Yes, you're right. Good night, Manu."

"Sweet dreams, Persi." He winked, and the image of him blacked out, leaving only her reflection in the glass. She yawned and dragged herself to bed.

THE MISSION WAS in less than twenty-four hours. Twelve hours and thirty-six minutes, if Persinette were keeping count—which she was. As the seconds ticked away, and the departure time got closer and closer, a knot tightened in the pit of Persinette's stomach. She couldn't help but worry about what would become of her if all did not go according to Manu's plan. If there were no Enchanted in the locations Manu had given her when MOTHER arrived, the agents would know something was amiss. In the end, if the plan failed, it would be Persinette who would be executed or sent to the camps. No one.

"We'll just send you down to the labor camps; I'm sure you'll be more useful there." Some of Gothel's words finally registered to Persinette, turning speculation about failure to failure's actual consequences.

Because if Persinette failed, she would lose everything she had grown to love about her life as a MOTHER Asset. She would lose her friendship with Wyn, who would no doubt see her assistance to the Uprising as a betrayal. She would no longer be allowed to read books from the library, and any she owned would be left behind. Above all, whatever faint illusion of freedom she'd conjured in the compound would evaporate. In the labor camp, she would be told when to wake, what to wear, where to be, and her existence would be nothing more than a cog in MOTHER's production machine. The very thought of it sent a cold shiver down Persinette's spine.

"Persinette. Are you listening?" Gothel asked with a glare.

"Oh, yes. Sorry, Gothel." Persi nodded. Gothel was now watching her suspiciously. "I was just..." she started, casting her eyes around for a plausible lie. "I had a vision!" The words slipped almost too easily from her lips, and her heart pounded.

Gothel's glare turned to a look of confusion. "You did? Just now?"

Persi nodded again and reached for the pen in front of her to jot down one of the addresses Manu had her memorize. "A werewolf lives here. I think his name is Owen."

Gothel took the piece of paper and looked at it with a satisfied sneer. "That's four."

"Yes, it is."

"You've never given us four before," Gothel said, a bit of surprise in her voice.

Persinette shrugged slowly, buying herself a little time to prepare another lie. "I guess going out into the field helped?"

Brow furrowed, Gothel looked back to Persinette. "Perhaps it did. Maybe all you needed was a change of scene to shake things loose." She sounded thoughtful. Like she believed Persi.

"Maybe," Persinette agreed.

Silence fell as Gothel transferred the new information over to her files, the only sound her pen scratching away against the paper. "Right, then. Good work Persinette. Go and get some rest. We have a big day ahead of us." She didn't even bother looking up from the file as she dismissed her charge.

"What about training?" Not that Persi *wanted* to go to training with her stomach feeling the way it did, but she supposed she ought to get official dispensation to take the evening off. Otherwise, it might be seen as deserting her duties, which would no doubt end with her in more trouble.

Gothel's dark, beady eyes lifted from the file to scrutinize the girl. "I suppose you can skip it for this afternoon," Gothel conceded after a moment. "Just be sure to get plenty of rest."

Persi swallowed down the giggle—half manic, half genuinely excited—that threatened to take over and somehow managed to keep her face impassive as she dipped her head. "Thank you, Gothel." Then she rose carefully and collectedly from her chair and headed out into the corridor. Once out of Gothel's sight, it was a struggle not to skip down the hallway toward her rooms in the Tower, where incantations and Manu were waiting for her.

19

CAPTAIN MANU KELII & PERSINETTE

MANU, for his part, had worked to set everything into motion. In spite of Benard's protests that what they had come to call Manu's "secret plan" was utterly ridiculous, everything was in place. The captain was taking no chances with the life of his new friend, and Benard would help his captain whether he liked it or not.

"Eight hours. Eight hours. Eight hours," Manu was chanting to himself as he paced up and down the length of his quarters, wringing his hands into nervous knots. Dark irises flickered to gold and back once more in agitation. "Eight hours."

"You must calm down, sir, or you'll tear through another waistcoat. I cannot afford to keep mending them, and the last one you split right in half," Benard said placidly.

Manu's Enchanted form was far less forgiving than some—like Benard's natural goblin shape—and he had indeed torn through three waistcoats already. It was beginning to get expensive. "Right, sorry." He took closed his eyes and focused on his breathing. Yet neither the apology nor the deep inhale calmed the tension that vibrated off him.

"Why don't you sit and have a drink, sir?" Benard asked as he rose from his chair and made his way to the small cabinet beside the captain's desk. He pulled from it a little bottle of amber-colored liquid and a glass. "To calm your nerves."

"I don't want a drink," Manu said, dropping onto the well-worn leather sofa.

Benard blinked, motionless, still holding the glass and bottle. "I'm sorry, sir?"

"I said, I don't want a drink. I need to be clear-headed going into this thing tomorrow." When the first mate still didn't move, Manu let out a long-suffering sigh. "What is it?"

"I just don't think I've ever seen you turn down a drink before, sir," Benard said, with genuine surprise. "That is, I'm glad you're not drinking—it'd be irresponsible to drink right now—but still."

"Still what?" Manu said, eyeing his first mate.

"Nothing, sir," Benard said, replacing the bottle and glass in the cabinet. "Miss Persinette seems to be having a positive effect on you."

The captain huffed and shrugged his well-muscled shoulders as he slumped further back into the sofa. "I guess so."

With a nod, Benard settled back into his chair that faced the couch. A little smile had appeared on his weathered face, but Manu pretended not to notice. "Your girl will be quite all right, and everything will go according to plan. You're getting yourself worked up over nothing."

"It is not nothing!" The captain sprang forward, his teeth grown and pressing sharp points into his lower lip as he glared at Benard.

Benard simply lifted a dark brow and shook his head,

with no more words to ease the captain's fears. "All right then, let's go over it again. To be sure." He grabbed the rolled-up parchment from the table.

The idea of having something to do and think of other than the worry of what could or would go wrong eased the captain. He released a relieved sigh, feeling his fangs retract and his shoulders relax a little. The rest of the evening was spent hashing and rehashing the plan to be sure that the two men hadn't missed anything. To make certain that there was a contingency plan for anything that might go wrong. And, hopefully, to ensure that Persinette would be safe no matter what.

When the captain finally slumped into bed late that evening, it was only with a small amount of struggle that he found sleep.

THE FOLLOWING morning Captain Manu Kelii was up with the sun. Avoiding breakfast for fear that he might throw it up from his nerves, he headed directly to the flight deck to begin the process of lowering the anchors that would keep the *Duchess* docked. Once he'd checked—and double-checked—and was that the ship was indeed firmly anchored, he headed to the deck below to check on the crew's preparations for the mission.

The hold was loud with the bustle of activity as the crew moved this way and that to prepare for heading to ground. Could-be-Paula bumped the captain in her hurry to get to the other side of the room.

"'Scuse me, sir," she said, adjusting her glasses and brushing a strand of dark hair from her face as she stumbled on her way.

"Sir, maybe you should head back up to the main decks." Benard drew to the captain's side. "The crew knows what they're doing down here. They haven't failed you yet."

Manu nodded, deflating a little as he fidgeted with the buttons on his waistcoat. He needed something to do with his hands, *anything* to do with his hands. "It's not them I'm worried about," he said.

The young captain hadn't yet admitted why he'd been up so early, not even to himself. He hadn't been able to acknowledge the fear that loomed inside of him like a fog. It hadn't been his crew's competence that had brought on the fear; no, it was his own competence, and the potential lack thereof, that troubled him most. The crew of the *Defiant Duchess* was battle-tested and ready for this, from the most seasoned mate right down to the youngest deckhand. Her captain, however, was another story. Although Manu had been captain of the *Duchess* for over six years, he had never been on a mission of this sort before. And the fear was bigger and newer now, too: What if he failed Persi? What if he did something wrong and she got hurt?

Benard snorted softly, shaking his head. "Well, don't worry about yourself either," the old goblin said. "Now, go on and set this boat into a nice hover so the crew can do their jobs."

"Right," the captain. But he stood there fidgeting with the ends of his neatly pressed shirt. His dark eyes were following Could-Be-Paula when a thought occurred to him. "Hey, Benard, what's her name?" He nodded in the woman's direction.

Benard turned to Manu and frowned. "Janette. Why do you ask?"

"Hm. Not even close to Paula," Manu murmured.

Benard stared at his captain. "Of course it's not even close to Paula. Where the hell did you get Paula from?"

"Not even close," the captain repeated to himself. "I have to tell Persinette!"

Back in his quarters, he shut the door with a faint click and he pulled the little compact from his pocket. His fingers slid over the detailed cameo on the outside, but didn't open it. When Benard had told him Could-be-Paula's actual name, the need to tell Persi was immediate, urgent. Now, he realized how foolish that was. The *Duchess* and her crew were just an hour away from the meetup with her. She wouldn't have brought the compact with her through the portal, either, lest one of the MOTHER agents catch her with it. So telling Persi about Janette's real name would just have to wait.

For now, Manu grabbed his pistol and dagger and headed back to the flight deck.

EDDI PLANNED to just put a few of Manu and Ivy's men in place of civilians so they could deal with MOTHER's Collection party. That part, Manu was sure, would go off without a hitch, but he had his own plan in place. Eddi and Ivy had made it very clear that they saw no reason for Manu to meet his Asset in person again. What need would there be for that? Still, Manu had always been one to skirt the rules, and he wanted to get to know Persinette a little better. He wanted the chance to show her a bit of the world she was risking her life to help save; it only seemed fair. Also, he reasoned, it couldn't hurt to have the chance to pass her a weapon just in case.

Thus, the young captain set his own plan into motion.

Because, most importantly of all, he had promised Persinette she would get to try pineapple, and he was going to deliver, damn it!

"I'm not overly excited about this plan, sir," Benard remarked as they wove through the streets of Pascal. The crew had run surveillance all over the city and found out where MOTHER set up their base for the mission. The base—where they would be keeping Persi.

"Oh, come now, Benard. You don't even have to do anything. Just sit in her chair and make it look like she's in her room. You could do that in your sleep. Hell, you probably will do it in your sleep." Manu let out a jovial laugh as they stopped across the street from the glass-covered building. "Ethan set everything up for me?"

"Yes, sir." Benard nodded, but didn't move, as though he had one final attempt to make his captain see sense. "I don't think I like using my abilities this way."

Manu threw him a blank look that hopefully conveyed that he was not in any way concerned with whatever moral implications Benard might be struggling with.

"And all this so you can go and see some girl," the goblin added.

The captain exhaled sharply. "That's not why, Benard." There was no killing his mood at this point, a fact that seemed only to make Benard grumpier.

"Oh? Then why?"

"She's never had pineapple, Benard! Can you imagine all the other things she's never been able to do? They've kept her locked up in headquarters for God knows how long, maybe since she was a baby! She deserves a little fun now that we're asking her to risk her life for the cause. Doesn't she?"

Benard's expression remained grumpy, but a kindness

had settled into his eyes that told Manu he'd won. "Oh, I suppose."

Manu released an excited little squeal and pulled his first mate into a bone-crushing hug. "Oooooh, thank you! Thank you! Thank you! You're the best, Benard!" The goblin just grunted and pushed Manu away. "I knew you'd come around, you old softy." Manu released a laugh that was all teeth and sparkling dark eyes—an affair of ridiculous proportions that seemed to take over his whole body instead of just his face.

Once inside, all of them—the two men and the small crew that was waiting for them beside the building—split up. A few headed off to cause a distraction to draw the guards away from Persinette's room. Manu had instructed that the disturbance didn't have to be destructive; it just had to make a ridiculous amount of noise. Thus, a few of the crew headed to the abandoned apartments, grabbed as many pots and pans as they could, and banged them together they ran up and down the halls.

As chaos ensued, Manu heard a delighted laugh leave the old goblin, his eyes gleaming with excitement. If there was one thing goblins loved, it was wreaking a little havoc. While Manu waited below, looking up at the windows, Benard stood in the hall, watching for when the guards stationed before Persi's door cleared out. It didn't take long for the clanking of metal on metal to grab their attention, and just like that, the two hulking MOTHER agents ran from the room to see what was going on. Benard took the opportunity to slip into the room behind them.

The door creaked gently shut, and Persi whipped around, terror pricking at her eyes. Though she had no weapon, her hands flew up to defend herself.

"Relax, Miss Persi. I'm Benard, Captain Manu's first

mate. He sent me." Benard held up his own hands to show her that he meant her no harm.

Persinette watched him suspiciously, her hands glowing with sparkling purple magic. A soft tap on the glass behind her drew Persi's attention away from the goblin in front of her to the window once more. There, on the balcony, stood Manu. A bright toothy smile had split his face and his eyes were lit with mischief. "Would you be a darling and open the window?" he shouted through the glass. "We haven't got much time before they come back."

Persi furrowed her brow, trying to understand what was going on. At last, she nodded and opened the window, allowing the captain to step through with an exaggerated bow. "Wh-what are you doing here?" she asked. "The plan hasn't changed has it? Oh no—does the Uprising not want me to help anymore?" Her words came out in a jumbled, quick mess of thoughts tripping one over the other as fear gripped every part of her insides.

Benard said nothing, frowning more and more deeply the more worked up Persi became.

"Persi," Manu said, grasping her hands in an attempt to anchor her. The girl's breath continued to come in shallow gasps, but her wild eyes met his. "Persinette, calm down." The captain's words were calm but firm.

Persinette nodded, taking a inhaled deeply to force the panic back down into the depths of her mind where it belonged.

Once she appeared to have calmed down, the captain allowed himself a little smile. "There now. Isn't that better?"

She nodded again and even offered him a smile. "Yes, thank you."

"Good. Now, the plan has changed a little. But only in

that, I plan to take you on a bit of an outing while you're in the city. You deserve to see some of it while you're here."

Just like that, the panic came back threefold. Persi let out a strangled sound. "An outing? I can't go on an outing! There are MOTHER agents just outside that door! They are going to notice if I'm not here, Manu!" Persi wasn't sure what kind of harebrained logic the captain had in his head to make him think a field trip was a good idea, or that a field trip was even something they could pull off, but she didn't like it. It most definitely would not work, and it was certainly a horrible idea! They would notice! They would notice *and* they would question her, and in the end, Persi knew that she could not resist a real interrogation. The little white lies she had been telling thus far were nothing compared to what she'd have to concoct to make it through rigorous questioning.

A sharp pinprick pain in her scalp caused Persinette to yelp loudly. Her panic forgotten, she rubbed her head as she glared at Benard. The goblin held between his green fingers a single strand of lavender hair, and he was grinning at her.

"You let me worry about the MOTHER agents," he told her in a voice that sounded...like hers? A shiver ran up her spine at the sound of her own voice coming from the goblin's mouth, a shiver that only intensified as she watched Benard's dark greenish skin lighten and turn freckled, much like hers. His features reformed themselves into a mirror image of her own, and a moment later her own forest-green eyes were blinking back at her with an expression of impassive annoyance. "Now, please do be a dear and get the hell out of here before they notice there are two of you. You too, Cap'n." Benard-who-looked-like-Persinette pressed one pale hand to each of their backs and shoved the captain and the girl out onto the balcony.

Persi did not attempt to argue; she was still too shocked at what she had seen. Once the window was shut, and she was looking back at her face from behind glass, she shook herself and tried to focus on something else. It was eerie. "So, how do we get down?" she asked, leaning over the railing of the balcony and peering at the street several stories below.

"Oh, that part's easy." Manu climbed over the railing and stepped out onto thin air.

Persi yelped, grabbing for him, but she stopped suddenly when the captain, instead of falling to his death, just stood there wearing that roguish smile of his. He whistled softly and a copper hovercraft appeared beneath him. The machine was strangely silent—or perhaps she just couldn't hear it over the noise of the street below—but she could see briskly whirring gears within it, working hard to keep it afloat.

Persi gaped as she reached for the machine. The surface was cool and smooth, and she found herself enthralled by the very idea of it. She had never seen such a thing in person! "Wow, it's so quiet," she said.

Manu shrugged. "A little bit of magic keeps it from being noticed." He offered her his hand, or not so much offered as hauled her onto the hovercraft without any warning. Persi yelped, but once her feet found purchase on the smooth, skid-free surface, she let out an excited giggle. "I have some amazing mechanics on my ship," Manu bragged, his arms wrapping tightly around her waist, hugging her from behind, to keep her steady. "Now, off to find some pineapple!"

He whistled again, this time a slightly different note, and the machine plunged toward the ground with the pair of them firmly attached to it by where magic had melded their shoes briefly to the surface. Persinette shrieked as her stomach flew up into her throat, and she squeezed her eyes shut. Her hands flailed, vainly seeking something to hold onto, but there was nothing, so she just gripped Manu's arms, knuckles white.

At ground level, the machine zipped through the streets at a speed that made her eyes water and her breath nearly still. Manu seemed to be putting as much distance between them and Persi's holding cells as he could, and doing it as quickly as possible. They were some blocks away from the building where MOTHER had been holding her before the hovercraft finally slowed down to a speed that Persinette found bearable, and she loosened her grip on Manu's arms.

The young captain let out a loud whoop of laughter, tightening his arms around her to in a little squeeze. As he did, Persinette found herself laughing too. The fear of dying from a fall finally faded away, and the excitement at being free, even if just for a moment, took over. "All right Miss Persi, where to? The ship? The market? What do you want to see first?"

"Let's go find some pineapple first, then to the ship," she exclaimed, unable to hold in her enthusiasm.

The two laughed again as they zipped through the streets toward the market. The wind whipped Persi's long lavender hair free from its braid, and it flew out behind them. Sixteen years—that's how long it had been since she'd left MOTHER and was truly free. A lightness blossomed inside her inside her in a way she hadn't thought possible.

20

CAPTAIN MANU KELII & PERSINETTE

PERSINETTE'S HEAD spun as they turned a corner, and then another, and then another all in quick succession. At last, the little ramshackle market came into view, made up of rickety-looking lean-tos and threadbare canopies. Manu whistled and the hovercraft slowed to a stop. He jumped to the ground, took her hands, and helped her down. Persinette's legs felt wobbly and unstable, but she let out another breathless giggle in spite of herself.

"You all right?" Manu asked.

"Yeah, just need to get my land legs back." Persi laughed softly.

Manu nodded and held out an arm. "Well, hang onto me until you do. I'll keep you steady." At the touch of Persi's arm looping through his, a warm feeling settled into his stomach. Benard's warning rang through his head, and he hoped that warm feeling was just hunger. "All set?"

She nodded, and together they headed into the bustling marketplace. All thoughts of pineapple immediately flew from Persi's mind as she tried to take in everything there was to see. She had only ever experienced markets through books, which meant she was not at all prepared for the noise that rushed her, or the crowds of people. Her arm pulled Manu's closer, using his steady presence as an anchor while her head swiveled this way and that like an owl trying to see everything in at once. The urge to wander off and explore was quickly taking over.

There was a moustached man selling rugs, bragging loudly that they were "hand-woven by royal dwarves"—whatever that meant. Then there was a small table with a bitter-looking little troll behind it, velvet boxes full of rows and rows of glistening silver rings sitting in front of them. Each ring was shouting, "Pick me! Pick me!" to the hustle of people.

Past a few more few stalls—mainly displaying gears and other machinery that didn't hold Persi's interest—there was a tattered and washed-out blue canopy that covered two tables laden with elegantly dyed silk scarves. The owner of the little stand was a woman with her face shrouded in a bright teal scarf, showing only a dark pair of kohl-lined eyes. The bright colors caught Persi's attention, and soon she was dragging the captain through the crowd toward the table to get a closer look. Manu merely chuckled and followed her as they went.

"I've never seen something so beautiful." Persi gasped, widening her eyes as she took in scarf after scarf, each more vivid and inventive than the last.

"Would the lovely lady like to try one on?" The owner's eyes crinkled at the edges, hinting at a smile beneath her veil, and she lifted a purple-and-mint-green-colored scarf from the pile. As the scarf billowed from her fingers, its colors seemed to shift and rework themselves like ripples in water right before Persinette's eyes.

"Gods!" Persi breathed. With little thought for her utter

lack of money, Persinette took the scarf. The fabric felt light and cool to the touch as she wrapped it loosely around her neck.

"It suits you very well," the woman said, holding up a mirror for Persi to see for herself. "The colors are beautiful with your hair, Miss."

As Persinette regarded herself in the mirror, she blushed a little. "My goodness," she said.

"How much?" Manu pulled a pouch from his pocket.

Persi's eyes flicked from her reflection to the captain. She frowned. "No, Captain...I couldn't. I can't even take it back with me. It'd be a waste."

But it was too late; he'd already handed the woman the coins she'd requested and put his money away once more. "Nonsense. I'll hang onto it for you. Then when you're out here, you can have it back. Promise." He gave her a playful wink.

"Oh...okay." Persi looked in the mirror again. The scarf was lovely, and there was no denying that it did suit her, but she couldn't help the guilt of allowing Manu to buy her something when she had no hope at all of repaying him.

"Now come along. I know my guy is here somewhere." Manu offered her his arm again to pull her away from the table and back out into the crowd. Persi waved to the woman behind the table as they headed off.

"Wait. You have a pineapple guy?" she asked suddenly.

Manu looked down at her with a devilish smile. "Of course I have a pineapple guy." He winked at her again, and she felt herself blush once more.

"How does one go about getting a pineapple guy?"

"See, now, that I can't tell you," he said.

"Why not?" Persi asked, completely missing the teasing note to his voice.

"Because I can't just tell you all my secrets, Miss Persi! Then you wouldn't think of me as amazing, mysterious, and roguish as you currently do." The smile broadened, revealing a handsome dimple in his cheek.

"Oh," was all she managed to get out past her embarrassment—because she definitely *did* think of him as amazing, mysterious and roguish in equal parts. A deep flush settled into her cheeks, and she ducked her head.

"Ah! Here he is!" Manu dragged her to the end of the market and a tiny stand with a tiny man behind it. The stand was barren of any signage or product on display; it was just the stand itself and the man—who, for his part, looked twitchy and unwashed. His pale eyes darted from one passing shopper to the next, and his feet were tapping as though he might take off at any moment.

When those eyes landed on Manu, however, they narrowed in recognition. "Whatsit yooooou want?" he asked in a scratchy, high-pitched voice, dragging out the word "you" in a way that Manu wasn't quite sure was intentional.

"Oh come, come, Otis, you know what I'm here for," Manu said. He leaned against the stand, which shuddered as if threatening to fall at any moment. Undeterred, the captain plastered a friendly smile on his face and met the man's narrowed eyes. "And I know you've got it. You're the only one around here who sells it."

An uneasy tension tightened across Persinette's shoulders. She shifted from foot to foot and cast her eyes around to see if anyone was watching them. Otis, as Manu had called him, looked at her, his pale eyes now narrowed in suspicion more than familiarity. "What's on with her? She MOTHER?"

Manu let out a loud laugh. "Persi? MOTHER? That innocent little sprite an agent? That's a good one, Otis.

Come on. You're paranoid." It was a lie—both Persi and Manu knew that—but it also wasn't entirely *not* the truth. Persi was with MOTHER, yes, and she was technically an agent. But she would not be arresting or shooting Otis for whatever illegal thing he was doing, and Manu knew that was all that mattered. "Now, show me the good stuff."

The dealer kept those pale eyes on Persi, bobbing his head to look her tip to toe, perhaps to check if she was carrying a weapon. But he must have been satisfied, because he whipped his head back to the crowd, loosening a greasy strand of blond hair from his low ponytail into his eyes, making him look more unhinged.

Manu whistled and waved his hand in front of Otis's face for attention. "Come on, man, she's with me. Just get us the damn pineapple."

Otis sniffed distastefully—a sniff that, to Persi, sounded a little wetter than it should have. She cringed. Otis dipped down behind the stand, presumably to rummage through a cabinet or basket or something, and when he came back up, he held a strange thing that Persi could only assume was a pineapple. It was roundishly oblong, golden in color, with dark green spiked leaves and prickles all over it. It looked like it might very well jab to death anyone who tried to eat it.

Persinette gaped. Her feet stepped her toward the strange thing, as though she instinctively needed a better look at it. The sudden movement seemed to spook Otis, who yanked the fruit out of reach and held it protectively to his chest. Though she couldn't be sure, Persi thought she heard a hiss come from him like a feral cat, which was enough to freeze her in place, awkwardly mid-step, hoping not to scare him further.

Manu didn't seem to notice. He was already digging

through his little purse for some coin to pay the man. "Same price as always?"

Otis's milky eyes remained fixed on the lavender-haired girl, gleaming with obvious distrust. "Double."

Manu looked up from the coins to glare at him. "Double? *Double*?! No way! That thing's half the size of the last one you got me! If anything, you should be giving me a discount!" The captain gave the fruit merchant a fierce scowl.

"I said double," Otis spat. "Or no sale."

With a deep sigh and a dramatic eye roll, the captain counted out double the amount of coins he'd intended to pay and slammed them onto the rickety table, which once again shuddered. "Fine. Double. But I won't forget this next time you want something shipped for you, Otis."

The little man shrugged and scooped up the coins, one of which he lifted it to his lips, where, to Persi's utter confusion, he bit it.

"Don't trust me, Otis?" Manu asked.

"No. Las' time you tried to pay me wif fairy gold," Otis said through his teeth.

"I didn't *know* that was fairy gold," Manu said—not unreasonably, he thought. "I told you that. Now, let's let bygones be bygones." He snatched up the pineapple before Otis could get it into his head to take it back and keep the coins besides. "You know, next time I'll go to Milo two towns over for it. She didn't give me this much grief." Pineapple secured under one arm, Manu offered Persi the other and dragged her away from Otis and his black-market fruit stand.

"Fine! You go to Milo!" Otis shook his little fist in the air. "That old wench will probably give you one full o' maggots! Idiot!" He kept up his screaming as they made their way away from the stand, although said screams quickly devolved into incoherent curses.

"Don't mind Otis; he's a suspicious little bugger," Manu said. "He's been raided too many times by MOTHER to trust anybody these days."

The notion struck Persi as odd, and she knit her brow. "Raided? Why would he be raided? I thought MOTHER just...Collected?"

Manu snorted. "No, they do far more than that." He frowned and shook his head. "But let's not talk about that anymore. We've got a pineapple to try, and I have a ship to show you around!" He vowed to himself that he would not bring up MOTHER for the rest of the evening. The subject was a dismal one, and it would only remind them both that in a few short hours she'd be going back there, whether either of them liked it or not.

The pair loaded onto the hovercraft and headed to the ship. Most of the crew, Manu knew, would be out and about putting the final touches on their plan, and the ones that were aboard were either in the rec room playing cards or in their quarters resting up for the mission—all of which meant Manu was free to take Persi anywhere and everywhere aboard the *Duchess* without being disturbed.

As the airship came into view, Persinette's eyes widened and her mouth dropped open. She had never seen an airship in real life before; it was breathtaking. "Is this your ship?" she asked, her voice barely above a whisper.

If Manu hadn't been paying attention, he wouldn't have heard her at all, but as it was a slow smile spread his lips. He snuck a glance at Persi as her green eyes passed over the *Duchess's* worn wood and the metallic balloon that held her aloft. "Yup, this is her," he said, with no small amount of pride.

Persi just nodded and followed him to the loading platform. As it slowly dragged them up into the ship, she looked around, still amazed. "What's her name?" she asked, a dazed smile still on her lips. Ships had names—she knew that much—so she was curious what a ship like this had been named. Although, honestly, when *wasn't* she curious? It seemed that she would be curious about everything for the rest of her life given how little of the world she had seen while she was with MOTHER.

"The *Defiant Duchess*," Manu said proudly. Persi's excitement seemed to spark the same feeling inside him, and he felt unable to contain his own happiness. "Do you like her?"

"She's stunning, Manu! Give me a tour? I want to see all of it!" Persi turned her bright eyes to him, happiness and curiosity sparkling in them as she smiled widely. "Please?"

"Of course!" Once the platform stopped, he grabbed her free hand and pulled her up the steps out of the cargo hold. "We'll just drop our pineapple off in the galley first, and then we'll swing back to eat it after the tour."

Persi followed eagerly. With her hand in his, he showed her the flight deck, his quarters, the small library, the rec room, and everything in between. She drank it all in like a sponge, her eyes wide in amazement. She was doing her best to remember every detail so that when she was back at MOTHER, she'd have something to hold onto.

By the time they made it back to their pineapple in the galley, Persinette had fallen in love with the *Duchess*. She wanted nothing more than to never go back to MOTHER and live aboard the ship as one of its crew. "Do you go on many adventures?" she asked as she settled onto one of the stools at the counter.

"Oh, all the time! It's constant with the adventuring,"

Manu said, stretching the truth just a little as he made skillful, quick work of the pineapple.

Persi sighed wistfully and propped her chin on her fist to watch him. "I wish I could live a life like that. There's so much of the world I've only ever seen in pictures in books. And even more of it I've never seen at all."

The captain regarded her, his brows furrowing a little. He'd never heard anyone talk about seeing the world like that before, as something unreachable and outside four walls. Everyone he knew had the freedom to come and go as they pleased, and he wondered what it must be like to see the world through Persi's eyes—where everything was new and exciting, and the problems of the world hadn't jaded you yet.

"What? Do have I something on my face?" Persi rubbed self-consciously at her cheek.

Manu cleared his throat and shook his head. "No, you don't have anything on your face." He focused intently on cutting the pineapple in wedges. "I was just thinking—someday you'll get to see all of it."

She just shrugged. Better to not say anything at all than to argue with him. She knew he was wrong. She knew that there was a considerable chance that this little taste of freedom might be all she'd ever get. In all likelihood, she'd probably die before she was free of MOTHER's control—that was the simple truth of her circumstances. Still, it was a nice thought that maybe one day she might—a sweet dream to have and keep her from completely losing hope.

"I'll make sure of it."

She blinked at him for a moment, then nodded hesitantly.

He nodded back. "I'd like to see it all like you do."

"Like I do?" she asked, her cheeks flushing brightly. "What do you mean?"

Manu shrugged. "Just...you seem to see everything with this excited, optimistic, curiosity. Like everything in life has the potential to be a daring adventure."

"Well, doesn't it?" She giggled.

Manu stared at her, then smiled. "Yeah, I guess it kind of does." He watched her a moment longer before he shook himself and turned back to the pineapple at hand. "Ready for some pineapple?"

"Yes!" She giggled again. Maybe, for Manu, pineapple was the most exciting of adventures. He took her wrist and put a wedge in between her fingers, then pulled back to wait with his lip between his teeth for her to take a small bite.

Persi studied the bright yellow slice, the juice making her fingers sticky. Lifting it to her lips, she took a careful nibble and wrinkled her nose in thought. The fruit was crisp, tart yet sweet, and she chewed it slowly, trying to think of something she could compare it with...but nothing came to mind. Pineapple was wholly unlike anything else she'd ever tasted before. She'd had jams, jellies, and preserves made from more common berries, apples, and pears, of course—she'd even had a banana once!—but nothing like this. The more tropical fruits like oranges, grapefruits, and pineapples were so hard to get that they were reserved solely for those MOTHER deemed worthy. She was not worthy. After chewing as long as she could make the bite last, she swallowed and took a second one.

"Well?" Manu asked. He was eager to know how she felt about his favorite fruit, even though he wasn't sure why it mattered so much whether or not this girl liked pineapple.

"Ifth's really goob!" Persi said around a mouthful. She

offered Manu a closed-lipped smile that grew when he let out an excited laugh.

"It *is* good!" He took a wedge for himself, which he quickly demolished.

THE REST of their evening was spent finishing off the pineapple and chatting. Manu found it easy to talk to Persinette about pretty much everything, although much of their talk that evening was about nothing in particular.

"I can't believe you've never had fresh apple pie before," Manu said, aghast, as the hovercraft made its trek back to the apartments through the now-sleeping city. Buildings loomed dark and tall over them.

Persinette shrugged. "I don't even know if they can even *make* apple pie at headquarters."

"What about pineapple upside-down cake?"

"Manu." Persi laughed a tired laugh. At some point exhaustion had crept in, but she found it was a good tired, a happy tired. "If I've never had pineapple..."

"Oh, right, right." Manu set the hover to rise to the window of the apartment. Benard was there, still sitting in the chair, cloaked in his Persinette glamour. A look of irritation was etched on his borrowed Persi-features, and when he saw the two of them, he let the glamour fall away so he could glare at them with his own face.

There was some clatter out in the hallway, and they heard the guard hurry off. Benard stood to open the window, grumbling. "Took you long en—"

His words were cut off by the tiny girl launching herself at him. Persi wrapped her arms tightly around Benard and gave him what Manu figured was the biggest hug the cantankerous goblin had ever had in his long life. Benard threw Manu a pleading look, but the captain did nothing to save him, and Benard let out a soft *oof* as the girl hugged him tighter. He patted her back awkwardly.

"Thank you! Thank you! Thank you! A thousand times, thank you!" Persi exclaimed over and over, hugging the goblin around the middle one last time before pulling back and pressing a quick kiss to his cheek. "You are such a sweet man, and I am so very grateful you're my friend."

Manu wondered if Benard would argue with her about whether or not they were friends, but he was pleasantly surprised when Benard simply nodded. "You're welcome, Miss Persi. Now, if you'll excuse me, I have to be going." He slipped past her, waved goodbye, and climbed out onto the balcony, giving the pair a moment alone.

Persinette turned to the captain, looking up at him with a smile so wide it ached. She wasn't sure why, but now she suddenly felt so shy. "And thank you too, Captain. I had a lovely evening." Her words were soft, so much so that if the room weren't wholly silent, he wouldn't have heard her at all.

"That's really not necessary, but you're most welcome Miss Persi." He dipped his head, removed his hat, and gave her an exaggerated bow, like something a musketeer or pirate might give to a beautiful noblewoman.

Persinette snickered, her heart thudding in her chest, and, as Manu bowed, she clenched her hands to calm whatever nerves might be lingering. Then, when he had straightened up once more, she took a quick step to him, tipped onto her toes, and gently pressed her lips to his. The kiss lasted no more than a second or two, but she could feel the tingle of his lips against hers even after she pulled back. Her fingers lifted to brush her mouth, her face flaming. "Good night, Captain."

"G-Good night, Miss Persinette," Manu stuttered. He stumbled back toward the window. With some difficulty, he climbed out onto the hovercraft, this time nearly falling to his death in his utter distraction.

Benard snickered and set a course for the ship. As they sped off, Manu pulled out the mint-and-purple scarf from where he'd tucked it away and smiled.

21

PERSINETTE

THE CAPTAIN and his first mate flew off to the outskirts of Pascal, leaving Persinette by herself with no one but the two MOTHER agents outside her door for companionship. Disappointment twinged in her chest at the realization that she wasn't going with the captain and his first mate, that she might never get to. She wanted nothing more than to soar off the night with them and never come back to MOTHER. To leave her responsibilities as a Seer behind. To live and adventure in the real world, surrounded by real people and things. It had been so hard to hand over the beautiful scarf Manu had bought. It would have been a pleasant reminder of their adventure. But if she were caught with it...well, it wouldn't end pleasantly for her, that much she knew.

She cast her gaze to the threadbare cot in the corner and released a heavy sigh. Persi knew she should curl up and try to get some sleep. The following day's mission would be long, arduous, and full of potential pitfalls, but she just couldn't bring herself to lie down. There was just so much to think about, so much to *fret* about. Her chief worry was that Manu and his crew could be found out. MOTHER could realize that they the "visions" she'd had were fake, that the crew members were acting as decoys and thus needed to be captured or killed.

Something about the risk Manu's men were taking didn't sit quite right with her. All of them were putting their lives on the line just so that MOTHER wouldn't find her out. Her stomach gave a sick twist as she thought about what might become of people like Janette, Benard, and the others she'd seen in the rec room just enjoying their evening. She swallowed to keep the pineapple down.

"There isn't anything you can do about it, Persi," she told herself. The crew believed in the cause just as she did. This is how they wanted it.

And if that worry wasn't enough to keep her awake, there was still the tingle of her lips. She smiled a little to herself as pale, freckled fingers tapped her lower lip.

"Well," she muttered. She hadn't thought she'd be the one to kiss someone first. It hadn't been much of a kiss—not that she had anything to compare it to—but it had been her first, and *she'd* been the one to initiate it! Plus, there had been something sweet about the light blush that settled into the captain's cheeks, and how he stumbled, flabbergasted, through the window. She giggled just thinking about it.

She wished—very badly, she realized—that she could tell Wyn. But that wasn't a possibility. It just wasn't. Persi heaved another heavy sigh, her shoulders drooping. To share this with Wyn would be a death sentence for both of them.

Persi shook her head, her long lavender hair falling into her eyes as she forced her mind away from such sad thoughts and dropped onto the dingy cot. Instead, she let her mind play the events of the evening over and over again. She clung to the few hours of freedom she'd had like a lifeline, hoping to burn them into her memory forever. Maybe then she'd have something to sustain her when she returned to MOTHER.

When the sun finally rose through the lingering steam that shrouded Pascal, Persi allowed herself a moment to enjoy the beauty of the city around her. The thin layer of moisture hanging over the mismatched buildings seemed to glow when the sun shone. The buildings closest to her window were of the traditional Daiwynnian style—crisp columns and grungy lintels that gave the buildings a dirty, hulking appearance—but on the outskirts of Pascal, the buildings were so tall they seemed to scrape the sky above them. The sunlight reflected off their innumerable windows as if the walls were covered in mirrors. In the distance, dirigibles and other steam-powered ships drifted to and from the docks—sailors making their early morning runs. The sight alone drew a soft gasp from her lips.

She wondered idly if every city in Daiwynn was this lovely in the morning. "I'm going to see them all one day," Persi said, wishing she knew how to make the statement come true.

"What was that?"

The sound of Gothel's voice made Persinette whip around. The older woman was standing in the door, arms crossed. "Good lord, child, you look absolutely haggard. Did you sleep at all last night?" Gothel's nose wrinkled in disgust as she surveyed her charge.

Persi shrugged. It didn't really matter what she looked like. Nor did it matter what Gothel thought about her appearance. She'd had her first taste of freedom and her first kiss the night before. Nothing could bring her down. "Is it time for breakfast?" she asked. Her stomach gave an irritable grumble.

"No," Gothel said briskly, glaring accusingly at Persi's growling stomach. "We won't be eating breakfast this morning. We are going straight to the Collection site. Now get up and make yourself at least marginally presentable. We leave in five minutes."

"Yes, Gothel," Persinette said, bowing her head. There was no point at all in arguing that she needed breakfast or complaining that she was hungry. Neither would get her fed any sooner.

Gothel made for the door, but stopped. "Have you had any other visions?" The words sounded almost casual, like they may have been an afterthought, but Persi knew better than that.

Persi felt her stomach drop. Manu had provided her with two other addresses for this very situation, but that didn't make faking a vision any easier. She knew this was the purpose of her being brought out into the field. She knew this was what she needed to do to help the Uprising. Still, it was hard to acknowledge that, despite her best intentions, she possibly be sending MOTHER after someone.

Persi calming inhale and closed her eyes.

"Well?" Gothel asked, annoyed. "Out with it! We don't have all day!"

"If you have a bit of paper, I had a vision of an elf and a troll," Persinette said, keeping her voice low even as her stomach twisted violently. She wondered if any of the crew members she'd met the night before would be acting as bait. All she could hope was that they were ready for what was coming their way.

Gothel procured a bit of paper and a pen from somewhere in the small apartment and held them out to Persi, who dutifully jotted down the two addresses Manu had made her memorize. She held the paper out to Gothel, silently praying to the gods that this would be enough. Maybe now MOTHER wouldn't surveil her so closely and she could focus on learning spells instead of watching her back.

Gothel snatched the bit of paper up quickly, her dark eyes flicking over the words. "Right. Get up. Get Ready. Now."

"Five minutes, I heard you," Persi said, sighing with exhaustion as she rose from the chair and stretched.

"No attitude," Gothel barked. The door slammed behind her.

Persi sat motionless for a moment and then shook her head. She pulled on her boots, straightened her skirts, and deftly tied her hair back in a braid, ready to head out in just a few moments. When she reached the door, she could hear Gothel was busy relaying the information to the other agents, so she allowed herself one more long look out the window. She would miss this view when she was back in headquarters. Manu had promised this wasn't forever. He had promised that she'd get to see the world. If she wanted to stay sane, she had to hope that he was right.

She shook herself and faced the agents. "I'm ready," she announced to draw their attention. They all glared at her, and Persi felt the color wash from her cheeks. It was evident they didn't give one whit if she were ready or not, but she held her head high nonetheless.

The three agents barely looked her up and down before completely disregarding her and returning to their conversation.

"Change of plans," Gothel said. "You won't be coming with us this time."

Persi frowned. "What? Why not?" The words left her

unbidden, and even she was surprised by them. Why would she *want* to go out into danger?

Gothel stared—perhaps wondering the same thing—before narrowing her eyes on Persi. "You're too much of a risk. You'll stay here with these agents on guard, and we'll come back for you when we're through the Collection."

Persi wrinkled her brow, and stood up straighter. "I want to go. I promise I won't get in the way this time. And I won't run away." Her tone was level and serious. She didn't know that she could help any of the crew if they happened to get into trouble, but it had to be better to have someone there watching their backs than not.

Right?

"Please, just give me another chance."

Those dark, beady eyes flicked over Persinette as if calculating exactly how much trouble she'd be. After a moment of thinking, Gothel's lips curled into a sneer. Persi held her breath, afraid that one twitch of her face might cause the MOTHER agent to change her mind. At last, Gothel shrugged.

"Fine. It's your neck on the line."

And that was that.

PERSINETTE JOINED the formation of MOTHER agents and the group headed out to the first Collection location. All the way there, Persi stayed tucked deep within the ranks—protected on all sides by agents—just as she'd been instructed to do. Her gaze darted every which way as they navigated the back alleys of Pascal to the apartment complex. Her hands tightened into fists at her sides, longing to use some magic to protect herself if need be, but she refused to reach for it.

When the envoy reached the location—the address Manu had given her and she'd in turn fed to Gothel—there was no fight. Manu's man had made sure she was seen, but not much more than that. The woman for her part acted every bit as surprised as anyone would be with MOTHER breaking down the door to ground floor door, but she quickly disappeared before the agents could get within spitting distance of her, as of those magical bloodlines were wont to do. Persi hid her relief as the agents grumbled and groused.

"It didn't even give us a chance to shoot at it," one of them muttered. He kicked the legs from under a side table, sending the lamp atop it to shatter on the floor.

"We don't have to...ruin her things, do we?" Persi asked softly. All this earned her was a glare from the agents, and so she fell silent once more. Still, it seemed at least this time the plan had gone her way. No one had gotten hurt, and the Enchanted who had been living in the apartment before could return without fear of MOTHER for a little while.

"Let's go to the next one. Werewolf. Should be fun," another of the agents offered with a dark gleam in her eye. The rest all nodded, and the whole formation did an about-face to head to the next address.

Persinette shifted nervously and prayed that there was an easy out for the werewolf in question—a window, a back door, *anything*. But as they approached the next building, that hope was swiftly dashed. The facade was covered in windows too narrow for a human man to escape through, let alone a full-grown werewolf. "Maybe he'll just run," she whispered.

"What was that, 11-24-10?" the agent nearest her asked.

"Nothing." Persi shook her head and averted her eyes. Her heart beat wildly in her chest as they made their way to the fifth floor, the stairs creaking beneath them. Once in front of the door, an agent procured a small hammer from a satchel, and Persi watched in mute wonder as the woman leveled the tool with the door, tapped it once, and sent the door flying inwards, clean off its hinges, with a mighty bang. The dust hadn't even settled by the time a snarling wolf lunged for the agent holding the hammer, snapping its massive jaws. The woman growled back and used the hammer's magic to throw the wolf across the room.

The wolf hit the wall with a hard thud and fell to the floor. But he only lay there for a moment before he was up again. *Run. Run,* Persi tried to beg him with her thoughts. *Just get away while you can.*

He didn't. Instead, he snapped his jaws and snarled at the approaching agents, all of whom had drawn a weapon as they circled the growling wolf. When one of the agents got a little too close, the wolf bit viciously at them, unaware of Gothel right behind him. Light flashed off the sharp blade as Gothel raised it above her head, ready to bury it in the wolf's back.

Persi didn't stop to think about what she was doing; she just reacted. She reached for the magic within her and it reached back. The spell flew to her lips and sparkling purple light lifted a small ottoman from a few paces away, scraping across the floor until it was right in Gothel's path, perfectly positioned to trip her. Which it did. The agent went down to the floorboards with a loud curse, the knife flying from her hands and clattering to the floor. The shouting drew the attention of the wolf, who spun and launched himself at Gothel.

Gothel screamed. The next thing Persi knew, the agents were pushing her back, charging the wolf in an attempt to get him off Gothel. But they were too late. The scream died with a gurgle.

Persi's stomach lurched. The room spun around her. The whole world seemed to tilt as everything grew louder— so much louder—and the room went white with light.

Then—nothing. Inky blackness.

It all came back into focus in fragments. First, the sensation of movement, of being carried. Then, the smell of that recycled air that meant they were back in headquarters. Finally, the barely cushioned support of a bed beneath her. When she blinked her eyes open, one of the infirmary nurses was standing above her.

""She's awake," the woman announced.

"Good. She can go to her room, then," growled someone out of Persi's line of vision. "Get up, 11-24-10."

As Persinette sat up, she saw that it was Agnes who was standing against the wall, his eyes narrowed in annoyance. "A-Agnes? What happened?"

"Doesn't matter. You'll be debriefed later. Go to the Tower and get some rest."

"But—"

"What did I just say to you, 11-24-10? I am your superior and I gave you an order!" Agnes's dark brows were tense with irritation. "Now move it!"

With a raspy gulp, Persi nodded and slid to her feet with a little wobble. She began a slow trek back to the Tower, mind still elsewhere. Once she was back in her quarters, and her boots discarded under her bed, Persi fell onto the hard mattress. She stared up at the ceiling for a long while, the light that streamed in through the window slowly fading.

The soft chimes of the compact under her pillow finally pulled her from her stupor. Not bothering to sit up, Persi pulled it out and popped open the lid.

"Oh, thank the gods!" Manu exclaimed when his eyes met hers. He held a hand to his heart as if to slow it. "I was terrified something had happened to you! Henry got back, and he said the mission didn't go well, and then I didn't hear from you. And all I could think was the worst. That they'd found you out. Or that you'd gotten caught in the crossfire." He was rambling, as all of his words jumbled over one another in their attempt to explain. Persinette only half-listened; she found she didn't have the energy to keep up. It took him a moment to realize she wasn't following, but when he did, he frowned. "I'm sorry, Persi. Are you all right?"

She stared at him, trying to process the question. *Was she all right?* She supposed so. She wasn't injured; they must have gotten her out of the line of fire after she'd fainted. So, as far as that went, then yes, she was all right. But then there was the matter of Gothel, and what Persi was sure had happened to her. Over her sixteen years with MOTHER, Persinette had sent many to their deaths—that she knew. But she had never directly caused someone's death before. And never before had it been someone she'd known as she'd known Gothel. Granted, Gothel was a ruthless, cruel, human being who had slain countless Enchanted. But did that mean she too deserved to die? Especially so horribly?

"Persi?" Manu asked, drawing her attention back to him. "Are you all right?"

It took her a moment to realize that she hadn't answered

him. She frowned. "I think I killed someone today." The words were quiet when they drifted from her, uncertain. Perhaps a part of her hoped that if she didn't say them too loudly, they would cease to be true. She shook her head—no, that wasn't possible. Gothel was dead—she had caused it. She was a murderer.

Manu stared at her in silence. "No," he said finally. "You didn't kill anyone, Persi."

"Well she's dead, isn't she?" Persi half-shouted the question and swiftly sat up. She felt surprisingly angry that he'd suggest that she wasn't, in fact, a murderer.

"Well, yes. She is." Manu spoke slowly, as if he were afraid of spooking her. "But you didn't kill her."

"I did! I tripped her! That stupid ottoman! That stupid spell..." Persi's words trailed off. She rubbed her eyes, which were now burning with tears. She had so much blood on her hands, she knew, from her many years with MOTHER, but she'd never thought of herself as a murderer before. She gulped loudly, trying to suck back the tears that threatened to turn her into a blubbering mess.

Manu sighed. His hand twitched where it rested on the armrest as if, perhaps, he longed to reach out to her. "Persinette, you did what you had to. If you hadn't acted, the agents would have killed Henry. You saved his life."

"You weren't there! How do you know?" Persi said savagely. Finally, tears trickled down her cheeks.

Manu's brows furrowed and he shook his head. "No, I wasn't there. But Henry gave a full report, and although he didn't know you interfered, he did say that had that agent not fallen she would have killed him. As far as I know, he didn't deal the fatal blow. She was caught in the crossfire due to her injuries, so one of the other agents probably pulled the trigger."

"That doesn't make it better, Manu!" Persi felt her face growing red with anger.

The young captain blinked at her in surprise. Persinette never thought she'd be capable of yelling at someone like that, yet she just had, and Manu looked as though he, too, never thought she'd yell, let alone at him in particular. Still, he remained calm. Licking his lips, he nodded. "No, it doesn't make it better. Nothing I say will make it better, I know that. And I'm sorry you had to choose between two people's lives today. You shouldn't have had to do that; it's not fair that we asked that of you. But Persi, you did save Henry's life, and he's very grateful for what you did. So hopefully that makes it a little worth it." His words were even, steady, and they calmed her a little. "Were you two friends? Do you want to talk about her?"

Persi inhaled through her mouth, and out through her nose, to steady herself and shook her head. "No, we weren't friends." She spoke more measuredly now as she remembered Gothel. "Gothel was my handler. She'd been my handler since I first came to headquarters. But there was... there was no love between us." Those words stung a little. Sixteen years and Gothel had never so much as shook Persi's hand. They weren't friends. They weren't family. They weren't...anything. So then why did it hurt so badly now that she was gone? "She didn't even like me." Persi snorted. "I was just an Asset to her, a means to an end. And with the information I gave her—" She let out a shaky breath. "I think our count was over a hundred last time I checked. We sent over a hundred people to the camps. But still, she didn't deserve to die that way."

Manu nodded, listening silently. "I'm sure she didn't Persi, few people do. I wish there were a more peaceful way to solve all of this. But there doesn't seem to be, and a lot more people are going to die before it's over."

Persinette scrubbed at her eyes again to get rid of the rest of the tears and nodded. "I think I'm just going to go to sleep. I'll talk to you tomorrow," she murmured. Now that the anger had passed, she felt drained. She knew she wouldn't sleep, but she didn't really want to talk anymore either.

"Of course. Get some rest," Manu said but didn't close the connection. Instead, he waited for Persi to shut her compact and end it herself.

She stuffed the mirror back under her pillow, rolled away from the mirror, and stared off into the darkness, praying for sleep to come. Or, at the very least, for her thoughts to stop

22

CAPTAIN MANU KELII

MANU STARED at the glass dejectedly as Persinette's face disappeared. He lifted his hand to run through his hair, his shoulders sagging. All he wanted was to make Persi feel better, to promise her that she'd never be forced to do something like that again, but he couldn't. So long as MOTHER and the Uprising waged war, the people caught in the middle would have to make tough decisions.

"It's not going to get any easier for her," Benard murmured as he watched his captain. He lifted a hand, paused, then patted Manu's shoulder.

"I know that," Manu said after a few minutes of just staring at his reflection. He had known that going into this. He had known that in taking this on Persinette would have to surround herself with death and danger. Yet, somehow, he thought that wouldn't be an issue for him. It wasn't his neck on the line. He wasn't having to make those choices or, killing people he'd known all of his life. So why should it matter? "I'm such an idiot." He pinched the bridge of his nose. He'd been so excited to get an Asset all his own, to start really doing something with his Uprising status, that he hadn't thought for one moment at the relationship he'd develop with the Asset. He hadn't even considered that this could break that poor sweet girl, and even himself, in the process.

"Do you still think she can do this?" Benard asked.

Manu raised a brow at his first mate. "Don't you?"

Benard inhaled a deep, long-suffering breath. "I had decided to reserve judgment until after a few missions." The captain cut him an annoyed look, but Benard continued. "I believe Miss Persi is much stronger than people give her credit for, but I don't know if she'll realize it in time."

Manu nodded thoughtfully. "There was never a doubt in my mind that she could do it," he said. "She's strong, and good, and kind, and she wants to do the right thing." He spoke his words with all the conviction of a man who truly believed in another. He focused on everything that made Persinette completely capable and did his best to ignore the genuine possibility that this was too much for her.

"Then you're going to have to help her work through the bloodshed part. War is messy," the old goblin reminded him. "And you can't fake it till you make it like you usually do, Manu. You need to take this seriously." His tone was stern, but not unkind.

"I know that," Manu said rather petulantly. He had known all along the cost of this war, but then, he'd also never considered that it might cost him anything more than it already had. He'd lost his family, his home, and what little history still lingered in his family's stories. What was even left? He deflated into his overstuffed chair. "Any suggestions as to how to help her?"

Benard's wiry form sank into another chair across from him. He exhaled hard. "Just...try to take her mind off of it as much as you can. Give her something to look forward to, something that'll make her happy. It won't be easy. Sometimes all there will be to talk about is this damn job and the blood that's on her hands because of it. But you've always been good at getting people to talk, so do that."

It sounded so easy when Benard laid it all out that way —all Manu had to do was talk to her. But he knew there was no way it could be that simple. "There has to be more to it."

"There isn't. Don't you remember when you first came to us? That's all I did then, I talked. I talked you through the loss of your family. I talked you through joining the Uprising. Just *talk*," Benard insisted.

Manu wrinkled his brow as he thought back to that time, all that had happened when he'd first come to the *Duchess*. It hadn't been easy. His losses had all but dragged him into an inescapable hole. But when it all seemed ready to swallow him whole, there was Benard, always talking. It helped to ease the weight and the sadness. It hadn't been easy to adjust to a whole new home, a whole new family, a whole new life, but Benard had helped. And he'd become the family Manu needed. He and Owen both.

"You do that for her," Benard said, interrupting Manu's thoughts. "And she'll be okay."

Manu nodded, inhaled deeply, and leaned back in his chair to think.

What the hell could he talk about to keep Persi's mind off her handler's death?

AS THEY HAD YET to receive a new heading from Eddi, the *Defiant Duchess* was on her way to the nearest city for a supply run. Manu hoped that he would be able to drop Ivy and her Unit off there. If nothing else, losing them would at least make him feel less spied on.

For perhaps the twentieth time in three days, Manu pulled the compact from his pocket and to contact Persinette. It had been too long since they had talked, and he hated to think that she was still dealing with that trauma by herself.

"Don't," Benard warned as he walked through the rec hall.

Manu pouted a little. "You told me to talk to her."

"Not here," the first mate reminded him. He tilted his head toward where one of Ivy's unit was sitting in a corner reading. "You're not supposed to be just *chatting* with her. Business only."

Manu huffed and tucked mirror back into his pocket. Nevertheless, he waited until he was back in his own quarters, away from prying eyes, before he murmured, "Persinette," to the mirror.

It took a few long minutes before Persi answered. She was lying in her bed again, her usually bright green eyes unfocused and fuzzy. His shoulders relaxed in relief. "Talk to me," he begged.

"I really don't want to, Manu." Persi rubbed a hand over her mouth. Her eyes were red and puffy from crying, and her voice came out a little strangled. "I'm tired."

Manu frowned a little, but nodded. "I'll do the talking, then. Will you listen?"

She nodded back.

And so he just started talking about the first thing that came to mind. "My family once lived on the islands in the South Pacific, a long time ago. Before the war of the realms ripped the world apart and reshaped it. They were well liked, and for centuries, they were chiefs of the tribes that lived there.

"When the war came, my family had to pack up what little we could carry and run. I don't remember it—that was before I was born—but my mother told us the story. What I do remember is living on the streets my entire life and never staying in one place.

"We always had to stick to the shadows and hide what we were, so we couldn't do anything legitimate to make money. So we picked pockets, stole, and took whatever odd jobs we could find in an attempt to survive. I remember my grandmother used to talk about what a travesty it was that we were reduced to hiding. We always had to stay one step ahead of MOTHER and their registration." He spoke quietly and calmly, hoping his family's story would help her understand that what she was doing was the only option. For many like them, resistance was the only way out.

Persi listened as she'd promised, her expression gradually turning to confusion. He could see the questions forming one after another on her tongue, so he paused to give her time to ask. "So what are you?" she said.

Curiosity was good, Manu told himself. He could work with curiosity. It was something, at least—far better than apathy. "Where I come from, we're called Cindaku."

Persinette sat up a little more, her eyes wide now. "What's that?"

"That's my little secret." He winked playfully and tapped the side of his nose. "Anyway, we're very rare, and Tutu always said that if MOTHER ever found us, they'd turn us into weapons. So we hid. Hiding made everything harder, and my mom was in charge of our education, so we weren't as well educated as some. But it was nice being together as a family."

"What's a Tutu?"

"That's what we called Grandmother. She hated that we had to hide. I remember her telling me over dinner all about how we were once a *proud and noble race*." He mimicked his grandmother's voice, high and scratchy, which made Persi wrinkle her nose. Not the response he was hoping for, but it was something! He'd take it!

"So that's where my family came from," he concluded.

"You poor thing," Persi murmured. "Do you have any siblings?

The question caught Manu off guard, and he swallowed as sadness began to claw at his throat. "I uh—I had a little sister named Amara." His eyes burned. It had been so long since he'd really talked about Amara. It had been even longer since he'd seen Amara; he'd almost forgotten what she looked like.

"You don't have any family on the ship?" Persi asked with a sniffle. "Oh Manu, I'm so sorry."

The captain pressed his lips together. "No, it's fine."

"What happened to them?" The question spilled out of her, and her hand immediately flew to her mouth. "I'm sorry, you don't have to answer that. That was insensitive."

"No, it's okay. I don't know what happened to my family. I ran as far and as fast as I could until I was out of reach and didn't look back. I never saw them again." He cleared his throat to dislodge the sadness that seemed to have gotten stuck there.

Persinette stared at him, her eyes heavy and tired. "That's terrible."

Manu nodded. "It is. But that's why I'm doing this. I want to make sure no one else has to suffer through that."

Persi nodded. A giant yawn left her, and she moved too late to stifle it. "Oh, excuse me," she said, embarrassed.

Manu smiled a little. "No, it's all right. It's getting late. Maybe you should get some sleep?"

"No."

"Why not?"

"Can't. Nightmares."

"Oh," Manu said. "Here, let's try this then." Manu began to sing in a clear, smooth voice. The lullaby was the one his mother had sung to him when he was a child, and in a few short minutes, her head sank deeper into her pillow and it lulled her to sleep. He smiled again, watching her breathing deepen, finally peaceful. "Good night, my little hala kahiki," he murmured before closing the connection. Stretching his arms over his head, he got up from his seat.

"That was nice, sir," Benard said from where he was standing just inside the door—just arrived from his nightly chores.

Manu shrugged. "She needs sleep."

"She does," Benard agreed. "And so do you."

"Yes, I do. It has been a long couple of days," Manu said. The worry over how Persinette was faring, and whether he could actually do anything to help her, had worn on him, leaving him exhausted.

"You have a call scheduled with Eddi in the morning to talk about Ivy and her Unit."

"Oh, thank the gods. Hopefully, Eddi will decide we don't need them anymore and we can just drop that witch off at the nearest town." Manu headed to his extensive closet to dress for bed.

"Yes, we can hope, sir." Benard stayed where he was and raised his voice so that Manu could hear him. "Well, good night, sir."

"Good night, Benard."

The first mate disappeared into the corridor once more,

leaving Manu alone to his thoughts. The captain slunk to his bedroom, dropped heavily onto the bed, and, for the first time in days, fell asleep instantly.

AS THE SUN rose over the horizon, the captain pulled himself from his bed and readied for the day. When he made it into the flight deck with his plate of toast and pineapple jam, Eddi was waiting on the old projection screen.

"Good morning, Eddi." Manu nodded politely.

The Uprising Leader opened and shut their magnified dark eyes a few times. "Good morning, Captain," Eddi responded at last. "This is...a change of pace."

Manu raised a brow as he took a bite of his toast. "What is?" he asked through a mouthful.

Eddi blinked again before shaking their head. "Never mind. What is it you wanted to talk to me about? I heard the mission did not go quite according to plan."

"No, it did not." Manu set aside his toast and turned his full attention to the Uprising Leader. "I'm worried about Persinette. Her handler died during the attack and she's dealing with quite a bit of guilt. Plus, as a result, we don't know who her new handler will be, or what they'll be like." He had decided to broach all of the topics with Eddi in one chat. Hopefully, he could get as many answers and solutions as possible.

"I don't think we have anything to worry about her new handler, and her guilt will fade over time." Eddi shrugged their narrow shoulders as though they didn't care one whit what Persinette might be struggling with. In all likelihood, the Uprising Leader *didn't* care. What was one Enchanted

Asset when there was a whole monarchy to topple? "Something else is bothering you," they went on.

Manu tensed his face, but he nodded. "I'd like to submit a formal request for a grimoire."

There was a long silence as Eddi considered his request. "What for?"

"I want to be able to feed Persinette spells so that she can protect herself, should the need arise. She's already shown proficiency in learning to use magic on her own. All she would need is a few—"

"No."

Manu stilled, trying to understand for perhaps a few moments too long. "No?" he repeated at last.

"Request denied. I will not provide you with a grimoire or any pieces of one so that you can feed spells to the Asset." Eddi's stern tone left no room for argument.

Not that it would stop Manu from arguing. "Well, why the hell not? You just expect her to live among people who hate her, go on missions with them, and not have any sort of escape plan? You can't just leave her in there defenseless! She'll die!"

"Don't be so dramatic, Manu. She's hardly defenseless. According to our intel, MOTHER is training her in hand-to-hand combat as well as several classes of weaponry. This Persinette girl doesn't need magic to take care of herself, and even if she did, she doesn't need you feeding her spells to learn if, as you've said, she's already shown proficiency in the craft."

To Eddi, Persinette was just another Asset, that was it. His breakfaster turned to lead in his gut. To them, she was not a person, a friend, or even someone that Eddi cared about—she was a means to an end. Disposable. How did that make Eddi any better than Persi's Gothel?

It didn't.

"Now if that will be all, I have much to do," Eddi said.

"No, that is not all," Manu said quickly. "I want to know when I'll be able to get your unit off my ship. It was my understanding that they would only be aboard for the first couple of missions with Persinette, and those are over. I think myself and my crew can handle it from here on out."

"My unit will remain on your ship indefinitely."

"Indefinitely?"

"Until I can be sure that you aren't going to screw this up, Manu." At that, Manu growled softly and opened his mouth to argue, but Eddi swiftly cut him off once more. "Now, you are to stay out of trouble until I can provide you a new heading. That will be all, Captain."

The projection went fuzzy as Eddi closed the link between them. Manu growled again and threw his breakfast at the projection screen, splattering pineapple jam everywhere and shattering the plate into half a dozen pieces.

"Something wrong, Cap'n?" Benard asked, taking a tentative step onto the flight deck. His glowing eyes flicked from the ruined roast and shards of the former plate to his captain. "Did your meeting not go well?"

"Eddi refuses to give me access to any magic so that I can help Persinette! I can't protect her. I can't provide the tools she could use to protect herself. What good am I to her?" Manu shouted and threw his arms wildly in the air.

Benard eyed his captain and sighed. "Honestly, I'm not surprised."

"Not surprised! You're not surprised!" Manu seethed and cast his eyes frantically about for something else to throw, but found nothing.

"No, I'm not surprised. It would draw a lot of attention to Persinette if she suddenly knew a whole bunch of magic she didn't know before. It'd put her in more danger than ever." Benard was trying to be reasonable, but Manu had no desire to be reasonable. None at all. He wanted to throw a tantrum. "Please sir, don't pitch a fit," Benard added, as if reading Manu's mind.

"A fit? A fit? *Don't pitch a fit?* I am not some spoiled child! And you know what, Benard, I damn well *will* pitch a fit if I want to!" The captain rose from his chair to his full height and glared down at his first mate before storming off to the ship's small library.

And there he stayed until well into the evening, researching anything and everything he could on magic and Seers and trying to formulate some way to help Persinette. He was still there when Ivy slunk into the room, a smug, knowing look on her face.

"What do you want, Ivy?" Manu asked cagily.

"A little birdy told me you're looking for spells to pass along to your pretty little Seer." Ivy settled into the chair opposite him, crossing one long leg over the other.

"Was the little birdy Benard? Because if it was, I'll kill him."

Her only reply was a dainty shrug.

Manu darkened his gaze at Ivy as he tried to sort out what she was getting at. There had to be an angle to this; he didn't see Ivy as the benevolent type. If she was offering help, she would want to get something out of it. "Talk."

"First, I want an assurance that you won't go to Eddi with this." She held her hand out, and it glittered with pale green magic. "You have to swear an oath."

Manu's frown deepened. He eyed the extended hand. He didn't like the idea of making a magical oath to anyone, least of all Ivy. But if it would help Persinette, he'd be willing to try it. "Fine. I swear." He shook her hand. The magic ran through him like electricity, binding him to his promise. Now, even if he'd wanted to tell Eddi about whatever Ivy was about to reveal, he couldn't.

The witch pulled her hand back with a nod and settled it in her lap. "Very well. I may know of a tracking spell that could help us find the Great Library."

Manu goggled at her, trying to process what she'd just said. When the words finally registered, he laughed loudly. "The Great Library? That's just a legend. It doesn't exist, and even if it did, the legends say it moves constantly. It is both everywhere and nowhere all at once. Is this your idea of a joke?"

Ivy crossed her arms with a huff. "It's not a joke! It's real. And I know how to find it."

The captain schooled his features back to seriousness. "All right, say that I believe you. What do you get out of us finding it?"

She shrugged. "The same thing you get. Access to every grimoire ever written."

He flicked his eyes over her face he pondered this. It was clear Ivy thought the library was real. He himself wasn't sure that it was real, but what did he have to lose by trying? It wasn't as if they were on a mission at this point, and when one came up, they could merely pause in their pursuit of the library to complete it. No muss. No fuss. So why not? "What do we need to do to find this damn thing?"

The smug smile returned to her face as she leaned forwards. "First, we set a course for Hugo."

"And then what?" He raised an eyebrow, still not convinced this wasn't a horrible scheme cooked up by a vindictive woman to...steal his ship or something.

"Then we pay a visit to my old friend Maeve. She's a bit of a hoarder...but she'll have exactly what we need to find it." There was a gleam in Ivy's eyes when she spoke. Manu wasn't sure if it was a gleam of excitement or one of hunger, so he decided to ignore it. For now, they had a heading!

He rose from his chair and dashed into the corridor in a flash. "Benard!" the captain shouted as he skidded toward the crew's quarters. "Benard!" Several crew members stuck their heads out of their rooms to glare at their captain as he shouted for his first mate all the way down the hall. "Benard!"

When Benard opened his door, stood wearing a pair of pajamas and a tight expression for his captain. "What is it, sir?" he asked.

"We have a heading!" Manu told him excitedly, ignoring the glower of death he was receiving.

"Very good, sir. We shall be off in the morning," Benard said, annoyance lacing his tone.

"What's going on?" Owen asked, poking his head out of the cabin. His hair was a mass of mussed copper curls and his bright blue eyes were heavily lidded with sleep.

"Nothing, Owen. Let's go back to bed." Benard pushed Owen back into the room and slammed the door in Manu's face.

Manu stood dumbly for a moment. "Well then!"

"Go to bed, sir!" Benard shouted from inside the cabin.

MANU DID NOT GO to bed. Indeed, the captain could be found the next morning sitting at his desk with dark circles under his eyes as he downed at least his third cup of coffee of the morning. He had spent the rest of his evening poring over books, maps, and journals in the hopes of finding out a little more about the library. In the end, having found very little, he knew he would have to use Ivy's information whether he liked it or not. All he could hope was that this was not some elaborate scheme to screw him over.

"I don't think this is a good idea, sir," Benard said. He snatched the half-drunk cup of coffee just as Manu raised it to his lips.

"I was drinking that!" the captain whined, grabbing for the cup that Benard was keeping out of reach.

Benard firmed his mouth into a tight line. "Yes, and I'd say you've had quite enough of it. A drop more and you won't sleep for a week." He sat the cup far out of Manu's grasp and settled into one of the chairs opposite the desk.

"Maybe I don't *want* to sleep for a week," Manu muttered. All this earned him was a soft motherly *tsk* from Benard. "Anyway, *what's* a bad idea?"

Benard rolled his eyes. "Oh, I don't know, trusting Ivy to lead us to the Great Library, trying to find the Great Library in the first place, going against Eddi's orders. Take your pick; you seem to be full of bad ideas this week."

The captain thought to argue, but realized Benard was very right. None of those ideas sounded like good ones, but at the same time, he felt like a bad option would be his *only* option at this point. If he wanted to help Persinette, he was going to have to do some things he usually wouldn't. That included trusting untrustworthy people and going against orders. "Come now, let's have a little bit of faith, Benard. I'm sure it'll all work out for the better."

"Famous last words," Benard said under his breath.

"What was that?" Manu frowned at him.

Benard's only response was a trademark expressionless stare. Fortunately for him, a soft tinkling from the compact in Manu's pocket drew his attention away and spared the first mate a dressing-down. "Saved by the bell," Benard remarked.

"I'm not done with you, Benard. You will explain yourself." Manu wagged his finger at the goblin, who was already making a beeline for the door.

"Aye-aye, Captain," Benard said cheekily and gave a little salute before disappearing into the hall.

Manu glared at the shut door before he opened the compact and smiled softly at Persinette. "Persi! How are you? I hope you're feeling better."

Her gaze still looked heavy, but it seemed that at least one of them had gotten some sleep; her eyes no longer had dark bags under them. "A little better," she murmured.

The captain set aside the maps he'd been looking over to give her his full attention. He wanted nothing more than to comfort her, but he knew that it wasn't a possibility. Not yet, anyway. "You look like you got some sleep."

She nodded. "I did. Training started back up today, and that left me tired enough to take a nap."

"Any word on your next mission yet?"

"No...not yet." Persi shook her head, then wore on her lip nervously. "I'm supposed to meet my new handler tomorrow," she said, shifting uncomfortably. Then, after a moment, she seemed to decide something and asked suddenly. "How did you become a pirate? Tell me."

The sudden topic change took Manu aback, but he nodded. He would give Persi this. He would take her mind off of her worries, at least for a little while. "All right." He settled back in his chair, propping his boots up on the desk. "So, I told you that I got separated from my family, right?" She nodded as she too settled into an easier position in her seat, and Manu waited until she was settled before continuing. "I ran and ran as far and as fast as I could, and that night I slept behind some crates on one of the air-docks in town. It seemed like as good a place to hide as any—why would MOTHER bother to check out near the air-docks? And I figured the Pirates would leave me alone. I wasn't any use to them."

Persinette nodded, her brow creased in thought. "I've never been to an air-dock before," she said.

"One day you will, Persi, don't you worry about that. You'll be sick of air-docks soon enough and begging to be landlocked for a while." He offered her an encouraging smile.

"Do you ever feel like that?"

A laugh left the captain, and he shook his head. "No, I don't. If anything, being landlocked makes me crazy. I don't think I'll ever want to settle on land again."

She nodded her lavender head a second time as her lips pursed in thought. "I may not either."

"No, I don't suppose you would. You seem to have a touch of the wanderer in you too." He smiled a little. "Like calls to like, I guess." He studied her, feeling his smile grow into a grin, and she returned it, her face brightening.

"Then what?" she asked, breaking the silence.

Manu nodded with a soft chuckle. "Then I nearly froze to death, and probably would have, too, if Benard and Owen hadn't been coming back to the ship late that evening. I'm still not sure how they saw me. I must not have hidden very well—"

"Benard? But Benard is so young," Persi said, sounding surprised.

At that, Manu positively guffawed. "Oh no, dearest, no he is not. He just *looks* young — damn good goblin genes for you. No, Benard is ancient. He was probably around before the Great War."

"Oh."

He grinned a little more, recalling how Benard and Owen stumbled upon his scrawny, half-frozen self. It certainly had been a strange evening. "Anyway, so there I was, twelve years old, terrified, on the verge of hypothermia, and this creepy-looking goblin and gigantic man scoop me up and drag me onto the ship."

"Was it scary?"

"Oh, you have no idea." He huffed a laugh. "I'd never seen a goblin before, and Benard's eyes were all glow-y and nightmare-inducing. Then Owen is—well, you haven't met Owen yet, but he's enormous. Even taller than me and built like a troll." Manu felt a part of himself unclench as Persi released a soft snort of laughter. "You laugh! But you'll see when you meet him!"

"I'm sure I will." She grinned that bright grin at him. "He's probably a friendly giant."

"Well, he is that," the captain agreed. "Owen is perhaps the sweetest man I've ever met in all my life. Anyway, so then they asked me where my family was, and I told them what happened. After that, they dragged me before the captain, and he offered me a position as a cabin boy."

"What was the captain like? Was he handsome?" Persi leaned closer to the mirror as she listened, her eyes focused firmly on his face.

"Not half as handsome as yours truly." Manu offered her a wink, eliciting a tiny giggle. "In all seriousness, he was already pretty old at that point and a grumpy imp to boot. So no, not handsome."

Persi wrinkled her freckled nose a little as those slightly gapped teeth wore on her lower lip once again. "But how did *you* become the captain?"

"Ah, right." He tapped his temple. "Now, I'm getting there, just let me finish."

"Sorry, I'll be quiet." She pressed her lips tightly together.

Manu beamed, relishing the charge to tell the story. "So, by the time I was fifteen I'd worked my way up the ranks to deckhand and I was the old coot's favorite. By the time I was eighteen, he'd decided to retire and head over the wall to the Waste—"

Persi gasped loudly at the mention of the Waste, and Manu paused, confused. "Sorry, sorry. I was supposed to be quiet," she said.

"No, ask your question."

"Well, I didn't know people went there by choice. MOTHER always makes it sound like the Waste is dark and twisted, and no one can survive it. It's...scary," she whispered.

Manu cocked his head as she spoke. "Well, it's all of those things, but so much more too! Humans can't survive there, but with our magical blood, Enchanted can. There is a whole band of people who live there pretty happily. Don't you worry about our dear old captain. He will be getting on just fine there—I have no doubt." He did not continue until she had calmed. "Benard and Owen suggested me for the position, and the rest—as they say—is history." He finished his tale with a flourish.

"*Wow,*" Persi breathed, sounding completely amazed, which drew a proud smile to Manu's lips. Ever since their first night chatting, Manu had recognized that Persi was the perfect audience for storytelling. She ooohed and aaahed at all of the right times and allowed herself to be fully engrossed in the story. "And you've been the captain since you were eighteen?"

At that, his smile turned cocky. "Yes, ma'am, I have." He dipped his head forwards in a mini bow, which made her giggle again. "By the time I came aboard, the *Duchess* was already a part of the Uprising, so I just picked up where they left off when I became captain. Of course, Eddi didn't seem to trust me right off," he added, unable to stop his lip from curling.

Persinette's face fell. "What? Why not? Is this your first mission with them? I'm your first mission!" A note of panic seemed to take over her tone as her breath picked up and her eyes grew wild.

"Calm down, Persi, calm down," Manu said gently. He waited until she was breathing normally again. "It's not my first mission working directly with them, but not my first for the Uprising. Besides, it's not Benard's first. You're in good hands. You're safe with us. I swear."

She nodded, but her eyes were still a little panicked. "Promise?"

"You have my word. We won't let anything happen to you. You're going to be just fine. Now, breathe." She obeyed and inhaled deeply through her nose, letting her shoulders relax. "There, attagirl. Much better," he said bracingly.

"I'm glad Benard and Owen found you," Persi said.

"Yeah, me too." Manu meant it. Remembering the hour, he glanced down at his pocket watch and frowned. "It's late. You have training in the morning. You should get to sleep."

A long sigh left her as she flopped back onto her bed, causing the image of her in the mirror to jerk awkwardly. "I don't want to. Sleeping means nightmares."

Manu rubbed his face with a tanned hand, his own exhaustion finally catching up with him. "I know, Pers, but you need your rest. Trust me, a good night's sleep will make you feel better."

"Will you sing as you did before? That was nice."

Amused, he felt his lips twitch a little. "Yes, I'll sing again. And then tomorrow I want to hear all about how you became a MOTHER agent. We'll trade stories, yeah?"

"Yeah, I'd like that." Her words were melting together and her eyes drooping with sleep now that she was lying down. She yawned and tugged the blankets up to her neck. "Good night, Manu."

"Good night, Pers." He began the lullaby, singing low and evenly.

"Such a pretty song," she murmured. "Where'd you learn it?" One bright green eye peeked open again.

"My Tutu and Mom used to sing it to us when we couldn't sleep at night. Now, no more questions. Go to sleep," he ordered kindly.

A tired laugh left her. "Aye-aye, Captain."

Manu tipped his head in mock frustration. "No sass from you, young lady." He began to sing again, and this time she closed her eyes and didn't open them again. Her breathing steadied and quieted as she fell deeper into sleep. Finally, once he was sure she wouldn't wake, he stopped singing and closed the connection. And if his fingers lingered perhaps a little too long on the swirling cameo of the mirror, who was to know but him?

23

PERSINETTE

A WEEK HAD GONE BY. Seven days of training. Seven nights of stomachaches and uncertainty. One hundred and sixty-eight hours during which Persinette had no idea what would become of her. Every day she was told that they were finding her a new handler. Every day she went to bed uncertain about her position in MOTHER and, by extension, in the Uprising. The anxiety of not knowing wore on her, making sleep elusive and food tasteless.

Now the wait was over. Persi's schedule that day had listed a meeting first thing in the morning—before breakfast, thankfully so she didn't have to worry about being sick. Studiously avoiding the mirror, she tied her hair back in a low-hanging ponytail, repeating the room number over and over to herself.

Room 324. Room 324. 324. 324. 324.

The repetition steadied her, giving her something to focus on that wasn't the terror gnawing at her tired muscles.

With a soft hiss, the door opened to reveal a dark-haired young man standing behind a chair. His nearly black eyes lifted from the papers he'd been looking over to pin her to her spot with a cold smile. Persinette felt a shudder wrack her spine, and her toes pinch inside her boots.

Those black eyes and that cruel smile faded away as a memory flooded her mind. She'd seen that smile before...

Persi couldn't remember where she'd been going, or what she'd been doing. But she could remember the busy corridor of MOTHER filling with the sounds of screams. Persinette stood on her toes to see what was going on, but it was no use. Eventually, the crowd parted to let whoever it was through. When she finally got a good look at them, she saw that it was two agents dragging a young nymph boy with the boy's handler behind them.

The boy couldn't have been more than sixteen, and he was screaming at the top of his lungs. "I'll do better! I swear I'll do better! Please don't send me there! I'd rather die than go there," he begged, his head twisting and turning in an attempt to make eye contact with his handler. "Please, Andrew! Please, I promise to do better," the boy sobbed, his eyes brimming over with tears.

The dark-haired man swept before the nymph. Those near-black eyes met the boy's, and his lips curved into a cruel smile. "You'd rather die?"

"Please Andrew, I swear." The boy hiccupped as his body sagged against the hold of the two guards. "I swear I'll be better."

Andrew's cold smile crawled further up his face, making his dark eyes squint. "Answer the question, Felix. You'd rather die than go to the camps?"

The nymph sniffled wetly and nodded his blue head. What happened next went so quickly that no one could have stopped it even if they had wanted to. Andrew pulled his pistol from the holster, aimed, and fired a single shot into Felix's chest.

Persinette bit down on her tongue to keep from crying out hard enough to draw blood. She watched as the MOTHER agent casually holstered his pistol and pulled a handkerchief from his pocket to wipe the blood from his face.

Yet what was worse, impossibly worse than the guards carelessly dragging the boy's body off, or Andrew wiping the blood away as if it were nothing, was that after the body was pulled away, everyone in the hall just went back to business as usual. It was as if it had never happened, as if that boy's life meant nothing. Felix. She had had vowed to remember him.

Persinette shook the memory away as she heard someone calling her name. "I'm sorry, what was that?" she asked.

"I said, 'Hello, Persinette. I'm Andrew Gothel.'" The agent chuckled mirthlessly as he held his hand out to her to shake. She stared down at the pale, outstretched hand in confusion. She didn't think a MOTHER agent had ever shaken her hand before. It seemed strange that now would be the first time. "It won't bite," he teased.

"Hi," Persi whispered, taking the offered hand awkwardly to shake it. She dropped it as quickly as she could without seeming rude.

"You seem surprised. Had my sister never spoken of me? I suppose not. She wasn't really the social sort, was she?" Andrew's tone was friendly and polite as he gestured for her to take the seat beside him. "Please, sit."

A cold sweat had settled onto Persinette's hands, slippery and chill. The hair on her arms raised in panic, every instinct in her body telling her to run, but she forced herself robotically into the chair beside him. "No, she didn't talk about you," she said evenly.

"I thought not." Andrew chuckled. "Always all business, that was my sister. That's what made her a good agent."

Persi nodded numbly. Was he expecting her to say something? She wasn't sure, but she thought it was probably safer not to.

"Regardless." He straightened. "I'll be your handler from now on. In case you hadn't figured that out yet," he added.

She looked over at him nervously before nodding once more. From the dark eyes to the dark hair, he looked like Gothel, but everything else was an entirely different person. Andrew Gothel was handsome in a way she'd never thought a MOTHER agent could be. He was not attractive in the way that Manu was, though. When Manu smiled, it reached his eyes, but when Andrew smiled it was as if he'd just carved a smile onto an expressionless mask. There was no real emotion behind it.

"Do you have any questions for me before we get started?" Andrew's tone remained friendly, bordering on helpful. *Had he acted like this with Felix, too?*

"What should I, um, call you? Gothel never told me her first name."

"Oh, just Andrew will be quite all right. I want us to be on friendly terms, and I think that'll be the best way to do that. Don't you Persinette?"

"Yes, sir."

"Andrew," he corrected.

"Andrew," she repeated, hoping to make the first name feel less strange in her mouth. It didn't.

"Better. Shall we?" Andrew Gothel didn't wait for a response. He motioned for the projector and the robot dutifully turned it on. With whirring and clicking, the gears and fans warmed up quickly to cast the image of a large city on the opposite wall. "We're headed for Maximus," Andrew said as he slid a file to her.

Persi flipped it open. There were statistics for the overall population and pictures, as per usual. But what surprised her was an estimate of the Enchanted populations broken down by species. Gothel had always kept those statistics from her, and Persi didn't want to ask why she'd been given them now and risk having it taken back. It'd be useful information for when Manu placed people and fed her addresses and names later on.

"We expect that with such a large population, and the rumors of an underground Enchanted city, you will be able to compile a list of at least ten Enchanted for Collection," Andrew continued, businesslike. His words bore no underlying hint of a threat, just clear-cut facts. None of which did anything to ease the terror blossoming in her belly.

"Ten?" she asked. Persi realized that the file in her hands was shaking and quickly dropped it. She tucked her trembling hands into her lap, hoping that Andrew hadn't seen.

"Yes, ten." He looked puzzled. "Is that going to be a problem?"

"How long do I have to put together this list?" Persi asked, avoiding the question. She licked her dry lips, trying rising panic in check. And likewise settle the magic inside of her reacting to her emotions.

"Six weeks should suffice." There was an air of finality to his words—this was not a negotiation. Andrew Gothel would not be giving her more time and he would not accept any fewer than ten Enchanted. She didn't want to know what would happen if she were to fail.

"Right." She nodded curtly. "I'll do my best."

"I expect better than your best." His words turned icy. Perhaps he was showing his true colors now. "We have many other Seers able to produce at this rate. In fact, you are our lowest-producing Seer in residence, Persinette." The ghostly chill of a threat lingered in the air—not quite fully formed, but clear enough to lower the temperature of the room. "You will have ten names and addresses for me in six weeks."

Persi's eyes widened in fear in spite of herself. "Yes, sir," she choked out.

"Andrew."

"Yes, Andrew."

His lips spread into a handsome smile, his eyes dancing without any lightness. "Wonderful. I cannot wait to begin our work together, Persinette. I can see now that we are going to have a productive partnership." Andrew suddenly sounded absolutely delighted. He ducked his head to jot down some notes in his own file. "We will meet again in one week so that you can update me on your progress. How does that sound?" Those black eyes peered at her expectantly.

A week. Persinette had a week to prove that he shouldn't shoot her in the chest just as he had Felix. She felt bile surged her throat and staved it off with shallow breathes through her nose nose. "Sure."

"Fantastic! I'll see you in a week. You are dismissed, Persinette. Enjoy your training session!" The agent had a too-bright smile on his lips showing too-white teeth as he looked at her. Then he went back to his file, dismissing her entirely.

Persi gave a quick dip of her head. No words, no sounds beyond the quick clicking of her boots as she abandoned all illusion of normalcy and rushed to her bathroom. When she reached safety, her knees hit the cold tile as she bent over the toilet and promptly threw up what was left of last night's dinner.

A thin sheen of sweat spread over her face and neck, and little hairs stuck to her skin. Persi took a moment to sob before retching again. This time nothing came up, but she couldn't seem to stop. She was still there, kneeling on the floor when she heard the soft pad of boots approaching the bathroom door.

"What in the heavens is that ghastly sound?" A voice carried through her quarters and into the bathroom. It was muffled through the door, but unmistakable. Agnes poked his vibrant head through the doorway and took her in, nose wrinkled. "It's you. Of course, it is."

"Get out," Persinette gasped out as she struggled for breath around the wrenching sobs.

"Now is that any way to talk to a guest?" Agnes asked, looking her up and down with his lip curling more. "You look awful."

"I said *get out!*" Persi stood and slammed the door in his face. With the door between them, Persi was finally able to catch her breath and regain some of her composure. She bent over the sink to rinse out her mouth and her face.

When she finally emerged from the bathroom, Agnes was sprawled in her chair, looking utterly disdainful. "You done?"

"How did you get in here?" Persi asked.

"You were late for training, so your handler gave me access to your rooms." Agnes's blue eyes examined her once more before his lip curled. "Which, by the looks of you, you'll be missing today. I hope whatever you have isn't catching."

Persi expected him to swan out after that, but he didn't. He remained where he was, splayed in her well-worn leather chair. "What do you want, Agnes?" she asked, feeling weary, as though all of her fight had been expelled with the contents of her stomach.

The well-tailored shoulders of his jacket shrugged, and for a moment his brows creased as if he were battling with his words. "How did your meeting with the new handler go? Are they sending you down to the camps?" If she didn't know any better, she'd say he looked a little worried. But she did know better, and his tone made it clear that "not that I care" should have been added to the end of those questions.

"No," Persi said. At this point, though, the camps might be a relief. At least in the camps, her fate would not be uncertain. At least there she would not be forced into whatever mind games Andrew seemed intent on playing with her. She also wouldn't have to feel the guilt over having to send anyone else there. Maybe that was what she deserved after what she did to all of those people, to Gothel —a short existence of misery. "My next mission is to Maximus. I'm expected to help them Collect ten Enchant-ed." The words left her throat feeling rawer than it had from being sick.

Agnes gave a light sniff of some emotion—what it was, Persinette couldn't be sure—but his expression remained unchanged. "Guess you better hop to, then." Agnes rose from the chair, straightening a waistcoat so fine she was sure Manu would be envious, before he headed to the door. Just as he reached it, however, he stopped. "You do what you have to, Persinette. We all do. That's the only choice we've been given." He didn't bother to wait for an answer.

A moment later the door shut behind Agnes the ornery unicorn. Agnes, who had just used her name for perhaps the first time ever.

Persinette took a slow breath and ducked into bathroom

to brush her teeth. A few minutes later she stood staring at her pale, freckled face in the mirror.

"You do what you have to, Persinette," she repeated.

AGNES MUST HAVE TOLD Andrew that Persinette wasn't feeling well, for she received no formal reprimand for missing training sessions. Still, she was more grateful for the normalcy of Agnes standing in the middle of the mats waiting for her than for any reprieve from Andrew's wrath. Training kept her mind clear of the memory of that cold smile on Andrew's face, and of his sister's death. Though Agnes seemed to be going easy on her, she refused to go easy on herself. She worked herself into a bone-tired state, praying that when she finally made it back to her rooms, she would just pass out.

Hours later, she melted into her bed—although not without changing, complete with fuzzy socks—and closed her eyes, hoping sleep would take her right then and there. The momentary peace was broken by the tinkling of chimes coming from under her pillow. Persi reached beneath and popped the little compact open, smiling despite her exhaustion. There, in the center of the glass, sat Manu behind what seemed to be a large wooden desk covered in documents. "Persi! How was your day?" he asked, sounding eager.

She hadn't known him long—a few weeks maybe, a month perhaps—but Manu had become a fixture in Persi's life. Her life had changed drastically, from one of a quiet existence to a continual struggle, but she had gained Manu as a constant. "Better, now," she said sheepishly.

Manu looked up from his papers to fully take her in,

and what he saw must have been horrendous for it drew his face into a worried scowl. "What happened?"

Inhaling deeply, Persi closed her eyes. "I met my new handler this morning." The words left a sour taste in her mouth. She swallowed, hoping to keep down her dinner.

The captain waited for her to continue. When she didn't, he asked, "And?"

For a brief, fleeting second Persinette thought maybe she could keep her fear of Andrew from overtaking her again. But after one more second, the burn of tears pricked at the corners of her eyes. "Manu, I'm scared." Her voice shook.

Manu's well-cut jaw tightened. "What's wrong?"

"It doesn't matter. There's nothing you can do about it," Persi said. Her hands shook now, too. She rolled onto her side, setting the mirror on the bed before her so her hands would be free to swipe at her watering eyes. "None of it matters. I just need to focus on the mission."

"Persinette." The way he said her name had her lowering her hands so that she could focus on him once more. Once the captain had her full attention, he held it. "I need you to take a deep breath and tell me what happened. Can you do that for me?" She nodded awkwardly against the pillow, her lavender hair curling beneath her cheek. "Good. Now close your eyes and breathe in."

She did as she was bid, closing her eyes and inhaling deeply. Then she released the breath, letting some of the tension go with it. "Okay," she whispered, her voice no longer shaking.

"That's my girl." Manu nodded. "Now, tell me what happened."

"My new handler is Andrew Gothel. He's my former handler's younger brother. And..." The words drifted off for a moment as the memory of Andrew shooting that nymph boy at point-blank range came flooding back. Manu gave her a moment to gather herself. "I watched him execute his last Asset in the middle of a crowded corridor not a year ago," she whispered.

Manu's handsome face twisted into a scowl once again, but he took his time to find the words to say. "That won't happen to you," he said firmly.

His utter certainty stilled Persinette's nervous movements. The memories drifted away in her confusion as she looked at him with wide eyes. "How do you know?"

An arrogant smile split Manu's full lips, and he winked at her. "Because you have Captain Manu Kelii on your side, of course!"

A startled laugh left Persinette unbidden. "Then I suppose I have nothing at all to fear?" The teasing question flew from her lips before she had the chance to stop it.

"Not a damn thing." That cocksure smile only widened.

"Okay then." She giggled. It was silly, Persi knew it was, but the realization that she wasn't alone did make her feel better. She didn't have to face Andrew and his pistol on her own. She had someone out there in the world willing to help her evade that cruel smile for as long as possible. Manu was on her side.

"Right. What's the next problem I can solve for you, m'lady?" The captain bowed his dark head in a gesture of overdramatic chivalry. "I live to serve."

Persinette's lips twitched, wanting desperately to smile, as she released a sigh. "The next problem is that I need a list of ten Enchanted for Collection in six weeks."

Manu's aquiline nose wrinkled in disgust. "Ten? What's the largest number you've ever helped Collect before?"

"Successfully?" He nodded. "Four."

"More than double!" His shout startled her enough that she jerked, nearly toppling the compact to the floor. Manu inhaled deeply as though to steady himself and rubbed at the bridge of his nose. "Sorry. Sorry. I'm not shouting at you. I'm sorry."

"It's all right," Persi said, trying to steady herself as well. Manu's sudden outburst left her a little worried. What if he couldn't get her ten names? What if she failed? What if the next person Andrew executed in front of the entire compound was her? Gods, she was going to throw up again. "*Berightback*," she mumbled, and rolled from the bed quickly. She skidded into the bathroom to retch into the toilet for a few long minutes.

"Persi? Persinette? Are you all right?!" She could hear Manu shouting into the mirror from the bathroom. When she was done, she laid back down, rubbing at her eyes. "Pers?" Manu asked. The single word was so full of concern that it her heart ached.

"I'm all right," she said shakily. "I'll be all right."

"Are you sure? If you can't do this..." Manu's words drifted off. They both knew he couldn't finish that sentence. If she couldn't do this, then what? What could he do about it? Nothing. She either did this or Andrew Gothel punished her for failing him.

"Don't worry about me."

Manu snorted softly. "Can't seem to help it. That's all I seem to do these days. I worry about you. I worry about the *Duchess*. I worry about Benard. I worry, Persinette! It's all I do!" He sounded a little manic, but the feeling behind the words made her feel a bit better.

"Well, I appreciate it."

"Oh, you had better, missy." He wagged his finger at her

in a mock threat. "Now, you tell me right now if you can do this or not. Because if you can't, I'm coming to get you." It was a radical proposition, yet Manu spoke with all the conviction of a man who had well and truly made up his mind.

"You-you are?" Persi saw her lavender brows raise in the mirror before her.

"Yes, I am. I'm not going to let MOTHER lock you up in one of those camps or shoot you in front of a bunch of people who don't care. Uprising be damned, I will come in there and get you."

All Persi could manage was a small, "Thank you."

"Of course, Persi. That's what I'm here for." He offered her a broad grin. Persi knew that just because he promised he'd get her out didn't mean he'd actually be able to. Still, it felt good to have an exit plan, even one that was plainly impossible. "Now, I believe there was some talk of you giving me your life story. You know, since I told you mine the other night." Manu's tone turning light and teasing.

Persinette let the change in subject lift some of the weight off her. Even though her life story was sad a sad one, and would only prove to him how little she knew of the world, it was a better topic than death. "There really isn't anything to tell. I don't remember much before MOTHER."

"Nothing?"

"I didn't say nothing; I said not much." She chuckled. "I was six when I was abducted by MOTHER, so it's mostly just glimpses of memories."

"Tell me about those."

Persi nodded, tugging forward a strand of hair to fiddle with as she spoke. "I remember my mother singing to me. She had the most beautiful voice. I remember my father smiling at me—he had freckles just like I did, all over his nose and cheeks." She grinned fondly at the memory, letting the images briefly overtake her. "And I remember my brother..." Her words drifted off. "I don't remember much about him. Just that he had red hair and freckles like Father and me. It's all...a blur." Her voice faded as she did her best to try to put their faces into focus, but the years made it impossible. "I don't even remember his name."

"We don't have to keep talking about this," Manu told her gently.

Persi shook her head. "No. I promised to tell you." She swallowed hard and continued. "The next thing I remember was a room in the Tower that just had a bed, and nothing else. I felt like I was there for days as I waited to find out what was going to happen to me. Then Gothel came in to tell me that I would be helping them Collect others like me." A little sob left her at the memory of Gothel. For all her harshness, Gothel had been the closest thing she'd had to a family for the last sixteen years, and now she was gone too.

"She told me if I didn't, I'd never see Mother or Father again. For a little while, that was enough of a threat, but eventually, I realized I was never going to see them again no matter what I did. So I stopped telling them about my visions and then...and then...then..." She stumbled over the words as she remembered what came next. "Then they took me to the camps to show me what happened to Enchanted who weren't useful. It was dark and cold, and everyone there looked half-dead inside. Even the children." The last word was barely audible. "I started helping again, because I didn't want to go there, ever." She'd been selfish, she told herself, and she deserved this guilt gnawing at her insides, threatening to stop her breathing any minute now. She'd been just a child herself, and she'd doomed others to that fate.

"Persi, you didn't have a choice. You were just doing what you had to, to survive." Manu's words were sweet, empathetic, as if he knew the guilt she felt—as if he had felt it himself. She supposed he had: He had survived where his family hadn't, just as she had. That must have worn on him. It hard certainly worn on her.

"That doesn't make it better."

"No, it doesn't, but we can't feel guilty for what we have had to do to survive. All we can try to do is change things now. You were too young then, and so was I."

Persi dipped her head, sucking in air through her teeth "Tell me something nice now, please?" She needed something light again.

Manu opened his mouth, closed it, then let the subject drop. "Like what?"

"I don't know, just something...else," she finished lamely.

He screwed up his tan face, rubbing the stubble of his chin in thought. After a moment he said, "For a long time I didn't realize that Benard having a boyfriend was unusual."

"Wait, Benard has a boyfriend?" Persi felt her brows fly up in surprise. "Isn't that technically illegal? I mean MOTHER doesn't—they don't *allow* that."

Manu snorted. "There are lots of regulations that MOTHER's put in place that are stupid. Outlawing same-sex relationships is one of them." His tone held nothing but disdain for the very idea as he rolled his eyes. "Closed-minded idiots."

"Who's Benard's boyfriend?"

"Owen! The giant, remember? Our boatswain. They're tooth-rottingly adorable together." Manu said fondly.

"Benard's grumpy with everyone else, but he's actually really romantic with Owen. Whenever we're in port, he brings Owen back a gift. Sometimes it's flowers, sometimes it's a new ratchet. Whatever catches his eye."

Persinette smiled dreamily as she imagined Benard doing just that. "That's sweet. I can him being very thoughtful."

"You can?" Manu barked out a bright laugh. "*I* can't. He's such a little jerk to everyone else."

"What's a boatswain?" Persi yawned and rubbed the corners of her heavy eyes.

"The boatswain keeps track of all the equipment on the ship and makes sure it's all in working order at all times. You know, if you wanted a lesson on the ins and outs of a Pirate ship..." He let his words drift off teasingly as he smiled.

Persi rolled her eyes, though the idea pleased her. "What's Owen like? He's nice, isn't he?" Exhaustion was beginning to pull at her. There had been too much of everything today, and she needed sleep. But she knew the moment she closed her eyes to rest, she'd hear Gothel's scream again. If she could just put it off a bit more...

"He's a nice guy—a little snarky, but not sarcastic like Benard is. He laughs a lot, and he makes Benard smile more than I ever thought possible. When I was younger, he was always good to me, like I was family. I'd like to stand up at their wedding one day." Manu was smiling now, a far-off look in his eyes. "I hope it's made legal again soon."

"Well, you're pirates. They could just have a wedding, and you could officiate it. Couldn't you? Since you're a captain?"

"Yeah, I guess I could." Manu sounded intrigued at the thought. "You'll have to suggest that to Benard next time you see him. Or better yet, to Owen when I introduce you. Then he can propose."

"That'd be adorable." Persi yawned again.

Manu gave her a fond smile. "All right, that's two. I think it's time for you to go to bed miss."

Persinette shook her head, frowning. She didn't want to go to sleep. Not like this. If she were going to sleep, she wanted it to happen without her putting in the effort to do it. She wanted a dreamless sleep and a dreamless sleep alone.

"I'll sing you to sleep again?" Manu offered, sounding almost hopeful.

"Okay," Persi breathed. She pulled the blanket up to her chin, letting her eyes fall closed heavily as Manu began his gentle lullaby. It wasn't long before she had drifted off to sleep.

24

CAPTAIN MANU KELII

THE YOUNG CAPTAIN was a little nervous about his conference with Eddi that afternoon. He wasn't particularly good at giving bad news. He'd much prefer to be the person who people came to after they had heard bad news—as Persi had the night before—so that he could cheer them up. Still —Manu reminded as he looked himself over in the mirror— this is what he had to do to help Persi, so he would.

"It's a part of your job, sir," Benard said reasonably from where he sat on a stool in the captain's expansive closet. "And there was nothing at all wrong with the navy blue waistcoat you just took off," he added, a bit less so.

Manu ignored Benard's comment as he grabbed a chartreuse waistcoat from one of the racks. "Too somber. I don't want to seem too somber. I want to have an air of hope about this whole thing."

"Then perhaps the puke-green one is not the right choice."

"It is not puke-green!" The captain gasped in utter horror at the mere insinuation. "It is *chartreuse*, Benard! How dare you!" Manu narrowed his dark brown eyes at the goblin, who merely rolled his own glowing eyes in response. "But perhaps you have a point." He replaced the waistcoat on the rack. "Maybe chartreuse is a bit too lively a thing for such an affair. What about fuchsia?"

"Don't you have anything that doesn't look like disco shat it out?"

"Disco?" Manu paused his wardrobe-browsing. "What is disco?"

The goblin only shook his head.

The captain brushed off his first mate with a broad-shouldered shrug and turned back to the long rack of waistcoats. From the lot, he plucked a waistcoat of a burgundy silk in an intricate paisley pattern. "Is this good enough?" He held it to himself as he looked in the mirror.

"Yes, sir, much less garish. Now, please do hurry along and get ready. We do not want to keep Eddi waiting." Benard headed to the door of the closet. "I'll go and set up the call."

"Yes, thank you, Benard," Manu said distractedly as he turned this way and that, considering the waistcoat at every angle. "Perhaps it's not about the waistcoat," he muttered to himself. Indeed, it really *wasn't* about the waistcoat at all; it was about his worry for Persinette. But he couldn't let anyone else know that.

Pressing his mouth into a firm line, he replaced the hanger and pulled from the rack a lilac-colored waistcoat instead. The gold trim and delicate swirling pattern reminded him of Persinette's long locks and sunshine smiles. "This is it." He nodded, pulled it on quickly, buttoned the front, and strode off for the flight deck.

Eddi was already on the screen. "Kelii. I expected you twenty minutes ago."

"Yes, well, you know what they say about perfection."

Manu offered a ridiculous bow and plunked himself into the captain's chair.

Grey magnified eyes blinked at him in an unreadable expression as Eddi seemed to process his words. "Benard tells me that you have news from the Asset."

"Persinette," the captain reminded. There was something about the way that Eddi talked about Persi. He didn't like it.

"What?"

"Persinette. Her name is Persinette. Or Persi. Don't call her the Asset." Anger was building in Manu's gut. To MOTHER, Persi was just a tool. Just something they would use until she ceased to be useful. He didn't want that for her with the Uprising. He wanted—no, he *needed*—to believe that the Uprising was different. That he was on the right side of things.

"Right, Persinette," Eddi amended. "So, what information did Persinette have for us?"

The captain could feel those dark eyes on him, as if the Uprising Leader were trying to decode something about him. What, exactly, Manu wasn't sure, but he didn't care for being surveyed like this. It left him feeling exposed in a way he wasn't used to. He shrugged, attempting casualness, and moved on. "She's been assigned a new handler, a certain Andrew Gothel, of whom she is utterly terrified. And their next mission is to Maximus. Persi has been given six weeks to provide Andrew with a list of ten Enchanted in Maximus for Collection." The words left him in a whoosh of air as if he'd been holding them in far too long. Manu told himself he was just excited to get a move on, ignoring that nagging feeling in the back of his mind. "They think they can get a better Collection there, I assume because of the rumored underground community."

Eddi nodded, then looked down at some paper sitting on the desk. "Of course that would be their next target," the leader said pensively. "There has never been a successful Collection in Maximus. This is probably a test for Persinette."

Manu swallowed hard, the nagging at the back of his mind getting bigger and much more naggy. "That was Persi's concern. She is worried that this new handler has set her up to fail." In that, Manu couldn't help but agree with her. Persinette had caused the death of Andrew's sister. so why wouldn't the agent try to get revenge?

"That, or they want to see how good she really is." Eddi adjusted their goggles.

"Right, so, we need to prove she's worth keeping," Manu declared with more conviction than he'd felt about much else in many, many years. "That way they have no reason to get rid of her."

"You still have a small unit of my agents on your ship, correct?"

"Yes, Ivy and the others are still aboard."

There was a rustling of papers. "Good. Then you and Ivy can work out the logistics. If you need more agents, just let me know."

"Yes, sir." Manu nodded firmly. "I believe that's all, sir."

"Oh, one more thing." Eddi looked up from the papers once more to fix Manu with a cold, dark stare. "You and Ivy are to cease your attempts at finding the Great Library immediately." The Uprising Leader said nothing else before the transmission ended and the screen went blank.

Manu stared at the staticky screen, then released an inhuman growl and stood abruptly from his chair. "Benard!" he shouted as he made his way down the hall to the first mate's quarters. "Benard!" He burst through the door to glare at Benard who was sitting behind his desk with Owen sat alongside him.

"Cap'n?" Benard asked, looking at him impassively. "Is there something I can help you with?"

"Did you tell the old bat about the damn library?" The captain's eyes flashed golden as he accused the rather unperturbed-looking goblin.

Benard rolled his glowing green eyes and Owen scooted his chair away from him presumably to get out of the captain's line of fire. "I did not, nor would I ever betray your trust in such a way. I'm unsure how Eddi knew about it, but that tends to be what happens when you are the leader of an organization such as the Uprising. You know things. Now please do take a breath...sir."

Manu's eyelid twitched. He let out a breath and allowed himself to deflate into the chair across from Benard and Owen. "I'm sorry Benard, I just..." He trailed off, leaned forward, and pressed his forehead to Benard's desk.

"It's all right, sir. You're worried about Persinette. We understand." Owen's chair legs scraped the floor as he settled back next to Benard. "Now, what did Eddi say?"

"To sort things out with Ivy. Then call back if we need more men," Manu muttered, not bothering to lift his head.

"Then I suppose you should go and have a meeting with Ivy, shouldn't you?" Benard said.

Manu rubbed his forehead against the smooth surface of the desk in a sort of nod.

"And see where her witch friend is whom she plans to meet with so we can find the library?"

"Right," the captain said.

"Maybe you should go and do that...now?" Benard suggested.

When the captain didn't move, the two men let out a

synchronized sigh. "Persinette will be all right, Manu," Owen said kindly.

"And the sooner we get to the Library, the sooner we can give her spells so she can protect herself," Benard added.

"Right!" Manu sat up quickly, his eyes crossing when all the blood rushed to his head. "Whoa." He squinted, then laughed. "Right! I'm off to see Ivy and get this all under-way." He threw himself to stand and launched for the door.

"He's in a bit of a state, isn't he?" Owen whispered to Benard.

Benard sighed. "It's that girl."

"It's cute."

"If you say so."

"I'm still here, you know!" Manu cried, stopping at the door. "Next time you want to talk about me, do it after I've left the room!"

"Now what's the fun in that?" Owen asked. He laughed softly. Benard snickered a bit as he stood.

"I'll see you later, love," the first mate murmured, and dipped a little to press a kiss to the boatswain's temple. He gestured at the captain to follow. "Come on, you big baby, let's go get this sorted."

THE CAPTAIN, first mate, and Ivy spent what felt like hours holed up in Manu's quarters, hashing and rehashing anything and everything that could possibly go wrong.

"Is that all of them?" Manu asked, peering over the neatly written list of names.

Benard consider, then nodded. "I think so, sir. These are the best of the volunteers."

"I don't see why we can't use more of my unit," Ivy groused. Her arms were crossed and her lips were drawn into a scowl. Typical. "They would clearly be more qualified for such an endeavor."

Benard looked as though he were holding back a snort. "Yes, well, we don't really—"

"That may be so," Manu cut Benard off quickly, shooting the first mate a warning glance. "But we don't want to waste our Assets. We can't afford for MOTHER realize Persi's pointing them to the same five people over and over again." It was a valid point, he told himself. One that surely Ivy couldn't argue with.

"This is because you don't trust me, isn't it?" The witch narrowed her kohl-lined eyes at Manu as if in a threat. "Because if that's the case, I can just take all the information I have and go help someone *else* find the library."

"Of course that's not why," Manu said, offering what he hoped was a soothing smile. "It's just as I've said, we don't want to waste your talents. Who knows how many they'll demand of Persi in the coming months. No sense in drying up all of our resources right away."

"Mhm." Ivy sounded skeptical.

"Shall we move on to something else?" Benard prompted. "Our new heading perhaps?"

Manu and Ivy stared each other down for a good ten seconds before Ivy smiled and turned to Benard. "Yes, Benard, onto other things."

Manu felt his broad shoulders relax at her words and let himself blow out a whoosh of relief. Good. "Wonderful. So you said there was a witch we needed to visit?"

"Well, more like a witch we need to *rob*." Ivy smiled a canary-eating smile as the words slipped from her lips.

"E-excuse me?" Benard stammered. Both he and the captain stared at her.

Ivy waved nonchalant hand through the air. "Like I said, Maeve is a bit of a hoarder. She keeps literally everything."

"And that means we have to rob her...why?" Manu asked. He hoped there was a point to all this. Or maybe Ivy was messing with them. Perhaps she'd laugh and say they could just ask this witch nicely for whatever they needed. He had no desire to be on a witch's bad side. Curses did not require a witch to have her victim in her sightline, and he did not want to be cursed.

Ivy tossed her green hair with evident exasperation. "Because she doesn't let anything go. Ever. She doesn't throw things away, and she sure as hell doesn't give anything to anyone."

"Can't we just pay her for whatever it is?" Benard asked hopefully. Then he wrinkled his brow. "What is it we're going to steal anyway?"

"A hair."

"I'm sorry, did you just say a hair?" The captain sat up straighter, gobsmacked. "We are going to steal a *hair*?"

"Why in gods' name are we going to steal a hair?" Benard's thin lips twitched in irritation. "I've got a whole head of them!"

"Well you don't live in the Great Library, do you, Benard?" she replied nastily.

"No," the goblin muttered awkwardly.

"Well then that wouldn't be very helpful would it?"

"Whose hair is it?" Manu asked, genuinely curious.

Ivy's eyes shifted from Manu to Benard and back again, then flicked her wrist dismissively as if batting the question away. "I don't know, someone in the Library. Maeve never said who; she just said it was someone in the Library."

Suspicious, the captain narrowed his eyes. "Oh? Is that all she said?"

"Yes," Ivy said firmly. "Now do you want to know where she lives or what? It won't be hard to break into her house."

Manu scratched the back of his head, out of options. "Fine, where is it in Hugo? It's not going to take us too far out of the way of Maximus is it?"

Ivy leaned over the desk and surveyed the map sprawled out in front of them. "It shouldn't. It's a town over, just on the outskirts. Maybe a week out from Maximus." She pointed.

The two men stared down at the spot and frowned. "A week out *in the wrong direction*," Benard clarified, glaring at her finger like it had personally offended him—perhaps it had.

"I never said it was on the way," Ivy said. "Just that it wasn't far."

"You really should have led with that! We can't just go a week out of our way for a hair that may or may not belong to someone who lives in the Great Library in the hopes that we'll be able to find a place that is both mythical and, according to legend, consistently jumps from one place to the next!" Benard's voice had escalated into a near-shout.

"Oh, come on, it's not like it—"

"ENOUGH!" Manu roared, and the others shut up instantly, both sets of eyes wide. "If we change our heading tonight, we can get to Hugo, retrieve the hair, and still make it back to Maximus with a week to spare. That will leave us plenty of time to prepare for the Collection." Benard and Ivy's mouths snapped shut at Manu's authoritative tone. "Now, Benard, I want you to go and set our heading."

"Aye, Cap'n." Benard nodded firmly and left to follow his orders.

Then Manu turned to Ivy. "I need to know everything you can tell me about Maeve. I want an exhaustive list of what kinds of traps she may have laid to keep her property secure. Leave nothing out."

The witch bobbed her green-haired head, grabbed a piece of parchment, and began to write. "I don't think it'll be that hard. She's a crazy old coot, but she's not nearly as paranoid as most witches."

"So you claim," Manu muttered, and leaned to look at the list.

A COURSE WAS PLOTTED for Hugo, the list of all the tricks and spells Maeve had used before written, and Manu was finally sitting before the fire in his room. It was well into the evening by that point, and he felt exhaustion down to his bones, and the pulsing of a headache in his temples. He poured himself the first drink he'd had in well over a week and sat back to stare out the curved windows of his quarters at the night sky.

At that moment, he would have loved nothing more than to give the Uprising, MOTHER, and this whole damn kingdom the middle finger. Then he would promptly fly off into the sunset with his crew never to be seen or heard from again. But that was the hitch—there was no place to fly off to. This was his world; there was no escaping it. The only choice he had was to make it better with the help of people like Benard, Owen, and...Persinette.

The glass sat forgotten beside him as he rubbed his fingers to his throbbing head. He frowned, desperate to settle the ache now raging behind his eyes. This—working with the Uprising, trying to change their world, helping others—is what he knew his family would have wanted from him. So even if there had been some place to fly off to, he had no choice but to stay the course.

The soft chiming of the mirror in his pocket yanked the captain from his thoughts. He hurriedly opened it, eager to lay eyes on Persi's freckled face. Offering her a tired, fond smile, he greeted her. "Good evening, Miss Persi. How are you?"

The girl breathed out, sounding tired but relatively content. "Sore from training, but I slept better last night. I didn't have the nightmare about Gothel until it was almost morning."

"I'm glad," Manu said. "I should have that list for you very soon, but my crew has to make a brief stop first in Hugo."

Her lavender brows drew together at his words. "What for? There isn't anything wrong, is there? Or are you picking up more Uprising agents? Should I be worried?" Her questions came in a tumbling rush, each one fighting to get out first.

"No, nothing to worry about. We are just going to pick something up from a witch."

"Ooooh. A witch? What kind of witch?" Persi leaned forward like she was settling in for another story.

Manu shrugged, but felt his smile grow. "Just a hoarder witch. Apparently, she has the key to finding the Great Library among her stash of junk."

"The Great Library? Is-isn't that just a myth?"

Manu laughed. "Guess we'll find out soon."

"Why are you looking for it? Do you think you'll find it? How are you going to find it?" Her green eyes had gone wide with excitement as another onslaught of questions made him chuckle.

He shook his head and pushed a strand of dark hair from his eyes. "So full of questions. Were you always like this?"

Persi snapped her mouth shut and ducked her head in shame. Her slim shoulders heaved and fell. "I guess so. But around here you get into trouble if you ask too many questions, so I just...don't bother."

There was a sadness to her words that tugged at Manu's heart. Sighing, he nodded. "You don't have to worry about that with me. I'll always do my best to answer your questions."

"Thank you." She breathed out, her lips lifting into a soft smile once more. "So...why are you looking for the library?"

"For you, of course." He laughed at her startled squawk. "Now give me another one. I've got time."

He kept his promise. He let Persi pepper him with question after question about the Library, their plans to find it, the hoarder witch, Ivy—anything and everything she could think of. So much so that at some point he moved to his bed to get more comfortable. Eventually, she yawned so loudly that he told her it was time for bed and they bid each other good night. Then Manu rolled over and did his best to fall asleep as well.

Although Persinette's chatter had eased him, it wasn't enough to soothe him completely. The upcoming mission and the desire to escape all of it pulled him in opposite directions, plaguing him with nightmares of a tiny space where he was boxed in with no hope of escape. He could hear pounding as someone hammered the lid shut. His mouth opened to scream, but nothing came out. No words, no cries, no sound at all. Just silence. But that wasn't the worst part. The worst part was the darkness that closed in around him. His vision narrowed further and further until there were not but two tiny specks of wood before him. And then nothing. Just the darkness.

In a moment of sheer panic, Manu clawed at his eyes to tug away whatever was hindering his vision. A low voice called to him, familiar though he couldn't place it, and a sense of peace settled over him. Suddenly, the darkness did not seem so terrifying, and that sense of peace enveloped him until morning.

25

PERSINETTE

FOURTEEN DAYS of relative peace and routine passed Persinette by in what felt like a flash—a flash during which she trained, visited the library, ate her meals in the cafeteria, and met with Andrew Gothel semi-regularly as was expected of her. It would have been easy to allow herself to settle into the routine of things and become complacent. Yet she couldn't ignore the feeling that all too soon the other shoe was going to drop. There had to be more to Andrew's plans than to Collect a few more Enchanted. Then there was the very real issue that she hadn't actually helped him Collect any Enchanted yet.

The uneasy feeling continued to nag at her the entire week until she woke up one morning to find an early morning briefing with Andrew on her itinerary. Rushing down the hall, Persinette arrived at the conference room door panting and ten minutes late. When the door opened, Andrew was sitting at the table waiting for her—looking oddly unperturbed.

"Sorry I'm late. My alarm didn't go off this morning," she explained as she flung herself into the chair across from him. Her pale fingers lifted to brush staticky lavender flyaways back from her face to no avail.

"It's quite all right, Persinette." Andrew gave a smile she thought was meant to be a reassuring, but that only made her skin crawl. Persinette forced herself to meet his gaze and nod. "We're just going to go over the information you've already provided."

She nodded once more and forced her shoulders to relax. She didn't see why this song and dance was necessary. Perhaps he thought if they went over what she'd already given him she might have more visions. She wouldn't, but these meetings seemed to be a tactic all of the MOTHER agents used. "Okay."

Andrew slid some pictures across the table to her. Not pictures of the actual Enchanted—that would have been impossible—but crisp black-and-white photos of the addresses Persinette had given him. "These are the locations you've supplied in Maximus. Right now, we have a mermaid, a vampire, and a wood nymph on our list for Collection. Is that it?"

Persinette wrinkled her brow as if she were trying to remember something. Then she nodded. "Yes, for now, that's all I have. But I still have another month to have more visions." She did her best to sound hopeful. As if there were nothing more in the world that she wanted than to help Andrew Collect as many Enchanted as possible. As if she weren't lying like her life depended on it—because it did. She slid the photos back to him, expression carefully neutral.

The agent gave a curt nod as he tucked the photos into the folder. "I do hope we actually Collect some this time. It's bizarre that even though we have come close enough to see the Enchanted you've indicated, we are never close enough to Collect them." His tone was offhanded, but his dark eyes flicked over her face with unmistakable suspicion. "Don't you think?"

Persi folded her narrow shoulders inward in an attempt to make herself too small for him to notice her. When that didn't seem to work, she swallowed hard and shrugged. "Well, I mean, it's not like MOTHER goes unnoticed when they move into a city or town." It wasn't a lie, but she could still hear her heart hammering against her ribs as she uttered the words. She hoped he didn't hear it too.

Andrew eyed her for a half a second too long, and she felt the beginnings of sweat gathering at the nape of her neck. "Very true," he responded finally. "I suppose we'll have to be stealthier this time." Then he lowered his attention to make more notes on his papers and spoke without looking up. "You are dismissed."

Persinette stood on shaking legs as she did everything in her power to remember to breathe. He knew. She could see it in his eyes. He knew she was lying. The question was... did he know *why* she was lying?

And if he did know why, then how long before he did something about it?

SURPRISINGLY ENOUGH, the run to the training arena calmed Persi a little. She listened to the repetitive thud of her heart beating in her eardrums and allowed herself to feel the breaths coming deeper and more steadily as her mind cleared. By the time she reached the arena and its clusters of fighting agents, she had decided that of *course* the Uprising would have a plan to deal with something like this. Manu had promised her that he would help her. He'd sworn up and down that he wouldn't let anything happen to her. She'd have to have faith in him.

"Took you long enough," Agnes drawled from where he sat, rolling his sleeves up over his forearms. She wasn't sure how he'd gotten there before her and concluded it was better not to ask. "Let's get started, shall we?" He peeled off his well-tailored waistcoat.

Persi bobbed her head, swept her lavender hair out of the way, and moved to the center of the mat. "Hand-to-hand?"

"Yes." Agnes faced her, and Persinette fell into the fighting stance.

He attacked in one precise motion, a quick jab to her stomach. Persinette spun such that he hit her hip instead. And thus a long battle of wills began. Agnes would jab and Persinette would duck. He would kick and she would block. But Persi remained defensive the entire time, merely reacting to Agnes's attempts to knock her off her feet, and never actively attacking him.

Finally, Agnes fell back and glared at her. "What the hell are you doing?"

"I'm training." She frowned. Her hands fell away from their protective positions and her stance loosened. "I'm doing what you taught me."

"No, you're acting like a punching bag! Do you want to be a punching bag your whole life, 11-24-10?" Agnes struck out at her again. This time he landed a hard punch to her shoulder that brought a whimper from her lips and sent her feet stumbling backward, tangling one over the other until she hit the mat. But that wasn't enough. Agnes kicked her swiftly in the hip. "Get up! Do you want to survive out there? Get up and fight!"

"I-I-I can't!" Persi sobbed, struggling to get away from

him as he kicked at her ribs and ripped a yelp from her lips. "Leave me alone!"

Agnes snarled and yanked her to her feet by the collar of her shirt. "You're a worthless punching bag who deserves every bad thing that has ever happened. *Useless* is what you are. Gothel is going to send you to the camps, and you're going to die there like just another nameless, useless—"

A sob fell from Persinette's throat as something within her finally snapped. One small hand tightened into a fist, and before she could stop herself, she punched Agnes right in the nose with every last ounce of her might. He dropped her immediately, his hands flying to hold his nose and his astonished eyes watering in pain.

"That's enough," she said quietly and got to her feet.

"Again." Agnes dropped his hands from his face to reveal a red and bruised—but still intact—nose.

"Wh-wh-what?" she sputtered.

"I said *again*. Plant your feet and fight me just like that. Like you mean it. Like your life depends on it. Because one day it might."

Taking a deep breath, Persinette nodded and did as she was bid. The next time Agnes lunged at her, she didn't just deflect the blow; she landed one of her own as well. She learned quickly how he left himself open when he attacked, and how to use that opening to her advantage. It was either learn or let him kick her again, and she had had enough of that.

When Persinette finally limped back to her quarters, she was exhausted, but she felt a deep sense of determination. She would save as many people as possible, even if it killed her, and at least now, she thought she might stand a chance.

"HE'S JUST BLUSTERING, Persi. Don't let him get into your head," Manu assured her. She was eager to soak up any comfort he might provide, but in truth, she knew there was nothing he could do to erase her fear. Her fear sat at the back of her mind like a block of stinky cheese on a shelf—slowly making everything else reek until she became numb to the smell.

"Well, he wouldn't be blustering if he didn't suspect something," Benard piped up from where somewhere in Manu's cabin.

"You're not helping, Benard," Manu growled. He glared at the goblin, who was carrying a stack of balled-up shirts. "What are you even doing in here? Isn't Owen waiting for you somewhere?"

"I am helping, sir. You haven't done laundry in at least two weeks, and you don't want to go off on a mission in rumpled shirts, do you?" The goblin paused only long enough to raise a brow at his captain.

In spite of her fear, her situation, and all logical sense, Persinette found herself giggling at the banter between the pair. At the sound of her laughter, Manu's eyes jerked from Benard to her. He was frowning.

"Well, he's got a point," Persi said, biting back another laugh.

"Don't you start." Manu shook a finger at her in a mock threat, which only teased another soft snicker from her lips. "You aren't supposed to take his side. That's not how this works."

"Says you." Benard put a waistcoat on a hanger. "Why don't you put these damned things away when you're done trying on everything you own?"

Manu growled again, balled up a piece of parchment, and threw it at Benard's head. It bounced off, and Benard glared at his captain.

"Rude." He narrowed his eyes.

Persi bit her lip to hold back another chortle as the exchange played out. There was a feeling of family between the pair, a feeling she'd never experienced herself, and she found herself longing to be a part it. Manu sighed and turned back to her. Lifting a tanned hand to rub at his temples. "We should get back to business."

"Right, business." Persi nodded.

"As I was saying—before I was so rudely interrupted— you have nothing to worry about. Your new handler is just trying to scare you so that you don't challenge him. Try not to let him bother you too much." Manu's tone was confident. He knew without a sliver of a doubt that Persinette would be all right. Or he sounded like he did, anyway.

"Still..." Persi sucked in a deep inhale, wishing that she could be half as confident that Andrew was just fishing. As Benard had said, Andrew wouldn't be fishing if he didn't suspect something. "I would like you to bring it up with the Uprising Leader, please. So that we're all on the same page."

"Eddi? You want me to tell Eddi that your handler is itching to catch someone?" Manu's brows rose as he shook his head. "I don't know if that's a good idea, Pers."

"Regardless, you had better!" Benard shouted from somewhere out of sight.

"Are you telling your captain what to do, sir?" Manu called back, sounding more than a little irritated.

"Please," Persi said. "I don't want anyone to end up in the camps, but Andrew's gunning for results. So maybe if one of the agents could—I don't know, get caught and then escape?" She exhaled as freckled fingers moved to tug at the end of her braid. Guilt crept up her spine at the idea of crew members putting themselves in that kind of jeopardy for her. "That's...that's horrible of me. Forget I said anything," she said hurriedly. How could she have even suggested such a thing? Her life was in no way any more important than any of the Uprising agents. She shouldn't ask them to volunteer for courting death just to save her skin. Persi's eyes fell to the desk in front of her as she felt Manu's gaze survey her. She was sure all he could think was how utterly horrible she was.

"I'll bring it up," Manu said finally. "Look at me." Persi lifted her head and met his dark eyes. "I promised you that I would do whatever I had to do to keep you safe, remember?"

Persi nodded and released a relieved sigh. "Maybe you're right. Maybe he's just trying to scare me."

"Even still. Better safe than sorry," Benard remarked from over Manu's shoulder. "And don't you worry Miss Persi. We'll keep you safe." He winked one glowing green eye.

Persi smiled at Benard's image as it floated on the glass of the mirror. "Thank you, Benard. I very much appreciate both of you."

Manu rolled his eyes and half-gently pushed Benard out of view. "You really have nothing to worry about, no matter what Benard may think. I have little doubt that this mission is going to go off without a hitch. Your handler will very well be so impressed that he may even give you a medal!" He chuckled.

Now it was Persi's turn to roll her eyes. "I don't think he's going to do that, but maybe at least he'll keep me around long enough to help some more people," she said.

That was the best that she could hope for, she supposed: to evade notice long enough to make a difference. She knew that she couldn't give Andrew Gothel the slip forever, certainly not long enough to see the end of MOTHER, but if she could at least help *some* people before she was dragged off to the camps...that would be something.

"You're going to be all right, Persinette," Manu said, breaking her daydream.

"We've got your back, Miss Persi!" Benard had appeared in the room again.

"Thank you. Both of you." In spite of her fear, she laughed softly.

26

CAPTAIN MANU KELII

IT WAS the dead of night when the *Defiant Duchess* arrived in Hugo. Her captain and crew docked her quietly on the outskirts of town, where she would hopefully remain unnoticed until they left for Maximus.

"And you're sure Ivy's anti-curses will work?" Benard asked, casting a wary look at Manu.

"No, I'm not," the captain answered as he brushed a lock of dark hair back from his handsome face. "I'm not sure about anything as far as this mission goes."

"But?"

"But we have no other options. We either trust Ivy, or we leave Persinette to find some more useful spells in the MOTHER library and hope for the best." His eyes flicked over to Ivy who stood a few paces away, giving her Unit instructions for while she wasn't on board.

"Right, no good options." Benard nodded.

Manu nodded as well and tore his suspicious gaze from Ivy. "You know what your orders are if things go south?"

"Yes, sir. But let's try to keep that from happening, shall we?" The first mate offered Manu a mischievous grin.

Manu snorted. "I'll do my level best."

"You do that, sir. And remember if she gets out of line —" The words cut off as Benard's eyes lowered to the pistol on Manu's hip.

"Oh, I hardly think it'll come to that, will it, Captain?" Ivy had appeared at Benard's side, her arm flung around the goblin's shoulders for a hug that looked rather unwanted. "We're going to be just fine, Benard. Your captain is in good hands. Trust me." She gave them both a wink and planted a kiss on Benard's cheek that left the goblin scowling.

"That's enough teasing, Ivy. Let's go." With a sigh, Manu strode toward the platform that would lower them to the ground in Hugo.

"Are you sure you don't want to take extra men, sir?" Owen drew to Benard's side, his tall frame engulfing the Goblin in a reassuring half-hug.

"Quite sure," Manu said. "The fewer people there, the less likely we are to get caught. You two just keep the ship idling so we can get out of here in a hurry if need be." The order flowed smoothly from his lips. Manu was finding himself more and more comfortable with his authority as captain. It was strange that it took him these many years to feel like he was in complete control of his inherited ship, but now that he felt that way he wasn't going back.

"Yes, sir." Owen bowed his head in respect.

Manu stepped onto the platform, with Ivy close behind, just before it began to lower.

MANU FOLLOWED Ivy through the sleeping city streets of Hugo. They had docked the *Duchess* strategically on the opposite side of the small city—closer to Maximus, but further away from Maeve's house. The only trouble with that plan was that they had to make their way to Maeve's before the sun rose.

Still, the streets were blessedly empty, and so the captain and the witch made quick work of the distance between the ship and the small hut on the outskirts of town.

"Is that it?" Manu asked as his eyes fell on the tiny cabin. "It doesn't look like much." He wrinkled his nose. From the outside, the one-room hut seemed to be nothing more than a shack. A shack that very well might fall down around the ears of whoever tried to enter it. A shack that in no way resembled the home of a powerful witch. The only person Manu could imagine living there was some sort of wizened hermit.

Ivy scoffed. "No, it doesn't *look* like much, but trust me, Maeve is good at hiding the truth of things. It's one of her specialties." She closed her eyes and pressed her palms together. As she concentrated, the pale green magic began to wind itself around her in a sparkling stream. She murmured words under her breath, the stream spun tighter and tighter around her until finally her dark eyes flew open, glowing softly with resonating power. "This way," she ordered.

Manu watched with healthy skepticism as she set off in a wide circle around the little hut. "Where are we going?"

The witch glared at him. "The safest route. Now come on. The longer you stand there, the more likely her wards are to notice you." She spoke over her shoulder, still walking and not bothering to check if he was following.

"Oh, right, of course." Manu moved reluctantly but carefully in her footsteps. Together, they crept slowly around the little hut to a back door that was creaking off its hinges in the breeze. "Are you sure she even still lives here? It looks abandoned," Manu whispered.

Ivy's gleaming eyes fixed him with a death glare. "Will you shut up and just trust me?" She lifted her arms, palms up, and blew softly above her hands. As her breath mingled with the air, it formed into a small glowing green canary, which twittered bitterly at Manu as it cut him what seemed like a birdy glare. Ivy's lips twitched and she addressed the bird. "Now, none of your sass, little miss." The glowing creature peeped petulantly and cocked its head at her. "You know the drill. In you go."

The bird gave one more irritated chirp before hopping off Ivy's hands and flying toward the creaking door.

"Now what?" Manu asked, shifting antsily from foot to foot.

"Now we wait." Ivy crossed her arms.

Manu narrowed his gaze at the creaking door. "I'm not very good at waiting."

"Well, this will be good practice, then."

SECONDS TICKED BY INTO MINUTES, and the longer they stood there, the more uncomfortable and impatient Manu became. "Stop fidgeting," Ivy muttered. Her eyes were still fixed on the spot where the bright canary had disappeared.

"How much longer?" Manu asked as he rocked back and forth on his heels in an attempt to disperse the boredom and anxiety vying for control of his body.

"It's only been a couple of minutes." Ivy released her hard gaze just long enough to shoot him a look of annoyance. "Just be patient."

"I don't know *how* to be patient," Manu grumbled.

"Clearly."

The captain opened his mouth to scold her, but his incipient tirade was cut off by the reappearance of the bird. "Took her long enough," he said instead.

The bird cheeped peevishly and perched on Ivy's shoulder.

"Well, you *did* take a long time," Manu said, suddenly feeling defensive enough to argue with a magic bird.

"Enough." Ivy plucked the bird from her shoulder and released it into the air once more. "Show us the way."

A soft twitter of agreement left the bright green bird and it flew back toward the house, where it hovered at the door, waiting for them.

"Are we supposed to just follow it blindly?" Manu asked. "Even after it yelled at me like that?"

The witch sighed. "You can stay here if you want, but I'm going in to get the hair." She followed the bird to the door and into the space beyond.

Manu stared at the darkened doorway for a moment before he followed, but not without a huff. "Hey, wait for me!" He jogged after Ivy, slipping past the swinging door and into a barely lit room. Across from him, a long narrow hallway that looked nothing like the run-down outside stretched into the depths of the hut. About midway up the walls, a row of flickering orange sconces provided the only light, revealing ornate purple wallpaper bedecked with swirling black patterns that whirled and winked as Manu hurried past. "This doesn't look like somewhere a hoarder would live," he said.

"Don't be fooled. Maeve has appearances to keep up," Ivy said from in front of him, still following the little bird.

The canary had stopped to tweep-tweep noisily at random point on the right side of the wall.

"Appearances for who?"

"For clients, of course. No witch worth her salt lets her clients see the mess that comes with magic." Ivy cocked her head at the swirling wall. "This must be it."

"Must be what? It's just a wall." He blinked as the pattern on the wall moved again, making his eyes cross. "Gods, how can she stand this wallpaper? It's horror on the eyes."

"It's meant to keep people disoriented, so they don't see the doors." Ivy grabbed a doorknob Manu hadn't even seen and pushed open a door he also hadn't seen. "Really clever trick. Too bad I taught it to her."

"Of course you did." Manu sighed and followed her into another dimly lit room. This time the lights flickered in a faint green color that tinged the place with a sickly glow. And instead of another neatly kept hallway, Manu found himself in a room surrounded by mounds and mounds of what was, for lack of a better word, junk: mountains of trash, broken potion bottles, ripped book pages, and even old magazines from the era before Daiwynn. "Now how do we find a single hair in all of this garbage?" he cried.

"It won't be here in *all this*," Ivy said condescendingly. "It'll be in her personal collection."

"So, this isn't her...personal collection?" Manu's eyes caught on a rolled-up poster of what looked like a half-naked woman.

Ivy snorted. "Hardly. This way." She darted between two mountains so massive that Manu had thought they were a single, extra-large mound.

As Manu took a step after her, a screeching whistle rent the air and the mountains of garbage began to grow, and grow, and grow. No. Wait. *He was shrinking*! "Ivy! IVY! Change me back! Help me!" he shouted as what looked to be a huge aluminum can with a blue and red logo it loomed over him. Ivy spun around, her giant foot almost crushing the tiny captain. "HEY! Watch it!"

Ivy's massive eyes flicked down to him and she released a delighted cackle that was now boomingly loud. "I have to say, Captain, this is a good look for you. You're positively adorable." She bent down, plucked Manu up by the back of his shirt, and planted his tiny boots on her palm. "You know, I could put you in my pocket, and no one would ever be the wiser. Or just leave you here and tell your crew you died valiantly in the line of battle. I doubt they'd believe me, though."

"Turn me back!" Manu whined.

"Tsk, tsk, Captain. I hardly think you're in any position to be giving orders now." One pale finger gave the top of his head a patronizing pat, which he swatted away with a growl. "Still, you'll never trust me if I do that, will you?" With that, she unceremoniously dumped him out of her palm.

As he tumbled down, down, down to the ground, the tiny captain released a scream that grew into a bellow. When his feet finally hit the floor, Manu found himself looking down on Ivy once more as she finished murmuring the spell he supposed had saved him. He snapped his mouth shut mid-scream. "Do you think I woke her?"

"Probably not. Woman sleeps like a log. But even still, we should keep moving." Ivy grabbed his hand and dragged him through a maze of piles: old magazines, newspapers, and books in languages he couldn't pronounce.

Finally, they emerged from the junk labyrinth and reached a large wooden door with a heavy lock on it. Ivy's little canary squeaked annoyingly before flew from her shoulder to the bolt and into the keyhole. A soft click echoed through the silence and the door creaked open. Beyond that lay a circular room full of bookshelves, themselves full of little vials, that covered every inch of the wall and extended so high that a ladder stood in the middle of the floor to reach the upper levels. Manu craned his neck to take in the rungs of the ladder—up, up, up—and his jaw dropped. The thing seemed to disappear into the atmosphere. "Hell, how will we find the hair in here?"

"Oh, how you underestimate me, Captain. Would I have come in here if I didn't know exactly where the hair was?" Ivy walked to the ladder and set a foot against the first rung

"Maybe?"

"Just shut up and hold the ladder."

"Right." He shut up, held the ladder, and waited. Ivy climbed up several rungs—at least a foot above Manu's head —before she seemed to find what she was looking for, grab it off the shelf, and descend toward him.

"Now, let's get the hell out of here before she wakes up." The moment one of Ivy's well-polished boots hit the floor, a rumble sounded overhead. The pair looked up. A sheer wave of magic was barreling down right for them.

Ivy let out an *eep*, and Manu wasted no time. He grabbed her and dragged her from the room. Together, they raced through the piles of antiques from a forgotten era, which were now teetering dangerously. "Run faster, Ivy! We have to get out of here!" Manu shouted above the roar as he launched himself toward the door. When they were both back in the hall, panting hard, Manu looked down toward the way he was sure they'd come, but saw nothing but hallway. The swirling wallpaper and glowing sconces seemed to stretch on forever. "Now how do we get out?"

Ivy shrugged. "I don't know."

"Excuse me?" Panic laced Manu's voice. "You had all these plans to get in and none to get *out*?"

"I thought getting out would be the easy part!" Ivy argued. "Let's just start opening doors. I'm sure we'll find the way out eventually."

"EVENTUALLY?"

Ivy huffed and folded her arms. "Look, I got us in here, *and* I got the hair." She held aloft the vial containing a long strand of red hair aloft. "You do something!"

"Like what? Sniff out the exit?"

"Yes! Exactly! Do that!"

"I am not a bloodhound, Warner," the captain growled, his eyes flashing golden with irritation.

"No, but you should at the very least be able to follow your own scent back to the door. Shouldn't you?" She sounded decidedly hopeful.

He blinked at her. "I mean, in theory," he said. "I've never actually used that particular ability before. There's never been much call for it."

"Well now's as good a time to try as any, isn't it? Before Maeve finds us, preferably!"

Manu rolled his eyes, but opened his mouth a little, inhaling the scent of the hall. There was the cakey scent of dust, the tangy taste of magic, but above all of that, there was the distinctive note of himself and Ivy. Once he had the smell, he followed it, with Ivy close behind him. The trail faded abruptly right below a sconce that looked just like every other damn sconce along the hall, but when Ivy reached out, a doorknob appeared. With some struggle, the door swung open, revealing the shabby lot surrounding Maeve's hut.

"Good job Kelii!" Ivy cheered, to Manu's surprise.

Manu grunted a response, and they hastened to put some distance between themselves and Maeve's hut of horrors.

EDDI WAS WAITING for Manu when he returned from the mission. The Uprising Leader's wrinkled face looked very much like that of a disgruntled pug dog as their eerily magnified eyes took in the young captain's disheveled appearance. Manu did his best not to look guilty and sat in the chair opposite the crackling screen. "Eddi, what a pleasant surprise."

"Where have you been, Captain?" Eddi asked sharply. Those abnormally magnified eyes pinned him to the spot and dared him to lie.

"Oh, you know me, Eddi." Manu grinned. "Just off at the bars scoping out the latest in Daiwynn's fine cocktails."

The Uprising Leader blinked their bug-like eyes. "Uh huh."

"Don't you believe me?" Manu asked. "I'm hurt, Eddi! Hurt!" He clutched his chest dramatically.

After another hard, searching stare, Eddi appeared to let this go and move on. "Benard mentioned that Persinette's handler indicated that their unit was to Collect an Enchanted on this upcoming mission. Yes?"

"Yes. That was Persi's concern." Manu sat up a little straighter in his seat. "But she also does not want anyone sacrificing themselves for her. Her thought was that perhaps someone would get captured and then escape before were taking all the way back to MOTHER HQ."

Silence fell once more. Eddi blinked, seeming to process the information. "That won't be possible," was all that left those thin lips.

"What?" Surely Manu had heard wrong. Surely Eddi couldn't mean there was nothing they could do to help Persinette. "What do you mean?"

"I mean that if one of ours is captured to save your Asset's ass, then that person will have to be processed and sent to the camps before escaping. There will be no coming back from it any earlier. The person we choose will effectively be going on a suicide mission."

Manu frowned. He realized what it meant. He had a choice to make: Persinette's life or someone else's. Whose meant more to him? He had to think. And would Persinette be angry at him for making this choice for her? Very likely. Still, he found himself nodding. "Fin. Who do you have on the shortlist for something like that?"

"Are you in Maximus already?" Eddi asked, their dark head of bob-cut hair had ducking to consult some bit of paper on the desk.

"Very nearly, we're about two and a half days out." The words left Manu easily without the hint of a lie—because they were not a lie. They were, in fact, two and a half days or so from Maximus. He just didn't specify in which direction.

"Right, then, I'm sending you an address. There is an agent in a town near Maximus. His name is Sullivan. You'll meet him before the upcoming Collection. He'll act as your bait." With a light clicking and whirring, the printer beside Manu spat out an address. "He's on the list of people who've volunteered to go inside."

The fact that there was a list of people who had volunteered to infiltrate the camps shouldn't have surprised Manu, and yet it did—likely because he couldn't see *himself* ever making such a sacrifice. Especially, if it was for someone he had never met. Manu Kelii liked to think of himself as far too selfish for such a thing.

Eddi was still rattling off instructions, but he had mostly stopped paying attention at that point. He had an address and a name—what else did he need? After a while, he realized that Eddi had decided that the call was over and terminated the link, because he looked up to find the screen empty.

"What did Eddi have to say, Cap'n?" Benard's question made Manu jump and frown. He hadn't even heard the first mate enter.

"We have a new heading," he responded, and cleared his throat. He handed the paper with the address to Benard and waited. It would take them more than two and a half days to reach the location, but they would still make it in enough time to get back to Maximus for the Collection.

Benard took the paper so that he could look at the address and nodded. "Who are we meeting here?"

"An agent who will help us maintain Persi's cover," Manu said quietly.

Benard took a moment before he nodded. He walked deliberately to the control panel to set the new heading. "I'm glad Miss Persi will be safe."

"Yes, but for how long?" The question left Manu before he could stop it, fear clawing at his insides. "How many more of ours will we have to sacrifice to keep her safe? How many more will Eddi be willing to sacrifice for her?" His eyes flickered golden as his control over the beast slid away from him. "And you know, you just *know* she's not going to like this."

A sigh left the goblin as he moved before his captain once more. He met Manu's eyes. "No, she will not like this. But this is the only solution we have for her at present, and she'll have to deal with that." The first mate's words were soft but firm, and above all else, they were right—this was their only option to keep Persinette safe.

"Gods, you're annoying." Manu chuckled.

"I'm sorry, sir?" Benard stared at his captain in confusion.

"You always have to be right, don't you?" The captain let another small laugh relax the tension that had settled between his broad shoulders.

A chortle left Benard's full lips. He shook his head. "It would seem that is my lot in life, sir."

Manu sighed. He leaned back in his chair, brushing his fingertips through his neatly coiffed black hair. "I just...I don't know how I'm going to tell her, is all." He hated how his voice sounded much smaller than it ever had before. Yet he hated more how he *himself* felt smaller than he had in a very long time—not since he was that lost little boy Benard and Owen had found.

"You'll find a way sir. You always do."

27

PERSINETTE

PERSINETTE'S HEART plummeted when those words left Manu's lips. She knew that they would haunt her for the rest of her life.

"I'm sorry, what?" She sent up a silent prayer that perhaps she'd just misheard him. Although she knew that someone needed to sacrifice themselves so she could stay safe, she had still hoped, with an overwhelming part of herself, that no one would volunteer. With all the blood already on her hands, she wanted to save people by helping the Uprising, not ask people to surrender themselves to the same fate as the others she tried to rescue.

"I'll be meeting with an agent in two days who has agreed to deliver himself to MOTHER so that we can maintain your cover," Manu repeated slowly.

"No!" The word left Persi in an angry shout. Her eyes flashed and she felt the magic inside of her responding to her upset. She glimpsed the tiny sparks of purple magic glimmering off her hands, and she swallowed, trying to calm herself. "Th-there has to be another way," she said more evenly.

The captain's dark eyes pinched shut and he rubbed his jaw with a sigh. "I'm afraid there isn't," he said. Tired lines creased his face as he met her eyes again. "If we're going to maintain your cover and continue to save innocent lives, we have to be willing to make sacrifices."

Persi's hair fell into her burning eyes as she shook her head quickly. "I can't ask that of another person."

"Well, you aren't asking. He volunteered." Manu's tone had gone from tired to a little grumpy in seconds, and the change brought a frown to Persi's face.

"I'm sorry. I didn't mean to upset you," she said. In all of the time, she had known Manu—which admittedly hadn't been that long—he had never been anything but sweet, or occasionally impish, with her before.

His lips twitched into a grimace, marring the handsome face she'd become so familiar with. "No, I'm sorry. I shouldn't have snapped at you," he murmured. "There is just a lot going on, and I wish I could make you feel better about this."

She nodded in understanding. "Did Eddi say anything else?"

"Nothing. But it seems there is a plan in place. I don't know what it is—they never tell me half of what's going on—but I feel like they're up to something. Sullivan, the person who volunteered, is sacrificing himself for a reason."

Persinette inhaled deeply to calm herself. "Then I hope none of this is in vain."

"As do I." Manu looked down at something on his desk then back up at her. "I should have more details about where we have him set up once we pick him up and get to Maximus. Until then, please try to get some rest?" His words were quiet, pleading.

"I'll try," she promised. "Good night, Manu."

"Good night, Pers," he replied. "Sweet dreams." He offered her a gentle smile.

Persi closed the compact, rolled onto her side, and curled up tightly around the thin pillow between her arms. He was right, of course. There was probably some other plan in the works that neither of them was privy to, but that didn't make her feel better. She laid there—for how long, she didn't know—staring through the bars of her window and into the darkness.

THE FOLLOWING morning brought training with Agnes —and he didn't go easy on her. She hadn't expected him to, and with the weeks slipping away from her, she had grown to appreciate his dedication. Of course, it was only to make himself look good. That didn't matter. Whatever is motivation, Agnes was putting everything he had into making sure that Persinette could defend herself if she needed to, and she was grateful.

The rest of the day sped by quickly—as did the rest of the week.

She supposed that it was for the better. The more quickly time passed, the less time she would have to worry about what she was going to have to do. She had sacrificed countless other lives in the name of keeping herself alive, but this was somehow different. She wasn't sure how; it just was.

That Friday, when Persinette curled up in bed, sleep evaded her. Her mind raced with everything that could and would go wrong, and when her mind finally settled, it landed on the image of a woman's pale face with black eyes, framed in dark curly hair.

It had been a while since Persi had thought about Gothel, what with everything else going on, but now there she was. For the first time since Gothel's death, Persinette allowed herself to linger on that face. Gothel had never, ever been kind to Persinette, but she had been a sort of family, strangely enough. The bitter, angry woman had been the only constant in Persinette's life since she was a child. And now—now she was just gone.

The thoughts gave way to tears as Persi allowed herself to mourn the loss of the closest thing to a family she'd ever had. Had Gothel ever loved her? No. But the truth was, *no one* had ever really loved her, except maybe Wyn. Soft tears became sobs as the loneliness threatened to engulf her.

When she woke up in the morning, she felt sore and groggy. Everything from her head to her toes ached. She pulled herself from her bed to prepare for the day ahead anyway. With a meeting with Andrew scheduled for early that morning, she had no time to waste.

Her meetings with Andrew had become more frequent than she would have liked, but still, she had no choice. So she dragged herself to the conference room to settle across from him at the table.

"Have you anything new for me, Persinette?" he asked once she had been seated. The question constantly loomed over her. Three weeks had passed, and he asked this of her every day—sometimes twice a day. All she could hope was that the remainder of her six weeks until the mission would go by quickly.

"Not yet, Andrew." Persi bowed her head in what she hoped would be perceived as respect.

She felt those dark eyes on her, the ones that were at once eerily similar to his sister's and somehow colder than hers had ever been. "I do hope you'll have something for us soon. Collecting only a handful of Enchanted in Maximus would be very disappointing to MOTHER—and to me."

Gulping, Persinette forced herself to meet his eyes. "I understand," she said.

Andrew's handsome face was arranged into an expression of what, to a person who didn't know any better, might have looked like compassion. "I'm sure you're trying your best," he said bracingly. "But might I suggest less time in the library?"

Persinette wrinkled her brow. "I use that time to research the area in the hopes that it'll stir a vision," she explained, the lie flowing from her lips with well-practiced ease. "My library hours were already cut as it is, to accommodate my training schedule."

""Yes, and now I believe you should focus more on your visions and training. I'll have the on-staff librarian deliver books about Maximus to your rooms in the Tower. That way you'll have fewer distractions. Aside from that, for the time being, your library privileges have been revoked. That is all." Andrew said nothing more—and didn't try to act like he cared—as he ducked his head to the papers before him.

Persinette felt her heart sink to the floor.

Revoked.

How was she going to learn any more spells? How was she going to strengthen her magic to the point that she could protect herself? How was she ever going to escape MOTHER?

She wouldn't. That was the short answer.

Nodding grimly, Persi left the room. The door shut with a hiss behind her and she forced her chin upwards. She would just focus on the handful of spells she had in her rooms already and learn to bend her magic to her will as best she could. It was the only hope she had.

"Persi!"

Persinette turned to find Elwyn running after her. She forced a smile. "Wyn!"

Wyn's dark eyes flicked over every inch of Persi's face before she sighed. "He's told you," she said flatly. There was no question; it was a statement, a simple fact. "I'm so sorry, Persi. I told them they didn't need to do that."

Persi shrugged as she started down the corridor. "It's not your fault. I suppose I'm lucky I was allowed to use the library this long. They could have revoked my access right after the first mission."

"It still doesn't seem fair." Wyn kept in step with Persi, shaking her head. "You're just trying to do what you're supposed to—have visions!"

"I know, but it's fine." It wasn't, but Persinette knew that nothing she said or did was going to change matters. Making Wyn feel bad wouldn't help.

Wyn leaned her tall frame in for a hug around the shoulders and a kiss pressed to Persi's freckles. "Hey now, don't look so down! If you have any special requests, just let me know. I can probably get them for you."

And there it was, warm like the sun—a glimmer of hope. Persi looked at Wyn thoughtfully. Could she ask this of her friend? To put her neck on the line for a favor? And if Persi *did* ask for what she really needed, how would she ask without setting off any alarms in Wyn's mind? Maybe if she just played it off as a passing interest, like her curiosity about history of horses when she was thirteen. "Even spell books?" she asked in a hushed tone, so no one would overhear them.

Wyn stopped dead in the middle of the hall. Her eyes widened and her mouth opened a little. Persi's heart sank for the second time in barely twenty minutes. This was it;

this was how she got caught. "What would you need those for, Pers?" the librarian asked carefully.

Persi thought faster than she ever had in her life. Her survival depended on the next words that left her lips, and so she needed a lie—a good lie. Letting out a heavy sigh, she let her shoulders sag. "They won't let me have a weapon when I go out there, Wyn." She ducked her head in shame as the words left her barely above a whisper. The shame, at least, was real. She didn't like lying to her only friend, but she also didn't feel like she had a choice. Persi either learned enough magic to protect herself and escape MOTHER, or she would die here—very likely sooner than later.

So she swallowed down the guilt and continued. "I need to be able to protect myself out there. What if...what if..." She wasn't sure if she was stuttering on purpose or if she was just having a hard time lying, but her hesitation seemed to have helped. Wyn's suspicious look had changed to one of pity. "What if one of those creatures attacks me?" she finished, feeling the bile rise in her throat. Talking about Enchanted like that made Persinette feel sick, but drastic times called for even more drastic measures.

She waited for a beat to see if it took, and when Wyn leaned in to hug her tightly, she allowed herself to breathe again. "Okay. But only protection spells, right? Just defensive—shields and stuff. Promise?" Wyn's voice was serious.

"Promise," Persi agreed.

Wyn nodded and pulled back as they started waking once more. "I'll sneak a couple into your stacks tonight. But Pers..." Her dark eyes met Persi's in earnest. "Be careful. If you get caught with them, we'll both be in a world of trouble."

Persinette threw her arms around Wyn in a grateful hug. "I know, Wyn. I'll be careful."

WHEN PERSINETTE DRAGGED herself back to her rooms after training with Agnes that evening, a stack of books was waiting on the table next to her chair. "Wyn kept her promise," she said with a small smile. Now, she'd have to keep up her end of the bargain—or part of it at least—and ensure no one found out. If Persi accomplished nothing else, she wanted to keep her friend safe, at least.

With tired eyes, she skimmed over the titles to see what Wyn had selected for her. There were geological maps of Maximus, a history of the city, and what looked to be a book of the most recent censuses. In the middle of the stack was a single, thin, volume with a cracked purple spine. It couldn't have been more than twenty pages. Persi pulled it from the stack carefully, her fingers brushing reverently over the wordless front cover.

She inhaled sharply and flipped it open. There, on the first page where a title ought to be, was just the word *spells* written in scrawling handwriting. Kicking off her boots, Persi settled into the chair. Her index finger ran slowly over the word for a moment—imagining the witch who might have written it—before she began to flip through the pages to browse everything now at her fingertips.

The pages held a few spells she had already worked with: fire messages, creating flames, and even the levitation incantations. But there were others still she'd never seen before. One, in particular, caught her eye: a shield charm. Persi murmured the words, foolishly hoping that maybe something would happen the first time she tried it. But nothing did, which seemed to be the way of things when she first started working with new magic.

A couple of hours whizzed by as she worked with the

charm. She would reach for the magic, call it to her hand, and say the words. Slowly, a shield began to form. First, it was just a tiny plate of glimmering armor that would do very little to protect anyone, but the more she practiced, the bigger and more steadily it grew.

When Persi finally forced her tired body to bed, she pulled the compact from under her pillow to call Manu. Somewhere along the line, this had become routine. She would spend the entire day working herself into weariness, and then in the evening, she would call the captain. The regularity of it relaxed her.

"Have you met up with him yet?" she asked as soon as Manu's face appeared in the glass. A part of her hoped that maybe the agent who had volunteered simply wouldn't show up. Then she wouldn't have to deal with the guilt of his sacrifice.

One finely sculpted dark brow rose up the captain's handsome face at her question. "Am I not enough for you now, Persi? Must you have more men in your life?" He sounded playfully scandalized as his hand went to his heart. "Truly, I'm heartbroken! How will I survive?"

Persinette giggled at his dramatics. She rolled her eyes and she shook her head fondly. "You know what I mean."

A chuckle left the captain. His hand fell away from his chest and he nodded. "Yes, I do know what you mean. We are in the town now and are scheduled to pick him up tomorrow. I'm sure he's absolutely delightful, as most Uprising agents are," he muttered sarcastically.

"Aren't they? I mean...they're the good guys, right? And you've had a whole unit on your ship for a while now." Persi didn't quite understand what he meant. The Uprising was trying to save people—that's what she'd thought, anyway. That's why she had joined forces with them to try to combat

MOTHER. But the longer she thought about it, the more she realized that maybe there weren't any real good guys in this fight. Maybe there was just a bunch of okay guys trying to make the world better for their own kind.

The captain closed his dark eyes for a moment, his brows wrinkling. When he opened them again, he seemed to have made up his mind about something. "Of course we're the good guys, Pers. It's just that sometimes even the good guys can be a little more extreme than they need to be."

"Extreme." She repeated the word slowly, trying to grasp his meaning completely. "You aren't in trouble are you, Manu?"

He gave a nervous laugh and a less-than-casual shrug. "No more than usual, my dear. No more than usual."

Persi scrutinized his features, trying to decipher his real feelings. But she couldn't, and exhaled in frustration. "Extreme how?"

"Oh, you know," he said breezily, clearly trying to brush off the topic.

"No, I don't know. I've never met any Uprising Agents other than you and your crew." Persi made a point to meet his eyes; she wasn't going to let him wriggle out of this one. She needed to know, *now*, if she was working with the right people.

The captain let out a harsh sounding exhale, his proud posture slumping a bit. "They'll do what it takes to save as many of our kind as possible, and it doesn't matter to them what they have to sacrifice for that. Which means that sometimes they might do things that someone as honest and good as you would find morally questionable."

"Oh." The word left her in a breath. She felt her body

sag, suddenly even more exhausted. "What about the ones on your ship?"

"Ivy and her gang are all right..." Manu let the words drift off with a little shrug.

"But?" she prompted.

"But there have been a few threats of mutiny since they joined my ship. Nothing serious. Let's move on?" His tone was almost pleading, and she couldn't find it in herself to keep pumping him for information.

Instead, Persi changed the subject. "Okay. Tell me about this Agent Sullivan?"

"I don't know. I haven't met him. But he's probably an asshole." Manu sounded petulant.

Now it was Persi's turn to chuckle. "You just don't want me to like him as much as I like you," she teased gently.

He snorted. "Please! As if anyone could be as charming or handsome as Captain Manu Kelii!"

Persi found herself laughing—honestly laughing—for the first time in what felt like decades. From there the conversation descended into lighthearted banter and silliness. All of which, Persinette realized, she desperately needed.

28

CAPTAIN MANU KELII

A NIGHT of restless sleep yielded a tired and drawn Captain Manu Kelii at dawn. He stood before his closet mirror to assess the damage his insomnia had caused. The dark bags under his eyes and the wild hair did nothing to ease the sense of foreboding that had taken up residence his chest. Looking his best always helped him to feel better in any situation, no matter how dire. But judging by his appearance, it would seem wouldn't get that small comfort today.

He ran his long, tan fingers over the waistcoats rack, stopping at a bland, grey vest made of silk. It displayed no embellishments or trappings of any kind. It was just a plain grey vest. A deep exhale left the young captain as he made quick work of the buttons. Once dressed, he looked himself over in the mirror again. "Well, here goes nothing," he muttered to himself and straightened the vest unnecessarily. As he made his way through the *Defiant Duchess* to the loading bay, he tucked his hands deep into his pockets to keep from fidgeting.

"Are the pigs flying today, Owen?" Benard called across

the open room. Manu's eyes flicked to his first mate in irritation.

"Uh—no? Why?" Owen asked. He took in the captain's disgruntled expression, which only seemed to further his bewilderment. "I don't get it."

The captain grunted, hardening his gaze on Benard. "Is something funny, First Mate Benard?" His tone skirted edge between annoyance and all-out ire, but even he wasn't sure how much of it was genuine agitation and how much was mere anxiety. He almost wanted to laugh right along with Benard, if only to shake loose the feelings of guilt lingering in his belly.

The goblin's blank face tightened just slightly and he stood up a little taller. "Nothing sir. I just...didn't know you owned a grey suit." His thin lips twitched as he waited for Manu to break.

Normally such tactics would have worked, goading Manu to respond and lightening his mood, but today there was just too much weighing on the captain for such light-hearted jests to help. "I thought it inappropriate to wear something flashy to a meeting with a fellow agent." He tugged down on the vest once more and kept his tone gravely serious. "There is no need to draw unwanted attention to myself. Is there?"

Benard cleared his throat, the teasing gone. He seemed to realize—immediately—what was going on within Manu, as he often did. "You look very nice, sir."

With a gulp, the captain straightened his waistcoat a third, entirely unnecessary time, pulled himself up to his full height, and tipped his head at his first mate. "Thank you, Benard. You are in charge while I'm gone. Try to keep Ivy from running off with my ship, won't you?"

"Aye-aye, sir." Benard dipped into a respectful bow.

"Right, then, I'm off to meet our new crew—er—this agent." The words he'd almost said choked him, and he shook his head to try to clear it. Would that this were as simple as going to recruit another crew member—a new friend– and a part of his ever-growing makeshift family. But he was not.

No, he was going to pick up a lamb for the slaughter.

MANU DIDN'T REALIZE how utterly ridiculous that description was until he was sitting in a booth at the back of a tavern, and a very tall, muscular, dark-skinned man walked toward him. The man must have been at least six foot four—if not more—and his very presence seemed to take up the whole room. He was less of a lamb to the slaughter and more of a wolf circling the flock. All of it added up to make the hairs on the back of Manu's neck stand on end in a way that would have made any sensible person run.

Conveniently enough, Manu was not overly sensible, so he swallowed his terror and stayed put.

"Captain Kelii?" The man's voice practically vibrated through the air, smooth and velvety enough to cause anyone to forget how imposing he was.

"Sullivan?" Manu resisted the urge to stand and to close some of the height difference. He most certainly was not feeling inferior in any way, thank you very much. Not a whit.

The man—presumably Sullivan, if his silence was affir-mation—sat across the table. Manu felt the sudden need to push his chair back to put some distance between himself and the Uprising agent, but unfortunately, he'd selected a booth. He settled for crossing his arms over his chest.

"I hear you got an airship headed to Maximus?" Sullivan's words lilted through the air once more as if they were sung instead of spoken. This back-and-forth was the dance of the Uprising. Manu had danced this dance once or twice before, and by now he knew how it went.

"Maybe I am. What's it to someone like you?" Manu snorted and flagged down the waitress.

She flounced her way over. "What can I get you boys?"

"Beer," Sullivan said.

"Rum and coke," Manu ordered at the same time.

The waitress stared at them. "Run that by me again?"

"I'll take a rum and coke and he'll have a beer," Manu said. Sullivan gave a grateful nod, and the waitress walked away again.

The two men returned to sizing one another up.

"You mean a kelpie like me?" Sullivan's tone had turned cheeky as his large form leaned back in his side of the booth, completely relaxed. He seemed to swallow up space around him as he moved, and the word kelpie—well, now, at least, Manu knew why the hair on his neck had risen and everyone suddenly seemed to be avoiding looking at them.

The captain swallowed, battling the fight-or-flight reflex that was trying to take over. Kelpies had a nasty habit of ending their conversations with death, and Manu liked being alive, thank you very much. "There isn't any water around here to drown me in." The words—which trembled more than he would've liked—seemed to have left him of their own accord. He wasn't sure why he needed to tell Sullivan that.

Sullivan let out a short, loud, sharp laugh. "Don't worry

your pretty little head about that, Captain. I'm not looking to drown anyone."

A quick breath left Manu, although he told himself he hadn't been scared. He shook himself and tried to refocus on the task at hand. It was hard to remember what he was actually doing here when faced with an honest-to-gods kelpie. He'd never seen one with his own eyes before. "Then yeah, I guess I'm headed to Maximus."

"It's Sully, if you don't mind," Sullivan offered as he held out one large hand.

"A pleasure, Sully." Manu took his hand and squeezed it perhaps a little harder than necessary. Their drinks arrived, and Manu found himself feeling a little more at ease with the cool glass in his hand. "So, how'd you get into this?"

Sullivan's—Sully's—broad shoulders shrugged at the question. "I was born into it, sorta. My adopted parents were a part of it, long before they had me. I guess it was just...meant to be, yeah?"

The captain found himself nodding in understanding as he listened. He had always liked to hear people's stories of deciding to join the Uprising. Everyone had their own reasons, but since the war had been going on for so long now, he found that more and more of the Uprising's agents were second-generation fighters.

"How'd you join up?" Sully asked.

Manu shrugged half-heartedly. "About the same. After I lost my family, two pirates adopted me, and they brought me into the fold."

A little smile tugged up the kelpie's lips as he nodded. "Funny how that happens, isn't it?" he said. He twirled his glass idly, and a moment later, lifted it in a toast. "To being adopted by the right people at the right time, then."

The captain chuckled, clinked his glass to Sully's, and drank.

WHEN MANU and the kelpie finally made their way to the ship sometime later, Benard was waiting for them. His face creased with amusement as he raked his eyes over the two men, grinning crookedly without a trace of fear. Manu supposed old-as-dirt goblins weren't affected by the instinctual reaction of terror most others had to a kelpie.

"What's so funny?" Sully asked, his brows raised in curiosity.

Benard seemed unable to get words past his chortling. His glowing eyes pinched shut, and he shook his head without another word.

"Maybe because Manu looks so short next to you," Owen offered. His long strides brought him to the three other men. With a shake of his head at Benard, he turned his attention back to Manu and Sully.

Manu's eyes narrowed on the two men as he frowned. "Don't," he said brusquely. "Just don't." Then he stalked off toward his quarters, leaving his two crewmen snickering in his wake. Inhaling sharply, he turned to check if Sully was following him.

"Those must have been your dads," Sully said with a good-natured smile. "Are they always like that?"

"No. Sometimes they're worse." Manu snorted. "And yeah, I guess you *could* call them my dads."

"Well if not that, then what?"

"I don't know. I've been with them for almost twenty years now, but they've never really sought to replace my family. I just always call them Benard and Owen." Manu shrugged, leading Sully down the narrow hall toward the crew quarters. "It was a little different with us because I was already almost a teenager when they adopted me."

"Right." Sully's smile turned yet more gentle. "Mine were Hazel and Henry, and they were wonderful."

"What happened to them?" Manu asked, hoping too late that wasn't rude to ask.

The smile on Sully's face may have grown sad, but it didn't slip away. "They were human, so they did what humans do. They got old and they died." The words left him quietly, but without any to-do, as if he'd said it a million times before.

Manu gazed at Sully, wondering how long it had been since he'd lost them, but decided that would indeed be too rude to ask. "Well, you can share my Benard and Owen. Benard is going to outlive all of us, the ridiculous little goblin." He chuckled, surprised when Sully, too, released a low rumbling laugh. "We should probably go check in with Eddi."

"I mean, I guess we've gotta." The taller man winked at him, and they both laughed again.

Manu felt a strange friendship forming between them, even as he tried to tell himself getting attached a bad idea. It was only going to make sacrificing Sully for Persinette that much harder if he grew to like the kelpie. Even still, he couldn't seem to help it. Sully was just likable.

With a curt nod, Manu led the kelpie to the flight deck.

Benard had already set up the call, and Eddi was sitting there waiting for them when they entered. "You're late," the Uprising Leader announced with clear irritation.

Sullivan pulled a weathered pocket watch from his pants pocket. "I suppose we are a little behind," he said with an unbothered shrug. "But then, we had to make it look convincing that we were vetting one another before I hopped on a ship with the good Captain Kelii here." He nudged Manu in the arm, causing him to stumble a little.

"Exactly," Manu agreed, regaining balance. "We had to maintain some semblance of a cover."

The gnarled face of the Uprising Leader stayed impassive—an expression with which Manu was all too familiar. "Very well then. Let's get to business."

Both men nodded, and they each moved for the captain's chair. There was a moment of fumbling and grumbling as they both tried to sit in it. In the end, Manu sat while Sully stood behind him—crouched over a little so that he could be seen by Eddi, of course. Eddi watched the little rigmarole, no trace of amusement on that wrinkled face and no hint of a laugh from those thin lips. Just as Manu had suspected, they had no sense of humor.

"Please, do go on, sir," Manu said. Despite Eddi's gravitas, an overconfident grin threatened to take over Manu's face, and he could almost feel the kelpie behind him snickering.

Eddi lifted a greying brow—barely—before moving on. "Sullivan, you are headed for Maximus. Once there, you will be set up in an apartment that we've readied for you. Manu, I have sent your first mate the rest of the addresses we've cleared for us. I think that covers everything. Are there any questions?"

"No, sir," Sully replied.

"Good. Then I believe we are ready." Eddi's gaze flicked down to something on the desk before pinning Manu to his seat once more. "Manu, you have abandoned all attempts to find the Great Library?"

"Yes, sir," Manu lied, not missing a beat. "We are

focusing solely on the mission to maintain Persinette's cover."

Eddi stared at him for a moment longer before speaking. "Good. As I am sure you are aware, if you were to go against my orders, I would have every reason to confiscate your ship. She belongs, after all, to the Uprising. And every reason to discharge yourself and the crew from all further Uprising operations."

"Yes, sir, I am aware."

"Good," Eddi replied with a curt nod. The transmission cut off to a blank screen, and Manu scowled.

"The Great Library, huh?" Sully whistled as he stood up to his full height once more. "That's a bit of a risky heading, isn't it? Especially without the Uprising's blessing."

"Yeah, well...some people are worth the risk." Manu rose from his chair and straightened his clothes again.

The kelpie smiled as he looked down at the captain. "Yes, they are."

"You think Eddi bought it?" The question left Manu far more nervously than he would have liked.

"Probably not. They don't trust much of anyone. But..." Sully shrugged. "Not a lot you can do about it now."

"No, guess not." The captain sighed.

"What's your plan then? I assume you have one. The Great Library isn't just going to fall into your lap," Sully said.

Manu ran a hand through his hair. "There is a witch aboard who says she can track the library. So we're going to start trying to track it down after this mission in Maximus. Hopefully, then we'll have a little more free time to do it."

Sully nodded. "Well, good luck. I don't think I know of anyone who's ever found it."

"Yeah, thanks." They would need more than luck,

Manu knew, but he wasn't going to worry about that yet. They needed to get through this mission first. "Come on. I'll show you to your room." He padded across the flight deck, his soft leather boots nearly soundless, and led Sully through the corridor and down the hall toward the crew quarters. "I've got a question," Manu announced, taking even himself by surprise.

Sully cast him a doubtful look. "Okay."

"Why are you doing this?"

Another soft, sad smile split Sully's face as his eyes grew distant. After a moment of reflection, he shook his head and shrugged. "Like you said, Captain. Some people are worth risking everything for."

It wasn't a direct answer, but Manu understood.

29

PERSINETTE

"I WANT TO MEET HIM," Persinette declared.

"I'm sorry, what?" Manu halted his explanation of the overall plan. "Meet who?"

He stared at her as she sucked inhaled deeply. Persi knew he would try to dissuade her from this. She knew that he wouldn't want to add to her guilt. But she had thought a lot about it over the last few days and had realized that she needed to meet this agent. She needed to know about the man who was sacrificing his life to maintain her cover. *Sullivan.*

The captain shook his head, expression serious. "Pers, no. You don't need to do that."

"I do," she insisted. "I need to know what he's like."

"Does it matter what he's like? If you like him, it'll just make things harder knowing you're sending him to the camps. If you don't like him, you won't trust him to do his job. It's a lose-lose situation here." Manu's tone had flattened, and there was something about his eyes that looked a little sadder than usual, though she couldn't tell why.

"Do *you* trust him to complete the mission?" she asked

"I do. I think he's a good man, and he'll do everything in his power to make sure MOTHER doesn't suspect you. Can't my opinion of him be enough?"

"Your opinion is important," she said, but tightened her jaw in determination. "But I still need to meet him."

The captain sat more rigidly at her words. He didn't argue again; he merely nodded and disappeared from view for several minutes. When he returned, it was with a large, dark-skinned man who hardly seemed to fit into the frame of the mirror from far away.

"Persinette?" the man asked as he settled into the chair that Manu had just vacated.

She blinked at him wide-eyed, trying—and failing miserably—not to look as shocked as she felt. "Persi, this is Sully." Manu stepped in to provide introductions. "Now tell me he's not more handsome than I am."

The joke seemed to break Persi from her stupor. She shook her head and giggled. "It's nice to meet you, Sully. Please, call me Persi."

"Persi." He nodded and smiled warmly. "The pleasure is all mine."

"Enough of that, you two. Now you've met one another, can we go back to the discussion of the plan?" Manu sounded irritable. Perhaps because Sully had taken his chair.

Sully chuckled. "Don't worry, Manu. I'm not trying to steal your girl. I was just saying hi." The tall man winked at Persi, eliciting another bright giggle from her lips. "But I'll leave you two to your plans."

Persinette watched him stand, awed into silence by his impressive height before she remembered. "No, wait! I had a question."

"Right. Well, be quick about it before the captain blows

a gasket." Sully's teasing words earned him a glare from Manu.

"I just wanted to know that you really volunteered. You weren't...bullied into this were you?" Persi twisted her hands anxiously.

Sully gave a little snort "No, darlin', I wasn't bullied into this. I'm a kelpie; we don't get bullied into anything. Don't worry your pretty little head about that. You worry about making it look believable yeah?"

"Okay," Persi said. "I will."

"Great. Now I'll let you two get back to it. I'm sure Manu has plenty to fill you in on." The kelpie disappeared from view, and Manu threw himself back into his chair.

"I don't know...he's pretty handsome, Manu."

Manu narrowed his dark eyes and grumbled something indistinct. "You be quiet, little miss." His mock threat dissipated into laughter that they shared.

Persinette allowed the merry sound to lift her up and out of the dark hole threatening to drag her down to its depths. If she could just do this—laugh, and joke, and be happy with Manu—then perhaps she could avoid thoughts of the mission altogether.

AFTER THAT, the weeks seemed to wear on in a slow but consistent trudge. Long days of training with Agnes bled into long nights of talking with Manu and practicing spells until she had mastered them. Little by little she added names to Andrew's list of Enchanted in Maximus until one day he had a full roster.

The morning before the mission Andrew had scheduled

one final briefing, and Persinette did her best not to worry about it. She told herself that it was normal for a handler to check about any potential additional visions. His sister had done the same thing. But there was just something about a meeting with Andrew Gothel that made Persinette's stomach turn.

She took a steadying breath—in through her nose, out through her mouth—entered the room, and settled into her usual chair across from Andrew. All of this had become routine, but even the routine of it didn't calm her nerves. Nor did the fidgeting of her hands on her corset stays, or the sting of her teeth biting her cheek a little too hard.

"This briefing is just a quick check-in before we head out, no need to worry." Andrew's little smile was not reassuring, though he likely meant it to be. "All right?"

Persinette nodded, though she wasn't sure why she bothered to agree. Disagreeing wouldn't change anything. She would have to sit through the meeting, the Collection would still come, and Sully would still be captured. There was no stopping the events set in motion now.

Andrew took her silence as an invitation to continue and quickly ran down the list she'd given him. There was a total of eight names and addresses; she'd reserved two more for when they reached the city, to make things look more convincing.

"Are there any we've missed? Have you had any visions since last we spoke?" Andrw asked when he'd finished.

Persi shook her head quickly. "No. But I may have more for you once we reach the city," she offered with faux hopefulness.

"Of course." He nodded. "Proximity does seem to help some." Andrew jotted down some more notes, and for a moment, Persinette thought she was being dismissed. There was nothing else to discuss; surely, she was free to go now. She gathered her ruffled skirts to stand.

"I see that Agnes has reported much progress in your training." The words came suddenly and glued her back to her seat.

"Has he?" she asked softly. A twinge of dread crept into her, making her body itch to curl in on itself.

"As that is the case, you will be outfitted with some gear and brought along as a real Asset—not just luggage." His tone was nonchalant, almost bored. "Please don't make me regret this, Persinette."

"No, sir, of course not."

"Andrew," he reminded gently.

"Of course, Andrew." She balled her hands into fists under the table. Being forced to treat him with familiarity bothered her. They were not friends. "Is that all?"

"It would seem so," he said. She rose from her seat and headed for the door. Just as she stopped before it to press the button to open it, he added, "Oh, and Persinette?"

"Yes, Andrew?" She looked back at him over her shoulder.

"Do try to get a good night's sleep. We leave bright and early in the morning." A smile had dragged up his lips as if he were trying to look friendly. But the corners of his eyes didn't move, so instead, he looked sinister.

She gave him a firm nod and got out of the room and out of his presence as quickly as she could.

THAT NIGHT, as she wrestled with the knowledge that in the morning she'd send a kelpie to certain doom, sleep evaded her. Persi laid there, blinking at the ceiling for hours until she watched the sunrise glow through the bars on her Tower window. She flicked her gaze to the clock on her bedside table before she rose to prepare for the mission ahead. Showered and appropriately dressed, she headed for the weapons room where, she assumed, she would be outfitted with gear for the trip.

Once there she was given ill-fitting armor and one small pistol with a similarly small amount of ammunition. They trusted her—just not that much. She counted each bullet, one by one, as she loaded them into the pistol.

One. Two. Three. Four. Five. Six.

Only six bullets. Enough to fill the little pistol and not a single more.

Persi slumped half-heartedly. Then again, she wouldn't use it against the MOTHER agents anyway. She supposed it didn't matter that there weren't enough rounds there to take out even a quarter of the agents going out for Collection with her. As far as the Uprising was concerned, killing MOTHER agents wasn't her job—and she wasn't sure she had it in her to kill one on purpose. An accidental death had been bad enough. So, she focused on her directive which was to keep innocent Enchanted from being Collected and sent to MOTHER's labor camps.

The platoon of MOTHER agents moved through the portal swiftly. Their path through Maximus was one of back alleyways and silence. They had commandeered a building on the outskirts of the city to act as their home base, and that is where they set her up for Collections.

That first day seemed to go perfectly according to plan. The MOTHER agents went in quickly and quietly and just in time to find their prey slipping through their fingers out the back window, or side door, or a hatch of some sort. Manu had cleverly set his people up in buildings where it would be harder for MOTHER to sneak up on them, making it look like a complete coincidence that they were able to escape—all of which Persi was grateful for.

When the platoon returned to their quarters at the end of that first day, she found herself once again locked in a room with two guards outside her door. She settled into a chair in front of the window and peered out at the sprawling city of Maximus. Unlike some of the other cities in Daiwynn, Maximus was entirely new. None of the old pre-war buildings were mixed in among the modern Daiwynnian ones. Every building around her featured buttresses, small windows, and gargoyles.

She made herself comfortable, fully expecting to be in the seat all night with nothing else to do but watch the people below.

But her quiet time was quickly cut short as the door swung open, smacking against the wall beside it hard enough to leave a dent. Persi whipped around just in time to see a furious Andrew Gothel stalking toward her. She leaped from her chair as he drew closer, but she wasn't quick enough. The next moment, he was upon her. He drew back his hand and slapped her across the cheek with all of his might. "You've had something to do with this." His tone was soft but deadly.

The sting of her reddening cheek brought back the memory of the first time she'd seen Andrew Gothel in action. Her gut writhed as she tried to hide the growing fear from her eyes. Over the last month and a half, she had almost forgotten how dangerous he really was. He'd hidden it away underneath charisma and pleasantries, but now she remembered—remembered all of it. "I don't know what you're talking about," she rasped as she fought to keep her voice even. She lifted a tender hand to her cheek. "Had something to do with what?"

"The escapes! We've been to Collect four of the creatures off your delightful little list, and each one has escaped," he spat.

"I couldn't have! How would I have?" Persi's voice went up an octave. Panic settled in and threatened to choke off the very air she breathed.

Andrew's dark eyes narrowed on her dangerously as if reading something written in her expression. "I don't know. But if you have, I'll find out. And if this mission is a failure, I'll see to it that you are sent to the camps, where they'll give you the most soul-crushing job they can find and you'll wither and die like the pitiful little thing you are." His voice was low and full of an emotion he hadn't shown her before, but that she recognized it all the same—hatred. She had seen it and heard it so many times when humans talked about her kind, and there it was, at last, from Andrew's lips. "Do you understand me, Persinette?"

She bobbed her head quickly, swallowing the scream creeping up her throat. Andrew gave a curt nod in response, spun for the door, and strode from the room without another word.

Persinette stood for several seconds, stunned and nursing her bruising cheek, before she dropped into the chair once more. It would have been a relief to be able to talk to Manu. To tell him everything that had happened. To let him assuage her worries with his easy chatter and over-confidence. But she knew better. It wasn't safe here, not with two guards posted so close outside her door. Instead,

Persi settled for a distraction, watching the people in the streets of Maximus as they moved through the night. The city never seemed to sleep. Even into the wee hours of the morning people were wandering the streets.

She wondered where they were going so late—or so early, she supposed. With wide eyes, she followed a well-dressed man and woman as they stumbled their way home. A soft pang twinged within her as Persi wondered what it must be like to go out for a night on the town, to have that kind of freedom. She shook herself and let her eyes drift to a short man in a newsboy cap who seemed to be off to work. Person by person, she allowed herself to get lost in their stories, their journeys, and daydreams of what it'd be like to live that way.

She slept fitfully, and just before day broke over the tops of the towering buildings of Maximus, the two guards from outside her room stormed in, grabbed Persi by the elbows, and dragged her from the room. Neither spoke a word as they deposited her among the ranks of the Collection party.

Persi held back any complaints or reservations to herself as she kept to the back of the group. She had no desire to draw any more of Andrew's attention if she could avoid it. Even from a distance, though, she could see the way his shoulders had tensed to his ears. He was angry.

Three more Collections came and went. Each one was a near miss. Each one left Andrew Gothel practically shaking with anger. By the end of it, his hand was resting on the revolver at his side, not moving. His dark eyes cut through the crowd to find her, and she felt fear run up her spine.

There was not a single doubt in Persi's mind that if they hadn't been surrounded by other MOTHER agents, Andrew would shoot her right where she stood—not that the agents would care either way. She sent up a silent *thank you* to the gods that this next Collection was Sully's. If it hadn't been, Persi knew Andrew wouldn't let her make it back to MOTHER headquarters alive. She tried to swallow the terror that rose inside of her. Now was not the time to panic, not when they were so close.

Andrew Gothel was the first one up the back stairs of the small apartment that was situated over a shop. Once there, he didn't wait a moment before he slammed into the door, knocked it off its hinges, and stormed inside. Leaving nothing to chance, it seemed, he shot first with the stunning pistol on his other hip. Persi heard, more than saw, the kelpie hit the floor as the MOTHER agents overtook him. She took a step forward out of instinct to help, but a firm grip on her wrist stopped her. Looking back, she saw it was one of the guards from her room, holding her tightly and glaring at her.

A few moments later, the agents dragged the dazed but imposing man down the stairs in iron shackles.

Persi's eyes widened, watching the tall man closely. *Gods, he's so much taller in person,* she thought before shaking the notion away. Now was not the time.

When Persi's eyes met Sullivan's dark ones, she felt her heart sink to her toes. Kelpies were deadly, yes, but for all their violent nature they were also rare and beautiful. There was something sad about the thought that she was sending a kelpie to the camps. "I'm sorry," she mouthed.

Sullivan shrugged his massive shoulders and let the MOTHER agents drag him off without a hint of struggle. Persinette wondered if the agents realized that if Sully were to so much as try, he could escape handily. For so long kelpies had been harbingers of death— bad omens—but this one had just saved her life. With some difficulty, she forced her eyes away from where they were carting Sully away.

The group split in two: half began to make their way through the back streets of Maximus once more with their captive, while the rest remained behind to continue the Collection. Persi searched the crowd for Andrew, but couldn't seem to find him. She'd been so sure he'd be doing victory laps that not seeing him felt odd. Once they stepped into MOTHER headquarters, Persinette did another sweep, scanning for his dark hair, his handsome features. But there was no sign of him. She supposed he had gone off to fill out paperwork of some sort. There would no doubt be a debriefing later, but for now, she could head back to the Tower and rest.

She could put some ice on her bruised cheek and let Manu's soothing voice lighten some of the load. She turned to leave the transportation room and start down the corridor toward the Tower without another thought.

Persi was halfway up the long narrow staircase that led from the basement of MOTHER HQ to the Tower level when a robot stopped right in front of her. She stepped aside to pass it, but it whirred irritably and jerked into her path again. She eyed it and frowned. "Excuse me."

"Asset number 11-24-10?" it asked in a metallic, monotone voice.

"Yes?" Persi responded, tilting her head at the machine.

"I am to escort you to your quarters." It reached out with one hard metal hand and locked her upper arm in a vise grip.

"Well, I was just head—"

The robot started dragging her down the hall toward the Tower.

"Hey, you don't need to drag me! I can walk!" she protested. "I was going there anyway!"

"I am under orders to escort you to your quarters," the bot repeated, still dragging her down the hall.

"By who? Who ordered you? Why do I need an escort? What's going on?" Panic was taking over, making her voice grow shaky. The robot didn't answer; it just followed its orders. As they went, they passed several other Assets in the hall. No one stopped to help her, or even bothered to make eye contact.

When they reached her rooms, Persi found that her door sitting wide open. The hard grip on her arm gave a shove that practically threw her to her knees in the middle of her living quarters, and the bot moved to block any hope of an exit.

Persinette panted, taking a moment to regain her senses before she lifted her head and looked around the only home she'd known since she was eight years old. All of her books were ripped from the shelves and scattered everywhere. But even that didn't scare her as much as when her eyes landed on her chair, where she'd taken tucking spells away when it'd gotten too hard to move her mattress. Someone had taken a knife to it and torn the stuffing from it. All of the spells—oh gods, the spells!—were everywhere.

The soft tread of boots drew her attention, and Persi turned to find out who was behind this—who it was that had condemned her to death. A sob ripped from her throat as Persi's eyes met the Elwyn's eyes—no longer kind, but flinty.

"Wyn?" Persi choked out the word in question. Surely this was a mistake. Surely Wyn was just here under orders. Her friend hadn't turned her in—had she?

Wyn twitched one dark brow at Persi. Her lips had

drawn into a hard line. "11-24-10." The number left Wyn a little awkwardly. "You are charged with multiple counts of treason against the crown."

"But...you're my friend." Persinette gave a strangled half-sob, like an invisible hand was choking the life out of her. The only friend she'd ever had in this place had been the one to betray her.

"You did this to yourself, 11-24-10, the moment you decided to help those monsters." Wyn's words were cool, detached. Which somehow made all of this so much worse.

"They're *people*," Persi said firmly as she pulled herself to her feet.

Wyn blinked, visibly shocked. "What?"

"I said, they're *people*. They're not monsters! They're people! *We* are people!" She hadn't even reached for the magic, but it rose to the surface anyway. Her hands glowed with power and her eyes narrowed on Wyn in rage. "*We* are *people*, and we do not deserve to be treated as less than."

Wyn took a step back, and whether the retreat was involuntary or not, Persinette could see that her friend was afraid of her. She'd proven herself a monster to Wyn, she realized, but no sooner had the fact settled in than Persi felt the cold metal of the automaton's hand on her wrist. The magic flared with rage.

"Take her to Processing. I'm sick of looking at her," Wyn spat.

The robot was dragging her again, and before Persi could even think, the spell fell from her lips. Brilliant purple magic flung the clockwork creature across the room, and she bolted down the hallway. She didn't know where she was running—there was no escape. Nevertheless, she ran and ran and ran.

Persi sprinted until her lungs felt like they would burn

up from lack of oxygen and the adrenaline of rage and shock drained from her. She felt her legs turn to jelly and stumbled down the hall. But before she could let herself tumble to the ground, a hard grip caught her with a bitter growl. She looked up to find the bright rainbow hair and dark, angry eyes of Agnes.

"You're a damn fool," he muttered as he pulled a pair of iron cuffs from his overcoat. "I tried to warn you that anyone could just go into your room anytime they damn well pleased. But no, you kept on."

Persinette widened her eyes at him. "Warn me?" she asked, confused.

"I've got her," Agnes announced to some other agents further down the hallway. "I'll get her down to Processing and put into a holding cell. You two can handle the paperwork, since *I* did all the hard work."

There was no struggling. Persi didn't think she had any struggle left in her. She hadn't slept in days and hadn't eaten for even longer. All of her energy had gotten used up in that brief bid for freedom. So she let Agnes drag her through headquarters without any fuss.

"You're a real pain in my ass, Persinette," Agnes grumbled after a while.

"I don't understand," she said. *What was Agnes trying to say? What did he mean?* Her mind tried to put two and two together to make four but was somehow coming up with five.

The unicorn took a cursory look around the empty processing room before he leaned in close. "*I'm* the agent on the inside. And now you've gone and ruined all the work I put into making you a viable Asset, you daft little girl."

With that, he shoved her into a cell, slammed the door, and trotted off, leaving Persinette alone with the dark, the cold, and the thoughts of what was going to become of her next.

There was a brief moment when she thought to shout after him. To beg him to tell Manu that she was here and to come to save her. But then she thought better of it. Agnes wasn't going to help her, not now. Because she was no longer any use to him.

30

CAPTAIN MANU KELII

CAPTAIN MANU KELII sat in his chair on the flight deck, his eyes unfocused as he stared out the bubbled window-pane and into the starlit sky. He twirled an old-fashioned glass in his right hand, drumming his fingers nervously on its cool, smooth side. The glass had been empty for hours, but he'd made no move to refill it as he waited for a call about how the mission had gone. If he got up to refill his glass, there was a chance he might miss the call when it came in. He couldn't afford that. He had to be there when Eddi called, when the screen flicked on. He had to know right away.

At some point, Benard came in and asked Manu if he was going to bed any time soon, but he was informed that no, Manu would sit there until Eddi called, and that was that.

Manu lost track of time in between when he'd finished his drink and when the screen finally flickered on. He knew it was late, but he had no idea how late. Strangely enough, the Eddi sitting there looking at him looked no different than Eddi ever did—well-rested and alert. Manu, on the other hand—judging by the reflection in the metal on the panel in front of him—looked exhausted, sporting dark circles, an impressive five o'clock shadow, and disheveled hair. He had discarded his waistcoat hours ago, and in his troubled state, the shirt beneath had become thoroughly wrinkled.

"Good morning, Captain," Eddi said in greeting, perhaps a little too alertly for how the captain was feeling. Manu felt those dark eyes take him in, noting his appearance, but he didn't bother to react. Eddi was judging him, but there was no use trying to stop them. What did it matter now? All that mattered was if Persinette was safe or not.

"How did it go?" Manu's voice cracked from hours of disuse and fatigue, and he cleared his throat. He wondered if perhaps he should have tried to get some sleep while he'd been sitting there. The light from the call might have woken him. But no, that hadn't been a chance he'd been willing to take.

Eddi's nose wrinkled—perhaps at the lack of good-humored teasing from the captain—but they continued nonetheless. "MOTHER came and Collected Sullivan just as we planned—"

The rest of Eddi's words were cut off by a loud sigh of relief as Manu melted against the chair. His heart sank from his throat to the usual spot in his chest. Everything had gone according to plan, then—and that meant Persinette was safe. He had nothing to worry about until their next mission. Which meant that he could focus his full attention on using Ivy's powers to track the Library. Things would be good, if just for a little while.

"However."

Manu's heart throbbed right back up to his throat. He

sat forwards, back painfully straight in an attempt to look more alert.

"It would seem someone found out about Persinette working to wield her magic," Eddi continued. "They have pegged her as the reason Gothel died and made the leap that she's an Uprising Agent." The words had a flat, no-nonsense tone, without a single note of regret or sadness.

And each word felt like a death knell. "What will they do to her?" Manu asked as sadness tugged his body back into a slump. He'd failed her.

For the first time in the many years Manu had been with the Uprising, he saw an actual emotion flicker across Eddi's face. One corner of the Uprising Leader's thin lips tugged down into a grimace. But just like that, it disappeared. "Since the late Gothel was her new handler's sister, it would seem he's out for blood. Persinette will be stripped of her rank and sent to the hardest of the labor camps to spend what remains of her life mining for coal and precious metals."

In a split second, Manu's sadness lit into a rage like he'd never felt before. His eyes flickered golden and he let out a harsh growl. "And what are we going to do about it?"

Eddi blinked. "Excuse me?"

"I said, *what are we going to do about it?*" Manu repeated. He could feel his pupils contract to narrow, cat-like slits, the teeth in his mouth sharpening enough to cut. But he kept himself in check.

More blinking. Gods, that was beginning to grate on his nerves. He'd never realized how much Eddi blinked before, but now he found the action infuriating. "Nothing. I'll find you another Asset, and we'll move on," Eddi said.

"Unacceptable," Manu growled. He clenched the arms of his chair in a bid for control.

"Excuse me?" Eddie repeated.

"That. Is. Unacceptable." His tone had gone from calm to edging on manic as his knuckles tightened their grip. "We were responsible for her. *I* was responsible for her. And I made her a promise. I promised her that she wouldn't go to one of those camps. I told her I wouldn't let that happen. We need a plan to get her out before they transfer her." His words left no room for argument, or so he thought because he had made up his mind.

"That is not within our capabilities at this time, Captain," Eddi said, voice frustratingly flat. "We are nowhere near ready to tip our hand to MOTHER just yet."

"I don't care!" Manu roared, leaping from his chair. "We promised her! And I will not see her die in one of those damn camps for the sake of keeping your secrets!"

Eddi simply looked at him, their thin lips curving down once more. It was evident that the Uprising would be of no help to him, as their leader would not waver. He would have to do this alone.

"Give me your point of contact within MOTHER head-quarters," Manu ordered.

"Give you what?"

"Your inside man. I want their contact information. Whoever it is must be close to her, and I'm going to need all the help I can get if I'm going in there to get her out," Manu said, almost as much to himself as to Eddi.

Eddi shook their head—a passive gesture that made Manu want to reach through the screen, grab the Uprising Leader by the shoulders, and give the old bat a good shake. "No. But I will let him know you're coming."

With that, the call terminated. Manu had been left to his own devices. He would receive no aid from the Uprising, and in all reality, he very likely would not get any help from Eddi's contact within MOTHER, either.

But that wasn't going to stop him. He had a promise to keep.

"BENARD!" the Captain shouted as he stormed down the corridor toward the living quarters. His booming voice brought the crew from their beds, peering from their doors at their fierce captain with his tired eyes and mussed hair. "EVERYONE UP! WE HAVE A HEADING!"

His crew sprang into action—still clad in their nightclothes—as Benard appeared at his side in a pair of mint-green silk pajamas, alert and ready to go. "Where to, sir?"

"We are headed to the capital," Manu announced. Benard nodded and scurried off to map a course, no questions asked.

"The capital, huh?" Ivy asked as she peeked from her door, her long green hair tied up in a tight bun. "What about the library?"

"There will be plenty of time for that later, after we get Persinette the hell out of there. You better get yourself and your unit ready for a fight. I need all hands on deck." Manu offered her a sharp-toothed smile before he returned to the flight deck. Suddenly, he didn't feel tired at all.

"Aye-aye, Captain," Ivy murmured with a grin of her own.

31

PERSINETTE

TIME PASSED, though Persi just didn't know how much. Her muscles had begun to ache from the cold hard floor, but she refused to move from where she was curled up in the corner of her cell. Some small part of her thought that if she just made herself small enough, maybe she would disappear altogether. To cease to exist would surely be better than rotting away in the damp cell, or worse, being dragged down to the work camps to rot away there. And at least if she disappeared, Persi could save Manu the trouble of having to save her. She would prefer that, wouldn't she?

She'd weighed her options and decided she didn't know which she would prefer. And at that point, she didn't care. Whatever was going to happen, would happen. What little control she'd had over her life was gone. All that was left was a glimmer of hope that everything would work out in the end. But just a glimmer.

Persi sniffled, tugging her legs in tighter to her chest. She scooted herself toward the only light in the cell, a sliver shining through the slit in the door. She supposed the guards would yell through it when they finally decided to come and process her, but for now, Persinette clung to that little bit of light.

The thumping, muffled sounds of guards dragging bodies down the hall, and the kicking and screaming of the Enchanted, bled through the door. Was anyone in the cells around her there because of her?

"No," she whispered, trying to reassure herself. It would have been impossible for anyone she helped to Collect to still be there at this point. They all would have moved on to the camps by now. That thought froze her for a moment until a loud moan from one of the cells near her jolted it away.

Instinctively, her hands flew up to cover her ears, and Persi hummed to herself to block it all out. Because that's how she felt too. She longed to slam her body against the door until it, or she, gave out. She wanted to scream, and cry, and moan, and whimper, and do everything within her power to escape. But in the end, what power did she really have?

With her eyes closed tightly, and her humming in her ears, Persi could almost pretend she was somewhere else— anywhere else.

Someone called something, something vaguely familiar, but her humming and covered ears muffled the sound. Then the person shouted again. "11-24-10!"

Persinette jerked to alertness. A pair of eyes glared at her through the slit in the door. "My name is Persinette," she replied shakily as she stood.

"Right." Whoever it was snorted, and the sound of rustling paper came from the other side of the door. "Turn around and face the wall." The order managed to sound bored yet also leave no room for argument.

"Where are we going?" Persi asked anyway.

The person didn't answer, nor did they wait for her to turn and face the wall as she'd been instructed. Heavy steel squealed as the door flung open, revealing a young man no more than twenty years old on the other side. His pale eyes flicked over her as his upper lip curled in disgust. Persinette wondered for a moment how she had gone all her of her life without seeing that expression painted on every MOTHER agent that surrounded her. They had all seemed to hide it so well for as long as Persi had remained useful to them. But now that had expired, and the veil slipped away. She wasn't any different in their eyes than those they Collected.

"I said, *face the wall!*" With three quick strides, he was in her face. He grabbed her by the shoulders and forced her to face the wall. "You will do as you are told, 11-24-10." He bent her hands behind her back and shackled them together.

"Where are we going?" she asked again, this time louder, but still, she received no answer. Instead, the young man shoved her from the cell and dragged her down the corridor. "Where are you taking me?" She shouted the words at him now, loud enough that they echoed off the cell doors surrounding her.

The young man pulled her to a stop so that he could fix her with a steely glare. "Processing." He sneered.

Processing. The single word sent a shudder down Persinette's spine. She had never seen a person be processed before, but she knew exactly what it entailed.

"Nothing to say now?" he asked as the expression twisted his features into something frightening.

No. Persinette didn't have anything else to say. She was one step closer to the labor camps. One step closer to the thing she'd feared all of her life, the slow death of being treated more like a machine than a person. She shook her head, teeth gnawing the inside of her cheek.

"Good. Now move it." The guard gave a hard shove to her lower back. She stumbled on legs still half-numb from being curled up on the hard floor, fighting to maintain her balance without the use of her arms.

"H-h-how long was I down there?" Persi asked as she choked back the fear blocking her throat. *What if a week had already come and gone?* some irrational part of her asked. *What if Manu wasn't ever coming to get her out?* continued the small, nasty voice in her head. It took her a moment to realize it sounded eerily like Gothel, but that didn't seem to make the questions any less valid.

The guard didn't answer; he just continued to push her down the corridor. A heavy iron door loomed at the end of the hallway. As it drew nearer and nearer, Persi could feel her dull fear give way to shimmering, unrelenting panic.

The door opened when they were still some feet away, seeming to spit out a young girl with bright blue hair. The girl stumbled as her guard shoved her in the opposite direction, back toward the cells. Her brilliant hair had been buzzed to the quick, with barely an inch of electric-blue fuzz left to show it'd been there at all. Persi's fingers twitched, longing to reach out to the other girl and provide some comfort. She wanted to tell that girl that she wasn't alone, that someone would be coming for them soon. But her guard gave her another hard push toward the looming iron door.

Persinette's own lavender head turned to follow the girl's progress—a small gesture that nevertheless caused her to trip as the guard shoved her again. She blinked, and suddenly the heavy iron door swung shut in front of her, blocking the girl from view and sounding an ear-splitting bang.

Wincing, Persi turned to look at the room around her. Along one wall was a workbench of some kind, laden with thick shackles and other instruments she couldn't name. And in the very center of the room was an old wooden chair with restraints lashed to the arms and legs. Littered around the chair was something that made Persinette's eyes prick with tears: long locks of electric-blue hair.

"Sit down," the guard ordered from where he stood with his back to her at the workbench.

"Why do you have to cut our hair?" she asked, refusing to move. The question would do nothing to help her, or anyone else, but she felt a certain amount of defiance in asking it.

The young man turned toward her slowly. Instead of answering, he strode across the floor and grabbed hold of her long hair. Pain shot through her scalp, and she cried out as he dragged her to the chair by her hair. Her restrained hands jerked, and her shoulders screamed in agony when he shoved her down into the chair. "Trust me, little girl, I could do a lot worse than cut your hair. So shut your damn mouth and let me do my job. Have I made myself clear?"

With a hard gulp, Persi bobbed her head in a quick nod. She squeezed her eyes shut to will away the tears that burned there, which only made them to trickle down her cheeks. But she bit down hard on her tongue and didn't make a sound.

She didn't make a sound even when the grating squeak of rusted shears filled the room and large chunks of lavender hair joined the electric-blue locks on the floor. She didn't make a sound as the soft buzz of an electric razor added more hair to the piles on the floor. But Persinette swallowed and the tears kept trickling down her cheeks. She had never cut her hair before, never thought she would, and now she could feel the chill of the room what felt like a million times over as it washed over her bare scalp and neck. *It will grow back,* she told herself. *You will escape this awful place, and it will grow back.* The words resonated through her mind like a vow, and they calmed her a little.

Persinette counted her breaths now as she once had her footsteps. *One. Two. Three. Four.* She forced herself to remain calm while the guard unshackled her wrists, to remain calm as he secured them to the arms of the chair. But that calm disappeared when her eyes landed on the knife-sharp object whirring toward her faster than a hummingbird's wings. An ink-filled needle, massive and medieval-looking, pushed closer and closer to the tender skin of her forearm.

Surely, he isn't going to—

All thoughts ceased when the stab of the needle seared her freckled skin as the guard carved numbers into it. A soft whimper left her, the tears flowing more freely now.

Through the pain, she sucked in a shallow breath, reaching for her magic, hoping maybe it would save her. For the first time in months, it didn't reach back. In the place where magic should have been, there was only emptiness.

"Sorry, 11-24-10. No magic in here. The walls are lined with iron." The guard snickered softly. He began to hum a merry tune as he dragged the needle painstakingly slowly across the soft skin of her arm, etching the numbers *1-1-2-4-1-0* into it.

A wave of dizziness washed over her, threatening to knock her out, but Persi gritted her teeth and focused. "I have a name. My name is Persinette," she asserted through a clenched jaw. The words echoed away in the room, but it didn't matter; they weren't for him anyway. They were for her, a reminder that in spite of the number burning its way into her skin, she was a person, not a thing. They could brand her, but they couldn't take her name away. And she would get out of here—with or without Manu's help.

When at last the agony of the branding was set into her skin, the guard fitted her wrist with an iron cuff. Stripped of her dignity, and unable to use her magic at all, Persinette was released from the chair. The guard yanked her to her feet, and they made their way back down the corridor once more until he threw her to the hard ground of her cell.

"There you go 11-24-10. Have a nice—" The guard stopped as he thought for a moment. "Hey, what's the going life span down at the labor camps now?" he called down the corridor to someone at the end. There were a couple of shouted responses, each with a different number, and the guard merely shrugged. "Whatever. Have a nice life. Whatever's left of it." He sniggered.

Persi lifted her chin and met his pale eyes with her own unwavering ones. "Thanks. I will," she said firmly.

The guard just scoffed. "That's right; get uppity. See how that attitude serves you down at the camps, 11-24-10."

"You let me worry about that." Persi felt her lips curl into a taunting smile.

For a moment, the guard stared at her in utter disbelief. Then he shook his head. "Whatever," he spat as he slammed the door shut. "You keep telling yourself that, *Persinette.*" He said her name like a dirty word and left her to the silence of her cell once more.

In the corner was a small, dirty cot, and Persi sat on the edge. But this time she resisted the urge to curl up and cower. She was done cowering. Gingerly, she lifted a hand to brush at the lavender fuzz atop her head, like a final, too-late farewell to the long hair she'd known all her life.

It would grow back, one day.

But for now, there were other things to focus on. Her hand fell away, and she focused on the door, ears alert to any goings on in the corridor beyond. If she was going to get all of these people out, she needed to know the guards' routine, and how many of them there were. Her keen eyes narrowed on the slit that the guard had left open, and she began to count.

One. Two. Three.

The sound of sobbing broke her concentration. Standing up from the dirty cot, she moved to the cracked wall, hoping she could peek through to the cell on the other side. When the crack proved too small to see anything, she smashed her shackles against it. "*Hey!*" Persi whispered through the crack. "Hey, are you all right?" She slammed her shackle against the wall a second time, chipping away just enough stone to just make out the person on the other side.

Surprised, the person scrambled away from the crumbling wall and into the narrow shaft of light from the door, illuminated just enough for Persi to see that it was the blue-haired girl.

"I'm fine," the girl said, quiet but proud, doing her best to hide a soft sniffle that could only be the product of tears. "What do you want?"

"I just wanted to let you know that it's going to be all right. We're going to get out of this," Persi whispered reassuringly. She wanted nothing more than to comfort the girl on the other side of the wall, and do it properly, but had to hope that her words would be good enough.

"Yeah? How?" the girl asked. She sounded annoyed, and Persi couldn't blame her.

"It just will be, trust me. I'm going to make sure of it." Persi nodded, not sure how much the girl could see, and wondered briefly who she was trying to reassure more: herself or the girl. She decided not to think about it.

The girl snorted, and Persi could just imagine her rolling her eyes. "Yeah, okay."

"What's your name?" Persi asked.

"12-04-05," the girl said, rubbing her face with a dirty sleeve.

"No, no. Your *name*. Your *real* name. Not that number they gave you, but what your parents named you. What your friends call you."

The girl stilled, blinking at the wall in confusion. "Felicity...just Felicity. I don't have a surname," the girl—Felicity—said awkwardly.

"It's nice to meet you, Felicity." Persi smiled. "I'm Persinette, and I'm going to get us out of here very soon. Swear."

32

CAPTAIN MANU KELII

IT HAD ONLY BEEN a couple of days since Manu had gotten word that Persinette was discovered and he made the life-altering decision to defy orders and go in after her. Eddi was right, of course—the Uprising Leader always seemed to be right. Any attempt to rescue Persinette would be seen as a direct attack on MOTHER. Any direct attack would be seen as an act of war, and that would be that. But Manu found himself unable to give a damn. Act of war or no, he wasn't going to let Persi rot in there. He had made her a promise, and he had every intention of keeping it.

"Sir, are you sure we have enough crew for this?" Benard asked as his eyes followed the pacing captain. A large map sat on the desk, where both first mate and captain had been examining it. That map had been sent over by the Uprising's inside man, and carefully laid out where the holding cells were in MOTHER HQ. All that stood in their way was a cement exterior wall, a short hallway, and some offices. Easy enough. They'd done more with less.

"Positive," the captain declared, in a tone that left no room for argument. It was clear to everyone in the room—

Manu included—that it didn't matter if they were ready or not. They were going in. No one argued, and Manu wondered if it was because they felt the need to save Persinette as much as he did or something else, but he didn't bother to ask. He felt a particular kind of anxiety, the feeling of being utterly trapped, burgeon inside him as they drew closer to the Capital.

Benard shifted, watching his captain. His face flickered with an emotion Manu wasn't able to identify. "Sir, what if they've already moved her to one of the camps?"

The question hung in the air. Thus far, no one had dared bring up that possibility. For his part, Manu had merely acknowledged it internally and moved on, which was easy enough only so long as the words weren't spoken aloud. Now, however, he had to pay the possibility some mind. It was entirely possible that MOTHER would have already transported her to one of the camps, or worse yet, disposed of her entirely. The very thought made Manu's stomach turn.

"Don't say that," Manu snapped, baring his teeth. He wasn't even sure why he was angry at Benard for stating the obvious, but he was. Rage was simmering just below the surface. "She's fine. She's there, and she's fine. And we're going to get her out. And that's it."

Benard nodded. "Very well then, sir. The crew is ready. We should be there in the next couple of hours."

Manu let out a shaky breath and he nodded as well. His hands tightened into fists at his sides as he could to maintain some modicum of self-control. It took everything he had to keep from shifting out of frustration. But he stood firm, gazing out the window as the city drew ever closer.

HE WAS STILL STANDING THERE, looking out the bubbled glass at the sprawling Capital, as they closed the distance between themselves and MOTHER headquarters some hours later. The large building cast a shadow over the entire city. It was anyone's guess how many floors were within, as it was well known that MOTHER had built several sub-levels deep in the ground.

A low whistle cut through the air of the flight deck, and Manu looked to find Ivy sauntering across the room. "That MOTHER sure knows how to build a building, don't they?"

"Are the explosives ready?" Manu turned back to the building ahead. He didn't care if MOTHER headquarters was imposing or impressive. It was a building, and he was going to blow a hole in it.

Ivy raised her eyebrows and nodded. "My unit is ready, and I believe your first mate has everyone else in place." She bit her lip, not speaking for once, which counterintuitively drew his attention.

"What is it?" he asked.

"Nothing." The witch's expression was cagey beneath her green locks.

Manu tightened his jaw. "Out with it."

"It's just...well, I just wonder if you've thought this all the way through." She shrugged.

"Excuse me?" His eyes flashed angrily at her words. "Thought *what* through?"

Ivy froze, opened her mouth, then shut it. "Nothing, sir, nothing." She looked away.

Manu focused his attention back on the looming building. Waiting, waiting. And once the *Duchess* was in range, he gave the order. "Now."

The witches aboard the *Duchess* made quick and quiet work of evaporating the headquarters' shields, drawing no suspicion—at least not yet. Then, with a nod from Manu, the boom of explosives shook the air. A swirling mix of magic and old-world dynamite rained down on MOTHER, filling the air with smoke and burning charms. Green flames licked at the building, dissolving the walls away.

"We are ready to head in, sir. Are you?" Benard asked as he looked down at the destruction. "It won't be long now before we've breached the wall."

The captain nodded, and together they headed down to the cargo bay where the hatch was sitting wide open, ready to let them into the building. Many of the crew had already strapped themselves with ropes to be lowered down, but not a one looked to their captain as he and Benard joined them. Instead, they focused on their orders, arming themselves to the gills.

Owen offered a dagger to Manu, but the captain shook his head. "No, thank you." He gave Owen a sharp smile. "I plan to go in claws blazing." Owen nodded and returned the dagger to its place among their arsenal without a word. "All right, Benard, strap me up and send me down."

Benard tipped his head, as if to ask if that were wise, but didn't bother to say the words. It was no use. He handed his captain the harness and watched to make sure he secured it correctly. "Good luck, sir." Benard tugged on the harness one last time to make sure it wouldn't give. "And sir...bring our girl home."

"That's the plan!" Manu nodded, then snapped his gaze toward the hole they'd blown in the building. MOTHER had finally caught on to what was going on, and the *Duchess* shook as shots hit its shields. With a long inhale, the captain stepped to the edge of the open cargo bay hatch and leaped toward the smoldering hole and the chaos below. Above and behind him, he heard the *whoosh* of his crew following suit.

Once Manu's feet were firmly planted on the ground, he unhooked the harness and took off. They didn't have much time; already MOTHER agents were setting up barriers to keep the captain and his men from the rest of the building.

With a roar, the captain broke the thin thread of control keeping the beast in check. He let go of the fear, and the anger, and the anxiety, and his human form altogether. What was left in his place was an oversized pale tiger, dark stripes only partially hidden by the breeches and shirt his human body had been wearing. He ought to thank Benard for convincing him to forgo his normal wardrobe—but no, not now. Now, he released another roar and led the charge toward the row of agents blocking him from Persinette.

Even the sting of a bullet grazing his shoulder did nothing to slow him down as he barreled toward them, teeth and claws bared. Seconds later, all that was left was a trail of broken and bloodied agents in his wake, the path cleared for the rest of his men. With the corridor cleared, he turned to the crew member who had been put in charge of the map, a young man with glasses named Henry. Henry pointed down another hall, and the group of rescuers took off in that direction with Manu at the head.

Hang on Persi, I'm coming. Just a few more minutes.

33

_____

PERSINETTE

PERSINETTE DIDN'T HEAR SO MUCH AS *feel* the
first explosion smash into MOTHER headquarters. The
entire building shook. She leaped to her feet and zipped
across the cell to peek out the little slit in her door. None of
the guards ran to protect her or the other captives. It looked
like they were running for the exit instead, leaving the prisoners alone in their cells.

Sucking in a breath, she dashed to the hole in the wall
again. *"Felicity!"* she hissed, and the young girl whirled
around. "Did they put one of those iron shackles on you?"
She held up her own wrist to demonstrate.

The blue-haired girl looked with puzzled brown eyes
before lifting a shackled wrist. "Yeah. They put them on
everyone."

"Damn it!" Persi said.

"Why? What is it? What *was* that?" Felicity stood from
where she'd been crouched on the floor and glanced from
their whispering hole to her cell door. "It felt like an
earthquake."

Persinette paused, wondering what an earthquake was,

what it sounded like, she supposed. *Not important*, she reminded herself. "I think it's the Uprising coming to get us. If we could just out of these cells." She glared at her door.

Felicity fell silent, and then she reached down, took hold of the metal shackled on her wrist, and wiggled her hand out of it with minimal difficulty. "They didn't have any more of the small ones left. I can get mine off."

Persi stood on her tiptoes, peering through the crack to get a better look at Felicity. "Really?"

Felicity displayed the empty shackle for Persinette to see. "I guess they figured I wasn't much of a threat." She shrugged. "But I don't see how that helps us any. We're still in a cell."

Persi's eyes darted to her shackle, wondering if she could maybe wriggle free of it. She tugged it as far as it would go, just below the knuckle in her thumb, but she couldn't seem to get it any further. Felicity's hands were smaller, still the hands of a girl who had not yet entirely left childhood. She couldn't have been more than fourteen. Persi let the shackle slip back down to her wrist and returned her attention to more pressing matters. "Have you ever done any spells?"

Felicity frowned and shook her head. "Not on purpose. Things just...happened around me, never anything I could control. I always tried to stifle it, not wield it, but that didn't seem to work either." She looked down at her lightly tanned hands. "That's how they found me."

Persi gave a quick nod and straightened. Now was not the time for shame or pity; now was the time for action. "Right, then, you're about to get your first lesson. Stand up," she instructed and waited for Felicity to get to her feet. "Ready?"

"Umm...I guess?"

"Okay," Persinette murmured and tried to remember how she had first learned to control her power. "Close your eyes and focus. Then reach deep down toward that soft humming that's somewhere in the pit of your stomach." She waited and watched as Felicity did as she was told. The blue-haired girl bowed her head, closed her eyes, and reached. It didn't take long for the magic to reach back, and tiny sparks of bright blue light fizzled off Felicity's fingers like static. "Good. Good. There it is." Persi gave her a bright smile. "Now, repeat after me," she directed, and said the words she'd learned what seemed so long ago now. Once Felicity had repeated them correctly, Persinette smiled even more broadly. "Now, say them, and then focus all your energy on that door."

Felicity nodded and faced the door. She repeated the words, her tongue twisting a little around the foreignness of the sounds. It took a handful of tries, but soon enough Felicity was able to hurl her glittering blue magic at the door. The first blow only made the door shudder a little— but it was a start!

"That's great! Good first try! Now do it again," Persinette encouraged.

Felicity nodded, took a clenched her fists, and tried again.

34

CAPTAIN MANU KELII

IT SEEMED that the closer Manu and his men got to the holding cells the fewer MOTHER agents stood in their way. The captain found the whole thing a little suspicious, but there wasn't time to thoroughly think about what it could mean. The plan was the plan, and Persinette didn't have time for him to deviate from it. His crew and he would just have to figure it all out as they went.

The crew of the *Defiant Duchess* fought their way through the halls—hurling magic, claws, even bullets when they needed to. They made no attempts to be quiet. What was the point? MOTHER knew they were there.

And Manu wanted Persi to know he was coming for her.

35

PERSINETTE

FELICITY SAGGED as her continued assault on the door left her more and more exhausted. Persinette wished there was another way, but she didn't see one. "I know it's hard," she said, trying to remain encouraging. "But you can do this, Felicity. You can get us out of here."

"I'm trying!" Felicity panted just as her knees buckled, but caught herself just in time.

Persinette sighed and stared down at the manacle around her wrist. If she could get the thing off, she knew she had the power to break the door down easily. "Take a break. Let me think," she told Felicity, scrunching her nose in thought.

After a good think, Persi returned her attention to the problem. She clanged the shackle against the stone wall, but only the wall gave; the metal stayed intact. She tried squishing her hand down as small as it would go and tugging the thing off, but once again it wouldn't budge past her knuckles. "Think, Pers, think," she muttered to herself as she spun the chunk of iron around her wrist. She gave it another sharp tug, and it stopped once more, wedging itself around the first knuckle of her pinky and thumb respectively. Persi ran through the limited number of spells she'd learned, but with the iron preventing her from reaching her magic there was nothing that would solve this. Nothing to expand, melt, cut, break—*break*!

"I have an idea!" she announced suddenly.

Persinette could feel a manic grin spreading across her lips. She walked toward the heavy metal cot in the corner and knelt beside it. Felicity, who was now leaning against the wall to watch Persinette through the gap, gasped. She must have come to the same conclusion that Persinette had. "I don't think that's a good idea, Persinette," she said, almost pleaded. "Please don't do that."

Persinette flicked a determined look back to the hole even though she could no longer see Felicity through it. Then she shrugged. "We don't have a whole lot of options."

"Well, we could just wait for your friends to get here. They're coming, and they'll get us out," Felicity said, not illogically.

The point was a reasonable one, Persinette had to acknowledge that. And she could also admit that it might make more sense. But desperate times and all that. "No. I want to be out of these cells and ready when they get here. We can't waste time waiting for them to get all of the doors unlocked once they're here. MOTHER will be hot on their tails as it is. We need to be waiting."

"But...that's going to hurt like hell." Felicity winced, as if imagining what Persi was about to do. But it was too late. Persinette had made up her mind.

"Yeah, probably." Persi inhaled and held it. She only had one shot at this—she knew that—because if it didn't work the first time she wouldn't have the courage to try it again. She grabbed the dirty blanket off her cot to stick between her teeth. Then she lifted the bed so that one metal leg hovered just above the joint of her thumb. With a harsh exhale she slammed the leg down onto the knuckle with all of her might. The dirty blanket did nothing to stifle the scream of agony that left her. She pulled her mangled hand from beneath the cot and cradled it in her lap, whimpering.

"Did it work?" came Felicity's timid voice.

Persinette swallowed down her tears, and pulled her hand away from her stomach to get a better look at it. Her thumb was hanging limply at a sickening angle, enough to make her feel a little queasy. Persi closed her eyes to will away her nausea, then, with her lip between her teeth, tugged the iron shackle carefully over the broken joint, gasping in pain when the metal brushed it lightly. But it worked. Once her hand was free, she dropped the cuff to the floor with a clatter.

"Yeah, it...it worked," she whispered haltingly.

Persinette nodded and lifted herself off of her knees. With slow, measured steps, she approached the door once more and closed her eyes. "Once I'm out, I'll grab a key and come right back to get you out," she told Felicity. She reached for the magic within her and it reached back eagerly, like it had been waiting there for her all along.

Her lips fought into a pained smile as she lifted her uninjured hand and watched it for a moment in the darkness. Power pinged off of her in brilliant lavender sparks, lighting up the dim, dank cell. The words left her in what felt more like a prayer than an incantation. Her magic flashed forward, blasting the door clean off its hinges and into a door on the other side of the wide hall with a loud bang—a bang that drew the attention of one of the remaining guards, who immediately came running.

"What the hell was th—"

The agent had no more time to shout before he, too, went flying against one of the steel cell doors. Persinette hoped she hadn't seriously hurt him, but she didn't have time to check, not now. She bent, hurriedly rummaging through his pockets in search of the key cards that would open all of the doors.

36

CAPTAIN MANU KELII

EVERYTHING MOVED SO QUICKLY. It had to, Manu knew, because every second they took could be one second too long. Every second could make the difference between another unit of MOTHER agents mobilizing or not. Because ultimately, MOTHER had more troops than he could ever hope to have. The crew of the *Defiant Duchess* had dealt a crushing blow to the building, and they had caught MOTHER by surprise. But that advantage would only last so long—if it hadn't been lost already.

"How much further?" he asked, a great white tiger with a guttural growl.

"Not too much further," gasped Henry, the map crinkling between his fingers, as he ran alongside the others.

"We don't have much more time," Owen panted softly from beside his captain. "They'll have already started to close ranks and mobilize their forces."

"Then I guess it's a good thing I found you," came a smooth voice from the end of the hall. The captain's golden eyes darted with animal instinct to the tall, lanky figure leaning against the wall as if he hadn't a care in the world and wore his long rainbow hair tied back into a neat bun. The man's lips were set into an expression of boredom—impressive, Manu had to admit, given the circumstances. "This way." He straightened up and motioned them down another corridor.

"And who the hell are you?" Manu asked when he finally caught up. He wanted to assume this was Eddi's inside man, but there was no way to be entirely sure.

The man gazed down at the captain, visibly annoyed. "I'm the best chance you have of getting her out of here. Now move it. My people can only act as a diversion for so long before it starts to look suspicious."

"Your people," Manu repeated with a derisive snort. One more glance at the well-dressed unicorn and the captain had decided he had no use for the man. Manu liked clothes, sure, but he also wasn't living within the walls of MOTHER and letting them provide for him.

A scowl darkened the once-impassive face. "Yes, my people. I have a carefully crafted network of agents inside. And all of them are putting their necks on the line right now because you decided to up and play hero. Now, if you'd please stop being a condescending little shit, I'll lead you to your Seer and we can both get the hell out of each other's hair. The longer you and your idiots are here, the more of my people will get hurt, and I don't need that. So can we move on?"

"Fine," Manu growled as they turned a corner down another corridor. They didn't have a choice.

37

PERSINETTE

AFTER SOME SHUFFLING AND CURSING, Persinette found the keycard in the inner pocket of the guard's waistcoat. Once she had it in her hands, she got to work. As promised, the next door she opened was Felicity's. The young girl with her stubbled blue hair launched herself at Persinette, wrapping her in a tight hug that nearly cut off her air supply. Still, Persi returned the embrace, letting herself enjoy it but for a moment before pulling back. She held the card out to Felicity. "Quick, you start getting everyone out. I'm going to see about getting us another card. Hurry!"

Felicity nodded and set to work. She dashed to the door across the hall from them, releasing a pixie. The next released was a werewolf and the next another witch, and so on. Persi allowed herself a little smile, then rushed up the corridor in search of another keycard.

At the far end, the guard who had processed her was waiting, pistol aimed right for her chest. But the young man's hands shook a little—maybe out of fear, she didn't know. She didn't back down either. "Sorry, 11-24-10. This is the end of the line for you." In spite of his trembling, his words came out with smug satisfaction.

He thought he still had her, and perhaps, had this all happened months ago—before she'd joined the Uprising—he would have been right. The Persinette who stood before him now was not at all the same scared, weak girl she had been back then. No, she'd seen too much now. She'd been pushed too far. What this guard didn't realize was that this Persinette had had enough of MOTHER and their games.

"I told you already. My name is Persinette," she uttered, anger flashing hot in her belly.

The young man snorted. "Trust me, when they put you in the burner, no one will care what your name was. You'll be just another dead Enchanted turned to ash."

That was it. In that moment, something inside of Persinette snapped. The realization of what MOTHER had done to so many before her. All of those people she had helped them Collect. Silas. That's what had happened to Silas. Maybe even what happened to her parents. That's what they would have done to her, to Felicity, to everyone locked in here. MOTHER had worked them to death and then disposed of the bodies in the most efficient way possible, leaving nothing but dust for their loved ones to mourn. And there this boy was, laughing at all of those lives wasted, at all that suffering.

"My name," she repeated as she reached for her magic, "is Persinette."

Her magic flung the pistol from his hand. The guard didn't look quite so fierce without his weapon. He scrambled for it, but before he could grab it, or do anything else to protect himself, Persi swung her uninjured hand back and punched him as hard as she could—just as Agnes had taught her. The blow caught him right the jaw, crumpling him to the ground. Persi snatched up the gun for herself and held it out just as one of the other prisoners headed her way. The young woman fumbled with the weapon for a moment before she caught on and aimed it at the guard.

"Don't kill him!" Persi ordered. "Just make sure he doesn't move." She leaned in to the guard and held out her hand. "Your keycard." The guard nodded rapidly and pulled the card from his pocket with one hand while the other nursed his already bruising jaw. Snatching it, Persinette rushed back to the other cells. "You heard me—don't kill him."

"Yes, ma'am," came the woman's voice.

They kept scurrying down the hall, opening more doors. They released bright-haired witches, and iridescent-winged fairies, and even a pale-faced vampire or two. Soon, Felicity came running from the back end of the corridor, her breath coming in pants. "That's all of them," she gasped.

Persinette surveyed the others, wide eyes flicking from one face to the next. There must have been twenty-five or thirty of them there. Each looked haggard, hungry, and tired. Each had their hair cut too short and a number tattooed onto their forearm. Yet, beyond the deep circles and drawn faces, their eyes told a different story. There was hope there, and the fire of a fight still left in them.

But then her stomach did a sick twist. Sully—the agent who had sacrificed himself for her—was not among them.

"Wasn't there a kelpie here somewhere?" Persi asked.

Felicity shook her head. "No, should there have been?"

One of the vampires, a beautiful woman with angular features and blonde hair, stepped forward. "He came and went through processing just after they brought him in. They took him to another holding area. One of the agents said they had special plans for him." She shifted uncomfortably at the thought.

Inhaling deeply, Persi swallowed down the guilt. There was nothing she could do for him now, but these people she could save. She would have to focus her attention on that for now. "Right, well then, we'll just have to come back for him later. As for the rest of you, are you ready to get the hell out of here?"

There was a resounding, "YES!" from the lot of them—a call that echoed like a battle cry off of the steel doors and cement walls of MOTHER's dungeon.

It brought hope to her heart and a smile to her lips. "Then let's go," Persi announced and turned to lead the way.

MANU & PERSINETTE

"HERE YOU ARE, Captain. The holding cells, as promised." The unicorn gave an exaggerated bow as he deposited Manu and his crew right outside the heavy-looking steel doors.

Manu opened his mouth to thank the other man, thought better of it, and instead simply nodded. He and his crew approached the door cautiously.

Ivy lifted her hands, bright green magic setting her fingers alight as she readied to tear down the door. "On your word, Captain."

Manu glanced around at his men, to make sure they were ready. But just as he inhaled to give the order, he snapped it shut. The door had flung open with a loud creak to reveal a small girl surrounded by a mob of very determined-looking people. It took him almost too long to recognize her without the long lavender braid, but when he did, he laughed loudly. "Persi!" he exclaimed. "Why am I not at all surprised?"

Persinette cocked her head as she took in the large white tiger, trying to make sense of the golden eyes and familiar voice coming from its jaws. Her lips parted in a wide smile when it all finally registered. "Manu?" she asked eagerly.

The tiger nodded with a chuckle that sounded more like a purr. "Yes, Miss Persi."

"What are you not surprised about?" Her question rushed out as she peered past him to crew who had come to save them.

"That you're right here. Ready for me, and leading a small army." The captain laughed and gave a sharp-toothed smile. Persinette laughed as well and leaped forward, ready to hug him, but stopped as someone cleared their throat.

"Well, as quaint as this little reunion is"—Agnes' words broke the relative silence of the group—"we need to get all of you out of here before we're stuck. Move it!" He jerked his head down the corridor and started off.

Persinette paused, then realized he was right. The longer they stood around reminiscing, the more likely it was that MOTHER would be upon them. "They've probably already started blocking our path," she muttered before she turned back to her small army of freed prisoners. "Do we have any willing to fight?" she asked, and those who were willing to go into battle raised their hands and stepped forward. Nodding smartly, she turned to Manu. "Manu, you and your crew will take the front, and I'll take this little group to bring up the back, so they don't pick off any stragglers. Everyone else, in the middle," she ordered.

Manu's crew stared at the small woman giving them orders, visibly confused.

"You heard Persinette! Move out!" At Manu's booming command, the crew of the *Defiant Duchess* about-faced and rushed down the corridor they'd come up. Persinette and her small group of fighters waited while the other Enchanted filed ahead of them. "I'm sorry, I didn't catch your name earlier," Persi said to the werewolf who was still holding the guard's gun.

The young woman laughed awkwardly and shook her head. "We were a little busy. I'm Drea, ma'am." She offered Persinette a respectful bow. "What do you want me to do with this moron?" She nudged the agent with the toe of her boot, her thin nose scrunching as if she had stepped in something particularly foul.

Persinette looked down at the guard. His jaw had turned a fantastic shade of purple and his eyes pleaded with her. "Put him in one of the cells," Persi said. "They can get him out when they come to check to see if any of us is left."

Drea didn't hesitate. She grabbed the man by his collar, hurled him into the nearest cell, and slammed the door behind him.

"They're going to find you!" the guard shouted through the slit in the cell door. "They're going to find you and burn each and every one of you!"

Persi stepped up to the door and peered down at him, her head cocked as she let a slow smile spread across her lips. "Let them try," she said coolly. Then she turned on her heel and motioned for Drea and the others to follow.

Persinette's group of fighters fell into formation behind the freed prisoners, looking wide-eyed and alert, ready for any attack that might come from behind. As they paced behind the others, Persinette could feel the adrenaline from her escape slowly dwindling. The further and further they traveled from the holding cells, the harder it was to ignore the pain in her injured hand. Every step jerked the broken finger enough to make her wince, and she was getting dizzy from the pain. But she swallowed it down and forced herself to focus. They weren't home free yet.

MOTHER's halls were quiet and vacant, and any little sound made Persinette and her army jump.

"Something isn't right," Drea whispered beside her, and Persinette had to agree. It was strange that none of the agents had come to stop them. They had escaped *how* long ago at this point? Five, maybe eight full minutes? And MOTHER hadn't sent reinforcements to gather them up before they got too far? It didn't sit right with her. Between the dizziness and the pain, Persinette found herself stumbling on the slick floor. Drea reached out to steady her. "Are you all right, miss?"

"I'm fine. Don't worry about me." Persinette brushed Drea off. "Pay attention to what's around us." She lifted her uninjured hand, calling the magic to herself just in case.

Quickly, they crept toward the hole Manu's crew had blown in the walls of MOTHER, and, for a moment, it seemed like they might make it without seeing another MOTHER agent. But then there it was—a blockade. Agent after agent, and some Enchanted Assets, had piled into the corridor to block their way, each one loaded with a weapon, ready to fight to keep them from escaping. Persinette turned —maybe they could just go around another way—and found yet another blockade moving toward them.

Time seemed to stop and everyone stood very still as they sized each other up—Persinette and Manu's group all trying to think of a way out, the MOTHER agents just waiting patiently for something, anything to happen—until they attacked. Bullets, fur, and the electric hum of magic filled the air, a flurry of movement that had both Persinette and Manu losing track of which way was up.

Persi and the handful of other witches in the group threw up shields to protect those that they could. But even she knew it wasn't going to be enough; there was only so much they could do with their shields. One of the fighters next to her nudged her, shooting pain up her arm from the damaged hand. She stumbled only momentarily, but it was enough; the shield she'd thrown up to protect herself, and a few others around her, fell, letting a handful of bullets through. One grazed Persinette's shoulder, drawing a wince from her lips. Another buried itself in the heart of one of the fairies alongside her, sending the beautiful young man to his knees, sputtering and choking out wet sounds. Persi let out a cry and threw up another shield just in time to save more lives.

Manu fought tooth and claw, growling and slashing his way through agent after agent, trying to carve a hole in the barricade big enough to get them all through. How far were they from the ship at that point? He wasn't sure. But he was sure that if he could just get everyone through this wall of agents, they could make it out alive. A scream left one of the wolves that surrounded him, but he forced himself to focus. There would be time to mourn the dead later after they had gotten the living safely aboard the *Duchess*. He would focus on that.

The building shook, drawing everyone's attention momentarily from the fight, which gave the witches just enough time to throw up another set of shields. A loud crash sounded, and the cement above them gave way to reveal the *Defiant Duchess* with a very pleased-looking Benard looking down at them through the cargo hold opening. Several of the MOTHER agents collapsed to the ground, unconscious from blows to the head, but they were quickly replaced by fresh agents, alert and ready to fight. All the while the energy of Manu and Persi's small band of fighters flagged. Their little group was growing tired, and MOTHER's forces seemed endless.

Someone shouted overhead, and several ropes descended into the middle of the small army Persinette and Manu had created, quickly sliding reinforcements to the ground. "Get the ones in the middle onto the ship!" Persinette shouted over the cacophony of the fight.

"Now!" Manu added.

The reinforcements moved quickly, gathering up those who weren't able to fight and dragging them onto the ship with ropes. Meanwhile, the opposing sides drew nearer each other, closing ranks so that the witches' shields could better protect those rising through the air in the hopes they wouldn't be shot in the process.

More shouting. More movement. More chaos. Persinette tried to keep her focus on shielding the fighters around her. Every bullet that hit the shield tinked softly and left her feeling that much weaker. She wasn't sure how much longer she could hold on; she could already feel her knees buckling under her.

One of the crew reached for Drea to take her next, but the werewolf brushed them off. "No, take her first. She's hurt." She pointed to Persi. As much as Persinette wanted to shake her head—to say no, she would keep on fighting—she also knew she wouldn't be able to keep it up much longer. Soon enough, her magic would fail her, and she'd just be nothing more than a target.

When the person moved to grab Persi she saw with delight that it was Benard. Despite everything, she couldn't resist a tired smile.

"Miss Persi, nice to see you again," he said, bowing quickly.

"No time, Benard! Get me out so you can come back for someone else!" Persi shouted over the din.

Benard chuckled as he swiftly harnessed her. "You've

gotten rather bossy since last we met." Then, with a short tug on the rope, a mighty force hauled them off their feet toward the *Duchess*, a rapid ascent that made Persinette yelp and cling more tightly to the first mate.

A sharp crack, loud as thunder, lit the room in magic so strong Persinette could smell it above the gunfire. She caught the bolt of magic coming from somewhere among their group of fighters, but she couldn't see who had fired it, nor did she have time to throw up a shield to protect herself and Benard.

Manu, who had been standing close to Ivy when she'd cast the spell, saw it too, and took off at a run. He leaped toward Persi and Benard, sending the pair swinging out of the way just in time to catch the spell himself.

"MANU!" Persi screamed, struggling to get free of Benard's grip so that she could check on him. It was too late; they were already being hauled into the cargo hold. "MANU!" she screamed again, and flew forward, ready to jump down into the fray. She would have, too, had Owen's arms not scooped her up and pulled her away from the opening.

The great white tiger had fallen to the ground; he managed to land on his paws, but only barely. For a moment, he thought the smell of magic was messing with his vision, and he shook his head to clear the blurriness. But the smell clung to him, and blurriness quickly gave way to nothingness as the world went dark. "I need to get out," he mumbled to whoever was closest as his form shifted back to that of a man.

"He was hit! Someone needs to go get him! Someone needs to get the captain back up here now!" Persinette screamed to any and everyone in the cargo hold, praying someone would listen.

Owen sighed and set her on her feet. "I'll go. But you have to stay here, am I clear?"

She nodded rapidly as tears stung her eyes. Owen reattached himself to a harness and launched himself into the fight.

Persinette watched from where she stood at the edge of the hatch, lifting her hands to wring them anxiously only to realize too late how utterly agonizing that action would be. She hissed as pain shot from her broken hand up her arm, and she wobbled, losing her balance quickly to the dizziness of the hurt. Darkness lingered at the edges of her sight, threatening to take her with it into the black and to the ground.

Benard was at her side a moment later, steadying her. "That girl said you were injured. What is it, Miss Persi?" he asked. With a wobbling sigh, she let him see the hand that was now red, swollen, and hanging limply at her side. Benard winced. "What happened?"

"I had to break it to get out of my cuff so I could get us free." She shrugged, trying to appear uninterested so she could remain focused on the fight below. The group of fighters was growing smaller and smaller, and many bodies littered the floor. She couldn't tell from this height which of them belonged to her and Manu's ragtag army and which of them were MOTHER agents.

"That doesn't look good, Miss Persi. We should get you to the medic and have it looked at." Benard's features contorted in worry, but Persinette didn't have time for that right now. People were still being brought up into the ship, and she needed to make sure as many of her people made it up as possible.

"It can wait." She brushed him off and pulled the damaged hand to her stomach to hold it still. She needed something else to do, something else to focus on, and her eyes flicked around the room to find the blue head of Felicity. She rushed to the girl's side. "Are you all right?"

"Yeah, I'm okay. They got me out in the first wave." Felicity nodded eagerly.

A relieved breath rushed out of Persinette, unbidden. "Good, good." With that, she began to make rounds. She checked in with every freed prisoner, every crew member, every *everyone* and made sure they were all safe. She made sure that those who needed it visited the medic and that everyone had water. Attending to others was the only way to ignore her pain and her worry about Manu—at least until he was aboard.

When the captain was finally dragged aboard his ship, he was worse for wear. He was fighting for consciousness as his crew surrounded him. "Where am I?" he muttered to no one in particular.

"You're back aboard the *Duchess*, sir. You're safe," Benard sounded like he was trying to be comforting despite an audible strain in his voice.

Persinette rushed to Manu's side, ignoring how the motion made her sway on her feet.

"And Persi?" the captain asked softly.

"I'm all right. I'm here, Manu," Persi whispered. The captain turned to look at her, and she gasped loudly at the image before her. Those deep dark eyes that seemed to suit Manu so well had been replaced—it would seem—with a pair of dull grey irises and washed-out pupils.

"Oh, surely it's not all that bad." Manu did his best to pull a smile to his lips. "I know I've got a few bumps and scratches, but I'll be fine."

"But what happened to—" Persi started, but found she choked on the rest of the question.

"My eyes?" he finished for her, shrugging. "Seems our friend Miss Warner tried to curse you and I got in the way. It'll be okay."

"Get him to the medic. Now!" Persinette ordered.

Owen nodded and lifted the captain onto a stretcher held by a handful of the crew, who carted him off to the medic.

"You should go too, Miss Persi," Benard said gently. Resigned, Persinette nodded and followed the captain down the hall.

With everyone taken care of, Benard was left to get the ship moving again. He set a heading, and soon the *Duchess* was waving a cheerful goodbye to MOTHER.

EPILOGUE

IT WASN'T until a few days later that Persinette was well enough to leave the infirmary. Manu had been whisked in and out much more quickly, leaving them no time to talk. It seemed injuries and the ensuing fatigue had taken more out of her than she'd thought. She'd spent days hooked up to IVs and being fussed over. So when the medic—a tiny gnome woman with eyes half the size of her face—finally cleared Persi to leave, she knew she had to hunt down Manu.

When she found him, he was in the crew quarters with Benard, trying to reorganize things to accommodate their new passengers. He stood at attention in the middle of the room, wearing a pair of pants that didn't match his waistcoat and looking around distractedly as Benard spoke.

"This will have to work until we're out of harm's way. I don't want to see the ground again until we're at least to the border between the Sixth and Seventh Provinces." Manu's words were clear and direct—in spite of how he might have looked, he was still in charge.

"How will we feed them all?" Benard asked, sounding worried.

"We'll figure it out. We can get some of our pirate friends to help us. I'm sure someone is willing to do me a favor." The confidence in his words made Persi relax a little. She hadn't thought about the negative effect of all the added people aboard the *Duchess*, but she was glad Manu had a plan in place.

"Yeah, they'll love having something to hang over your head," Benard muttered, turning back to directing the crew members rearranging cots.

Persi took the opportunity to approach Manu. "Manu," she said softly, and placed her hand on his arm so he would know that she was there.

"Persi?" Manu turned those eerily grey eyes down in her direction. "Good to see you up and about!"

Seeing that blank gaze made her stomach twist in guilt. That should have been her. *She* should have been standing there looking out at the world without seeing it, not Manu, but she didn't say as much. Instead, she just murmured, "I'm sorry."

Manu frowned, shaking his head. "You have nothing to be sorry for; this isn't your fault. It's Ivy's fault, and one day I'll make sure she pays for it. Until then, just enjoy the spectacular contrast of my eyes to my hair. Does it or does it not make me look even more devilishly handsome?"

A soft giggle left Persi as she shook her head. "Who lied to you?" she asked teasingly.

The captain gasped, clutching his heart. "Are you saying it doesn't?"

Another giggle left Persinette as she felt the anxiety of everything she'd suffered lift a little. "You're an idiot." Although she did feel guilty, she was glad he seemed to be taking it so lightly. She couldn't imagine how bad things would have been if he'd decided to mope.

"We're good here, Cap'n!" Benard called, and Manu nodded.

"Let's take a bit of a walk, yeah? It'll be the injured leading the blind!" Manu said, grinning, and held his hand out to her. She looked at him for a moment before taking it, and led him down the corridor away from other people in no particular direction.

"I didn't really plan to take on twenty new passengers," Manu offered conversationally, not meaning anything behind the comment.

Persinette huffed in spite of herself. "I couldn't leave them there."

A fond smile warmed the captain's face, and he chuckled. "No, I don't suppose you could have. Though from what I heard from them, you were a regular badass down there. Kicking down doors and saving lives and all. Benard said you broke your own hand!"

A flush spread over her cheeks, but she only shrugged, not that Manu could see. "I did what I had to," she said simply.

"Yeah, you did. Which is why I wanted to chat with you about something." Manu bit his lip as his nervous eyes swiveled to stare blankly down the hallway. She waited silently for him to continue. He seemed to struggle with the words for a moment then let out a soft sigh. "All right, so here it is. You did amazing down there with those people as a leader. Every person you helped to free respects you. Hell, that blue-haired girl thinks you're a warrior goddess or something."

Persi snorted at the very idea. That seemed entirely ridiculous. She was just Persinette. "So?" What was he getting at with all of this?

"So, what I wanted to ask is..." Manu exhaled. His

nervousness must have been contagious, because she felt her toes wiggle in her boots. "Will you be my co-captain?"

A surprised laugh burst out of her. The captain frowned.

"What?" he asked.

"I just—" Persi let out a long breath, rubbing a hand over what was left of her lavender hair. "I don't see myself as the captain type. I can't be in...*command* of a crew." The word came out with an awkward giggle.

"That's exactly what you did down there! You *were* in command! You were their leader! Manu exclaimed, his pale eyes wide. "Of course you can!"

Persi caught her lip between her teeth as she thought seriously about his offer. He was right; she *had* been their leader down there. It seemed insane that the soft-spoken girl who let everyone walk all over her not a couple of months ago had turned into "some kind of warrior goddess." She wondered when, precisely, that change had happened, but decided it didn't matter. What mattered was that she had given orders down there and the others had followed those orders without hesitating even once. She had been their leader, and if they were going to make the *Duchess* work with all of the new crew, he would need her.

So, with a deep breath, she nodded.

"It's fifty-fifty, co-captaining?" she asked, grinning impishly. "You won't be pulling rank on me just because you're old and know better than me?"

The captain gasped loudly. "I am not old!"

Tittering a bit, Persinette shrugged. "You know what I mean."

"I do." Manu nodded gravely, and he dipped his head as though trying to meet her eyes. "From here on out—if you say yes—my crew will take orders from you just as much as they do from me. And vice versa. So...we got a deal?"

"Deal." Persinette took his hand with her uninjured one and gave it a firm shake.

Manu wrinkled his nose. "That's it? I thought we'd seal the deal with a kiss."

Persi laughed, surprised but pleased, but she didn't say no or shake her head, even as she felt a blush creep over her face. "Oh, fine." She lifted to her tiptoes and placed her hands on his chest to steady herself. The captain's arms slipped around her waist automatically, and he dipped his head to meet her just as she pressed her lips to his with a soft murmur.

It was easy to fall into the captain with his arms around her and his lips lingering on hers. A shock ran all the way down to her toes and made her knees weak. A happy, shared giggle burbled up between them, which Manu silenced as he pressed her lips softly open with his own, his tongue pushing hesitantly into her mouth, and Persi found she lost all sense of time and all sense of herself. She melted against him entirely, allowing him to kiss her thoroughly enough that when he finally pulled back, they were both breathless.

"So, Captain, what's our heading?" Manu rasped with a soft smile.

"Wherever the wind takes us, I suppose," Persi responded with a dazed grin of her own. "Maybe the Uprising has some daring adventure for us to get up to?"

"I like the way you think, Captain," he said, and pressed his lips to hers once more.

ACKNOWLEDGMENTS

First off, thank you—the reader—for reading Persinette and Manu's story. The Girl in the Clockwork Tower has been two years in the making, and I'm so grateful to you for having read it. I hope you enjoyed your first glimpse into the world of Daiwynn, and are thirsty for more.

Although this book is over, Persinette and Manu's story is far from finished. The world of Daiwynn is large, and holds many more tales. Rest assured, this isn't the last you've seen of our favorite pirate and his lavender-haired co-captain.

Next, I'd like the thank my small hoard of beta-readers. You guys gave some excellent insight, and I really appreciate all of your hard work!

And last but certainly not least, thank you to my small writing support group. Tiss, Elle, and Jasmine—without you there would be no Lou.

ABOUT THE AUTHOR

Born and raised in a small town near the Chesapeake Bay, Lou Wilham grew up on a steady diet of fiction, arts and crafts, and Old Bay. After years of absorbing everything, there was to absorb of fiction, fantasy, and sci-fi she's left with a serious writing/drawing habit that just won't quit. These days, she spends much of her time writing, drawing, and chasing a very short Basset Hound named Sherlock.

When not, daydreaming up new characters to write and draw she can be found crocheting, making cute bookmarks, and binge-watching whatever happens to catch her eye.

Learn more about Lou and her future projects on her website: http://louinprogress.net or join her mailing list at: http://subscribepage.com/mailermailer

facebook.com/LouWilham

instagram.com/lou.wilham

MORE BOOKS YOU'LL LOVE

If you enjoyed this story, please consider leaving a review.

Then check out more books from Midnight Tide Publishing!

Lyrics & Curses by Candace Robinson

Lark Espinoza could get lost in her music—and she's not so sure anyone in her family would even care to find her. Her trendy, party-loving twin sister and her mother-come-lately Beth, who's suddenly sworn off men and onto homemaking, don't understand her love of cassette tapes, her loathing of the pop scene, or her standoffish personality. For outcast Lark, nothing feels as much like a real home as working at Bubble's Oddities store and trying to attract the attention of the cute guy who works at the Vinyl shop next door—the same one she traded lyrical notes with in class.

Auden Ellis silences the incessant questions in his own head with a steady stream of beats. Despite the unconditional love of his aunt-turned-mother, he can't quit thinking about the loss of his parents—or the possibility he might end up afflicted with his father's issues. Despite his connection with lyric-loving Lark, Auden keeps her at arm's length because letting her in might mean giving her a peek into something dangerous.

When two strangers arrive in town, one carrying a mysterious, dark object and the other playing an eerie flute tune, Lark and Auden find that their painful pasts have enmeshed them in a cursed future. Now, they must come to terms with their budding attraction while helping each other challenge the reflection they see in the mirror. If they fail, they'll be trapped for eternity in a place beyond reality.

Coming Soon
11.11.20

CREDITS

Tower Shape made by FreePik from
www.flaticon.com